VICTORIA DAHL

TAKING
THE
HEAT

HQN™

HQN™

ISBN-13: 978-0-373-77970-3

Recycling programs
for this product may
not exist in your area.

Taking the Heat

Copyright © 2015 by Victoria Dahl

This edition published by arrangement with Harlequin Books S.A.

For questions and comments about the quality of this book,
please contact us at CustomerService@Harlequin.com.

® and TM are trademarks of Harlequin Enterprises Limited or its
corporate affiliates. Trademarks indicated with ® are registered in the
United States Patent and Trademark Office, the Canadian Intellectual
Property Office and in other countries.

www.HQNBooks.com

Printed in U.S.A.

3 1907 00345 6679

This book is dedicated to Kate, for the advice,
and to Allison, for the ideas. Thank you.

CHAPTER ONE

OUT OF ALL the mistakes Veronica Chandler had made in her life, this was definitely the worst. Worse than moving to New York City after college, worse than dating that guy who'd dumped her via text after a hand job, worse than crawling back home to Wyoming with her tail between her legs and even worse than becoming a complete fraud of an advice columnist.

What the hell had she been thinking? She should have said no to her boss. She should have told him to take his horrible idea back to whatever hellish place he'd found it. But she'd been too afraid to say no.

Veronica lived every single day afraid that her boss was going to realize the truth about her. Each email she received from him seemed to pulse with menace, and when he'd called and asked her to stop by his office two weeks earlier, she'd known that had been the end of her charade.

But instead of firing her, he'd presented her with an *opportunity*. In her state of shock and relief, she'd stammered out a yes instead of screaming "Hell, no." Maybe she'd been in denial since then. Maybe she hadn't wanted to think about it. But there was no denying the truth anymore. She was supposed to put on a live performance tonight, and now she was racing to the Jackson Town Library as if the stacks of books inside could save her.

She rushed through the glass doors, head already swiveling to scan the main room of the library. Lauren Foster was a great friend, so when she hadn't answered this morning's panicked texts, Veronica had known she must be working. If she could just find Lauren, surely she would say it was okay for Veronica to back out of this mess and hide from the world in her apartment for a week or two.

She walked past the circulation desk and looked into the children's area, but Lauren wasn't hidden between the stacks of kids' books. What if she wasn't really working today? What if she was on a hike deep in the woods and wouldn't be home until late?

"No," Veronica said. No, that wasn't possible. Veronica needed her too much.

She adjusted the sunglasses hiding her bloodshot eyes and took a deep breath. She had to stay calm. She couldn't let anyone see her panic. Veronica Chandler was a goddamn bastion of good sense and cool remove. She'd handled New York City. She handled other people's problems every day. She could handle this.

After smoothing a hand over her newly cut hair, she walked to the circulation desk and did not trip over her own high heels. "Is Lauren Foster in today?" she asked the older woman she recognized from one of her previous visits to the library.

"I think she's over in Periodicals with the new librarian. Wish I could join them."

Veronica wasn't sure what the woman's waggling eyebrows were trying to convey, but she smiled with relief. "Thank you so much."

The smile fell away as soon as she turned and headed for the opposite side of the library. Logically, she knew her friend couldn't save her from this awful mistake, but Veronica's body still strained toward her as if Lauren were a life preserver.

Tucked into the far corner of the building, the periodicals section was arranged around a cozy grouping of armchairs and couches, and in the middle of it all stood Lauren and a stranger. Not a new librarian, though. This stranger had a beard and dark hair and a plaid tie and a hot lean body that immediately dried Veronica's mouth to ash.

The royal blue heel of Veronica's leather half boot caught on the weave of the industrial carpet and jerked her to a halt. She lurched forward, catching herself on a shelf of autobiographies before she could hit the floor.

"Oh, God," she breathed, bent over and staring at the carpet. At least she hadn't landed flat on her face or jammed her skull into the corner of a shelf. She glanced up, face already hot with color, but miraculously, they'd turned away from her. Lauren was gesturing toward a rack of magazines as she spoke, and the man was nodding. Veronica stood straight so quickly that the blood drained from her brain and left her dizzy.

She was not going to meet this gorgeous man like the spastic mess of a woman she was. In fact... Veronica set her mouth in a straight line. She wasn't going to meet this man at all. If there was anything that could make her current situation worse, it was introducing a hot guy into the equation. She actually winced at the thought.

Nope. She was going to be cool, ignore the way his wavy black hair flopped onto his forehead when he laughed at Lauren and pretend his trimmed beard didn't make Veronica want to pet his face.

Hoping to stay half-hidden in the stacks, she waited for Lauren to turn in her direction. When that didn't happen, she waved a hand, hoping she was at least in Lauren's peripheral vision. If she could just get her friend's attention and lure her away from this bearded wonder…

But of course, he was the one who turned toward Veronica. As his gaze rose toward her, she slapped her waving hand to her head and pretended she was only smoothing down her hair as she stepped forward. She kept her eyes off him and locked on Lauren, and her friend finally noticed her. "Oh, my God!" Lauren cried out in the hushed tone she used only at work. "Your hair looks amazing!"

"Do you think so?" Veronica asked, touching the blunt edges at the back.

"I love it. Did you lighten it?"

Veronica nodded. She was naturally blonde, but she'd had her stylist lighten the front to a shade closer to platinum. She'd been worried it had been another big mistake, spending the last of her savings on such a frivolous expense. "I did it for tonight," she said.

"Good idea. You're going to blow them away."

Veronica shook her head and tried to ignore the fact that Hot Guy was watching her with a friendly smile. "Do you have a minute, Lauren?" she asked. "If you're too busy, I can come back later."

"Sure, I have a minute. This is Gabe, by the way. Gabe MacKenzie, the latest addition to our little library. Gabe, this is Veronica Chandler."

He really was a librarian. Wow.

He reached out a hand, so Veronica had no choice but to take it. His hand was warm and strong and rough at the edges, as if he built the shelves he later stocked with books. "Nice to meet you," he said, his voice pleasantly rough along the edges, too.

Veronica didn't want to know any of that about him. She didn't want to know how he felt or sounded. He was way too tempting. She pulled her hand away as quickly as she could. "You're the new librarian?" she asked, not able to keep the shock from her voice.

"I am," he answered as if he was used to people being surprised by this librarian's hot young maleness.

"Veronica is a bit of a local celebrity," Lauren offered.

"No, I'm not," she said as quickly as she could.

Lauren snorted. "In fact, Gabe, you're standing right by some of her work." She gestured toward the local newspapers spread out on a table. "She's Dear Veronica."

His white teeth flashed in a smile. "I'm afraid I'm not familiar."

Veronica crossed her arms and shook her head, but Lauren kept talking. "She writes the local advice column. A smart take from a big-city girl, that kind of a thing."

"Cool," he said, looking at the papers now instead of Veronica. That was an improvement, at least. She shifted impatiently, jerking her head toward the door of the conference room to try to get Lauren to move along, but Lauren seemed to be on a mission.

"He's from New York," Lauren said. "You two probably have a lot in common. Veronica's a local but she lived in Manhattan for years."

Oh, God. Not a New York guy. No. No, no, no. She shook her head as if that could ward him off. When Gabe looked up, he was shaking his head, too. "I was born there, but I've been away for years. I came here from Cincinnati."

"Right," Veronica said. "Sure." She crossed her arms more tightly and waited until Lauren finally sent Gabe back toward the small office behind the circulation desk to fill out some paperwork. Then she led Veronica to the conference room.

"Good Lord, girl," Lauren said as soon as the door closed. "What the hell is wrong with you? If I was ten years younger and single... Did you *see* that boy?"

Veronica waved a frantic hand. "I don't have time for that right now!"

"Seriously? I think there really are too many hormones in our food these days, because you're not okay. And here I thought having firefighters right next door was distracting. Now none of us will get any work done."

Veronica shot a mournful glance toward the door as if she could see through it. "Did he just start today?"

"Yes, Jean-Marie sprung him on me. I knew she'd been interviewing for Sophie's replacement, but I didn't know she'd decided to import a little testosterone from Cincinnati. He's here to drag us into the twenty-first century, I gather. Ebooks. Digital audio. Maybe even a 3D printer. Basically, he's going to be a giant pain in my ass, but regardless, I'm going to hook you two up if it kills me."

"What?" Veronica gasped. "No, you are not! I have problems. Big problems!"

Lauren immediately sobered. "What's wrong?"

Veronica grabbed her arms. "You know what's wrong!"

Lauren looked so surprised by Veronica's freak-out that Veronica felt immediately embarrassed. This was who she was on the inside. This wasn't the Veronica she let other people see. She didn't want even her friends to know how weak she really was. She managed to lower her voice but she still couldn't stop the fear from bubbling up. "That stupid show is in eight hours and I can't do it."

Lauren rolled her eyes and then carefully extracted her elbows from Veronica's grip. "Calm down. You're going to be great. We're all coming."

"No. You don't understand. I…" She stared at Lauren's face, wanting to tell her the truth. Wishing she could. But this lie was all she had anymore. It felt like all she'd ever had.

She'd spent the first twenty-one years of her life waiting for her *real* life to start, planning and saving for it. She'd put off making close friends and falling in love and doing crazy things and taking chances, because she'd thought she would do all that once she got to New York. And what if she got so cozy and tied down in Wyoming that she never went? No. Too much of a risk. So she'd waited.

But then she'd finally gotten to the big city, and… none of that had been real, either. And now here she was back home, living the biggest lie of all.

So instead of saying, *I'm a complete impostor, and I can't pull that off in a live show*, she went with the almost-true version of it. "It takes me days to write a column and do research and get everything right and still be entertaining. I can't do all of that in front of people!"

"Then why did you arrange these shows?"

"I didn't! It wasn't my idea. My boss told me I was going to do them, and I needed the extra money, so I said yes instead of sobbing and running into the hills!"

Lauren was clearly trying to look patient, but she had to press her lips together to hide a smile. It didn't work.

"Help me," Veronica begged. "Laugh if you want to, but tell me I can back out."

"You can't back out," Lauren said immediately. "And you're going to be great. People like you. You're nice. You're funny. And it's at a martini bar. Everyone will be drunk and ready to laugh at anything."

Veronica nodded, trying to psych herself up. "Yes. All right. Count on drunkenness."

"Exactly! And didn't you say that you get to choose the questions?"

"Yes, but I only have a few minutes. Everyone will put their questions in a bowl, and I get to read them before I start."

Lauren's face brightened as if the whole problem were solved. "Perfect. Just pick some questions that are close to ones you've dealt with in the paper. Death of a parent, cheating spouse, best-friend drama. You already know those answers."

Lauren was right. Veronica did know those answers. Maybe she could handle this. "So I shouldn't back out?"

"Oh, my God," Lauren groaned. "Get out of here. I'll see you tonight."

Veronica didn't move. She couldn't actually think of a way to back out of the show, but she'd thought her more experienced, smart-as-a-whip friend would come up with a plan, and all she'd come up with was encouragement. "I have to do this?" Veronica tried one more time.

"Yep. No choice."

"Okay," Veronica whispered. "I'll be fine, right?" When Lauren's eyebrow rose in impatience, Veronica nodded. "I'll be fine," she said more firmly.

"You'll be great," Lauren insisted.

"Right. Thank you for the good advice. And thanks for trying to fix me up with the new guy. He really is hot, but I can't deal with that right now. Still...a boy librarian?"

"A supersexy boy librarian. Who just moved to town and probably needs new friends."

Veronica waved her hand. "I can't. Really." For so many reasons. "I'd better go. I've got to spend an hour picking out an outfit and then I'll reread my old columns. You're a genius."

"I know. See you tonight."

Veronica tried not to feel panic at those last words, but she was a failure at that, too. There was no escaping the fear, but at least Lauren had talked her out of an outright breakdown. All Veronica had to do was pick already familiar topics and she could fake her way through this just as she'd faked her way through everything else.

Tonight was going to be fine.

CHAPTER TWO

IT WAS A BAD start to a new job.

As a male librarian, Gabe knew the drill. He'd be a novelty at first, but that would wear off really quickly, and then his job was to work hard and not be an asshole. The biggest mistake he could make was to walk into an established library and announce that he'd arrived to save the place.

Unfortunately, his new boss had already done that for him. Not only had she sprung Gabe on his new co-workers as a surprise, but she'd announced right away that he'd been hired to shake things up and bring the small library into the twenty-first century.

Not ideal, but Gabe had smiled his way through the first day and done his best not to step on any toes. It had been immediately clear that Lauren Foster was the woman the other librarians looked to for guidance. Jean-Marie might have been the boss, but Lauren was the leader, so Gabe had deferred to her. When she'd asked him about his plans for ebook lending, he'd held his opinions and instead asked about the library's experience with ebooks so far. He had only a year here, but that didn't mean he could jump in and start tearing things apart as if nobody else's work meant anything.

A year. He'd come to Jackson to live his dream life for one year, and he'd planned on spending every pos-

sible moment outside, but that wasn't in the cards tonight. Lauren had invited him to go out with the rest of
the library staff, and he damn sure wasn't going to turn
down an offer like that on his first day. It was some sort
of special event involving that girl from New York City
and a martini bar. The worst possible way to spend an
evening, as far as he could tell, but it was a great opportunity to bond with his new coworkers. He'd told Lauren
he'd meet them at the bar by eight and he'd clocked out.

Gabe had no idea what the dress code was for a martini bar in Wyoming, but his work clothes would have
to do, because he didn't have time to change. He'd finally found an apartment—not easy in a town the size
of Jackson—and he'd headed immediately from work
to the leasing office to sign papers and make the de-
posit. He'd start moving his stuff in tonight after the
Dear Veronica performance.

Smiling at the charm of the wooden boardwalks of
downtown Jackson, Gabe ditched the tie and rolled up
the sleeves of his pale green button-down as he walked.
Even at seven-thirty the sun was still hot on his skin
in the cool air.

It was only May. Not only did he have a good five
months of rock-climbing weather ahead of him, he'd
have the climbing areas nearly to himself for a month
before the tourists arrived. His smile widened. He'd
been one of those tourists, but now he could call himself a local. For a while.

One year of living exactly the life he wanted. He'd
have to make it count.

A woman riding by on a muddy trail bike returned
Gabe's smile. He tipped his head in acknowledgment.

He hadn't dated much in the past couple of years.

He'd spent his days off camping and exploring the hills south of Cincinnati. But in Wyoming, the wilderness was right here, and the town was full of women who spent more time outside than Gabe did. His dating pool was wide-open. Maybe he'd make that count, too.

Not that he'd meet anyone at the martini bar tonight, he thought as he eyed the sign ahead with disdain. The Three Martini Ranch. Popular with the ski crowd, no doubt. People from the big city. People like Veronica. She might have been from Wyoming originally, but she was all Manhattan now. Styled hair and big sunglasses and high heels, all for a trip to the library. Wow.

The funny thing was that he liked Lauren a lot. She seemed down-to-earth and smart as hell. Not the kind of woman to put up with bullshit. So why was she friends with a high-maintenance girl like Veronica Chandler?

A mystery he wouldn't put much time into. He'd keep his head down tonight, try to have a good time with the other librarians and deny any connection to New York if it would keep Lauren from trying to hook him up with a city girl.

He took a deep breath and opened the door of the bar, noticing that the door handle was a metal sculpture of a toothpick with an olive on the end. "Cute," he muttered.

The noise of the place hit him as soon as he stepped in. Gabe was shocked. He'd been to Jackson often enough in the past few years to know that the high-end places were dead empty during the off-season, and he would've expected this to be one of them. But almost every table was full and people were gathered around a small stand at the front, stuffing notes into a blue vase. Free Advice! read the sign in front of the vase. Submit Your Dear Veronica Questions Here!

That part might be entertaining, at least. Gabe spotted the table of his new coworkers but was surprised to also see two people he knew at another table. The man and woman were both rock-climbing guides. He gave them a wave as he passed on his way toward Lauren.

"Gabe!" Lauren called as he drew closer. She seemed happy to see him, at least. He'd been the only male librarian around in most of the positions he'd held since grad school, and it wasn't always a comfortable fit. At his first job, he'd been tempted to have the word *interloper* tattooed on his forehead.

"You made it," Lauren said. "I wasn't sure you'd be up for hanging around a bunch of strange ladies at a bar."

"What can I say? I'm down with strange ladies."

"Then you came to the right spot."

He nodded to the other two women, both of whom he'd met today during his training. The library director wasn't around, and Gabe felt no surprise at that. He could already tell she was the type of boss who stayed holed up in the office with the door closed as often as possible.

Gabe was a little relieved that, so far, none of his new coworkers were part of his dating pool. He'd fallen head over heels for a coworker a few years ago, and that had ended badly. Not with spectacular fireworks but with a simmering, drawn-out death that had made work a misery for six months until he'd finally taken another job.

After that he'd instituted a no-dating-at-work rule that had felt a little unnatural for a while. As the only single male student in his MLIS class, he'd spent a *lot* of time dating peers. But he'd also been young and dumb. At thirty-one, he was marginally smarter, but he was relieved that his coworkers were all either in relationships or members of AARP.

"So what did you think of your first day?" Lauren asked.

"The library is great. You've made efficient use of the space, but it's still welcoming. It's amazing to be working in a small community library again."

Lauren smiled. "It's a big change from the main branch of the Cincinnati Public Library, I'm sure."

"It'll be a relief not to be in touch with social services for a while. You wouldn't believe how often we had to try to find help for people using the library as a shelter."

"Just because this is a small town doesn't mean it doesn't happen here."

"Right," he corrected himself. "Of course."

"Not on a daily basis, though." She watched him for a moment. "How old are you, if you don't mind my asking?"

"Thirty-one."

"That's a relief. I was afraid that beard was hiding a baby face. Did you concentrate on digital lending in Cincinnati?"

"I didn't spearhead it there, but I worked on it from planning through implementation. Have you guys been looking at it long?"

She shrugged. "We've talked about it. We checked it out last year, but we really needed to invest in our Spanish-language section. And personally, I think an e-reader is cost prohibitive for the members of the community who need the library most."

"I know exactly what you mean, but you have to keep in mind that a huge percentage of the community has at least a smartphone, and these——"

"Hold on," Lauren interrupted, and Gabe worried that he'd misstepped, already talking up his plans on the first day, but then he realized she was pulling a phone from her pocket. "Hey, Jake," she said, covering her other ear as she stood. "Just a second. I can't hear anything in here."

She'd taken only one step away when Gabe heard her name being called. Lauren kept moving toward the door, a hand still pressed to her free ear. Gabe looked toward the sound of a woman calling out "Lauren!" one more time.

It was Veronica Chandler, standing in the opening of a hallway that he assumed led to the bathrooms and the office of the bar. She stood up on tiptoe and waved toward Lauren, then lowered herself again, her face falling from hope to disappointment.

Her blond hair still looked the same, some sort of angled, stylish cut that would look at home in any big city, but her face looked younger without the sunglasses. In fact, Gabe was a little surprised at how young she looked. He'd placed Lauren somewhere around forty, but Veronica looked more like twenty now that he could see her wide blue eyes and round cheeks. She bit her lip and her worried gaze swept the room as if she were lost.

Shit. Gabe glanced toward the door, but Lauren was nowhere to be seen. Veronica crossed her arms and stared at the door as if her only hope had disappeared. Gabe excused himself from the table and wound his way through the crowd.

She was still frowning toward the doorway and didn't notice him until he stopped in front of her. "Jesus!" she gasped, slapping a hand to her chest.

"Sorry," Gabe said. "I didn't mean to startle you. Lauren got a phone call. She should be back any second."

"Oh. Okay." She crossed her arms again and stepped farther back into the hallway, then raised a thumb to her mouth to chew at the nail. He noticed that despite her smoky eye makeup and glossy lips, her nails were bare and cut short.

"Is there something I can do for you?" he asked.

When she finally gave up her vigil and looked right at him, Gabe was a little shocked by the vivid blue of her eyes. But he was the only one who felt that jolt, apparently, because her frown was decidedly suspicious.

"I'm Gabe," he offered. "We met today at the library."

"I remember," she said.

"Is something wrong?" Gabe asked. "Do you want me to grab Lauren for you? She's probably right outside."

She sighed and shook her head. "No, it's okay. I just need a drink, and I was hoping not to mingle." She waved toward the bar, and Gabe winced at the casual gesture. She really was a bit of a diva. Still, that didn't mean he couldn't be a gentleman.

"I'm happy to grab something for you. What do you drink?"

He expected a complicated order, but she shrugged. "I don't know. Just a cosmo, I guess?"

It came out as a question, but he nodded. "A cosmo. You got it. I'll be right back."

"Could you bring it to the office? I have to go through these questions. And I really need a drink."

He headed toward the bar, deciding he'd need a drink to get through this evening, too. Just as he got the bartender's attention and ordered a beer and a cosmo, a loud, friendly voice rang out over the PA system.

"Hello, locals!" the warm voice called.

He turned and was shocked to see that it was Veronica, holding a microphone, her arm draped over the big blue vase.

"I'm Dear Veronica, in the flesh!"

The crowd cheered and hooted as she laughed. Her face looked transformed again. Neither cool and haughty nor young and uncertain, her round face now held a friendly, open warmth and a wide smile.

She waved at the whole crowd. "It's great to finally meet you in person!"

That was a lie. She hadn't even wanted to step out of the hallway. Gabe shook his head and turned back to pay the bartender.

"I hope everyone has their questions in," she continued, "because I'm ready to judge all of you."

A moan swept through the crowd, and she laughed over it. "That was only a joke. I'm here to help, of course. So I'm going to steal all of your secrets…" Gabe glanced over his shoulder to see her scoop up the vase. A young woman darted up and dropped one last piece of paper in.

"Ooooh!" Veronica called. "You look like trouble!"

The whole place clapped as the laughing woman's face went scarlet.

"Okay," Veronica continued, "I'll be back to answer your most burning questions in a few minutes. In the meantime, I'm told the martini of the night is called Your Favorite Mistake, which is about as appropriate as it gets, so drink up!"

A cheer went up as she waved again before disappearing into the hallway. Gabe sighed and collected the drinks to follow her.

By the time he'd picked his way through the crowded room, the hallway was empty. He passed two bathrooms and a door to the kitchen before he came upon a closed door marked Employees Only. Holding the beer between his elbow and his chest, he managed the knob and the door swung open.

He'd expected to find that crowd-pleasing Veronica again, but the woman seated at the desk before a pile of folded notes was pale and chewing on her lip.

"Thank God," she said when she looked up and saw him. Actually, she wasn't looking at him but at the drink. Both her hands reached out for the cosmo, and they were trembling.

"Hey," he said when pink liquid dribbled over the rim and hit the desk. "Are you okay?"

"I saw my boss out there," she muttered, then sucked in a deep breath. She took a sip of the drink and closed her eyes. "I'm better now, thanks."

Was she an alcoholic? Had she just been jonesing for a drink? But no...she shuddered slightly as she took another sip. "God, that's strong."

"Do you want my beer instead?"

She grimaced at the beer. "No, but thank you."

After one more sip of her pink drink, she put both hands flat on the desk and blew air through her pursed lips. The notes trembled and shook. She breathed deeply in, then nodded. "Okay, I'll be fine now. Thank you very much."

"No problem," he said. "I'll see you out there. Break a leg."

She laughed, that big smile returning for a brief

moment before it went crooked and uncertain. "Right. Break a leg. I'll try, I guess. Oh, I should pay you back!"

Her hand swung around and hit the martini glass with an alarming chime, but she scrambled and managed to save the glass before it tipped. "Oh, thank God," she gasped, "That would have been a tragedy."

"Not an insurmountable one. I promise I'd have gotten you another."

She laughed again, her round cheeks going pink. "You're really sweet. Thanks for helping me out."

Gabe was surprised to feel his own face going slightly warm. "No problem." He backed out and closed the door, leaving this odd woman to her work. He knew less about her after their second interaction than he had after their first, but one thing was certain. She was high maintenance as hell. A drama queen, maybe. Or just high-strung. Whatever she was, he was staying far away from it.

His phone buzzed as he reached the end of the hall and Gabe took it from his pocket, smiling when he saw his sister's name pop up in a text box. Another high-maintenance woman, but one he couldn't bear to keep at a distance: his middle sister, Naomi.

How was your first day? she asked.

Good. I'm out with the other librarians right now.

She texted a big smiley face. Girls' night???

Something like that, he responded. Are you back home?

Yes, Paris was a blast, but now Mom's trying to feed me, and Dad's just...disappointed.

Yeah, Gabe was disappointed, too. But he was hopeful that once his sister got through a few more years of international modeling, she'd be ready to settle down and take over the family business. Then again, he'd been telling himself that for more than ten years. Unfortunately, Naomi had turned out to be one of those rare models who was even more popular in her thirties than she had been in her teens.

And their older sister? Yeah, she was an even bigger disappointment to their father.

It was all up to Gabe now.

Gabe shook his head and texted back.

Just eat one burger and make them both happy.

I tried that last time. It didn't get them off my back, and I had to run ten extra miles on the treadmill.

Tragedy! he responded, then added a crying face to the text.

Kiss my ass, little brother.

Love you, too, he sent before he tucked the phone back into his pocket. One hour of this Dear Veronica nonsense, and then he could head over to his new place, ignore family and work obligations, and get on with his new life.

VERONICA COULDN'T FEEL her own hands and she couldn't quite hear what she was saying. It wasn't the martini affecting her, unfortunately; it was pure, unadulterated terror.

Despite the numbness, her hands were still holding the letters she'd chosen to read, and the crowd was still clapping and smiling. She couldn't remember much of the past forty-five minutes, but maybe it was going fine. She might even be doing a good job, but she had a feeling the crowd approval had more to do with the alcohol. Not that she minded.

"And now, our sixth and final Dear Veronica letter," she said into the microphone, lowering her voice a little to bring down the noise level in the bar. It worked. The roar subsided.

She drank the last of her now-warm cosmo and took a deep breath. "'Dear Veronica, I feel like I'm a pretty good catch. I'm young, relatively pretty, educated and fun loving. Men ask me out. I wouldn't say I have any problem getting a date, and my standards are reasonably high. I expect a potential mate to be employed and funny and hot as hell—'"

"That's you, Steve!" someone yelled out, causing howls to erupt.

Veronica smiled and pointed in the direction of the noise. "Find me later, Steve." She waited for the laughter to quiet, then continued. "'So why do I always end up being the booty call? Why am I never the girlfriend? It makes me feel like I'm not good enough. Don't get me wrong—I love sex, but I'd like more than that, and the last three guys I've dated have all ended up being casual.' It's signed That Girl."

Veronica looked out over crowd. "Now…this letter might mean something to a lot of you."

There were moans of agreement.

"Let me start with this. There's nothing wrong with a booty call." Veronica laughed at the ruckus that caused, then shook her head and moved on. "Sex is fun. Sex is good. Booty-call your way through life if that makes you happy. But apparently, it's not making you happy, That Girl, so you need to figure out why you're willingly participating in this unfulfilling little dance.

"I notice that you referred to yourself as 'relatively pretty' and then referred to your dates as 'hot as hell,' which makes me think you could be flattered by their attention. Let's be really honest here—there is nothing flattering about someone wanting to bone you."

She paused to let the crowd react, and a server sneaked over to hand her another martini. "Oh, thank you!" Veronica whispered, surprised and relieved. Her mouth was drying out and her hands were sweating. She gratefully took a gulp, then turned back to the audience. "I hear some disagreement, but let me be clear. There are men out there who will put their penises in a tree. There are men out there who will put their penises in sheep. You do not need to feel flattered that a man wants to put his penis inside you.

"And as for women...think of all the slimeballs out there you see taking women home every single night. Those women are happy to sleep with a slimeball, so, men, don't be honored that they'll sleep with you, too. Sex is not flattery! It's one of our basic animal needs and people will do a lot of nasty shit to get it."

"She's talking about you again, Steve!" a man shouted.

"Okay, Steve," Veronica said, "don't find me later." She winked in his direction. "But for this letter writer... You describe yourself as 'fun loving' and I'm afraid proving that you're down for casual sex is part of proving just how fun you are." She paused to let that sink in and registered a couple of women who looked as if they'd just heard the truth.

"If casual sex isn't fun for you, then don't do it. It's not a requirement—it's an option. Buy a good vibrator and take a break from being the fun girl who's down for the superhot guy. Because if you think those men can't tell that you're flattered by the attention, you're fooling yourself. If *you* believe they're too hot for you, then you can bet your ass that they think so, too. And if you're smiling your way through a booty call and pretending it's a great way to spend a weeknight, those men are not going to try to talk you out of it."

She took a deep breath. Almost done.

"So take a break. Reevaluate your choices. Figure out what you really want. And if what you want is to get serious with someone, then you wait for a person who's serious about you. You wait for the guy who calls you when he doesn't want sex."

A few of the women frowned and Veronica smiled. "Okay, wait for the guy who's dying to do you and *also* wants to spend time with you not having sex. Is that better?" All of the women cheered. "All right. Thank you very much, everyone. This has been a blast. I'll see you in the paper!"

She waved blindly at the clapping crowd, then turned, meaning to grab her drink and retreat to the office to hyperventilate, but the glass was empty. Had she downed that whole thing in five minutes? No wonder she felt dizzy. Before she could retreat, someone rushed up behind her and squeezed her waist.

"You were amazing!" said Lauren.

"Was I? I think I'm going to faint."

"Everybody loved it! You're a natural."

"I'm not," she murmured, starting to see spots. She managed to smile toward a female voice that called out a quick thank-you, but then Veronica pointed her body toward the hallway and started walking. "I just need a minute," she said.

She felt Lauren pat her back, and then Veronica was alone in the cool hallway and the noise of the crowd receded. She made it to the office, shut the door and collapsed into a chair.

"Oh, my God," she whispered. "Oh, my God, I did it. It's over." Her heart began to calm. The spots in her vision faded.

The door opened on a loud whoosh, and Veronica smiled gratefully, ready to fall into Lauren's arms now that some of the shock had passed, but it wasn't Lauren. It was Gerald King, the managing editor of the paper.

Oh, God. What if he'd finally seen through her stupid charade? What if he'd hated it?

"I'm not going to beat around the bush, Veronica."

Oh, shit. Shit, shit, shit.

"We were hoping to promote the paper and help pump up the locals' specials advertising with tonight."

"I know," she breathed. Unfortunately, the spots were completely gone now and she could see Gerald's stern face perfectly. He was only forty-five, but there was something in his posture that always reminded Veronica of her dad. Some arrogant, implacable way he held himself. She wished she hadn't cornered herself in the office. There was no escape from his disappointment now.

"But this is going to work out differently, I think."

She was already nodding, conceding her awfulness.

Gerald grunted, but she couldn't decipher the noise. "Anyway, Thursday nights are fairly slow this time of year, and the place was almost full tonight. The owner is damn happy. I think we can make this a great summer tie-in for the paper. Hell, maybe we can even take it to a bigger location during ski season, though I'd much rather increase permanent circulation than just get a temporary bump in advertising rates. But hell, why not go for it all?"

"I don't understand," she said.

"Every Thursday. Locals' Advice Night with Dear Veronica. One hundred bucks a pop for you, paid as a bonus. Are you in?"

Are you in? He asked the question so casually. Almost as an aside, a formality. Of course she was in, because the paper wanted her to do it and she always said yes.

Veronica stared at him.

"Hey," Gerald said, snapping his fingers. "Are you in? The manager wants to announce it before everyone leaves."

She nodded, meaning that she understood what the manager wanted, but Gerald took it as an agreement. "Great. I'll let him know. Good job out there." And then he was gone, and Veronica had to come back and do this all over again next week.

The black spots swarmed again, descending on her like flies on a carcass. Could you die of regret and terror and stage fright? Veronica lowered her head to the desk and let the coolness of the fake wood seep into her face.

She'd succeeded and become a disaster in one fell swoop. The same fucking magic trick she'd been pulling off her entire life. But there was no running from it now. Jackson was home. She had nowhere else to go. She'd have to keep this charade going for a long while. And it had only *felt* as if everyone was watching before. Now they really were.

CHAPTER THREE

GABE STRETCHED OUT on the sun-warmed surface of the rock and let his sore muscles absorb the heat. The sky was a pale, pure blue above him and the breeze dried his sweat. His fingertips ached from bracing himself in a vertical crack after a misstep, but even that was perfect. He closed his eyes and melted into the mountain.

"Water?" his climbing partner asked.

Gabe opened his hand and felt a bottle hit his palm. "Thanks."

"You're out of shape, man."

"Fuck you," Gabe said, opening one eye just so he could glare at Benton. "You try living in Cincinnati and see how rusty your climbing skills get."

"We'll work on it," Benton said.

"Hell, yeah, we will," Gabe sighed. "Sunday?"

"You got it. Are you up for climbing Exum?"

Gabe sat up and stretched his left arm. "Jesus Christ, what is that? Eight hundred feet?"

"Sure, but it's six pitches. And I'll lower you down if you get too tired."

"You're an arrogant ass, you know that?"

Benton grinned. "That's why you love me."

"I don't think that's it," Gabe muttered. "Hell, I'm not even sure I love you."

"Don't tell me you're just using me as a route leader?"

Gabe shrugged. "You come at the right price. Free."

"Yet again, I'm just a cheap piece of ass." Benton adjusted the tie holding back his dreadlocks and slipped on the shades that Gabe's sister had once said made him look just like Lenny Kravitz. He tipped his head toward the cliff edge. "Ready?" he asked.

"Just give me another minute. I'm enjoying the hell out of this." He closed his eyes again and let the silence wash over him. It wasn't completely quiet, of course. Trees below them rustled in the breeze and Benton's equipment clinked when he moved. But it was more profoundly quiet on the rock than it was when hiking or camping. There was no rustle of chipmunks through brush, no chorus of birds singing, no crackle of dead leaves under boots.

He stretched and pulled himself up. "I'll see you Saturday morning, too."

"No shit?" Benton asked. "You're in?"

"I'm in," Gabe answered. He'd just gotten word that his application for Technical Search and Rescue had been approved. After a couple months of training, there was a good chance he'd be out there helping with mountain rescues during the summer months.

Benton clapped him on the arm. "I never doubted it for a second." He gestured toward the edge of the cliff. "After you."

Gabe hooked back into the line and stood at the edge, but before he leaned out, he took the chance to look around one last time. This was his first solid climb since getting settled in Jackson a week before, and it was the perfect day. Sixty degrees and unlimited visibility. Valleys and peaks stretched out beneath him, the trees looking like stunted bushes from this height.

A hawk glided by, not shifting a feather as it rode an air current down. "Christ, I'm happy to be here," he said quietly.

"I know. I still remember the day I decided I wasn't leaving Jackson. It's a great place to stay forever, even if I do have to live on a bartender's tips and the occasional guiding gig. I'm guessing librarian doesn't pay much more, but I guarantee you won't find a reason to leave."

Yeah. Unfortunately, Gabe already had a reason to leave. He couldn't put good views and crisp air over his family, no matter how much he loved living here. He didn't have the option to stay. Not forever. But he'd be damned if he'd waste his time here dwelling on that.

"Rappelling," he called out, checking the anchor, the rope and the lock on his carabiner one last time.

"Rappel on, my friend," Benton said.

Gabe turned around, stepped down and let his weight settle him into the right position. There was nothing but two hundred feet of air behind him and it felt perfect.

"Hey!" Benton called as Gabe began to descend. "You coming out with us tonight?"

"Absolutely."

"Great. We're heading over to a new locals' night at Three Martini Ranch. Dear Veronica hosts it. Supposed to be a blast."

Gabe's hand tightened reflexively around the rope, slowing his descent. He loosened his grip and shook off his surprise.

Between moving all his belongings into a new apartment and working his ass off at the library, he'd been too busy to think much about Veronica Chandler in the past week. She was a distraction Gabe didn't need. But she was definitely a distraction.

He had no idea what to think of her. She was pretty, a pain in the ass and absolutely not his type. She was also funny and smart as hell, if last Thursday's performance was any guide. She'd been transformed into that warm, welcoming version of herself once she'd started speaking, but more than that, she'd been bright as a star.

He'd agreed with every one of the answers she'd had for the letter writers, and he'd been looking forward to discussing them with her after the performance. So much so that he'd realized what a bad idea it was to stay, and he'd said his goodbyes and hauled ass before she could come out to join Lauren.

He'd figured that was the end of it, but apparently, he was going to see her again tonight. Not that he had to go, but…what good was a day off if he couldn't hang out with old friends?

Gabe slid past an overhang and kept up a steady descent until he was back on flat ground, then shouted the alert back up to Benton.

"Geronimo!" Benton yelled back. He was down in a few minutes.

"What time tonight?" Gabe asked.

"Starts at eight, but we'd better make it closer to seven. I hear it might be packed."

That would work in Gabe's favor. He could check out Veronica again, but he wouldn't draw her attention. He didn't want to date her. He just wanted one more chance to figure her out before he filed her away.

"Hey," Benton said, nudging Gabe's elbow as they began to pack up the gear. "Did you bring that book?"

"Sure." Gabe dug into his hiking pack and withdrew his worn copy of *The Curious Incident of the Dog in the Night-Time*. Benton's nephew had been diagnosed with autism and Benton had read through two dozen nonfiction books about the condition. Now he was looking for fiction, too.

"If you want anything else, let me know and I'll see if I can order it in to the library."

Benton shot him a narrow look. "I don't know, man. Will I have to sit in on circle time on the rug?"

"Benton, it's a library, not a preschool."

"Same thing, right?"

Gabe was used to this, but he still rolled his eyes. "I don't run the kids' section. Come on."

Benton shrugged. "All right. Since you're in the adult section, any sexy librarians I should be aware of?"

"Yeah," Gabe said, slipping on his pack. "Me."

"Tempting," Benton countered. "But I'm gonna need you to take the lead next time so I can get a better look at that ass."

"I'll wear running shorts," he promised, prompting Benton to groan.

"Now I'll never get that image out of my head."

Gabe grinned. "I like that you pretend it's awful. That's cute."

"Good Christ, man," Benton muttered. "Your hairy fucking thighs. To change the subject entirely…how's your sister?"

Gabe shook his head. "Naomi is great. Want me to pass her a note from you?"

"I can pass my own notes," Benton said. "I've still got her number from last time. Is she coming to visit anytime soon?"

"No idea," Gabe said, throwing Benton a wary look. He didn't want to know if his sister had hooked up with Benton three years ago when Gabe and Naomi had met up here with a group of friends. He didn't care who his sister slept with; he just didn't want to know any details.

"Fine," Benton said, holding up his hands. "How's your dad? Still pressuring you to take over the family business back in New York?"

"Always," Gabe answered, not adding more. Even Benton didn't know about Gabe's plans. He wanted to live the next year as if he wasn't planning to return to the city. He didn't want to field questions about MacKenzie's. He didn't even want to admit the truth out loud.

His dad knew, of course. It had been the only way to get his agreement to retire in a year. And his sisters knew, because Gabe had tried to talk each of them into stepping up and taking over the MacKenzie's chain of restaurants. His sisters were older, after all, and someone had to do it or their dad would work himself into an early grave.

But they'd refused, and so it had come down to Gabe, the one who liked to keep the peace and make things right.

"Well, if Naomi does come out here, let me know."

"Yeah, yeah."

Benton shouldered his own pack. "All right, you're not as pretty as your sister, but you'll have to do for now. Come on, beautiful."

Gabe laughed as Benton started down the trail, but Gabe didn't immediately follow. He was distracted by the echo of his own laughter off the rocks behind him. How long had it been since he'd heard that? His voice bouncing off mountains instead of being swallowed up by a cacophony of cars and air conditioners?

He took a deep breath and felt years of stress fall

away. If he'd been in any kind of shape, he'd have turned around and headed right back up the face again, taken a slightly different path, pushed himself a little harder. But his arms already burned and there was no way his hands would hold up. Sunday would be soon enough to push himself. And then every Sunday after that.

Gabe rolled his shoulders, stretched his hands and set off down the trail, suddenly eager to get out, have a beer and watch the Dear Veronica show from the crowd. He'd just be careful not to get too close.

VERONICA CHEWED HER gnocchi and watched as her father typed out an email on his phone. She didn't know why she'd accepted his invitation to dinner. It wasn't as if there'd been any chance that an hour with him would be relaxing. On the other hand, the stress of his disapproval did distract her from the stress of worrying about tonight's performance, so maybe that was what her subconscious had jumped on.

And he always chose great restaurants. Judge Chandler was used to the best.

He finally looked up, glancing around the restaurant before he looked at her. "Did you say something?"

"Yes, I said that it went so well I'm doing a live Dear Veronica again tonight."

He frowned. "For free?"

"No, Dad, I'm getting paid."

"Not much, I'd bet."

No, not much. Not as much as she'd get paid if she'd followed in his footsteps and gone to law school. "I told you I'd be happy to pay rent."

He waved a dismissive hand before picking up his

Scotch. "At least I don't have to worry about the unit being vacant during the spring and fall."

Yes. At least she could do that for him. Fill space in the smallest apartment in the building he owned.

"I only got you that job as temporary work," he grouched, settling back into his sweet spot of disappointment combined with magnanimous gestures.

"I'm a writer, Dad. It is an actual job."

"Is it?"

She stuffed more gnocchi into her mouth and stared hard at her water glass. If she'd been making even a few hundred dollars more a month, she'd never have accepted her dad's offer to live in his building. She'd known exactly what it had meant. But she'd spent her life savings trying to make ends meet in New York. When she'd come home to start over and try again, she'd thought maybe—just maybe— she'd find a soft place to fall.

She'd been wrong. "Just tell me the market rate on the apartment and I'll pay it," she said, not for the first time. "Then you won't have to worry about my job or my decisions."

He gave the same answer he always did. "You can't afford it."

The problem was that he was likely right. As small as the apartment was, it had a nice kitchen and a fireplace and it was in Jackson. It was a place she definitely couldn't have afforded during ski season, but she told herself that a yearly lease wouldn't be quite so much. It wouldn't be like living in New York. Nothing was that expensive.

She set her fork down hard. "I'd better go," she said. "I need to get ready for the show."

"Knock 'em dead," her father said, already looking at his phone again.

He was always like this. She knew it had nothing to do with her, but it was sometimes hard to believe it when he was directing his arrogance at her. "Sure, Dad," she said. She gave him a kiss on the cheek. He patted her hand, then got back to his phone.

Maybe her plan to see her dad tonight had actually worked. She was still nervous about the show, but she had a little anger to energize her now. She stalked toward her apartment, pissed that her dad was such a self-absorbed ass and mad at herself for failing so hard at life that she was relying on him again. She was living one of her Dear Veronica letters.

"Dear Veronica," she snarled as she jammed the key into her apartment door, "I'm a stereotypical twenty-something who couldn't quite make it out of the nest and now whines nonstop about it. What should I do?"

She slammed the door behind her and looked around at the furniture that had once filled a Brooklyn apartment she'd shared with two virtual strangers. "Shut your mouth," she told herself, "stop whining and find something you're good at."

Actually...

She stared at the stylish little chair she'd found on the curb in front of a nice brownstone near her subway stop. It had been one of her most triumphant moments in the city, sadly, and she still loved that chair.

Find something you're good at.

Hadn't she already done that? She was good at writing. Her editors in New York had rarely offered anything less than praise, and her boss seemed happy with her work here. She was a good copy editor and she was surprisingly good at giving advice, despite having zero qualifications for it. Aside from the normal trolls, commenters on the paper's website seemed thrilled with the column and eager to contribute their own thoughts. So maybe "Find something you're good at" wasn't the right advice.

It wasn't her work that was the problem; it was…everything else. And *everything else* was a lot harder to fix than the wrong job.

She needed advice. And she was good at giving it. She just had to dig a little deeper.

Veronica made herself move slowly as she got ready for her show. She couldn't rush or she'd panic and lose all this hard-won calmness. So she changed from jeans and a sweater to the dress she'd already laid out on the bed. It was a cute little blue A-line number she'd found at a charity store in New York.

She'd found a lot of her clothes there. So many women in New York would wear a dress only one or two times before they moved on.

She added high-heeled ankle boots and a silver necklace that looked expensive but had been on clearance at a department store. Her hair was already styled, so she freshened her makeup, darkened her eye shadow and put on some earrings that swung and sparkled when she moved.

Her transformation was complete.

She'd never thought much about her apple cheeks and blue eyes before she'd moved to New York, but once there, her look had drawn attention. Men had called her Heidi on the street, as if she were fresh off the mountains of Switzerland. They'd called her "baby doll," yelling out that they'd love to dirty her up a little. Her stupid round cheeks had flamed with mortification every time, which made the men howl with laughter and get even filthier. Catcalling was not something she'd grown up with in Wyoming, and it had taken months for her to school her response.

But she'd done it. Walk taller, tune them out, don't look at them, don't respond. She'd learned to put on heavier makeup, a mask to hide behind, along with high heels and a long black jacket anytime it was less than eighty degrees outside. Stare straight ahead. Look impervious.

It had worked moderately well with the catcallers, and the rest of New York, as well. Don't let them see the real you.

Don't let them see the real you… Wasn't that what she was doing in Jackson, too? Hiding behind this costume she'd assembled in the big city?

If she wrote in to her own column, the answer would be easy. *If you feel like you're faking your way through life, then stop faking it. Let people see the real you. Take a chance. If you don't open yourself up to others, then they won't be open to you.*

It wasn't even complicated. It wasn't something she needed to research. But it was still scary as hell. Letting people see the real you.

Veronica stared at the big-city version of herself in the mirror. The smoky-gray shadow made her eyes even bluer. The blush gave her cheekbones. The lip stain made her lips fuller. But she could tone it all down. Be the natural girl she'd been when she'd flown to New York all those years ago. Let people see *her.*

No.

She picked up her mascara and added another coat,

then packed her makeup into its bag and put it away. "Not tonight," she murmured to herself before she snapped off the light. But before she walked out of the apartment, she found a black marker and wrote a big note and stuck it on the fridge.

#1—Let people see the real you.

She'd start taking her own advice. Tomorrow, maybe. But definitely when she wasn't standing in front of the whole damn town.

CHAPTER FOUR

VERONICA CHANDLER WAS shining again when she took her place in front of the microphone. The wide smile made her eyes sparkle. Her earrings glittered as she waved to the crowd. "Good Lord, there are a lot of you tonight!"

The place erupted in cheers. Gabe didn't cheer, but he did clap for Veronica before picking up a beer to wet his suddenly dry mouth. Maybe it was because he was already buzzed or maybe it was because he hadn't seen her cool, bitchy side right beforehand, but she looked hot tonight. Her legs were bare all the way from ankle to midthigh, and his eyes followed the path up and down several times. Those legs made her look like his kind of girl.

He cleared his throat at the strange thought, but when he tried to look away, his gaze swung right back to those bare legs. They weren't thin and impossibly long like the legs of some of the fashion models his sister hung out with. Veronica's legs were tight. Hard. As if she used them to go places and do things. Her calf muscles were cut and the fronts of her thighs tightened when she shifted.

"How have I not seen her before?" Benton asked.

Gabe forced his eyes off her legs and looked at Benton. "She was living in New York for a while."

"You know her?"

"I met her last week. She's friends with Lauren at the library."

"Maybe I should be spending more time at the library."

"Because bartenders don't get enough female attention? Please."

Benton grinned and raised his beer. "Cheers to that."

Veronica spoke again, drawing their attention. "This first question is R rated. Do you guys think you're ready for that, or should we ease in with something tamer?"

When the crowd reacted, Veronica covered her mouth and shook her head, her cheeks going pink. "I actually didn't mean it to sound that way, but I'd say you're definitely ready."

"Hell, yeah!" a girl shouted from the left.

"All right," Veronica said. "This one's short and not so sweet. 'My boyfriend won't go down on me—'"

The place erupted in groans and boos and Gabe found himself laughing until his eyes watered.

Benton booed right along with the crowd. "What a punk ass," he muttered. Gabe clinked his glass in agreement.

Veronica's laugh echoed over it all. "Okay. Just listen. 'My boyfriend won't go down on me. He says he's never liked it with anyone, but I can't help but take it personally. What should I do?' Signed, I Need Love. Well, I hope your boyfriend is here to listen to this! But, letter writer, it doesn't really matter if he's here or not. Because what you need to hear is how many of these guys think he's a fool. Right, guys?" The place exploded with noise.

Once the cheers died down, she started again. "There

are lots of men who genuinely don't like going down, and there are also lots of women who don't like performing oral sex. These are not bad people—"

"Are you sure?" someone shouted.

"—and I don't think anyone should be talked into anything they don't want to do. I have no idea what your boyfriend's problem is, and it doesn't truly matter. If you have to talk him into it, I doubt he'd be very good at it and I doubt you'd have a great time."

Somebody muttered an "Amen."

"So, letter writer," she continued, "the truth is that your boyfriend doesn't really matter here. You matter. And what you need to ask yourself is 'Do I want to go my whole life without oral sex?' Because that's what we're talking about if this relationship continues. Since oral sex is the way the vast majority of women orgasm, I'm going to guess the answer to that question is no."

Gabe noticed her cheeks going pink again.

"So if you don't want to go your whole life without it, what's the point of going a year without it? Or five years? Maybe he's a really great guy, but he can be a great guy with someone he's sexually compatible with. Believe it or not, there are women out there who don't want that. They think it's gross or it makes them uncomfortable. I once even met a woman whose nerves were so sensitive that she found it too intense and didn't like it. Let him date that woman. Or better yet, he can hook up with one of those girls who hates blow jobs and they can live resentfully together for the rest of their lives."

Veronica smiled. "But you, letter writer, you can look around at this very large gathering of men who love to go down—" she swept a hand over the crowd, and several guys jumped to their feet with triumphant fists in the air "—and you can decide to choose another path. A path that involves cunnilingus, and lots of it. My hunch is that's the path for you."

Gabe thought of the Robert Frost poem about two roads diverging in a wood and shook his head in wonder. Probably not what Frost had had in mind, but who really knew?

Her next question was from a woman who'd received hateful messages online telling her she was fat and slutty and who'd then tracked down the IP address to her sister's computer.

Gabe half listened to Veronica's answer, but he was more interested in the way her voice changed from wry humor to serious concern. Was she only acting or did she really feel that deeply for these people? He couldn't tell, but the whole room went quiet as she talked about betrayal and pain.

"I can't begin to guess at her reasons. I'm sure she tells herself she has them, but she is consciously hurting you. She's trying to damage you on the deepest level. Now, people do that all the time. There are people online who spend every day swooping down on strangers just to hurt them and they find that entertaining. But this is your *sister*. You can't just ignore that. You're going to have to talk to her, because you're both adults and part of being an adult is doing difficult things.

"Tell her you need it to stop. And if you're open to the answer, ask her why. Find out what's really going on, because I guarantee that it has nothing to do with your body and what you do with it. It's all about her. Maybe she's having issues with your parents. Maybe they're using your success to shame her. Or maybe she's just depressed and angry and lashing out. Ask her why.

And if you don't like her answer, you have every right to cut her out of your life, but be honest with your family about why you've done it, or she will make you into the bad guy."

The applause was more subdued this time, but Veronica smiled. "Don't worry. The next question is about boobs."

When she started giving advice about living with a small chest, Gabe felt less guilty about checking her breasts out. She gestured to them as she was talking, after all. People were laughing so hard it was difficult to hear everything she said about bra shopping and dress styles, but he had a perfect view of her breasts the whole time. The neckline of her dress swooped only low enough to hint at cleavage, but she made clear that she didn't have much to show, anyway.

"Personally, I wouldn't bother much with water bras or miracle padding. What if you attract a guy who's really, really into C-cups and then your magic show ends with whipping off your bra and making them disappear? You can yell out 'Ta-da!' but I promise you won't get any applause."

Benton was laughing so hard that Gabe suspected it was a magic show the bartender had seen several times.

Half an hour and four more questions later, the show was over. Once the room started to clear out a little, Gabe took the opportunity to grab a free space at the bar and order another beer.

"We're heading over to the saloon," Benton said when Gabe returned to the table. "You coming?"

"I just bought a beer."

"Finish it and come on."

"I'd better not. I've got work tomorrow, and my shift doesn't start at 5:00 p.m., unlike yours."

"All right, man." Benton slapped his shoulder. "See you this weekend."

Gabe relaxed into his chair. If Sunday turned out to be anything like today, he might die of happiness. It was all so…simple.

But when he glanced up, it wasn't simple anymore.

Veronica stood in the opening of the back hall, leaning forward just slightly to look around the room. He realized then that she was part of the reason he'd decided to stay, even if he hadn't admitted it. Shit.

After a few seconds of peering toward the bar, she retreated and leaned against the wall, then closed her eyes and drained her drink.

Gabe watched her, confused by yet another sudden personality shift. She clearly didn't want to come out, which was odd considering she'd just spent so much time in front of these people.

She pushed off the wall again and her gaze roamed the room. Her eyes skipped over him, then returned and widened. He smiled and gave her a wave. She waved back but didn't move. Telling himself he was an idiot even as he did it, Gabe pointed at the empty chair next to him. She hadn't been looking for him, and he shouldn't want to spend time with her, anyway.

But Veronica smiled and seemed to wilt a little, the stiffness going out of her shoulders, and he was glad he'd offered. Relief seemed to glow from her face as she stepped out of the hallway and made a beeline for him.

"What are you doing here?" she asked as she set down her now-empty glass and took a seat.

"Some friends wanted to see your show."

"But not you?" she asked.

"Are you kidding? I've been following your live show since the beginning. You want another drink?"

"Oh, God, yes. Please."

He started to raise a hand to catch the server's eye, then realized the woman was already headed over with a drink. She winked at Veronica. "The manager says thanks for another great show. There's more where this came from."

"Keep them coming!" Veronica cried. When she reached for the drink, Gabe noticed her hand was trembling again.

"Do you get nervous?" he asked.

Her big blue eyes peered at him from over the rim of the martini glass as she took a long drink. "Nervous?" she finally rasped when she came up for air. "More like fucking terrified."

"I'm surprised." That might explain a lot of her odd behavior. "You seem totally confident up there."

"Seriously?"

He nodded as she took another drink.

"It's all an act. I'm scared to death." She took one more drink, then set the glass down. Her hand was still shaking.

"Hey, it's okay," he said. "Anyone would be nervous talking to a roomful of strangers about cunnilingus."

She squeaked and covered her face with her hands. Her cheeks went red behind her fingers, but when her shoulders began to shake, he knew she was laughing.

"Sorry," he said. "It was kind of the elephant in the room. That and your small breasts."

"Oh, my God!" she shrieked, her head bowing with laughter.

"Not that there's anything wrong with that."

"Gabe!" she scolded, and he grinned at the way she made him feel as if he was getting away with something. He couldn't deny that it was a turn-on having an excuse to talk to this girl he hardly knew about sex.

He smiled at the top of her head until she finally peeked up, her eyes still crinkled with amusement.

"Feel better?" he asked.

She sat up straight and shook her head. "I can't believe I'm saying this, but yes, I actually feel better."

"Makes sense. Oral sex is a great icebreaker. But I don't need to tell you that. You've probably given that advice a hundred times."

"You're awful," she said, still grinning.

"I know. I'm sorry. But your hands were shaking."

"Oh." Her smile faded. "I didn't realize."

The waitress interrupted with a new cocktail, and Gabe watched Veronica take a deep breath. She touched the new glass but didn't lunge for it the way she had with the first one. She really had been scared. No wonder she'd been so hesitant to join the crowd.

"You have no idea how good these drinks are. So good." She took another sip. "And you distracted me from the terror. Thank you."

He noticed how her dress had ridden up to expose more of her smooth thighs and made himself look away, if only so he wouldn't get caught. "I honestly had no idea you were nervous. It was a great show. You're a natural."

"Really? I can't tell how it's going when I'm up there. It feels like my brain shuts down and my mouth is working on its own."

"No, your brain is definitely working. Everything you say is really damn smart."

She blushed again, and Gabe liked that. A lot. That she blushed over sex talk and then blushed when he called her smart. She was…intriguing. And nothing like the first impression he'd had of her.

"You look like you got some sun today," she said.

"It was my day off. I finally got a chance to do some climbing."

She sat back in her chair. "Rock climbing? That's crazy."

"It's not crazy," he said, the same answer he'd given to a hundred other people. It was the most typical reaction. "It's fun. You should try it."

"Oh, sure. I've got the perfect body type." She flexed her right arm and pointed at it. "Check out these guns."

"You don't need much upper-body strength for the beginning climbs. It's all in the legs."

"Are you saying you're not impressed with my guns?" she asked, flexing again.

"I'm saying your legs look strong."

"Oh." Cheeks going pink again, she looked down at her legs. Her hands settled on her thighs as if to cover them, but then her fingers spread.

Gabe watched, wondering what her skin felt like. Warm, probably. Soft. Nice.

"Thank you," she said. "If that's a compliment."

"It's definitely a compliment."

"Are you flirting with me?" she asked, then immediately shook her head. "I'm sorry. I always ask weird questions like that. It's a problem."

"How is it a problem?"

"Well, it's a little awkward, isn't it? That's my flirting technique. Complete awkwardness. Look, it's happening right now. Are you entranced?"

"I kind of am," he said, smiling at her until she smiled back. "If awkwardness is your flirting technique, then you're clearly into me right now."

She threw back her head and laughed. "Clearly. But isn't everyone into you?"

He was the one who drew back this time. "What?"

She watched him as she sipped from her drink, her eyes still sparkling with laughter. Her gaze dipped down his body when she set her glass on the table. "Come on. Look at you. You're so damn hot."

"I am?" he asked, feeling his own cheeks get warm.

"Yes, with your little beard and your shoulders and all this." She waved her hand up and down, while Gabe touched his beard in confusion. "Never mind," Veronica said. "I'm drunk. Ignore me."

"Maybe you shouldn't—" But before he could finish his sentence, she downed the rest of the drink.

"No, I hardly ever get drunk. I want to get drunk. I want to have fun for once."

"You look like you've had plenty of fun in your life."

"Ha! You're wrong about that."

"Come on. You're just feeling sorry for yourself after all the excitement of the big city. But you can have fun here, too."

"Oh, sure," she huffed out on a laugh.

He bristled a little, used to hearing this kind of shit from his oldest friends. "It's not New York, but it's a good place. Aren't you having fun right now?"

She nodded and leaned closer. Gabe tried very hard not to glance down her dress to the slight rise of her breasts, if only because her gaze was locked on his face. "Gabe MacKenzie," she said in a loud whisper, "you're beautiful."

He'd been flattered by her attention, but with those words he realized she was just very, very drunk. Her bright smile was gorgeous, but her eyes had gotten a little hazy. "Okay," he said, "you're cut off. And I think I'd better walk you home."

She rolled her eyes. "I lived in Brooklyn. I can handle myself in Wyoming. And walking won't be a problem. I've got the legs of a Russian weight lifter." She slapped her bare thighs.

"That is not what I said."

"What did you say?" she teased.

"I said they were strong. Muscled. You look like you run or bike or—"

Her groan cut him off as she dropped her head to her hands. "I was going for cute tonight. Just cute. Why can't I even pull that off?"

"Are you kidding? You're just fishing for compliments now. You're really cute. The definition of cute. But your legs…your legs are sexy."

She raised her head, her eyes narrowing in suspicion. "Are you making fun of me?"

"Making *fun*? You really aren't very good at this flirting thing, are you?"

"No. But a guy in New York once called me corn-fed, then acted like it was a compliment."

"I'm not a guy in New York."

"You used to be!" she said, poking him in the chest as though she'd caught him in a lie.

"Okay, but I never felt at home there. I'm a country boy at heart. New York is just…where I was born." Not quite true, but that was what it felt like. A place his family lived. A place he loved from afar and visited occasionally.

Gabe caught sight of the waitress approaching with another drink for Veronica and he shook his head. The woman shrugged and headed back toward the bar.

"I'm sorry," Veronica said. "You called my legs sexy and I made it weird." She snagged his beer before he could grab it. "This is why I don't date. Look at me."

She got one swig before Gabe took it back and finished it off. "Come on, Dear Veronica, let's go."

Even though she collapsed onto the table with laughter, she eventually nodded. "Okay. Let's go to my place."

"I didn't mean…"

"Yeah, believe me, I know." Veronica pushed to her feet. "See? Steady as a tree."

In fact, she was swaying a little. If she was a tree, she was more a willow than an oak. "How many of these did you have?" he asked.

"One before the show. One during. Then…two more?"

"In the space of an hour?" Gabe reevaluated his options. "How far away do you live?"

"Only three blocks away. I'm centrally located." That set off a bout of giggling that had Gabe smiling as he wrapped her arm around his.

"Are you okay in those heels?"

"Sure. I had to learn to walk in them in New York. You know how it is. Spike heels everywhere. I bet you loved that, didn't you? Men love that."

He looked down at her as he opened the door of the bar. She was smiling as she stepped into the night.

"I'm not sure how to answer that," he finally said.

"Just be honest. I write an advice column. I know what guys like. You can't scare me."

"Okay, then. Women's legs look amazing in heels. Your legs look amazing in heels. But nothing beats the sight of a woman in hiking boots on the trail ahead. I could watch that for hours."

"And have?"

"Only with permission, of course."

She bumped him with her shoulder as they walked. "Does that mean you're an ass man, Gabe MacKenzie?"

"I—" he ran through all the possible responses in his head and decided discretion was the better part of ass valor "—am not going to answer that."

"You can tell me. Feel free to spill all your kinks. You wouldn't believe what I've heard."

"I'm sure I wouldn't." He looked around. "Are we even walking in the right direction? Where do you live?"

"Oh, shit," she muttered, then spun him around. "It's this way. I'm sorry. I haven't been this tipsy in a really long time."

He thought she was way past tipsy, but damned if it wasn't adorable on her. "So how does one become a professional advice columnist?"

"Overbearing father," she muttered, then shook her head. "I was a copy editor, but I also helped out with an advice column at the *Village Voice*. Screening letters, proofing the column, that sort of thing. When I told my dad I was moving back to Jackson, I suppose he wanted to help. He's friends with the owner of the Jackson paper, and Dad *inflated* my experience a little. So here I am. A fraud who gives advice."

"Well, you're great at it, so how could you be a fraud?"

"You'd be surprised."

"Does someone else write the column for you?"

She laughed, bumping into him again, her thigh rubbing against his and reminding him of how naked her legs were. "No," she said. "I write it all by myself. That I can do, at least."

"Which was your favorite column to write?"

"Hmm." They stepped from the sidewalk to the boardwalk and Veronica seemed to get distracted by the sound of her heels on the wooden boards for a moment. Then she shook her head and looked up again. "Last year a mother wrote in to slut-shame the woman her adult son was dating. She said that this harlot was luring her son with free sex."

"Oh, God," Gabe groaned. "Poor guy."

"I know. We can only guess at how much he was suffering. Anyway, I answered that letter, telling her that if she was disappointed in the behavior, then maybe she hadn't raised her son very well. I also said there was nothing wrong with sex and to leave the girl alone. Pretty standard stuff. Except that I became friends with the harlot later."

"Ha! Seriously?"

"It's a small town. These things happen. I probably know the guy who fell in love with his sex doll, too, but please don't tell me if it's you."

"I'd rather not talk about it, anyway," Gabe said. "It's over."

"Oh, no! Did it fizzle out?"

He shrugged. "We tried to patch it up a couple of times."

She tugged him to a stop, then leaned against a street lamp, wheezing with laughter.

He grinned as she wiped tears from her cheeks. "You okay?"

She shook her head, still struggling for air past her hysterical laughter.

"Was it that funny, or is it just the alcohol?"

"Both!" she gasped. Then groaned, "God, I must be a mess."

He looked over her tearstained face and the mascara smudges beneath her eyes. "Nah. You look great."

"Really?" She swiped at her pink nose.

"Really. Now, where are we going?"

"Right here," she said, gesturing toward a three-story condo complex.

He grabbed her hand and pulled her off the lamppost to walk her toward the entry. "I only live one block over."

"I'm not surprised. There are a lot of rentals around here." She dug her keys from her bag and led the way to one of the ground-floor doors.

"I won't come in," he said for clarity's sake. Even if he might have wanted to, she was way too drunk for him to feel right about it.

She stabbed her keys toward the doorknob several times. "Don't worry. I didn't think you wanted to."

"Okay, because I— What? Why would you think that?"

She waved her free hand and the keys jagged two inches to the right. "I'm not that girl. I get it."

"What girl?"

"You know." She finally got the key into the hole, and when the lock turned, she gave a little cheer. She pushed the door open and then lurched in before spinning back to him. "I'm not going to try to jump your gorgeous bones, Gabe. You're safe with me. I'm sexual kryptonite."

"What?" he asked again, even more confused.

She reached down to pull one of her high-heeled boots off, but the other ankle wobbled dangerously.

He jumped forward to grab her elbow so she could pull off the boot without falling. She smiled up at him and took off the other boot. He was surprised by how much shorter she was without them. He could now see straight down her dress. The view was lovely and so was her lacy black bra. He stepped back quickly.

She stared up at him. "It's true," she whispered.

"What's true?" he asked.

She watched him for a long moment, then leaned a little closer. "Can you keep a secret?" she asked.

He nodded.

"Promise?"

"I promise," he said, not sure what he was hoping to hear her say. Whatever he'd expected, her next words were not it.

"All that advice I give? All of the wise insights on love and sex that I helpfully hand out to strangers?" Her voice was getting softer.

Gabe put his hands on her shoulders. He wanted to lean down and kiss her. Her mouth looked so plump and her eyes so happy. But he couldn't. Not tonight. "Mmm-hmm," he murmured, using his hands to hold her steady instead of pulling her close.

"That's the biggest lie of all, Gabe. I've never even done it."

"Done what?" he asked, distracted by the pretty way her neck arched so she could watch him.

She moved even closer, going up on tiptoe to bring her mouth toward his neck. "Fucking," she whispered.

For a moment, his brain stuttered over the provocative word, guessing that she was trying to turn him on. Not that he'd act on it tonight, but it was a nice problem to have. Then the rest of the conversation caught up and overrode his libido.

He stood straight. His hands gripped her shoulders with more strength. "You *what*?"

Instead of reacting with the seriousness he thought the moment deserved, Veronica burst into laughter. "You should see your face!" she chortled, pointing at his face in case he'd forgotten where he'd left it. "Oh, my God, you're so cute!"

"You were kidding," he sighed, feeling a relief he didn't understand.

"Oh, I wasn't kidding. But it's still funny."

He blinked several times. "You're a virgin?"

"Pretty much," she said, her face suddenly getting serious.

"What does that mean? Can you even be pretty much a virgin?"

"I mean, I've done *things*. On occasion. But I've never *really* done things. Do you get it now? Look at me! I'm a fraud, Gabe. An undesirable, freakish fraud!"

He stared down at one of the most adorable women he'd ever met and wondered if someone had slipped a psychotropic drug into his last beer. "You're..." He couldn't think what to say. *Oh, my God, you're a virgin!* Or... *I don't know what you're talking about—you're totally fuckable!* His mind spun. He stayed silent.

"I'm sorry," she said. "I shouldn't have told you. You just have such a nice face. And everything else."

"Thank you," he said carefully.

"Maybe you'd like to help with my problem?" He wasn't sure what she meant until she waggled her eyebrows.

"You mean…with the…?" He pointedly dropped his gaze to a lower point on her body, then realized it was an extremely creepy gesture and snapped his eyes back to her face.

She nodded solemnly. "Yes. With *that*." She pointed at the spot he'd just eyed. When he didn't respond, her nodding slowed, then stopped entirely before she changed it to a negative shake. "No. Right? It's a no?"

"I don't… Veronica, I don't know what to say. You're really drunk. We shouldn't even be talking about this."

"I know. I'm sorry. I'm trying to let people see the real me."

He swallowed hard, wishing he had another beer to wet his dry mouth. Or maybe something with caffeine instead of alcohol so he could navigate this minefield more deftly.

"You're so cute," she said mournfully, reaching up to slowly pat his cheek. Her fingers lingered, stroking down his beard. "Huh. It's soft."

"Thank you?" he ventured.

She looked so startlingly pretty when she grinned at him that Gabe finally snapped out of his shock and stood straight. "Okay. That's it. Let's get you to bed."

"Yay!" she cheered, pumping her fists in triumph.

"Just you," he clarified. "Not me. You need to sleep this off. This might be a little more of the real you than you meant to reveal."

"The real me!" Veronica squealed, giggling as he retrieved the keys she'd left in the lock. "Look at her! She's horrifying!" He set the keys on the table closest to her and closed the door.

"She's not horrifying. She's just being a little more candid than she'd like if she were sober." Gabe gestured toward the open door of her bedroom.

Her hip hit the table when she turned, but she bounced off it and moved toward her bedroom. Gabe let his hands hover near her shoulders in case she started to lean. Once they reached her bedroom, he grabbed the blankets and pulled them back so she could just fall in. She tipped helpfully onto the mattress, then twisted around to look up at him.

"Are you sure you won't stay?" she asked with the sweetest smile.

"Something tells me you're not quite lucid," he said as he took the purse she'd snuggled up to and put it on her nightstand. He snapped the covers over her before he could let himself notice that her dress had ridden up to expose more of those soft thighs now. Soft, until she shifted and tension added muscle definition. "So…" he said, forcing his thoughts off her legs, "I'm going to get you a big glass of water, and then I'll leave."

"That makes me sad." Her bottom lip curved into a luscious little pout that made him want to taste her. "I want you to stay."

"We can talk when you're sober."

"Promise?"

When he nodded, her pout turned to a smile. But then the smile wavered. Her eyes glistened.

"Are you okay?" he asked in alarm.

"Yes. You're just so nice, Gabe." She sniffled and a tear escaped. Then another. "And so hot. Just so, *so* hot."

His laugh was half horror and half amusement. He handed her a tissue, then escaped to the kitchen to get a glass of water. "Here," he said when he returned. "I think you'd better drink some of this. Can you sit up?"

She gave him a thumbs-up but didn't move.

"Come on," he said, carefully sliding his hand behind her neck to help her raise herself up. She cooperated with another smile that was ruined by her having to sniff back tears several times, but then she dutifully drank a third of the glass while he watched.

He pulled the covers up again when she lay down, then backed away. "Need an alarm?" he asked. It was only ten, but she might sleep for quite a while.

"Nope. I work from home."

He smiled at her fit of giggles, then raised his hand. "Good night, Dear Veronica. It was a hell of a show."

She aimed a finger pistol at him and winked as she pulled the trigger. "Thanks, Gabe. Don't forget your promise."

"I'll make you a deal. I won't forget if you don't." He had a very strong feeling that she wouldn't remember any of this tomorrow. And an even stronger feeling that she'd be sorry if she did.

He turned off her lights and locked the thumb lock on her front door before he stepped outside, grateful that he had time alone to process what she'd said to him. Still, he was smiling as he hit the sidewalk and headed for his own place a block away. No, Veronica Chandler was nothing like he'd thought she'd be. And he was kind of…thrilled.

CHAPTER FIVE

VERONICA KNEW SHE was hungover before she even opened her eyes, but opening her eyes confirmed the state. Even the weak dawn light filtering past her blinds made her groan in pain. She'd had a hangover only twice before, but there was no mistaking the symptoms. Fuzzy tongue, queasy stomach, pounding headache.

Keeping her eyes closed, she sat slowly up and swung her feet over the bed. The room spun a little, but her stomach didn't protest too much, thank God. In fact, a glass of cold milk sounded like something she'd pay a million dollars for. Promising herself a reward of returning to bed in just a few minutes, she pushed to her feet and shuffled to the bathroom, not bothering to turn on the lights.

After the bathroom, she headed slowly to the fridge, hissing in pain like a vampire when the fridge light burned her retinas. She squeezed her eyes shut and managed to find the milk and get the door closed without having to brave the light again. She gulped down half a glass of milk, popped some ibuprofen and trudged back to her room.

She sank into her mattress with a sigh. "I should take off this dress," she muttered to no one, but it seemed like a Herculean task. She pulled the covers over her head and slept.

The next time she woke up, the room was much brighter, but her headache was gone. Her body still ached, and her stomach felt hollow, but that was the worst of it. She was bone-dry, though, and when she saw the water on her bedside table, she sat up and gulped the rest of it down.

"God, I'm an idiot," she moaned. She couldn't remember how many martinis she'd had, but there'd been at least two before the show, and two was really her limit. She remembered the nice waitress and she remembered sitting with Gabe, and then... Then she'd obviously stumbled home and fallen into bed without even taking off her dress.

Looking down at herself, she winced. There were deep creases all over the pretty blue knit. She'd have to hand wash it and hope it recovered.

Veronica climbed from bed and struggled out of her dress and bra, then dug out yoga pants and a big T-shirt. This time, when she got to the bathroom, she turned on the light and regretted it immediately. Not because of her hangover, but because of what she saw in the mirror.

"Oh, holy mother of God," she wheezed, staring wide-eyed at the hot mess that looked back at her. Her hair stood up in crazed tufts, as if she'd twisted her head into her pillow for half the night. Her skin was sallow and sickly looking, as befitted a woman with a hell of a hangover. But worst of all were her eyes, which were bloodshot and ringed with layers of purple and gray and black makeup that looked like a bruised rainbow.

Veronica dove for her bathroom drawer and frantically pulled out her makeup wipes. It took five minutes to get the eye makeup off, but the slight purplish tinge beneath her eyes wouldn't budge. Maybe it was just exhaustion. Her skin felt invigorated, at least, though after all the scrubbing, she now looked as if she had pinkeye.

"Never again," she promised herself. "No martinis next week."

She was craving a hot breakfast, but no way was she leaving her house to grab anything. Even a hoodie and big sunglasses couldn't cure her self-consciousness, so she ventured into her kitchen to see what she had. The inside of her fridge didn't present the best options, but she did find cheese and some egg substitute. A bad omelet, then.

She set her finds on the counter, closed the fridge, then turned to flip the light switch, wincing instinctively at the shock of brightness.

But it was fine. She was fine. Because she'd been smart enough to get up and take ibuprofen hours before. This wasn't so bad. Maybe she could handle a party lifestyle, after all.

She turned back to face the fridge, paused to feel her heart skip in her chest and then she screamed.

The white notebook paper stood out against the black door. Hand pressed to her mouth in horror, Veronica backed up until her ass hit the other counter. "No," she whispered against her fingers. "No, no, no, no, no."

#1—Let people see the real you.

"No!" she yelled at the paper.

Those bold black words were all it took for the whole evening to rush back at her. The way she'd flirted with Gabe, the way she'd *told* him she was flirting with him, the drunk, stumbling walk back to her apartment and then...

"Noooo," she moaned, pressing her hand hard to her

mouth as if she could somehow stop the words that had passed her lips the night before.

She'd told him her deepest secret. Confessed what no one could ever know. And then she'd asked if he'd *help her take care of it.*

Her stomach, which had felt merely hollow before, now churned with acid and sickness. It rose up and pushed at her throat. Veronica shook her head. She pressed her whole hand to her mouth, but there was no defeating it. She gave in and rushed to the bathroom.

She didn't feel any better after she was sick. She only felt more pitiful, more wrung out. She'd told Gabe MacKenzie, the new hot guy in town, that she had no experience with *fucking.* And then she'd practically begged him to apply his penis to her charitable enterprise.

He'd somehow managed to resist her siren song, even after she'd started crying.

Oh, my God, she'd started *crying* while she asked him to come to bed with her.

He hadn't come to bed. Thank God. What if he'd stayed? What if he'd spent the night and then woken up to find her goggling at him with her zombie raccoon eyes just before she vomited all over his naked body?

"Oh, God." Yes, that was one way to look at the bright side of things. She hadn't talked him into taking her virginity and then thrown up on his penis.

Veronica rinsed out her mouth, splashed cold water on her face and then tipped her head up to stare herself down in the mirror. Water dripped slowly from the pink tip of her nose. "I'll have to move," she said, watching the way her chin trembled. "I'll have to start over in a new place where no one knows my shame."

It was really the only solution. It was exactly what she'd tell anyone who wrote in to her. *Leave immediately. Take only what you can carry. Slip out of town under cover of night. Start somewhere new and this time try not to be a pitiful disaster.*

Except that wasn't what she would say. She was overreacting. A little.

So what would she tell herself?

She felt dizzy at the thought. Or maybe she was dizzy from having consumed nothing but martinis and milk in the past twelve hours.

Feet dragging, she headed back to the kitchen to make her sad omelet. She might be having the same thing for lunch and dinner. She obviously couldn't leave the house today.

She accidentally caught sight of the fridge as she poured the egg mixture into a pan. The black letters of the note glared at her. *Let people see the* real *you?* What a shitty idea that had been. She snatched the paper off the fridge and threw it into the trash. At least she could say she'd really tried it. The real her had been on full display last night. She'd given it her all. She'd practically shown him her real crotch.

She seasoned the omelet, flipped it over and added cheese. Then extra cheese.

Overreaction or not, she couldn't leave town. She had nowhere to go. Jackson was the place she'd already retreated to. Her safe zone. Not that it had ever felt safe.

She could flee to her dad's latest house. Abandon her pretense of independence and go live in one of his professionally decorated guest rooms. That wouldn't feel exactly safe, either, but she'd still have a lot of privacy. His "cabin" was in the mountains and the closest neighbors were almost a mile away. Granted, that closest neighbor was Isabelle, one of Veronica's best friends, but she was too much of a hermit to cause problems. And Veronica's dad wouldn't bother her. She'd hardly seen him at all the last time she'd stayed there.

Still...maybe she wasn't as destroyed as she thought she was, because the thought of moving to her dad's house lit a fire inside her, a burning fire that felt a lot like heartburn. She wasn't ready to give up yet. Not completely.

She ate her sad omelet and took a shower and put on a slightly less baggy T-shirt that made her small breasts look slightly more visible. She used some Visine and brushed her teeth and styled her hair. That was good, safe advice she could give herself. *You'll feel better if you make an effort, even if it's just brushing your teeth.*

She peeked out her front window, then backed quickly away when she saw people walking past.

Gabe knew where she lived. What if he stopped by? She'd made him promise, after all. But surely he never wanted to be in her presence again. Surely he'd play it safe and assume that a promise made to an insane drunk girl wasn't meant to be kept.

So she was stuck here. Her apartment was the safest place for her. She could do her work and sneak out only during Gabe's work hours. Maybe she could somehow get his schedule from Lauren. Yes. Avoidance. That was the best tactic.

Unless he decided to share his story. It was pretty funny, after all. Really funny. Veronica was the only one who wouldn't be laughing. And maybe Veronica's boss. He wouldn't find it funny at all.

"Shit," she breathed. Gabe didn't seem the type to

gossip. He seemed entirely trustworthy. But she'd met him only twice. Maybe he was a catty, cruel asshole. Maybe he was the kind of guy who would've hung out with Veronica's stepbrother in high school and laughed every time she walked by. Maybe he'd already texted his ten closest friends and then spread the tale around the library.

Veronica checked her phone to see if Lauren had texted or called. But no, there were no messages from Lauren. Or Veronica's boss. And there weren't any accusatory emails from readers, either.

But there were quite a few emails asking for help from Dear Veronica. She should really get to work.

Even so, she switched back to her texts and stared at Lauren's name. Maybe Lauren would have good advice to give. And Isabelle, too. Maybe Veronica could tell her friends at least some of the truth and see what they thought.

But what if they just stared at her in horror and then made excuses never to see her again? They were both a little older and a lot more together. Lauren had already raised a kid and sent him off to college, and her new boyfriend was a silver-fox fire captain. And Isabelle was a successful artist who owned her own land and was dating a studly US marshal. Veronica really had nothing in common with either of them, but they'd still included her, inviting her along for girls' nights out and treating her as an equal. She didn't want them to know that she wasn't an equal. Didn't want to admit she was a fraud.

But the next girls' night was on Sunday. And she was getting a little tired of always being on guard. What if she treated them like real friends instead of just women who intimidated her?

She had a few days to work up to it. She could always change her mind.

Taking a deep breath, she took her notebook and marker from the drawer.

#2, she wrote, *Ask your friends for help.* She stuck it to the fridge and stared at it for a whole minute. It looked wrong up there by itself, so she set her jaw and pulled the first note from the trash to put it back in its place.

Her stomach tensed at the sight of both notes together, but she nodded. Two tiny things. Two basic pieces of advice that she'd give anyone. Surely she could pull this off. She needed help from her friends, and the only way to get it was to reveal a few tiny bits of herself. No big deal. No problem.

She turned off the kitchen light and took her computer to her room. She had a few days. She'd start dealing with her issues on Sunday. But today? Today she'd hide.

She put in her earbuds, cranked up the music and started reading letters. And the letters started to help her feel halfway normal.

CHAPTER SIX

GABE EYED LAUREN as they shut down the library together. He'd been eyeing her all day, hoping that interacting with her would somehow help him understand Veronica better. Did Lauren know the truth? Did it even matter? It wasn't as if Gabe could ask her about it.

The girl he'd been flirting with last night was a virgin. The thought still stunned him, though he wasn't sure why. Maybe it was only that he'd assumed since college that any woman he might date was probably as experienced as he was, give or take a couple of partners.

But Veronica had never had sex. Or she'd "pretty much" never had sex.

He frowned at the shelves as he straightened a few books. What the hell had that meant? Had she said it just to drive him insane?

Clearing his throat, he watched Lauren as she shut down the computer monitors. "I saw the Dear Veronica show last night," he finally ventured as he hit the switch on the entryway lights.

"Oh, I was having dinner with Jake's family and I couldn't make it. Was it great?"

"It was pretty amazing," he answered, wincing a little at how accurate that assessment was. He grabbed some paper towels and helped Lauren wipe down tables in the children's section. "She's really good at doing that in front of an audience."

"She is!" Lauren beamed at him. "You wouldn't believe how worried she was about it. But I knew she'd be great. She's good at everything. She just needs a little more confidence."

Right. He nodded. "How long have you known her?"

Lauren shot him a curious look that he pretended not to see. "About a year. I didn't meet her until after she moved back to town."

"Why'd she leave New York?"

"I'm not sure. You should ask her about it." Her smile wasn't subtle.

Gabe shook his head. "I'm just curious." He left off the "because she asked me to have sex last night."

"Good," Lauren said. "She's very interesting."

That was putting it mildly. Veronica was so damn interesting, he couldn't get her out of his head. He'd thought about her all night until he'd fallen asleep. He'd thought about her all day. He'd wondered how she'd feel about their conversation once she was sober. He'd tried to figure out how he felt about it. He'd imagined what it would be like to sleep with her.

That had felt a little wrong since he hardly knew her and she was…*kind of* innocent? But that kind of wrongness didn't exactly put a damper on sexual interest. She was pretty. She had great legs. Her smile made him happy. And she thought he was gorgeous.

Shit.

He retreated to the office to shut down the documents he'd been working on, though he hated doing it. He was just getting into the good stuff of figuring out which ebook lending system would work best with the library, but there'd be plenty of time to work on it tomorrow.

"Ready?" Lauren asked, reaching past him to grab her purse.

"Sure. I'll walk you to your car."

She laughed over her shoulder as she hit the last of the lights and headed for the back door. "Seriously?"

"Right. I got used to working in downtown Cincinnati."

"Well, we do have to keep an eye out for bears. And there were rumors of a mountain lion in Jackson Square last year, but I suspect old Mrs. Smith was drunk again. She does love a good whiskey sour."

She held open the door, then locked it behind her once he was through. "Hey, guys," she called to the three firemen sitting in folding chairs near their door.

"Jesus, Lauren!" one called. "When I said you should hire a hot new librarian, that wasn't what I meant!"

"Gabe," she said drily, "that's William, and those other two are Henry and Elliott. I'm afraid they're a little disappointed with you."

"It's okay," he said. "They're probably just jealous because they can't grow facial hair."

"Hey!" William yelled back. "We *can*—we're just not allowed to."

"Whatever you need to tell yourself."

The other firefighters razzed William as Gabe walked away.

"We'll work this out on the court!" William called.

"You got it," Gabe answered, happy for the excuse to get in a little time on the fire station's outdoor basketball court. They seemed to pick up games at all hours of the morning and night, and Gabe missed the public courts near his apartment in Cincinnati.

"Night, Lauren," he said as she headed toward her car and he set out for his apartment on foot. He was keenly aware that Veronica's building was on his way.

If he took a right at the next street, he'd miss her place by one block. He could walk home, go for a run, relax with a book afterward. And be distracted the whole time that she might be waiting to hear from him.

He'd promised her, after all. He didn't have to take her up on her…request, but he did have to get in touch. Tonight or tomorrow or at her next performance.

The idea of leaving it until next Thursday tightened his shoulders into such painful knots that Gabe went straight through the intersection and headed toward Veronica's apartment. Hell, the most likely outcome was that she didn't remember anything and he could try to forget the whole thing, too.

"Yeah, right," he muttered. Still, at least he wouldn't have to wonder if she was worrying.

And there was the chance that she remembered every detail and wanted to pick up where they'd left off.

He took off his tie, freed the top button of his shirt and rolled up his sleeves as if he were preparing himself for an arduous task. Two more blocks and he was at her condo building. He turned up her walk and then knocked on the door without giving himself time to think about it.

The nearest window was sealed up tight, but he could see light through the peephole in the door. He waited a few moments, listening for the sound of footsteps, then rang the doorbell.

Still nothing. The street was quiet out front. He

leaned closer, trying to tell if the faint sound of movement he'd heard was coming from her place. Nothing. He was turning to leave when he saw the light in the peephole flicker to dark for a split second. He squared his shoulders, trying to think what he'd say when she opened the door.

She didn't open the door.

He frowned. Leaned closer. Lifted his hand to knock again, but he let his knuckles hover just above the wood.

"Veronica?" he called. She didn't respond. "It's Gabe. Gabe MacKenzie. From last night."

There was a soft sound, like a breath or the brush of fabric. He waited for the lock to click open. It didn't.

"Are you okay?" he asked. "Veronica?"

"I'm fine," she finally said through the wood.

His tight shoulders relaxed. "Good. I thought you might be a little hungover."

"Yes," she said, her voice more muffled now. "A little."

"Are you up for talking?"

The wood stared silently at him.

He winced and lowered his voice. "Listen, Veronica, it's no big deal."

The lock finally clicked. The door swung in. He was startled to see her without her heels again, inches shorter than he expected her to be. She looked different in other ways, too. Younger, really, her blue eyes naked of makeup and her face a little paler. She crossed her arms snugly over the plain gray T-shirt she wore.

"We don't need to talk," she said.

"Are you sure? I did make you a promise." He offered a smile, but she only cringed.

"I'm sorry about last night," she said. "Like, really, *really* sorry."

"Hey, it's okay. Honestly."

"No, it's not. But we don't ever need to talk about it. You're not going to tell anyone, are you? Because if you did, I could—"

"Hey." He started to reach toward her, but the tight way she was holding herself made him hesitate. "I'm not going to tell anyone. Why would I?"

"I don't know." One of her shoulders rose in a shrug. "Because I'm living a lie. Because it's funny. Because it's so fucking weird."

"Jesus, Veronica. That's crazy. I don't think it's funny or weird."

"It's a little funny," she insisted. "You know it is."

He thought of her confession and ducked his head to hide a smile. "Okay, I admit I'm intrigued by the 'pretty much' part."

She groaned, but when he glanced up at her, he noticed that her hands had relaxed. She wasn't gripping her arms nearly as firmly now.

Gabe leaned against the door frame. "I haven't said a word to anyone and I never will. I swear."

"Okay," she said, squeezing herself tight again. She looked tired.

"I just got off work. I'm starving. Have you eaten?"

She shot a look toward her kitchen. "Kind of."

"Kind of? Is that like 'pretty much'?"

"Shut up," she said, pouting a little now. He noticed that her lips were full and pink even without lipstick.

"Come to dinner. We can have a drink and talk."

"Nope. I never want to have a drink or talk again."

"Food, though?" he pressed. "Food sounds good?"

Her head dropped. She took a deep breath. "I'm not even dressed."

"You look dressed to me."

"I'm wearing yoga pants and a T-shirt."

"Throw on a hoodie and you've got a look. Let's go."

She finally cracked a smile, though she tried to hide it. Gabe ducked down and met her eye. "Come on. You've got to eat."

She shook her head. "I wasn't planning on leaving the house today."

"Why?"

She groaned and rubbed a hand over her face. "Because I didn't want to take the chance I'd run into *you*."

"Well, shit, I really screwed that up. No wonder you didn't want to see me. I've ruined everything."

"You're a dork," she muttered, but this time there was no hiding her smile. Her eyes crinkled at the edges and her gaze rose to his. He suddenly remembered the way she'd leaned close and whispered the word *fucking* to him the night before.

Gabe stood straighter and cleared his throat. "What sounds good? Mexican?"

"Oh, God, yes."

"Mexican is always good after a hangover. Come on. My treat."

Despite what he thought was an inspiring tone, she still stared doubtfully at him for quite a while. He wasn't sure why he felt so invested in getting her out for dinner, but he wasn't going to give up.

"I look like shit," she finally said.

"You're beautiful," he answered.

Her face flickered in a brief frown, but she hid it

quickly. "Whatever. I'm starving. Let's go before I change my mind."

Gabe stopped himself from raising a fist in triumph.

She slipped on flip-flops, took a hoodie from the closet by the door and grabbed her keys. Her toenails were painted bright blue. Gabe knew it was a bad sign that he found that impossibly cute.

They headed toward a place four blocks away that even Gabe already knew was the best Mexican in town. She had her arms crossed tight again, pushing her breasts up in a way that caught Gabe's eye.

Damn. There was no way to pretend she hadn't told him what she'd told him. She clearly wanted to forget, but Gabe might need electroshock therapy to shake last night loose. *Are you sure you won't stay?* He was afraid she'd never ask that again.

When they reached a busier street, Veronica pulled her fleece jacket on and tugged up the hood as if she was hiding.

"No one else knows," he said in a stage whisper.

"I know," she sighed, "but I'm supposed to have my shit together. I'm not supposed to be the depressed, hungover girl who hides in her house in old yoga pants all day. I really can't believe I'm dressed like this in front of you, of all people."

"Me? Why? My hobbies are basically sweating in the woods, reading in my underwear and nerding out on my computer. Flannel shirts and workout gear make up about fifty percent of my closet."

"Fine, but you're just…" She waved a hand up and down his body just as she had the night before. "Whatever. I told you last night."

"Sure, but I thought that was the alcohol talking. Are you saying you really think I'm beautiful?"

"Please don't tell me you're going to bring up every word I said last night."

"Not every word. But that one was pretty good."

"Like I'm the first girl to call you beautiful," she muttered.

Gabe laughed. "I swear to God, you're the first. And probably the last. So let me enjoy it."

Her face was pink with embarrassment, but she was smiling as Gabe reached for the door of the restaurant and waved her in. "How about a margarita?" he asked with a wink.

"You're a monster," she answered, not even looking at him as she breezed past.

"Sorry."

Service was quick, one of the benefits of living in a tourist town during the off-season. The full-time residents could eat cheap and fast at even the best restaurants because they were dying to get people in.

They both ordered quickly. Gabe got a beer, but Veronica stuck with water. "Lots of water," she explained to the waiter. She glared at Gabe when he smiled.

"I'm not laughing at you," he explained. "I'm laughing with you."

"I don't think I've quite reached the 'this will be funny someday' point."

"Wrong. You already pointed out how funny it was," he said before he popped a chip into his mouth. "God, they've got great salsa."

She took a bite and closed her eyes. "They really do."

"This is so much better than anything I could find in Ohio."

When the waiter brought his beer, Gabe took a long draw before sitting back in his chair. Veronica looked much more relaxed now. And pretty as hell. She'd pushed the hood off when they'd entered the restaurant and her hair was a little…askew. But he liked it. She looked touchable. Flawed. Fuckable.

"Can I ask you something?" he ventured.

"No," she answered immediately, but then she sighed, her gaze flashing up to him before she looked at the chips again. "Fine, go ahead," she said, then stuffed a chip into her mouth.

"How did you manage to get through high school and college and New York City without ever having sex?"

Her expression didn't change. She wasn't shocked by the question. She must have known that he would ask.

She folded her hands and leaned forward, her voice going quiet. "You have to swear you won't tell anyone, Gabe. Nobody else knows. I wish you didn't know. I don't know why I told you."

"I swear," he answered immediately.

"I was so drunk."

"I get it," he promised.

"You can't even tell Lauren," she said.

He felt his eyes go wide. "I guarantee that I don't discuss sex with Lauren. Or any other woman in my workplace."

"Of course. I just…" She waved a hand. "This is just embarrassing. And ridiculous."

"I'm sure there are a lot of people who've never—"

"No," she interrupted. "Not people who claim some expertise in the area!"

He nodded. "Okay. I get that."

"And even aside from that, it's just… It was okay

for a while, you know? I wasn't a popular girl in high school. It was complicated. I didn't really go out with anyone. Not seriously. I dated in college, but back then I thought I wanted my first time to be special. I wanted to be in love. Now I wish I'd just slept with that cute guy in my philosophy class during sophomore year. I can't even remember his name now. That would've been perfect."

Gabe smiled. "I'm sure he'd have thought so, too."

"After college I went to New York, and then… God, then it was like a weird weight I was dragging around with me. I felt like the only adult virgin in the whole damn city. I told one guy. Only one. And then I never told anyone again. Until you."

The last words could have been meaningful and sweet, but she said them with the rough edge of frustrated regret so that they sounded like "Until you, *asshole*." He tried not to take it personally.

"So what happened with that one guy you told?"

"He made a big speech about how he wasn't ready to settle down. After we'd been on *two* dates. I mean, he actually stood up to pace back and forth in his living room as he talked about his five-year plan. It was as if I'd presented him with my virginity wrapped in a spell of eternal connection and topped with an engagement ring. Jesus, he was trying to get a BJ—I just thought he should know!"

Gabe tried not to laugh. He really did. "I'm sorry," he choked out, trying to control his amusement, but when she rolled her eyes and smiled, he burst out laughing. "You're really good at painting a picture," he managed to say, but then he had to stop and wipe tears from his eyes. "And you're really, really funny."

"Thank you," she said, still shaking her head at his laughter. "That's sweet. But I swear it wasn't funny."

"But he was just trying to get a BJ!" Gabe gasped, then totally lost it again.

Veronica finally laughed, too. "God, it was like he thought I was going to superglue his penis to me forever. Because that's what I'd dreamed of my whole life. Getting my hands on a first-year stockbroker's penis. And *never letting go.*"

She collapsed onto the table, laughing too hard to stay upright. Once his own laughter had died, Gabe found himself grinning at her, he was that damn happy he'd cheered her up.

"I guess things didn't work out for you two?"

"No. I never saw him again. I'm sure we were both relieved by that."

Their food arrived, and they settled into a silence that was surprisingly comfortable considering how little they knew each other. In fact, he didn't know much about her at all, aside from maybe the most intimate of things.

"You grew up here, right?" he asked, deciding to drop the subject of her virginity for a while.

"Yes. My dad was an attorney here, then a judge. He's a federal judge now, but this is his district. So I lived here until I went to college in Cheyenne."

"Do you ski? Bike?"

She shrugged. "I ski, but it's not really my thing. I like it once I get up on the hill and it's so quiet. But you have to get through so many crowds and lines to get up to the quiet part. My first love is hiking. I can be alone. Clear my head. It's peaceful."

Gabe felt his heart thump dangerously at her words,

but mostly it was the faraway expression on her face. "I know you don't climb. Are you into camping?"

"Not really. My dad isn't outdoorsy. I never really had anyone to go with."

"We could go sometime."

Her cheeks went immediately pink. Her gaze dipped to her plate. "Maybe."

"It's a lot like hiking, except you don't have to go back to the real world within a couple of hours. And we've got so many great secluded sites close by. There's no reason to go to a campground unless you like a lot of neighbors with generators and RVs. The key is to ask a ranger on your way into a park. They can point you to great flat sites that are near a creek or have a view."

"It sounds nice," she said.

"I've got a ton of gear. You want to try it? Separate tents, of course."

Her pink cheeks went red. She set down her fork. "Gabe, I meant it when I said you were sweet. You are. But you don't have to feel sorry for me. I have great friends. I'm doing okay. You don't need to take me in. I've just never had a real lover, that's all."

"I don't feel sorry for you! Okay, I felt a little sorry for you today, because I knew you'd be hungover and maybe mortified—"

"Maybe," she scoffed.

"But...can I be honest?" Her flat mouth told him what she thought of that question. "When I met you, I thought you were someone else. Some high-maintenance city girl who'd sneer at a pair of hiking boots unless they were Burberry."

"Really?" Her eyebrows rose in pleasant surprise. "I passed as a high-maintenance Manhattan girl?"

"Yes." He gestured toward her plate. "Until you ordered an enchilada platter bigger than mine."

She growled, "Shut up. I needed it."

"I know you did. I'm just saying that you're nothing like I thought you were. You're funny and smart and down-to-earth. And I like the way you get shy sometimes."

"Oh." She was blushing again.

"And you're beautiful, of course."

"You don't have to say that, Gabe."

He drew his chin in in shock. "I'm not just saying that."

"I can pull off cute on a good day. That's it."

"We'll have to agree to disagree."

She nodded, then carefully chewed a bite of enchilada *Suiza* before setting her fork down again. "I'm not good at graciously accepting compliments. You can add that to your impressions of me."

"Not like me," Gabe said. "When you said I was gorgeous, I just accepted that you knew what you were talking about."

"You're never going to drop that," she moaned.

"Never. Will you go out with me?"

She glanced around, her eyes darting from him to the table next to him and then the front door. "Go where?"

"We could go for an evening hike sometime. Or we could go to dinner." He waited until she met his gaze again. "We could count this."

She swept another nervous look over the room. "I don't think we could. I'm wearing flip-flops."

"I think that still counts. To make it official, we could go do something highbrow afterward. There's a historical talk at the museum tonight. We might have missed it, though. Still, I bet some of the art galleries are open. We could go nod and murmur at the art."

She watched him for a long moment, her eyes narrowed, her brow furrowed with thought. She cocked her head a little. Gabe tried to look sincere and patient, even though he felt like squirming. "Or we could get ice cream," she finally said.

Hiking, enchiladas, ice cream. Maybe she was the perfect girl. Maybe he was in big trouble.

CHAPTER SEVEN

VERONICA WONDERED IF she could die from blushing. She hadn't been lying when she'd called him beautiful. Or gorgeous. Or sweet. Gabe MacKenzie was a fucking dreamboat and she was on a date with him. An embarrassingly honest date.

They strolled down the boardwalk with their ice-cream cones and every time her shoulder brushed his arm, she blushed. It was dark now, at least. And probably too cold for ice cream, but she didn't think that was why her nipples were hard.

God.

Maybe he'd been joking about the camping, but the idea intrigued her. What would that be like? To go camping with a hot guy? To be totally secluded in the pitch-black night, surrounded by wolves and bears and all sorts of terrifying things? Separate tents or not, surely she'd end up in his sleeping bag. She shivered at the idea of him touching her. She hardly knew him, but she liked the thought. It was strange, this awareness. She couldn't remember a time she'd felt like this before.

"I've been to sleepaway camp," she blurted out. "I don't want you to think I don't have any experience."

His cone drifted slowly down from his mouth. "I see. At sex?"

"No! What? I meant camping. Experience at camping!"

"Oh. Because sleepaway camp… I thought… I don't know." He grimaced and shook his head.

She thought she would blush again. Or die of embarrassment. But instead she laughed. Hard. "Wow. You're a pervert."

"I'm not! I was just thinking of…something else. And you were thinking about camping. And I assumed we were on the same topic. That's all."

Did he mean he'd been thinking about having sex with her? That was only fair, really. She'd been thinking about sex with him. After last night, it was the standard she'd set. The giant flashing sign she'd put down between them.

"Fine," she finally said. "Thinking about sex doesn't make you a pervert, but you also ordered butter-pecan ice cream. Clearly there's something wrong with you."

His face relaxed into a relieved smile. "There's nothing wrong with butter pecan. Even so, that was only the first scoop. The second is chocolate. Surely that redeems me."

"Maybe." She finished her ice-cream cone and crossed her arms against the chill.

"So how did you end up back in Jackson?" he asked.

Veronica thought of all the reasons she'd given other people. That New York was too expensive. That she'd been offered a great opportunity as Dear Veronica. That she'd missed her dad. She sneaked a look at Gabe. He was frowning a little, waiting for her answer. He looked…sincere. And he didn't love the city, either.

The dark gray mass of the truth was pushing at her chest, squeezing the life out of her. It felt as though she were there again, in the city, in her tiny room in her crappy apartment in her intimidating neighborhood.

"I hated New York," she said, and it felt good to finally say it out loud.

"Oh," he said, the word a little dark with shock. "Really? Why? Didn't you say you'd wanted to live there for your whole life?"

"I did, but that was the New York from movies. The New York my mom and I used to talk about visiting. It was *Breakfast at Tiffany's* and *You've Got Mail* and later *Sex and the City*. That's not a real place."

"Sure it is," he said.

"I thought you weren't a city boy," she said, suddenly suspicious.

"I'm not!"

"Well, maybe you don't remember what it's like to live there. It felt like…a battle."

He nodded. "I know it can be a rough place."

"It wasn't that, exactly. I knew it would be expensive. I knew it could be dangerous. I thought I had it all planned out, though. I found roommates through an ad on Craigslist. Single women like me. I thought… I don't know. I'd watched too many movies. I thought we'd be friends, and I'd landed this amazing internship at an iconic paper, and everything I was waiting for was right there in front of me—it was all about to happen, and then…"

She felt very alone for a moment, walking down the street with Gabe. She didn't know how to explain it. It was as if the city had betrayed her. "My roommates weren't friends. They kept to themselves. And the quirky neighborhood felt like a gauntlet of yelling men and piles of leaking garbage bags, and there were roaches *everywhere*. And at my amazing job, I was just a cog in the wheel, and even though I did well, nobody cared if I made it or got spit out. The city was nothing but noise and steam and shadow and millions and millions of strangers."

He nodded. "I get that."

"Do you?"

He nudged her with his shoulder. "Of course. It's too much sometimes even for people who love it."

He made her feel better. Of course New York wasn't for everyone. She should have known it wouldn't be right for her. And of course, there'd been things about it that she'd loved, but they'd been hard to think of at night in her lonely bedroom on her noisy street.

Their steps had slowed as they'd talked, but she and Gabe were still heading toward her place. This morning she'd vowed never to see him again, but now they were on some sort of date, and what did that mean? Did he think she'd invite him to her place? Did she want to?

Tension drew her shoulders tight. She didn't know what to say. She was going to start babbling again. She could feel it. She was going to start talking about virginity and dating and then tell him he didn't have to pretend to like her.

Maybe she'd start spouting off statistics. She'd looked them up. That was her job. Even if she felt like a freak, she wasn't alone. About 4 percent of women were still virgins at her age.

Her lips parted. The words pushed at her throat, wanting out. The awkwardness needed to escape.

Veronica snapped her mouth shut and shoved her hands into the pockets of her hoodie. Her fingers closed around her keys just as she and Gabe turned onto the narrow walk that led to her door.

She dropped the keys immediately, then snatched them off the ground before Gabe could reach down to help.

"Sorry," she muttered, as if she needed to be sorry for dropping her own keys on her own walkway. *Sorry, I was just thinking about sex statistics.* The words pushed again at the back of her teeth. *Did you know that a large percentage of women don't experience pain when they lose their virginity? And anyway, I kind of already took care of that part, so you don't have to worry.*

No. She wasn't going to say it. She wasn't going to respond to awkwardness by being more awkward. Not with him. Not after last night. She'd used up all her quirky points already. She had to be normal, at least for a little while. She'd try being herself again on the third date. Or the fourth. If they got to that point.

Let him see the real you. Right. *Get drunk, spill your deepest secrets, then let him tuck your drunk ass into bed while you weep over his handsomeness.* Solid advice.

She shoved the key into her lock and unlocked it with a loud clack.

"Thank you," she said, turning toward him so she could say goodbye like a normal person. "I had a great time."

"I'm not going to ask to come in, Veronica. I only tuck girls in on first dates. On second dates I have a strict no-tucking rule."

She couldn't help but smile. He looked so serious. "Last night wasn't a date."

His eyebrows shot up. "Wow, you're right. Tonight

is our first date. I hope you're ready for the tucking of your life, then."

She leaned against her door, her laughter helping her forget what she'd even been so tense about in the first place. "You're awful, Gabe."

"Thank you," he answered. He hadn't cracked a smile, and now his gaze fell to her lips. "You're cute, Veronica."

"Huh," she breathed, caught between humor and the unbelievable thought that he was about to kiss her.

"Really cute." He moved slowly closer. "And I like you in flip-flops. Your toes are blue."

She laughed a little, a huff of breath, and then he kissed her. His lips touched hers for only one soft moment at first, just a careful, tentative touch. Then another kiss, warmer this time, and waiting. She sighed, tipping her face up as his fingers touched her jaw.

Her heart tripped over itself then. The kiss was a world of sensation. The brush of his beard on her chin, the smell of his skin, her pulse pounding in her ears.

He lifted his mouth and looked down at her, watching her eyes as if he was searching for an answer. But he didn't need to search. She was already breathing too quickly, already stunned and aroused. Both of his hands framed her face this time, and when his mouth touched hers again, she opened for him.

He still tasted sweet from the chocolate, but his mouth was hot against her. So hot. She rubbed her tongue against his, wanting more of that sweet warmth.

His body shifted closer to hers. Veronica let her hands rise. She let them touch his chest. Lightly at first, but as he kissed her more deeply, she moaned against his mouth and spread her fingers over his chest.

God, his tongue was slow against hers. A slow, steady stroke that sent a wave of shivery pleasure through her body. Her nipples went tight. Her fingers pressed harder into his chest. There was barely any give to him at all. He was…hard.

She made a noise in her throat at the thought, some instinctive sound of satisfied surprise.

Gabe slowed the kiss, ended it, lifted his mouth from hers. She wanted to pull him back down. She wanted more.

His teeth flashed in a smile. "I thought it'd be good to see if we had chemistry."

She stared at his mouth, willing it to come closer again. "And?"

"And if you're not sure, I should check again."

"Yes," she breathed.

"Good idea," he whispered just before his lips fell to hers.

Their mouths were more urgent this time. Or maybe it was only her quickening the pace, because she slid a hand into the soft waves of his hair and urged him closer.

His hands moved from her shoulders to her back, and Veronica wished he were touching bare skin. She wished he'd slip his hands beneath the hem of her shirt. She wanted to feel the edges of his rough fingers on her naked back, and she wanted—*needed*—him to feel her heat. God, that would be so good. She pressed even closer to him, and his fingers dug faintly into her back as if he wanted her closer, too.

Triumph fizzed into her veins when he groaned into her mouth. To make a man like this groan. To make him *desperate*…

But then he pulled away. "Oh," she breathed on a sigh of disappointment.

He shook his head. "I've gotta go before I lose all my willpower."

"Oh," she repeated, slightly dazed. Willpower to resist *her*? "Okay. Wow. You're way better at that than any of those New York guys."

His laugh was a little strained as his hands finally slid free of her waist and he stepped back. "I'm pretty damn happy to hear that. I guess that means the chemistry is okay."

"It's all right, but we should probably try again soon to be sure."

"I was thinking the same thing. Tomorrow?"

"Tomorrow?" she repeated.

"I get off work at six. Are there any trails we could hit with just an hour or two of daylight?"

"Trails?" she said, aware that her brain wasn't quite back to working order.

"I thought we could go for a hike."

She stared at him for a long moment before a sweet happiness filled her up inside. He didn't want to go to an art show or an avant-garde movie or a noisy bar. He wanted to take her hiking. "That'd be great," she said. "There's a trail that starts a few blocks away."

"Then I'll see you tomorrow."

She reached behind her and twisted the doorknob before she could say anything weird, then let her body weight swing the door in. She closed and locked it in the same slow state. Her body felt heavy. Pulled down. It made her want to kick off all her clothes and slide into bed. Was that how so many women ended up accidentally sleeping with men they hadn't meant to? A lazy, languid slide into bed from the sheer weight of arousal?

"Wow," she breathed. She was going to have sex. Real sex. With him.

Well, she assumed she was. She wanted to. And he seemed...favorably inclined.

Veronica stayed pressed against the door for quite a long time, imagining that mouth on hers again. And then she imagined that mouth moving lower. Down her neck, over her shoulder and then lower to her breasts. She closed her eyes and tried to breathe slowly, but the thought of that slow tongue on her nipples made her pant. And then...

And *then*.

She tossed her keys on the table and slipped off the flip-flops, smiling stupidly down at her blue toenails. She went to the kitchen to pour a glass of water to take to bed, but she found herself standing in front of the fridge, staring at the notes.

#1—Let people see the real you.

Maybe that had been a good idea, after all. Maybe it had been genius. After all, if you wanted someone to fuck the real you, you had to be visible. Maybe her problem for so long had been that she'd dated guys who'd never known the real her. What was it she'd thought they would like about her, anyway? The wall she'd put up? The clothing she wore like a costume? The fake confidence?

She'd been herself tonight, as much as she could manage right now, anyway, and Gabe had liked it. So maybe...

#2—Ask your friends for help.

Girls' night was coming up. The same night as her

birthday. Maybe she'd feel more mature. Maybe she'd be more *experienced*. She'd have Lauren and Isabelle alone and she could ask for their advice about Gabe or her dad or her job. And she had days to work up to it.

But first she had a date with Gabe.

CHAPTER EIGHT

Dear Veronica,

I've received an amazing job offer that would allow me to move from Wyoming to a big city on the West Coast. I've always wanted to live somewhere fast-paced, and even though the budget would be tight, I could swing it. But I haven't mentioned this offer to anyone else. The problem is my fiancé. He can't move and he would never want to live in the city. I love him with all my heart, but if I stay here and get married, I'll never get to follow my other dreams. I'm only twenty-five. Maybe I'm not ready to live in Wyoming for the rest of my life.

—Torn

VERONICA STARED AT the screen. She'd already opened this email three times. And closed it twice.

She hadn't received many letters this week. It was a slow time of year, but she wondered if the live Dear Veronica readings were cutting into the normal mail she received. Maybe people wanted to save up their questions for the live event. Regardless, she hadn't yet found another letter that was compelling, sounded true and focused on a dilemma she hadn't answered already.

But she didn't want to answer this one.

She considered digging back through the letters she'd

received months ago but felt like a worthless coward even thinking about it. This woman needed help, and she needed it quickly. So…

Veronica opened a new text window, copied the letter into it and then stopped with her hands poised over the keyboard.

Unless it was a subject she knew nothing about, she tried to go with her first instinct when answering a letter. Her gut response. Then she'd close the letter, let it sit for a few hours and go over the question and her answer more deliberately later. She'd found that the key to being a good advice writer was recognizing which of her responses were based on personal triggers and then working through it from there. You could never be completely objective or you'd lose all the style and insight people were looking for, but you couldn't base every answer on "Here's what I'd do."

And that was her problem with this letter. She wanted to respond by banging out in all caps, "DON'T GIVE UP YOUR REAL LIFE FOR A FANTASY OF HAPPINESS IN THE BIG CITY, BECAUSE THE BIG CITY IS NOTHING BUT LIES AND LONELINESS."

Yes, it was her first instinct, but it was maybe a tiny bit too subjective.

She ordered herself not to close the text window, then flexed her fingers and rolled her shoulders. "Okay," she said. "Ready." Then she dropped her hands to her lap and let her head fall back until she was staring at the ceiling.

This woman had written in because she had dreams. Veronica knew what that was like. She'd lived for nothing but dreams for so long. Dreams that she could leave this place and find love and success and a spine. She'd wanted to find *herself*, as if her confidence and strength had been hidden in a scavenger hunt that wound through the dirty, damp streets of Manhattan. How many miles had she walked through the skyscrapers and the parks and the subway stations, looking for things that had never existed?

She'd never been anyone. Just an amorphous, undefined *child*. Who the hell was she to tell this woman what to do with her life?

Veronica closed the window and dragged the email into her Unanswered Letters folder. The letter behind it was still on the screen, yet another query stained with virtual tears over a cheating spouse. She got them every week. Some from men, some from women. Some were filled with nothing more than tortured suspicions. Some writers knew all the gritty details.

Maybe she should answer this one despite that she'd published another two months before. It was clearly a common problem. Veronica told herself she should be happy she'd never had a partner, because that meant she'd never been cheated on or tormented by the fear that she would be.

But when she thought of Gabe MacKenzie, she wasn't sure she cared what he ever did with other women, as long as he did it with her, too.

The thought of Gabe broke through her haze of self-hatred. After all, if she'd stayed in New York or even found herself a boyfriend here in Wyoming, she'd never have kissed Gabe. And kissing Gabe had been... priceless.

She smiled stupidly at her useless hands. They might not have much to type today, but they'd been smart enough to touch Gabe's chest. To explore him a little.

She turned her phone over and pulled up her text messages. His was at the top. I can't wait, it said.

He couldn't wait. For their second date. An evening hike tonight.

She wasn't quite sure what to think of that, a hiking date on a Saturday night. Her first impulse had been giddy joy that he wanted to do something she actually enjoyed. But now in the light of day it didn't seem very...sexy. And she desperately wanted to be sexy for him, but she couldn't wear a push-up bra or high heels on a hike. Then again, he did seem to like her legs, and they'd be exposed. Who the hell was she trying to impress with her not-quite-B-cup breasts, anyway?

And whether it was sexy or not, a hiking date would be *her*. The real her. Not the Veronica who'd gone on dates with stockbrokers and salesmen and middle-management bankers in New York. She'd faked her way through those dates just as she'd faked her way through everything. She'd gone to the same kinds of restaurants her dad liked instead of the homey, comforting dives she really loved. She'd gone to art shows instead of Broadway musicals, because corporate ladder–climbing twentysomething men couldn't schmooze at the theater. And she'd worn the highest heels she could stand, along with the nicest secondhand outfits she'd been able to assemble.

Looking back, she had no idea what those men were supposed to have liked about her, anyway. The layers of falseness she'd painted over her less-than-adequate self?

But with Gabe...with Gabe she'd laid it all out on their second meeting. And he was still around. And he was taking her hiking.

The thought made her smile, but the smile vanished

as soon as she looked back at her computer. Hot date or not, she still had no idea what to tell Torn.

She gave up on work and shut her laptop. The stupid column wasn't due until Monday evening, anyway. Maybe she'd have a different perspective by then. Maybe she'd be thoroughly fucked and altogether debauched and she'd tell Torn to run after her dreams as fast as she could.

Her phone buzzed and she snatched it up, pulse already speeding. But it wasn't Gabe; it was her father. That was a real heart-rate killer.

Charity auction Monday 8:00 p.m.

Oh, Christ, not another one. Ever since she'd returned to town, her dad had treated her like an extension of the family name, requiring her to make appearances, but this was his first request since ski season had ended. She didn't know how to say no to him. She never had.

A second text appeared with the name of the gallery.

She checked her calendar in vain. There was nothing on it. Okay, she texted back. See you then.

That was a good enough reason to start getting ready for the hike. She showered quickly, then styled her hair and put on the bare minimum of makeup. Despite Gabe's kind words, she wasn't going barefaced when she could wear a little mascara and lip stain. She didn't come by makeup skills naturally, but she was no idiot. Men could claim they liked the no-makeup look, but there was natural and then there was *natural*.

She grinned as she chose a pair of exercise shorts that covered only the top two inches of her thighs. If he liked her legs, he'd get her legs.

She didn't need sunscreen, as they'd catch only the last ninety minutes of light, but that meant she couldn't pick a cute tank top, either. She settled on a long-sleeved shirt that at least fit tightly across the chest. After packing a water bottle, a flashlight and a hoodie into a light backpack, she was ready.

He knocked precisely at six-thirty, which was a nice surprise. She hadn't expected punctuality from a guy who was so laid-back. Cerebral thoughts about how considerate he was fled when she opened the door. He was wearing cargo shorts and a faded purple T-shirt and lots of lean muscle. *Lots* of it.

"Hi," she said to his biceps. She looked up just in time to see his gaze sweep down her body, too.

"Ready?" he asked, eyebrow raised in a way that made his smile look wicked. He'd noticed her legs.

Yeah, she was so ready.

She locked up and led him down the street toward the hills. "Are you sure you've never hiked this? It's pretty basic and crazy busy in the summer, but the views are great."

"Never. When I've been in town before, all my hiking was heading in and out of climbing areas. I'm happy you know a trail we can hit with such a short amount of time. If we had to drive to a trailhead, the sun would be setting before we could start."

"Or we could've just hiked over to the brewery," she suggested.

"We can work our way around later."

She felt him watching her and glanced over. "What?"

"You look pretty today, Dear Veronica."

She didn't even try to fight the blushing anymore. She was just so aware of him. And she was crushing on him so damn hard. "You look nice, too. In fact, no one should look that good in a T-shirt. It's distracting."

He brushed a hand over his chest as if unsure how to respond. The hair on his forearm glinted in the sunlight. She wanted to pet it. She managed not to say that out loud, but she thought it really, really hard.

They turned left onto a street that ended at the base of the foothills. They were on the trail and gaining elevation ten minutes after leaving her place.

"Since I'm a librarian," he said from behind her, "you have to tell me your favorite books. It's required. And if you don't read, you'd better lie about it."

"I read," she said, noticing that he wasn't even breathing hard. She kept her breath as even as she could. "A lot of nonfiction, actually. But my bachelor's degree is in English. Maybe I've read more books than you have."

He chuckled. "Your favorites?"

"I hate this question. How am I supposed to choose? *To Kill a Mockingbird*, obviously—everyone loves that. Anything by Margaret Atwood. I adore narrative nonfiction like *In the Heart of the Sea*. I deal with a lot of relationship issues in my work, so I love romance. I hope you're not a book snob."

"No way. I've read romance."

She turned to shoot him a doubtful look. "Really?"

"I wouldn't say it's exactly my cup of tea, but I love some of the sci-fi romance. I mean, it's sci-fi with good sex. What's not to love?"

"Excellent point." She started up the trail again. "What else do you read?"

"Everything. Horror, thrillers, science fiction, a little fantasy. I read the big award winners every year, of course. That's part of the job."

"And your favorites?" She heard him stop and turned around to see why.

He was standing with his hands on his hips, looking back the way they'd come. "*Dune. The Sheltering Sky. 1984.* And *Gone with the Wind.*"

"*Gone with the Wind?*"

He turned to her with a smile that was only slightly chagrined. "It was the first really big book I read. I got it from the library when I was thirteen and had to renew it three times to finish it. I loved it like crazy. I haven't reread it, though. I'm pretty sure it won't live up to my memory. I've learned a lot since then about writing and storytelling, not to mention the brutality of actual history."

"I know what you mean. I feel that way about *Pride and Prejudice.* I loved it so much the first time—I don't want to change anything about the experience. What if it's not as good?"

"Yeah," he said, nodding, "that's exactly it. But you're probably safe with *Pride and Prejudice.*"

Conscious of the fact that she was just standing there, smiling at him, Veronica let her gaze drift to the view he'd been admiring a moment before. Jackson was already a couple hundred feet below them, spreading out toward the open space of the Elk Refuge beyond. The Tetons loomed above everything in the distance.

"Come on," she said. "The view's a lot better farther up."

"It's pretty nice from here."

"Are you talking about my ass?" she teased, then realized immediately that she'd relaxed and said something weird. She barely knew this guy and now they had her ass hanging between them for the rest of the hike, both literally and figuratively.

She stopped abruptly and stammered, "I'm sorry. I shouldn't have said that."

"Why?" he asked, his voice closer. "The view of your ass is fucking spectacular."

She groaned and pressed a hand to her forehead. "Maybe it is, but I shouldn't have said it."

When he chuckled, she realized he was standing next to her now. She peeked between her fingers and grimaced. "Every time I let my guard down, I say the wrong things, Gabe. Every time."

"I honestly have no idea what you're talking about. We can have an hour-long conversation about your ass right now. It wouldn't bother me in the least."

"You're just being nice," she countered.

"I'm not sure you understand the male mind. Maybe you really are a terrible advice columnist."

She laughed. He always managed to make her laugh. "You have a good point. Let's just keep going, and hopefully, I won't have the breath to say anything else."

She didn't have to wait long. They hit a portion of the trail that was steep enough for switchbacks and she was soon panting for oxygen. There wasn't much of it at this altitude.

She was able to push through to the top, but she stopped to breathe once she hit more level ground. "You wouldn't believe," she rasped, "how hard this was… when I got here from New York."

Gabe held up a hand and took a few deep breaths. "I just got here two weeks ago. I'm still—" he took another deep breath "—acclimating."

"Oh, thank God." She dropped onto a boulder with a

flat top and dug her water bottle from her pack. "We'd better take a break, then."

He joined her on the rock. At first she was distracted by the way his chest moved with each breath. It was strange to see him breathing hard and a little sweaty. Intimate and unexpected.

His knee brushed hers, and she tried to take in every detail of his muscled thigh in the quickest of glances. She liked the way it looked next to hers. He was tan and hairy next to her smooth leg. If they were already sleeping together, she'd put her hand on his knee and slide it up. She'd let her fingers edge under his shorts and tease him with a touch on the inside of his thigh. God. Would he get hard for her? Would he drag her hand higher and make her feel what she'd done to him?

She didn't know. She didn't know if sex could really be as good as she'd heard. Every time she'd messed around with a guy, she'd ended up disappointed. She'd been...removed. *Un*moved. Completely clearheaded and disoriented by how much the guy seemed to be into it when she felt as though she were acting out a scene from tenth-grade health class.

Hell, she'd been more aroused by Gabe's kiss than she had been by anything the last guy she'd dated had done, and that included the time he'd gone down on her. That had mostly consisted of her staring at the ceiling for two minutes before telling him she was fine. He'd popped up so quickly, it had been clear he'd been waiting to be excused.

But with Gabe...just looking at his thigh turned her on. She wasn't even sure she cared that he might be throwing her a bone. She'd take that bone. She'd take it good.

Veronica glanced at her phone. "We'd better go. We've only got about thirty minutes before we should head down. Are you ready?"

"I think I can handle it."

The trail widened as it looped through a high meadow, and Gabe could walk next to her now. The tufts of dried grass left after winter were pierced by green shoots, and a few tiny yellow flowers dusted the field. Almost all of the aspen were brightening up with green, though a few still shivered with fuzzy seeds.

"So you've never been up here for a climb?" she asked.

"No, there's only one decent rock-climbing area close to town. The rock in this area is too brittle. Not ideal to have chunks falling out when you're trying to anchor. All the decent climbing spots are a good hour out, and that doesn't include the time you might need to hike in."

"So it takes a full day?"

"Well, it depends how early you want to get up. During the summer, it pays to head out before dawn. The main rock faces are swarming with tourists."

Veronica remembered hearing that complaint when she was growing up here. How difficult it was to get space for climbing or skiing or camping once the season started, but she'd never paid much attention.

At the top of the meadow, the trail cut into the aspen. Veronica heard the rushing of fast water ahead and smiled. "The creek is still high," she said. "We're lucky. This time last year it was a trickle."

She hurried to get to the creek. It always looked like a postcard to her, the way the water danced and foamed over the jagged stones, dropping down in dozens of little waterfalls as it made its way down the mountain. The last of the sunlight glinted off still pools, and the shadows of shaking aspen leaves chased dark spots over the light.

"I love it here," she said.

"It's beautiful. But I think I should've brought rope."

"Nah, the log is fine. Just don't fall in." She winked and jumped up onto the thick trunk of the dead pine tree that had been here for a decade.

The smooth surface of the wood was slightly damp, but earlier in the spring it had been icy in spots, so this was a piece of cake. She rushed the fifteen feet across and jumped off on the other side. She turned around to see if Gabe was following, only to find him landing on the ground inches from her.

"I'm going to take you climbing," he said, smiling down at her.

"No, you're not."

"You weren't the least bit nervous about that. You're a natural."

"You're insane," she said, laughing as she followed the trail along the creek. It got steep again, but this time she hardly noticed. This part of the hike was magical. The switchbacks wound through the trees, so it looked as if you were walking into dead ends of dark ponderosa pines, but then the trail would turn sharply and head into spring-green towers of aspens.

She turned to grin at Gabe behind her. "Isn't it amazing? I mean, it's not Yellowstone or Jenny Lake, but it's right in our backyard."

"It is amazing," he said. "Thanks for showing me. It's the perfect place to run after work. No one could be tense after this."

"Is it a stressful job? I know Lauren hates preschool hour."

"It's not that. Kids are fine. It's just a little weird to be brought in to change things, you know? Especially because I'm male, and all the female librarians here have more experience than I do, but I have to come in and say, 'This is what you're doing wrong.' It's shitty on the face of it, but it's what I was hired to do."

"I can put in a good word with Lauren, if you like."

"It's no problem. Lauren is great, actually. If I didn't have her on my side, I'd probably beg you for help. I wouldn't want to fuck with Lauren."

"She is pretty badass," Veronica agreed. Both of her girls'-night-out companions were really badass, actually. "Have you met Isabelle yet? She's an artist. She comes into the library sometimes for reference materials when she's working."

"I don't think so."

"She's good friends with Lauren. A brunette. She's usually got paint in her hair?"

"No, I definitely haven't met her."

"Anyway, she was a federal fugitive for a while."

"What?" Gabe snapped.

Veronica laughed. "That's really all I can say. You'll have to catch us out for girls' night sometime. Buy her a drink and see if she'll tell you the story."

"Are you serious?"

She shrugged. "What, you don't have any wanted fugitives as friends?"

"I probably do—I just don't know it. But now I *know* you're kick-ass enough to handle climbing."

If her friends made her seem more interesting than she actually was, she didn't mind, but no way could she imagine herself climbing any higher than a ladder. She wasn't one of those girls. She'd known a lot of them. In high school and college, they'd been the amazing winter athletes, some of whom had moved here just to hone their skills for world championships. In New York, they'd been the girls unafraid to take on every challenge that the city offered. They'd been glamorous and magnetic and *brave*.

Veronica had felt as though she'd used up all her braveness just getting to the city. And she wasn't even sure it could be called bravery, when she'd had no idea how difficult it all would be.

The trail took one last turn and they had to climb up two big rock steps, but they finally made it to the clearing she'd been aiming for. The trail cut between two huge boulders, then edged around a little ravine. Right at the top of the ravine, she stopped and faced the town.

"Here we are."

"Wow," he answered.

The setting sun turned the sky pink and gold in the west, and the highest peaks of the Tetons clawed at the colors like dark gray talons. The lower hills that marked the natural boundary of the town were already black with shadow, but beyond the grid of city blocks, the Elk Refuge stretched out for green miles. The river cut through the refuge, a winding line of deep blue that looked like a silk ribbon dropped into the middle of the grass.

Veronica sat down on a flat rock and Gabe joined her, but they didn't speak for a long time. They just looked at the scenery.

The breeze picked up, shaking the trees around them.

For the first time in a while, Veronica felt totally at peace.

"You take it for granted a little when you grow up here," she said. "It's not like there are parts of the valley that are ugly. It's all beautiful. I didn't realize how much I'd miss it when I went to the city."

"Why did you move?" he asked, sounding totally dumbfounded.

She shrugged. She wasn't sure why she'd done it, why it had been so important to her for so long. Maybe that was one of the things she needed to unpack in her life. Why going far away had seemed like the solution to everything. "It's complicated. And it was a mistake. I can't imagine ever going back."

He was quiet and she looked up to find him watching her. He looked more serious than he ever had.

She shrugged again. "Maybe I just spent too many years living in paradise." She lifted her chin toward the view. As a teenager, she'd spent a lot of time outdoors, but she'd always thought of it as her only option for escape. She hadn't realized how much she'd loved it until she didn't have it anymore.

He still watched her, as if he was trying to puzzle something out, but she didn't want to reveal more. In the end he only nodded and bumped his shoulder gently against hers. "So…tell me what it means to be 'pretty much' a virgin."

Veronica gasped in horror. "I'm not telling you that!"

"Come on. I've been wondering about it. The things you told me that first night."

"When I was drunk!" she yelped.

"Yes, when you were drunk. And being honest. I

mean, I was obviously intrigued, but after that kiss…
I've been thinking about it a lot."

"Oh, God," she whispered, her face going as hot as
fire as she let her head drop. But her face wasn't the
only part of her heating up. That kiss had been so, so
good. And if he was interested in what she'd said, then
he was…*interested*. Hadn't she just been thinking that
she'd do almost anything to get her hands on him?

She felt him lean closer. "I only want to know what
you want," he whispered, his voice so close to her ear
it made her shiver. "What you're looking for."

Just his voice was enough to make her warm, but
then…then his lips touched the side of her neck. She
inhaled so sharply that it sounded like a gasp. His warm
mouth touched her again, and the brush of his beard
sent goose bumps scattering along her skin and down
to her hardening nipples.

"I don't want to tell you about that," she whispered,
but she was arching her head away from him now, giving him more room to work. No one had ever kissed
her this way. Softly. Slowly. As if he was exploring instead of persuading.

"Okay." The word whispered over the skin behind
her ear. She felt his fingers slide along the base of her
skull, then trail down the nape of her neck. "Just tell
me one thing, then. Anything."

His tongue was shockingly hot when it touched her
neck. Just a little flick that made her gasp again.

"I…" she tried, then groaned when his mouth opened
against her and sucked gently. "I…I know a lot of
things," she managed to say. "All of it, really."

"Mmm." The sound vibrated against her.

"And I've done things."

"What things?" he whispered.

Oh, God, she couldn't say any of this out loud. It was too much. She didn't want to tell; she just wanted to *do*. With *him*.

He drew back a little, and she followed him, her body leaning closer, chasing after his mouth.

"Come 'ere," he murmured. She wasn't sure what he meant until his arm slipped under her knees and he lifted her up and onto his lap.

She grabbed on to him in shock, feeling as if she'd slide right off his knees, but his legs were strong, and his arms stayed around her to hold her steady.

She wasn't sure that sitting on his lap was quite… appropriate. But when his mouth settled into the crook of her neck and he tasted her again, any thought she'd had for returning to her own side of the boulder vanished. She didn't want to go anywhere. She wanted to be right here on his hard thighs, with his hands spreading over her back and his mouth creating magic on her neck.

"Oh," she sighed, settling more comfortably into his chest.

"You've obviously kissed before," he said. "You're very good at it."

He kissed his way up to her jaw, and when she turned toward him, his mouth caught hers.

Was she good at it? She had no idea, but he made her feel hungry and languid and *right*. But she got to kiss him back for only a brief moment before his mouth left hers. "Have you come before?" he asked, his voice a little rougher than it had been.

Oh, God. She closed her eyes. "Yes," she answered.

He kissed her lower lip. Bit it gently. Let it go. "With a man?"

She didn't want to say. She couldn't. She was a challenge. Hard work for a guy. No one wanted to be hard work in bed. But she finally shook her head. "No."

He exhaled deeply. One of his hands slid up her back to cradle the nape of her neck. His fingertips felt textured against her skin. Calloused. "No?" he murmured against her mouth.

She shook her head, the tiniest movement, letting her parted lips brush over his. He kissed her again finally. An urgent, dark kiss, his hand still on her neck, keeping her close.

Wanting to be even closer, she twisted toward him, sliding her knee up, and then his hand was on her leg, lifting it over his thighs so that she straddled him.

Veronica held him now. Her hands slid up his shoulders and his neck, and she cradled his face and kissed him more deeply. His hands went to her thighs, and his fingers rubbed slowly up and down, up and down, from her knees to the tops of her legs. She wanted him to go higher. She was spread open, straddling him, and she wanted him to rub her there. Right *there*. She wanted it to feel the way she'd always hoped it would. But his hands stayed on her thighs.

When he raised his head, she followed him, and he gave in and kissed her again. Triumph flared bright inside her. He wanted her. He couldn't resist her mouth. His fingers tightened on her thighs. Yes.

When he pulled away this time, his breath was rough. She stroked her fingers down his beard and put her mouth to his neck. She wasn't done tasting him. She wanted more. She felt his moan through her tongue and teeth and she dragged her hands down to his chest and the hard muscles there.

"Tell me what you've done," he groaned.

"No," she whispered against his neck. She didn't want to. It was all silly. She'd done things that everyone else had done; it just hadn't been *good*.

One of his hands slid up her hip, her waist, her ribs. He cupped her breast through her shirt and slid a thumb over her nipple. Veronica groaned with sharp need. It felt so good and it was torture. A small, stingy promise of what she'd feel if he touched her clit.

But then he rolled her nipple between his thumb and finger and she hissed at the pleasure.

"I just want to know," he said. "I don't want to shock you. I don't want to move too fast."

"Shock me," she urged.

He tugged her shirt up and her bra down and he closed his mouth over her nipple.

Veronica cried out. She couldn't help it. The pleasure was so sudden and sharp that it nearly hurt. She threw her head back as he sucked at her. When she opened her eyes, she saw stars. Stars just starting to shimmer above them in the purple sky.

"Oh, God," she breathed.

Above the sound of her own pounding heart, she heard a chittering and closed her eyes to ignore it. But then Gabe's mouth left her breast. Her nipple ached at the shock of cold before he tugged her shirt down.

Her head swam with dizziness when he lifted her leg and swung her around to her original position.

"I'm sorry," he said gruffly as the chittering sound grew louder. A biker flew past them so quickly that it felt like a sudden storm, the wind hitting them hard. "I shouldn't have done that here," Gabe continued.

Veronica blinked, trying to clear her head, but she

was still stuck in the pleasure. She wanted to get back to it. Who cared about bikers or hikers or anyone else?

She kissed him again and took his hand to slide it back under her shirt. Her nipple felt cold until his palm covered it with heat.

Gabe groaned. "Men have touched you here before?" he asked.

"Yes," she said, no longer shy.

His hand slid down her belly and over her shorts. "And here?" He cupped her, his big hand holding her sex in a careful grip. His fingers pressed lightly.

"Yes," she moaned.

He kissed her neck again, and she arched into his mouth as the heat of his hand soaked through the fabric that covered her pussy. "Have they licked you here, Veronica?" His fingers pressed gently.

The thought of him doing that filled her head so completely that she squirmed against his hand. She wanted his hot mouth there. She wanted his tongue. She wanted to grip the messy waves of his hair and hold him to her pussy. "Yes," she finally answered. "Just.. just once."

His breath huffed against her throat. "I want to do that."

Oh God, oh God, oh God. She wanted that so much. His middle finger stroked her, a whisper of a promise that sent little sparks of pleasure flying through her. "Yes," she urged.

"Shit," he rasped. "You're killing me. Not here. Not now."

"But if you—" she started, but his pained laugh cut her off.

"And not on a fucking rock. Not this first time, anyway."

She was going to suggest that there was a meadow only a few yards back, but even in her ridiculous state that seemed too desperate. As desperate as she actually felt.

In fact, she felt so damn tight and needy that she wanted to suggest they skip that altogether. She wanted to say, *It's dark—just tug down your shorts and fuck me right here.* But that was crazy. *Crazy.* To get well and truly laid for the first time in some hurried, frantic fuck on a public trail.

She nodded, kept nodding. "Okay," she said as his hand left her. Her pussy felt freezing cold without the cover of his fingers. She was a little mortified to think she was so wet she'd soaked through the fabric of both her underwear and her shorts. Then again, she was utterly thrilled that anyone could make her that wet. For a while now she'd been wondering if she could even get that turned on.

She could. She definitely could.

He eased her closer, arms around her waist, and rested his forehead against hers. "I think we lost track of time," he said casually, as if her hip weren't now pressed against his erection. He was hard. So hard that she was having trouble forming a sentence and wasn't sure why it was so easy for him to talk. Maybe it was just experience.

She shifted, pressing her hip more tightly to him, and she was rewarded with the sound of breath hissing past clenched teeth. It made her smile.

"Don't torture me," he rasped.

"I just wanted to see if you were enjoying this as much as I was."

"Are you *kidding*?" he sounded slightly offended. "I'm in serious pain."

She should have felt bad, but a laugh bubbled up in Veronica's throat. He was aching and hard as a rock. For *her*.

She pressed her hip against him again, then laughed at the strangled noise he made.

"Holy shit, you're cruel," he complained.

"I'm sorry. But you just teased the hell out of me."

His teeth flashed white in the twilight when he smiled. "That's good to know."

"Almost as good as knowing this," she said. Feeling sexy and bold in a way she never had before, she brushed her fingers over the front of his shorts.

"No," he said immediately. "We're not starting again. I can't take it."

Her laughter was husky even to her own ears. "But I'm having *fun*, Gabe."

He growled something she couldn't quite make out and kissed her brusquely on the forehead. "We've got to go. It's almost full dark."

"I know," she sighed, but she turned to look out at the view instead of moving. The sky was purple and indigo in the west now, the Tetons nothing but silhouettes against the fading light. The Gros Ventre mountains to the east picked up the last glimmers of light on their snowy peaks, but above them the stars blazed in the dark sky. The lights of Jackson twinkled cheerily below.

Now that her heart rate was returning to normal, Veronica shivered. Gabe pulled her back against his chest and wrapped his arms around her.

"It's hard to leave," he murmured.

"Yes," she said. "It's hard." Her giggle ruined the moment and she didn't care.

He groaned and set her on her feet. "That's it. No more mocking my pain. Your fun is over, lady."

"God, I hope not. It just started." She dug in her pack for her fleece jacket and a flashlight.

"All right," he said. He'd brought his own flashlight and a circle of light appeared at his feet. "The fun is only over for tonight."

She pulled on her jacket and they started down the trail. "And here I was hoping you'd come back to my place," she said to his back. Adrenaline rushed through her body as the words left her mouth. She'd just invited him over. They were going to have sex. Tonight. And the thing was…she felt nervous about it in only the best way. In fact, she was so excited about it that she didn't notice his silence until he finally broke it.

"Not that I wouldn't love to," he said. "I mean, I'd really, *really* love to, but…"

She stopped. He took two more steps before he stopped and turned toward her.

"But what?" she asked.

He didn't say anything for a long moment. She wanted to shine her flashlight in his face in the hopes of reading his thoughts.

"You're not coming over?"

"I don't think I should."

"Why?" she asked, then wished she could take it back. *Why?* sounded too much like *Please.* Suddenly cold, she zipped up her jacket and then forced herself to start walking again. *Why?* Why wasn't she ever enough?

He cleared his throat as she brushed past him. It must be difficult to explain to a woman why you didn't want to sleep with her. She was utterly confused. He'd seemed so turned on only a few minutes ago. He'd said he was in pain.

It was the virginity thing. Or the pressure to make her come. Why the hell had she told him that? No one wanted to—

"Because," he started, interrupting her thoughts, "I want it to be really good for you, Veronica. If we have sex. If you decide you want to."

She stopped again. *If?* Was he insane? She wanted it. Really badly. "Gabe, I… I shouldn't have told you all that stuff. It's no big deal, honestly. I've even… I mean, it's hard to explain, but I'm not even technically a virgin, I guess. It's really—"

"You absolutely should have told me. Everything."

She shook her head. She knew he couldn't see her. They were beneath the trees and not even a hint of light got through. The circles of their flashlights bounced on the trail at their feet.

She shook her head again. "I'm not looking for some weird moment with candles and stuff. I just want to *do it.*"

"Get it over with?" he asked.

"No! Well, yes. But no, I mean, I *want* to. I wanted to do it back there. On that rock! You turn me on more than anyone ever has and—" Shit. Why did words keep coming out of her mouth? "I just want to have sex because I want to. Like anyone else would!"

A few heartbeats passed. Veronica wanted to kick herself.

"You were that turned on?" he finally asked.

"Oh, my God, don't pretend you didn't feel it." Her crotch was still cold.

Even his chuckle was sexy. She was starting to hate him and his sexiness. "It's different to hear you say it, though. It's nice."

"Shut up," she grumbled. At least her face wasn't cold. Her face felt hot enough to melt steel. If she turned off her flashlight, maybe she'd see the red glow of her face reflecting off the leaves.

"Listen." His hand settled on her shoulder. She was glad she couldn't see him in the dark. He was close, though. Close enough to slide his hand over her hair. "I'm not planning to show up with candles and champagne. I just don't want to rush it."

"I turn twenty-seven tomorrow. This hasn't been a rush."

"Tomorrow?" he asked. "It's your birthday?"

She waved a dismissive hand. "Yes, and I'll still be a virgin for some reason I don't understand."

Even in the dark, she could see his smile. "Okay, I'll be blunt. I want to wait because I want you squirming for it."

The vulgarity of his words hit her square in the belly. "Oh," she said.

"I want you thinking about what we did tonight. I want you so turned on you can't stand it. I want you dying for it. Because I don't think anyone's ever gotten you there before."

She shook her head, speechless.

"Guys rush things. I was like that for a few years, too. We all are, I guess. And I think you've been with those guys. Guys who get you turned on just enough so you'll give in and let them kiss you, touch you, see you naked. Give them what they need to come. I don't want it like that. I don't want you to get it over with. I want you to *come*. In my mouth. On my cock. I want you to come for me, Veronica."

"Oh," she said again. The words getting inside her, tightening around her pussy. "Oh, fuck."

"Yes," he murmured. "And when we're done, I want you very clear on whether you've been fucked or not." His mouth was so close to her now. She could feel his breath on her lips. "I don't want any 'pretty much' about it. Okay?" he asked.

She had to swallow to wet her mouth enough to let her speak. "Okay," she croaked.

He kissed her. One quick little peck. "Okay," he repeated. "But I'm hard as hell again. Does that make you feel better?"

Yes, it did, because it was warm between her legs again. He could get her wet with just words. And he was going to fuck her. He'd made that clear. She didn't have to doubt that anymore. But she didn't say yes. She just shrugged and started down the trail. "Hope you can walk with that thing," she called over her shoulder. And if she had a spring in her step, she tried not to let it show.

CHAPTER NINE

SHE COULDN'T STOP thinking about Gabe.

Veronica had spent 90 percent of her day thinking about what they'd done the night before, the words he'd whispered and exactly what they might do the next time they were together. She'd wasted hours. She'd fantasized. She'd *squirmed*. Just the way he wanted her to.

But she hadn't made herself come. Honestly, she hadn't even been that tempted. There was nothing new about her own fingers, and she'd broken in her shiny new vibrator two years ago. It was old hat now. But Gabe... Gabe might call at any moment. And she'd be damned if she'd preempt their first night together with yet another solo orgasm.

So she'd waited. But she had no idea when Gabe would get in touch.

He'd gone out for a full day of climbing today, but that hadn't stopped her from checking her phone every five minutes.

Squirming. She was squirming in every way possible. And she was very afraid that this was the start of a long wait.

"Not if I can help it," she muttered as she stopped in front of her fridge to look at the notes one more time. Her advice was actually working out so far. If she could pull off "Ask your friends for help," she'd have to move on to number three. She just had to figure out what that was.

Baby steps.

The 10 percent of her day she hadn't been daydreaming about Gabe had been spent on work. She'd roughed out answers to a couple of emails she'd received and line-edited two articles her editor had sent her, but she couldn't stop going back to that letter from Torn. It called to her, yet she'd flinched away every time. If she couldn't figure it out by Monday night, she'd use one of the other letters. If she did figure it out, she'd publish the other letters on the web-only version of her column, where her editor allowed her a few hundred more words of advice every week.

She grabbed a coat and headed out for the night, and for once she didn't feel like a complete fraud as she stepped into the real world. She might be almost a virgin, but not for long. Tonight she felt sexy. She felt desirable. She had let a man lick her nipples on a public trail while the sun set behind her, and goddamn if that wasn't something.

Grinning now, she sashayed down the sidewalk toward the north end of town. The restaurant the other women had chosen for girls' night out was more expensive than she could afford, but she deserved a treat.

It was her birthday, even if no one but Gabe knew it. She hadn't told her friends. She didn't like being the focus. She preferred to watch from the shadows. A faceless Veronica who could put her carefully edited thoughts onto paper and then duck out of sight.

Except, of course, when it came to being touched by Gabe MacKenzie. She definitely wanted the focus on her then.

She'd learned in New York City to always walk the streets with your spine straight and your eyes fixed on where you were going. You didn't look at the men who called out to you. You didn't make eye contact.

Jackson was different, of course. She'd never experienced any catcalling here, though she wouldn't put it past a drunk cowboy on a Friday night. Here she could smile at the people she passed. She could look around. And she did. Her eyes traced the boardwalks, looking for dark waves of hair and a trimmed beard.

The sun was setting. Gabe would be done climbing by now. He could be out with his friends, making the most of his day off. And Veronica was showing off her legs again. She'd never thought too much about them before, but now she wanted Gabe to see her in her short red dress. She wanted his gaze to drop. Wanted him thinking about fucking her.

So instead of keeping her eyes on her destination, she let her gaze search the streets as though she were a woman on the prowl. She felt taller tonight, and it wasn't just the heels.

As soon as she opened the door of the restaurant, she spotted her friends. They stood and waved at her from a table right in front of the window. Veronica noticed that even Isabelle was dressed up. Not normal for her when she was in the middle of a commission, but tonight she wore tight black jeans and heels and a turquoise top that shimmered when she moved. Lauren looked sleek and beautiful in a black sheath.

And there was a champagne stand next to the table.

"Happy birthday!" Lauren called when Veronica drew near.

"Oh, my God!" She automatically returned Lauren's

hug, though she was completely confused. "How did you know?"

"I snooped in the library records months ago." Lauren pulled back after one more squeeze. "That's a little illegal, though. Don't tell anyone or I'll end up with a record like this one." She gently elbowed Isabelle.

"Shut up," Isabelle responded, then gave Veronica a big hug. "Twenty-seven years old. You're almost a grown-up, V."

"Almost," she agreed, thinking of the old Neil Diamond song about becoming a woman soon.

Her eyes caught on the champagne again and then settled on a little gift box wrapped in white and blue. "You guys. I can't believe you did this. Thank you." She was surprised that her throat felt thick with emotion.

"Thanks for spending your birthday with us," Lauren said.

She nodded. If she'd wanted to spend her birthday with her father, she would've needed to remind him that it was her birthday. After her mom had died, he'd remembered only every other year or so.

Lauren gestured toward a seat. "Have some champagne and open your present. It's from both of us."

Isabelle groaned. "It's from Lauren. I was a complete shit. I meant to shop, but then I didn't leave my house all week."

"You're painting," Veronica said, waving a hand in dismissal. "I'm honored you're even here. And you showered!"

"Right?" she cried, gesturing up and down her body, eyebrows raised in apparent shock at her own appearance.

Veronica picked up the small box and ran her fingers through the sapphire-blue ribbons. "It's so pretty." She tugged at a ribbon and then carefully unwrapped the shiny white paper. The box beneath was black. She eased the top off and gasped. Inside was a silver pendant stamped with a drawing of a fountain pen. "Oh, it's beautiful!"

"Turn it over," Lauren urged.

She flipped the silver disk over and felt tears blur her eyes. *Dear Veronica* was etched on to the back in elegant script. "I love it," she whispered.

"Come on. I'll help you put it on."

Lauren eased the necklace over her head and fastened it while Veronica lifted the pendant to look at it again. "You're the best, Lauren. Thank you."

"Just drink your champagne," Lauren insisted. Veronica did as she was told and was tipsy before the server came to take their order. The champagne was good, and the waiter was cute, and Veronica's cheeks hurt from laughing before they even got their entrées. It was one of her best birthdays ever. And these amazing women were her friends. It felt a little like the life she'd always dreamed she'd have in New York.

She put down her fork, took a deep breath and set her shoulders. "Guys, I need a little help."

Isabelle gestured toward her plate. "I'll finish that steak for you, if that's what you're after."

Veronica pushed her plate toward Isabelle. "Go ahead, but that's not what I meant. I need help with a letter."

"For your column?" Lauren gasped. "Oh, my God, I've always wanted to help with your column. Is it a question about being a sexy middle-aged librarian? Because I know all about that."

Veronica laughed. "No."

Isabelle held her fork up. "Hot chick on the run from the feds?"

"No! I just… Well, here's the thing. A woman wrote to say she got a job offer in a big city, and she wants to go. It's her dream life. But she's engaged to a man here in Jackson who wouldn't be willing to leave, and he doesn't know about the offer. She wants to know if she should chase her dreams or stay here and marry the man she loves."

Lauren nodded. "So what's the problem?"

"The problem is—" Veronica cleared her throat "—I want to tell her to stay. I want to tell her that following her dreams is a terrible idea."

They both frowned at her. "Why?" Isabelle asked.

Here it was. The truth. Her ears buzzed with anxiety. "Because," she said, "I followed my dreams and it ruined my life. That's what I want to tell her, and I have no idea if it's the right answer or not."

Her friends stared at her. Veronica stared back. Or tried to. But her gaze flicked back and forth between the two women, then finally dropped to the table. They looked too shocked. And probably a little disappointed.

"What do you mean," Isabelle started, "that it ruined your life?"

She slumped. She'd never told them any of this. As far as they knew, she'd spent a few years living it up in New York and then she'd moved back here to work at her hometown paper. "I was a complete failure in New York," she admitted. "I thought that my life was going to be there, and the truth is I was miserable. It took me four years to admit defeat and move back here."

"But that's not defeat," Lauren said. "You got some

experience—now you have a job you're great at here in Jackson."

Veronica nodded, but it wasn't true, and eventually her nod switched direction and she was shaking her head. "I'd been planning to make my life in New York City since I was a little girl. It was all I worked for. I never even considered having a serious boyfriend, because I didn't want to end up in the position that this woman is in. I thought…"

She took a deep breath. "I never felt like I fit in here. Not with my family. Not in school. And I thought I'd fit in in New York. That people would get me there. But it was lonely and scary and isolating. I hated it. I moved back home, and I now live in a building that my dad owns and I work at a job that my dad got me. And the truth is that people write to me with their problems, but I've never even been able to figure out my own."

She took another deep breath. Gulped in air. When she looked up again, both of her friends were still staring at her. She shouldn't have told them.

"Ladies," the cute waiter said from behind her. "Care to take a look at the dessert menu?"

"Can I get a cosmo?" Veronica said too loudly.

Lauren held up a hand. "Leave the dessert menus, please."

He passed the menus out, and then they were alone again, both women watching her. She hoped the bartender wasn't busy. She hoped the waiter would reappear within seconds.

Isabelle suddenly leaned forward and took Veronica's hand. "Life is never what you plan for it to be," she said. "You know that, right?"

Veronica shrugged.

Isabelle squeezed her hand. "I was going to be a doctor. I was engaged to the man of my dreams. I'd never set one foot out of place my whole life. I had everything planned. And then I lost it all. I failed at family and love and school and a career. I stole someone's Social Security number and lived under an assumed identity and hid in the mountains for fifteen years. And last year I almost ran again. I had a fucking bag full of cash and I was ready to disappear. So don't tell me how much you screwed things up, V. I almost went to prison."

Lauren was nodding. "Yeah. I actually did everything I planned to do. School, career, marriage, a kid. And I was terrible at it. I hated being a wife. I was the mom who always forgot to send lunch money. My version of fleeing New York and returning home was getting a divorce and starting over again. You're not a failure, Veronica. The things you've tried, the things you've failed at, the dreams you worked toward, all of that is what makes you good at what you do now."

Veronica frowned. "I don't see how that can be. Maybe if I'd gone through all that and had it figured out now…"

Lauren rolled her eyes. "You're doing fine."

"I'm not! I'm just…pretending."

"Pretending what?" Lauren pressed.

She was going to tell them. She even wanted to. But how could they understand? They'd both been having sex for decades. They'd both had normal relationships. Hell, Isabelle had even managed to take lovers while she was hiding from the feds in a mountain cabin. Veronica couldn't manage to get laid when she was living in the middle of a city of eight million.

"Just everything," she finally said.

Lauren shook her head. "You're good at what you do, Veronica. If your life had lined up for you and you'd done everything perfectly, how would you be able to help other people with their problems? How would you even understand them? You'd just tell them to buck up and try harder. But you don't do that. You see people's problems through the lens of someone who's fucked a few things up. You sympathize. You feel for them. You *get* it. That's your gift. Your dad might have gotten you this job, but he's not the one who made you good at it. That's all you."

Her throat was thick again. She had to pull her hand away from Isabelle's grip, because Veronica was afraid that small touch would make her cry.

The waiter appeared and presented her drink with a flourish.

"Thank you," Isabelle said. "Now shoo. We need a minute." She leaned closer but didn't take Veronica's hand again. "Lauren and I both screwed up our lives, too. We both felt like complete failures. And look at us now. We're fucking spectacular."

Veronica choked out a laugh even if it did sound more like a sob. She looked up at Isabelle in her beautiful turquoise shirt that clashed with the streak of lime green in her hair. "You have paint in your hair, Isabelle," she whispered.

Isabelle shrugged. "I'm still fucking spectacular."

Veronica laughed again. Two hot tears fell from her eyes and rolled down her cheeks. "Shit. I know you are."

"I was hiding from the feds and I started sleeping with a US marshal. So please don't pretend you're more screwed up than I am. I clearly win at that game."

"She's got a point," Lauren said. "You're obviously smarter than Isabelle ever was."

"Hey!" Isabelle smacked Lauren's shoulder, but Lauren only laughed.

Veronica grabbed a napkin and carefully dabbed at her face. "I can't believe you guys are actually making me feel better."

Lauren snorted. "Look, you went after your dreams. It didn't work out. You're only twenty-seven. You'll find new dreams. But when you're answering that woman, I guess you need to consider how you'd feel about yourself if you'd never tried."

How would she feel if she'd never tried? She'd spent so many years beating herself up for her decisions that she'd never wondered about that. What if she'd stayed in Wyoming? What if she'd gotten a job in Jackson or Cheyenne and settled in? The idea squeezed her chest until she couldn't breathe.

She grabbed her drink and took a sip. Then another. She nodded. "You're right. If I hadn't gone, the dream would have stayed. It would've gotten bigger."

"Right." Lauren patted her arm. "And instead of wasting four years in New York, you would've wasted your entire life imagining it. You're fine, Veronica. You're starting over. Welcome to your new life."

Her new life. Wow.

Okay. She could deal with that. New York and everything that had come before i:...that was her past. Wasn't that what she would tell anyone who wrote to her? *You made mistakes. Learn from it and move on.*

Move on. That was a little too general to be number three on her list, but it was still good advice.

"You're right," she said. "Thank you. To my new life." She raised her drink and took a hearty gulp.

"No fair," Lauren complained. "We're all out and Isabelle scared the waiter away."

"Let's order dessert," Veronica said, sniffing back the last of her tears. "And another round. It's my birthday."

"Hell, yeah, it is," Isabelle said.

Veronica had just decided on a fancy version of strawberry shortcake that included liquor in the recipe when her phone beeped. She dug it from her purse and made a little wish before she looked. It paid off.

Happy birthday, Dear Veronica.

It was from Gabe. Her cheeks might have been sore from laughing but that didn't stop her from grinning with delight. She glanced up to see her friends still studying the dessert menu.

Thank you, she wrote. Hope you had a great day.

The phone buzzed immediately back. Can I call you?

Her heart picked up speed. I'm still out.

Of course. Maybe later?

Yes, she wrote back, making sure not to add fifteen exclamation points. There was no reason for him to know that she was tempted to walk out on dessert for him.

She looked up to find her friends staring. "Sorry," she said, tucking her phone away.

"Sorry?" Lauren repeated. "Sorry you haven't told us who you're flirting with?"

"I'm not flirting with anyone!" she protested. Her lie didn't work, apparently, because they both laughed at her. "What?" she demanded. "I was only returning a text."

Isabelle rolled her eyes. "Judging by how ridiculously excited you were to hear from him, we'll be getting some details soon. We can wait."

"Speak for yourself," Lauren countered. "I can't wait." But she didn't press the issue. Instead they ordered desserts and one more round of drinks and Veronica tried not to imagine what might happen later. But she had a feeling this was going to be a birthday to remember. No...not just a feeling. This was her new life and she was going to make damn sure this birthday went the way she wanted.

She had her number three now.

Try new things.

She couldn't wait to get home and put it on her fridge.

CHAPTER TEN

"BUT IT'S MY BIRTHDAY," she murmured, her voice a purr in Gabe's ear.

He nearly groaned. He had a plan. He was determined to go slow. He'd been fantasizing about it since the night she'd told him her secret. And now...now that he'd actually touched her, now that he'd actually felt how wet she got for him... Shit. He was determined to make it perfect.

"Please?" she whispered.

Gabe stroked his cock through his shorts and winced at the ache. "It's late," he said.

"I know. That's why you should come over now. Don't you want to?"

He did groan this time. "I'm hard as a rock, damn it."

"Oh. Are you really?" The seductive purr had left her voice. She sounded a little breathless, a little doubtful, and hell, if that didn't make him want to show her just how hard he was.

"Yes," he finally said. "And you? Are you turned on?"

Her voice dropped to a whisper. "Yes. I like thinking of you that way."

Oh, God, she was going to kill him. He gripped his cock through the fabric and squeezed it hard. "Have you touched yourself?" he asked, torturing himself further.

"No. I was hoping you'd do that for me."

Gabe blew out a long sigh. It was after eleven. He had to work tomorrow. His muscles ached from the climb today. And this wasn't part of his plan. He knew how to wait for something he wanted.

"Please?" she whispered again.

Fuck his plan. "I'll be right there," he said.

She was laughing as he hung up the phone, but he was in too much pain to laugh. If she wanted to be touched, he'd touch her. Hadn't the girl waited long enough? And it was her birthday, after all.

He grabbed shoes, a jacket and his keys and stalked out. She didn't want champagne and candles, but if this was part of her fantasy, he wanted to give it to her.

Gabe knew he had trouble with wanting to be an ideal. An ideal son. An ideal colleague. An ideal boyfriend. He wanted to be the kid his dad could count on. He liked being the male librarian who wasn't shitty and chauvinistic. He'd always loved being told he was a great lover. The problem with being ideal was that it got tiring. Sometimes he wanted to be selfish. But right now his desire to make it good for Veronica lined up perfectly with what he wanted. To get her naked, to touch her, to make her come.

Fuck, he couldn't wait to get his hands on her. Or… he could. He just didn't want to.

By the time he knocked on Veronica's door, he was calmer, at least. And when he saw her smile, he was damn glad he'd come over.

She looked different tonight. More confident. Her eyes sparkled and her chin was tipped up to meet his gaze.

She opened the door wider to let him in. "Did you bring me a present?"

Gabe laughed at her audaciousness. "Wait a minute. Are you drunk?" he asked.

She giggled as she shut the door. "Just enough to be honest."

"Yes, I seem to remember how honest you get when you drink. But if you're drunk…"

"I'm not! I promise."

"Come here," he said, reaching for her. When he leaned down to kiss her, she met his mouth with a happy eagerness that twisted his heart. She was so…bright. So sweet. Nothing like what he'd first thought of her. He bit her bottom lip, then licked at the spot he'd bitten.

"I'm not going to fuck you when you're drunk," he murmured.

She groaned, but before she could protest, he kissed her again. He wasn't going to fuck her. He was going to make her come.

Her hands rose to grip his head, to pull him down for a deeper kiss, as if she meant to change his mind. He loved the way her tongue rubbed at his, the way her fingers gripped his hair. He was instantly hard again, instantly aching.

He eased her toward the couch. He wanted to touch her, explore her body, and the couch seemed a little more comfortable than leaning against the door. Or sitting on a boulder. He sat down and tugged her after him.

She wore a cute little red dress that rose up her thighs when she put her knees on the couch and straddled him.

"Tell me what you did today," he said, dragging his thumbs up her inner thighs.

Her head dropped and she watched his hands. "I worked. Then I went out to dinner with my girlfriends."

"Lauren?" he asked, drawing little circles on her skin.

"Yes." Her breath hitched when he dragged his hands up and pushed her skirt to her hips. Her panties were black. "Lauren. And Isabelle."

"Did you get lots of presents?"

She raised her hand to her chest. "This necklace," she said, "and now you."

"Very pretty," he said, but his gaze dropped quickly back to her thighs. Her legs flexed when she shifted. He smoothed his hands over the strong muscles.

"How was your—" her breath caught when his rising hands brushed the front of her panties "—climb?"

"I'm sore, but it was great."

"Your arms?"

"Yeah. Arms. Shoulders."

"Take off your shirt," she said.

He wasn't going to say no to that. Gabe shrugged out of his jacket and pulled off his shirt.

"Mmm," she murmured, her hands going to his shoulders. She stroked him gently, her fingers trailing from his neck down to his biceps and then back up. Every nerve in his body tingled to life at the soft touch.

Then she gripped his shoulders more firmly and dug her thumbs into the muscles near his neck. "Here?" she asked.

Gabe closed his eyes at the shock of wonderful pain. "God, yes." She rubbed slow circles into his sore spots. He relaxed into it, letting his lips part to take in a deep breath. Her thumbs slid higher and pressed deep again. Gabe sighed.

"Is this what you look like when you fuck, Gabe?" she whispered.

His eyes popped open.

She was watching his mouth. She licked her lips. "I

like talking to you after I've had a few drinks. I get to say the things I'm really thinking."

"You can say what you're thinking anytime you want. Are you always this dirty?"

She smiled as if he'd complimented her. "No. Yes. I mean… I have these thoughts. I know all these things, Gabe. I've read so much about sex. I get turned on thinking about it. I look at beautiful men and I imagine filthy things. But it's always a little removed. Wondering what they'd be like in bed. Wondering if I'd actually like it with them. It's like…"

She frowned and shifted her hands again to find another place. Gabe shivered with pleasure as he waited for her to continue.

"It's like I want to feel dirty, but I can't. It's intellectual. Something I've read about. But with you, it's… real." That last word seemed to make her feel self-conscious. She winced a little and added, "Maybe."

"Veronica—"

"No. You don't need to say anything. I just want to touch you for a little while." One of her hands slid up his neck to dig into the muscles there. The other slipped over his shoulder and down his chest.

His brain couldn't quite process the two different kinds of pleasure. One deep and bordering on pain, and the other just the sweep of her fingers over his skin. Combined with the strange seduction of her words, Gabe's cock was heavy and hard.

He opened his eyes. "Don't you think you should take your shirt off, too?"

"I'm wearing a dress," she breathed.

"Let me help with that." He slid his hands around her

waist and up her back to find the zipper. The sound of it was loud as he pulled it down, an unmistakable prelude.

She didn't stop touching him until he tugged down the modest neckline and eased the dress off her arms. The red fabric pooled around her waist. Her breasts were still covered by the black material of her bra.

Gabe reached for the front clasp of the bra slowly, giving her a chance to stop him. But she only watched his hands as if he were performing a trick. With a twist of his fingers, the bra fell away, and her breasts were naked.

He'd seen her in the dark. Felt her. Tasted her. But here in the lamplight of her apartment, she looked impossibly pretty. Her skin was so pale against the black fabric. Her nipples were pink and small. Her breasts would barely fill his palm.

A tinge of red crept down her chest and she raised her hands to cover her breasts.

"Don't," he said.

"I'm not very…" Her words died away when he swept her hand aside and replaced it with his own. He teased her nipple with his thumb until the skin around it went even tighter. Then he ducked his head and sucked her into his mouth.

She was small. He couldn't tell her that wasn't true. But it was her and she was perfect. And he loved the way her hips bucked against him when he scraped his teeth over her nipple.

He moved to the other breast and tugged her hips closer, groaning against her skin when she pressed into his cock.

"I…" she gasped. "I want you to fuck me, Gabe. For my birthday."

Her words wound around his cock like a torturous stroke of a hand. God, yes. Yes, he was going to fuck her. But…

He let her nipple slide from his mouth. "I'm not going to fuck you for your birthday." He felt the way she stiffened in his arms, as if she were getting ready to protect herself. Gabe circled her wet nipple with his tongue. "I'm going to make you come for your birthday."

She made a soft noise, a quiet growl of need and frustration. "No. That's not…that's not easy for me. I just want to do it. Really do it. I don't want to worry."

"Worry about what?" he asked, easing her off his lap. Once she was sitting on the couch, he slid her dress lower on her hips.

"About trying to come," she whispered, suddenly shy after all the wicked things she'd said.

"You don't have to try, Veronica. Just relax."

"I can't," she said, but she lifted her hips and let him ease her dress off. Now all she wore were her little black panties. Gabe knelt on the floor between her legs. She shook her head when he pushed the coffee table aside.

"This is one of my favorite things to do in the world," he said. "You're not gonna let me have my fun?"

"What is?" she asked, watching him warily, her hands poised as if she didn't know whether to pull him closer or push him away.

He pressed a kiss to her thigh, then her hip, then on the front of the black fabric that covered her sex. "This," he whispered. Then he closed his mouth over her pussy.

Even through the fabric he could taste her. He pressed his tongue hard against her and was rewarded with her shocked gasp. He smiled against her, nudged her with his nose. "Just let me. For a little while."

He looked up and saw her nod. One tiny dip of her chin, but that was all it took. He tugged her panties down, slid them off her legs. He felt her knees squeeze in as if she wanted to hide herself, so instead of dipping his head again, he covered her dark blond curls with his hand. She was beautiful. So wet for him already. He stroked his thumb along the top of her pussy and watched the muscles of her thighs jump.

"You don't have to try at anything, Veronica. Just let me touch you. Even if you don't come, I still want to taste you. I want you on my tongue. I want to hear the sounds you make when I lick you. That's all."

It was a lie, but it was one she needed to hear. He meant to make her come if he had to eat her pussy for an hour. And he was good at it. He'd been one of only three men in his entire master's program who'd been straight and single, so he'd been used for a lot of late-night stress relief. More important, he'd heard hundreds of discussions about sex from the woman's side of things. And he'd always been good at paying attention.

Back then it had been a more selfish act. A twenty-something guy with a great reputation for going down? He'd loved it. Now he loved it for a different reason. He loved it because there was nothing hotter than making a woman come.

Veronica's thighs relaxed as he stroked her clit. Her eyes relaxed, too. She was watching him past heavy lids now, her lips parted as her breath came faster. He stroked a hand down her thighs, urging her to open more. She did, just a fraction of an inch at first.

He bent down to kiss the inside of her knee, then higher up, then the very top of her thigh, and the whole time he stroked her clit with slow, soft movements. He dragged his tongue up the tight tendon of her thigh that led right to her pussy.

She tensed again, but he wasn't going to do what she anticipated. Instead of licking the pink, wet center of her, he licked her plump outer lip, tasting how aroused she was for him already. She was so turned on he couldn't imagine what a poor job some asshole had done at this the first time. She was nervous, yes, but she was glistening with arousal.

Still stroking lightly at her clit, he sucked her lip and gently worked his tongue against her. Then he did the same to the other side. Her thighs widened without any urging from him now. Her pussy spread open. She was deep pink and so gorgeous. Gabe swept his tongue inside her.

Her sound of shock was muffled, as if she'd kept her mouth shut tight against it. The taste of her pussy flooded his tongue as he dragged it higher. He removed his thumb and replaced it with his mouth, and he sucked at her clit. The sound she made wasn't muffled anymore. It was a loud cry. When he flicked his tongue against her, she exhaled on a hiss. He watched her hands clutch at the edge of the couch cushions. And then he settled into it.

She wasn't loud. The noises she made were soft and subdued, as if she didn't want to disturb him. He started out with soft flicks of his tongue, teasing her a little, finding out what she liked. He eased his hands beneath her ass and held her to his mouth like a treat. He liked controlling her this way, holding her steady, feeling the way her muscles flexed and tensed at the pleasure.

When he licked her more firmly, she squirmed

against him, just the way he'd wanted her to. "Oh, God," he heard her whisper. "Oh, God, that feels good."

He quickened his tongue to see if she'd like that, and she did. He sucked at her again, gently at first, then more firmly, feeling her small clit swell against his tongue.

"Gabe," she groaned, her hips pressing up against his mouth.

He moaned against her pussy, letting her feel the vibration of it through her most sensitive nerves.

"Oh, God," she gasped again. He felt her tense, but when he glanced up, she was shaking her head. "I'm sorry," she rasped. "I'm sorry—I can't." She pressed her hands hard to the couch and eased away from his mouth.

"Shh," he murmured. "We're just getting started."

"No." She shook her head. "I can't, and I don't want you doing this just because you think I need it."

"Jesus, Veronica. Do you think I don't like this?"

She stared at him, mouth pressed together, forehead tight with a frown.

Gabe rose up on his knees. He tore open the button of his shorts. "You want to see how much I like it?"

Her eyes fell to his hands as he pulled down the zipper. She didn't answer; she just watched as he pushed down his briefs and eased his cock out. "Look how hard I am," he said, wrapping a fist around his cock. "That's how turned on I am from eating your pussy."

She was breathing harder again, the worry falling from her face. She licked her lips and they shone with a moisture that Gabe would die to feel around him.

"Here," he murmured. "Feel how hard you make me." He took her hand and slowly moved it toward his cock. She dragged her fingertips along the underside, making the breath shudder from his throat. Then her hand closed around him. Pleasure crashed over him.

"Oh," she sighed, such a gentle sound compared to the violent need that twisted through him. "You are hard."

He couldn't help his desperate laugh. Yes, he was hard. He was fucking dying. She sat up a little to get a better angle. Then she squeezed him. "You're big, Gabe."

Oh, Jesus. He closed his eyes to shut out the sight of her. Her pale hand around his cock, her glistening mouth and wide eyes and her pussy spread for him. He needed to push his hips forward. Needed her to guide his cock into her. He needed to fuck her hard and fast until he came deep inside her.

He couldn't.

She stroked him then, and he couldn't help the words that spilled from his lips. "Yes. Stroke me. Oh, fuck that feels good." He opened his eyes to watch her hand work him slowly. The movements were clumsy, uncertain and the best fucking thing he'd felt in years.

"Oh," she said again as her thumb slid over his head, smearing precome along his skin.

"I could come now," he growled. "Just from looking at your pussy, just from your hand. I can still taste you, Veronica, and the taste of you in my mouth makes me want to come. Right now. So don't think I don't fucking love it."

He backed away from her hand and shoved her thighs wide again, and he put his open mouth over her whole pussy.

"Oh!" she cried out.

She was going to come for him. He couldn't believe

she didn't know that. Wetness was practically dripping from her now. He licked her clit and teased the opening of her pussy with a sliding finger. She bucked against him.

He didn't want to hurt her, so he pressed only one finger in, being careful just in case. But he wasn't going to hurt her. His finger slid in easily. He stroked her with it, and she wasn't being so quiet anymore. She moaned and panted and her hands fisted his hair.

Gabe gently eased another finger inside her. Now it was tight. Now she squeezed against him, but her hips met the thrusts of his fingers eagerly, lifting up for more. He licked more firmly at her clit and quickened the push of his fingers, pressing up, stretching her a little, letting her body feel full, as if there were a cock inside her. As if she were truly getting fucked for the first time. But he kept his tongue steady. He kept it firm and quick and her thighs began to tremble.

"Fuck," she gasped. "Gabe. Oh, fuck. I…" Her fingers tightened painfully in his hair. "Please don't stop," she begged. "Please. I'm sorry, just… Oh, *fuck.*"

Despite that growled curse, she still sounded surprised when she came. She gasped, her cry going high in shock, and then he felt her tight pussy spasm around his fingers. Her clit jumped under his tongue.

She seemed to hold her breath for a moment, and then she screamed, a rough cry full of released tension. A sob of pleasure mixed with pain. He didn't slow his movements until he felt the pulse of her orgasm slowing. He didn't stop until her hands pulled his head up.

"Oh, my God," she sobbed over and over.

He smiled. He couldn't help it. He didn't mind that

his scalp ached from the fists she'd twisted in his hair. He loved it. "Feel better?" he asked.

She stared at him with glazed eyes, then slowly nodded. "That was…" she started. She shook her head in confusion. "That was better than a vibrator. I didn't think it would be."

"Ha. Should I be flattered or insulted?"

"Definitely flattered."

He rose up to his knees and watched her eyes widen. Gabe glanced down to his straining cock. "Just ignore that. It'll go away."

"I don't want to ignore it," she breathed, and Gabe almost groaned at the lust in her voice. He wasn't just horny; he felt fucking triumphant, his beard still damp from her come. He grabbed his crumpled shirt from between the couch cushions and scrubbed it over his chin.

Veronica laughed. "Come here. I want you to fuck me."

His pulse sped at the words, making the ache in his cock even worse. "Nope. Next time. You're not even squirming now."

The lax muscles of her thighs tightened again as if she was aware of the decadent picture she made, sprawled and satisfied on the couch. "You're right," she said, giggling. "I'm not squirming. I'm shaking."

He spread his fingers over her thighs and felt the trembling of her muscles. He'd done that. But he forgot his arrogance when she reached for his cock and stroked him.

"But I want you to come," she murmured.

"Okay," he agreed immediately, making her giggle again.

"Are you laughing at me?" he asked.

"Yes. I feel…powerful." She stroked him again, and his hips pushed toward her despite his effort to control himself. She stroked him one more time before letting him go. "Come here, Gabe."

She patted the couch and he rose to sit next to her, tugging up his shorts as he did so. But he needn't have bothered, apparently. She didn't stay put for long. Veronica went to her knees on the floor and slid her hand into his shorts to wrap her fingers around his cock.

"You don't have to do that," he protested, though there was no mistaking the rough need in his voice.

"Do you think I don't like this?" she asked, echoing his own words back at him. Smiling, she drew his cock free from his shorts. That was all it took. Gabe gave in and slid a hand into her hair.

"Well, if you like it…then kiss me."

EVEN AFTER WHAT they'd just done, heat rushed to her face at his words. The words made it real. She was really kneeling at his feet; she was really about to put her mouth around his thick, hard cock.

She'd done it with other men. One guy in college and one a couple of years ago in New York. But with Gabe, it was a different kind of nervousness. His hand was gentle in her hair, and he seemed patient despite the raw need that tightened the skin around his eyes. And he was so beautiful. His brown eyes and dark beard and his muscled shoulders. Everything about him was perfect all the way down to his erection.

For the first time ever, this felt like something she *wanted*, not something she was willing to do. Was that how he'd felt, kneeling between her legs? That he wanted his mouth on her?

She shivered a little at the memory of that pleasure. Then she leaned forward and pressed a kiss to the crown of his cock. He smelled delicious. That was the first thing she noticed. Like soap and clean skin, yes, but with a subtle, unfamiliar musk that made her mouth water. He smelled like sex.

She kissed him again, a simple press of her lips, and Gabe sighed.

"God, you look so pretty," he whispered.

Her face flamed again. She liked it. She liked him telling her pretty things while she did something filthy.

She squeezed his cock again, glancing at him to see if he liked it. From the way he gritted his teeth, she'd guess that he did. A clear bead of liquid appeared at the tip of his cock when she stroked. With one last nervous glance at his face, she pressed her mouth there and tasted him.

When she licked, the salt of his precome covered her tongue and made her mouth water even more. She slowly licked all the slick, salty liquid from his skin and loved the way he hissed in response.

Feeling more confident now, she lapped at the head of his cock one more time, and then she wrapped her lips around him. He was heavy against her tongue, heavy and warm as she slid her mouth over him.

"Veronica," he murmured. "God, that feels good."

Yes. Yes, she wanted it to feel so good for him. She thought of how he hadn't stopped licking her despite her protest. Of how he'd sucked and tasted and kissed her as if he'd loved every second. She thought of that and sucked him deeper into her mouth.

His fingers spasmed against her hair, but he didn't

tighten his grip. He only touched her, as if steadying her for his cock.

She moved her mouth up and down, sucking at him, but she felt unsure. She wanted to be as good to him as he'd felt to her, and there must be more to being good than this. Or maybe not. After all, she didn't get letters from men complaining about technique, only from women.

Still, her mind began to work. She couldn't tell if he loved it. She stopped enjoying it. She started to worry and lost all the tight, hot feelings that had started building inside her again.

She didn't want it like this. Not with Gabe.

She drew her mouth slowly up and let him slide free.

"It's okay," Gabe whispered. He closed his hand around the base of his cock. "Come up here." He sat forward and his hand tipped her head toward his mouth. "Just touch me." His lips brushed hers.

She sat back on her haunches. "No. I want this. I've… I've done it before. I just want to know if you like it."

His laugh was a shocked huff of air. "I love it."

"I mean…" She took a deep breath and reminded herself that she was tired of being self-conscious. She wasn't the same girl she'd always been. Hadn't she just come all over this man's gorgeous face? She took another deep breath. "I want you to show me exactly how to do it. Tell me. I want to know."

He stared at her for a long moment. He looked impossibly handsome and decadent. His hair mussed from the grip of her hands, his eyes dark with arousal. His naked chest and flat belly. And there was his fist wrapped around the dusky skin of his hard cock. It still glistened with moisture from her mouth, and she felt strangely proud of that.

"That's what you want?" he finally asked.

"Yes. Absolutely."

His gaze fell to her mouth. "All right. I'll teach you how to suck my cock."

His filthy words hit her square in the chest, and the shock of it shuddered through her body. She couldn't speak. She could barely breathe. She nodded as he lifted his hips and pushed his shorts completely off. His hard cock bobbed with the movement, and she felt almost mesmerized by it. She simply didn't do this kind of thing. And now she was...*squirming* for it.

Her heart, which had skipped a few beats in surprise, now thundered to life. She felt a little dizzy. But the heavy tightness was back, squeezing her deep inside.

He gripped his cock in his left hand again, and his right hand returned to cup her head. "Do just what you did before, Veronica. I loved it." He pulled her head down. "Lick me again. Taste me."

She'd been doing it right, after all. She just had to stop thinking and worrying and learn to *enjoy.*

She licked him just as she had the first time, circling his cock with her tongue, sucking at just the tip of him again, drawing more slippery salt into her mouth.

Gabe groaned when she did that, so she did it again. "Now," he rasped, "lick all the way down. Tease me a little."

She pressed her tongue flat to his shaft and dragged it down to the base. She sucked there, then kissed him. "Can I touch you?" she whispered. "Here?"

She cupped his testicles lightly, unsure about how sensitive they were.

"God, yes," he answered.

She ran her tongue all the way up his shaft to the top again.

"Slide me into your mouth. Just like before. Fuck. That's so sweet, Veronica. Suck me. Just like you did."

Heat fluttered through her in waves, starting like a blush in her face and then rippling down through her body. She sucked his cock, and this time she felt as if she was perfect. She just wanted to *know*. That was all.

She gently tightened her hand on his balls, and Gabe bucked up a little into her mouth. "Deeper," he murmured. "Can you take more of me?"

Yes, she could. Of course she could. It felt easy to take more of his cock. She could suck almost half of it into her mouth now.

He sighed with pleasure as she slowly moved her mouth up and down. "That's it," he said. "That's so good."

She closed her eyes and concentrated on the feel of him in her mouth, the heaviness of his arousal, the width of him stretching her. Each time she'd done this before, she'd felt as if she was being used. As if her mouth was a sex toy. But this felt…intimate. She felt close to him instead of further removed.

His hand tightened on her head and eased her up. She felt disoriented as he slid from her mouth and she opened her eyes. It was too bright in the room. Her mouth was too empty.

"Are you still liking this?" he asked, the words deep and ragged.

"Yes. Are you?"

"Oh, fuck yes." He let go of his cock and wrapped her free hand where his had been. "Tighter," he said.

She squeezed him harder as he framed her head in both of his hands and lowered her mouth again. She took him deep, then even deeper as his hands guided her down. His cock hit the back of her throat. She held her breath for a moment until he raised her back up and she could breathe.

She should have felt used, she realized as he guided her slowly up and down, fucking himself with her mouth. But she didn't. She felt…almost light. Shimmering. She felt as if she was being fucked for the first time, and she loved it.

"Is that good?" he whispered. "Is that okay?"

She hummed an answer around his shaft and pressed her tongue tighter to him.

"Jesus," he gasped. "You feel so good, Veronica. And you look so perfect. Fuck, I'm sorry, but I like seeing you like this. I like watching my cock slide in and out of your pretty mouth. *Fuck*."

The heat crashed over her again, some strange, incredibly arousing variety of embarrassment that made her groan with pleasure. She sucked him harder. Faster.

Finally, he cursed and drew her head up. He gripped himself again and stroked quickly, one hand still tangled in her hair, holding her still. She panted, trying to catch her breath.

"Oh, fuck," he groaned. "Veronica. Fuck." His cock jumped and come shot onto his belly, then another pulse of it. She watched in fascination as he jerked off right in front of her. Her heart raced at the sight, as if she were watching something forbidden.

His breath huffed from him in broken gasps until his fist tightened in one long last squeeze of his cock and his head fell back onto the couch. "Oh, my God," he said, half laughing around the words. "Holy shit."

She pressed her lips together to hold in a secret smile. She shouldn't feel proud. Hadn't she just been telling herself that men didn't seem very picky about blow jobs?

But while his eyes were closed, she took the chance to look him over. The muscles of his neck and shoulders had lost all their tension. His hands lay open and relaxed on his naked thighs, as if he were meditating. But best of all, the flat, ridged plane of his belly was streaked with come, and the sight of it filled her with an odd joy. It felt like yet another secret for her to keep, but this was a delicious kind of secret she'd never, ever had before.

She ducked her head and pressed a kiss to his thigh and she finally let herself smile against him.

CHAPTER ELEVEN

I AM A SEX GODDESS.

She smirked at the words she'd typed into her blank document. "A sex goddess," she whispered to herself. But no, that wasn't quite it. There were too many types of sex she hadn't had yet.

She backed the cursor all the way up and tried again. *I give the best blow jobs in the whole world.* Okay, that probably wasn't true. Yet. She'd only given one awesome blow job, after all.

I am a dick-sucking savant.

Yes. That was it. And she was the perfect match for a world-class pussy eater like Gabe.

Veronica smiled stupidly at the screen, blushing at her own vulgar thoughts. She had to get to work, but all she wanted to do was think about what they'd done the night before.

He hadn't spent the night. She understood why. It was just sex. It wasn't serious. And he'd been due at work first thing in the morning, so he hadn't stayed. But she wished he had. She wanted it again.

Hoping more caffeine would clear the haze of lust from her head, she got up and poured herself another cup of coffee.

Her new note stared her in the face. *#3—Try new*

things. She was really kicking ass at that one. She'd tried Gabe MacKenzie.

She sighed and leaned against the counter.

Holy mother, she was in trouble. One single orgasm and he was under her skin in a big way. Not that she was surprised. She'd waited a really long time for that orgasm, and it had been a good one. As far as she could tell. Maybe there were better ones. She wanted to find out.

Try new things.

She set her cup down and dug a pen from a drawer to add two words to the note. *#3—Try* all the *new things.*

But first she had to work. She grabbed her coffee and laptop and headed to the desk in her bedroom. It would be easier to think if she was away from the oral-sex couch.

She opened the email from Torn and started writing.

Dear Torn,

I struggled with how to answer your letter, because there is no easy answer. You have dreams. You have goals and desires that are about you and have nothing to do with a man. But you also have a relationship that you value and a partner you love. The truth is that these two very separate things may not fit together.

I could tell you to sit down and make a list of pros and cons, of risks and rewards, but real life isn't neat like that. If you follow your dreams, there's a good chance they won't work out the way you expect. You might hate the city, you might hate the job, or you might get sick in a year and find that career and location are your lowest priorities. Then again, we all know that marriage isn't exactly a permanent state anymore.

You can dedicate your life to someone and wake up to find that they're gone six months later.

But if you're keeping this from him, I'm not sure he's the love of your life. First of all, you're not communicating with him. Second, you don't trust him. What you're saying is "I'm considering giving up my dream to live where he wants to live, because I know he won't do the same for me."

Torn, you have to tell him about your dreams, your job offer and your fears. His reaction might help you make the decision. But there's a good possibility that this relationship is already on shaky ground, shaky enough that if you stay in it and don't follow the dreams that are just for you, your love may fade more quickly than you think.

She hit Save, then rolled her shoulders. It was only a first pass. She'd shower and go grocery shopping and then read it again.

Before she closed her laptop, she paged to the top of the document just to be sure she'd erased her self-help mantras. Her editor didn't need to know that Dear Veronica was a dick-sucking savant. It would make for some awkward meetings.

She managed to get through the next couple of hours. She did a good job of not obsessing over her superhot lover. She showered and took only a moment to look at her naked body and wonder what it looked like to Gabe.

There were other adult things she had to do. She went to the bank, did her grocery shopping, put everything away and then cleaned the kitchen. But after all that, it was only one-thirty and she had to sit on her hands to stop herself from incessantly checking her texts.

She'd thought he might text this morning. She'd been sure he'd text this afternoon. He hadn't, and Veronica was trying to convince herself that wasn't a bad sign. After all, as meaningful as last night had been for her, for Gabe it had been just another sexual encounter. It hadn't been a first for him. He hadn't waited for years.

She snatched up her phone and checked it. Gabe hadn't texted.

Veronica felt suddenly disgusted with herself. Why was she waiting for Gabe to text? Didn't her fingers work just as well as his? He'd said he wanted to see the real her, and the real her wanted to text him.

Thanks for last night, she typed, then hit Send. Alarm immediately flooded her veins. Was she flirting now or being awkward? Was there any difference where she was concerned?

After holding her breath as long as she could, she let it out and tried to breathe normally. When a full minute passed without a response, she groaned in pain. She was definitely being weird. Who sent a thank-you note for an orgasm?

Oh, God. She'd just sent a thank-you note for an orgasm!

She fell slowly forward until her forehead thumped the table. Then she thumped it again. "You are so bad at this," she muttered. The last thump must have jarred something loose, because her head buzzed.

The second buzz vibrated through her elbow.

She reached for her phone so quickly that it slid away from her and nearly off the edge of the table, but she caught the slippery bastard and flipped it over.

No, thank YOU, it said. The pleasure was all mine.

She grinned so hard she thought her cheeks might

cramp. Even though she told herself to wait a moment, she typed back immediately. Not true at all. Finally.

His response was much quicker this time: a smiley face that matched her own ridiculous expression. She wanted to play it coy, but too many things were bubbling up inside her. She couldn't fight her eagerness. It was too new and too sweet.

She gave in without a struggle. You're not still planning to keep me waiting, are you?

As if in answer, he didn't respond immediately this time. She bit her lip and tapped her foot. Then she glared at her phone. "Come on," she muttered.

It finally buzzed. Oh, I'm definitely going to make you wait.

NO! she wrote back. There's no need! I'm squirming RIGHT NOW.

It wasn't a joke. He was teasing her. Flirting with her. She was so damn delighted that she felt like a stupid teenage girl twirling her hair while she talked to her crush. But…with the added tension of knowing exactly what his mouth felt like on her clit. She squeezed her thighs together and laughed at the terrible tension already coiling between her legs.

God, don't say that, Gabe wrote back. Lunch break over in five minutes. I need to be presentable.

Veronica clapped a hand over her mouth to try to catch her scandalized laugh. She'd gotten letters seeking advice about sexting, and she'd always been a little scornful. It had seemed silly to her. But now she understood the appeal. If Gabe hadn't been at work, she would have teased him, tempted him, just to feel more of the hot power that pulsed into her blood. He was getting hard for her. She wanted him aching. She wanted him to touch himself and tell her about it. It was intoxicating.

Don't make me wait, she tried again.

Thursday's not far away. And you know I never miss a show.

Thursday??? She sent that text and then shook her head. She wanted to see him sooner, but she didn't want to beg. Then again, when she'd asked nicely on Sunday, he'd come right over. She glared at the smiley face he sent back. It looked so serene. So peaceful.

"Ha," she said, narrowing her eyes at the phone. She had something to offer now, too. She was a savant. Thursday is a long way off if you're already hard. Have fun remembering my mouth.

As soon as she sent it, she started laughing. She laughed harder when she saw his response. Damn you.

She was going to have to go back and pull that email she'd gotten last week about sexting. She'd type up a response today and post it on the online extras. She had a whole new attitude now.

If you can't wait that long, she wrote, I need a date tonight. Charity thing at a gallery. Interested?

Her phone stayed silent for a while. This time she didn't doubt herself. He might have more experience, but she wasn't powerless. His hands had been shaking last night. He'd wanted it so badly.

Finally, she got her answer. Yes.

Veronica took a deep breath, trying to steady her thundering heart. Yes. She'd see him tonight. She texted the details and said goodbye. Then she very carefully set her phone down on the table, opened her laptop and got back to work.

CHAPTER TWELVE

GABE WAS RUNNING LATE. He hated being late. He especially hated being late when he knew that Veronica was waiting for him.

He'd warned her that he wouldn't be there before eight and it was only seven fifty, but he had to get home to shower and change before he could meet her at the gallery.

Still, instead of rushing out of the training room of the fire station, he slapped Benton on the back. "You'd better work on that overhand bend," he said.

"Fuck you," Benton returned with a smile as he unraveled the climbing knots he'd been working on.

"I'm just saying. That knot took you three tries."

"It took two tries, asshole."

"Fine, but I should definitely take the lead next Sunday."

"Ha!" Benton grabbed his pack. "I'm sure I'll be safe in your arms. I've gotta get to my shift. See you next weekend."

Before following Benton out the door, Gabe headed over to shake William's hand. "Thanks for the refresher, man."

William shrugged. "You didn't seem to need it. You probably know more knots than I do."

"I practiced a lot during the winters in Cincinnati.

Not much climbing there." Gabe helped William recoil the last ropes that were piled on the table.

"I have to admit," William said, "I was surprised to see you. I don't think we've ever had a librarian on the technical rescue team."

"Yeah, well we don't get many firefighters in the library, either."

"Touché."

"Actually, I know you guys read all the time. The Cincy firefighters seemed big on ebooks. We're working on getting ebook lending set up, so I'll let you know when it's up and running."

"Sounds good," William said with a wink. "But then we won't have an excuse to come flirt with the librarians. Present company excepted, of course."

"Now my feelings are hurt," Gabe said, dropping a coil in the box of rope William had brought to educate the rescue team on rope safety.

William dropped the last rope in. "Thanks for the help. If you want to hang out a minute, we're picking up a game out back."

"Another time, thanks. I've got plans tonight."

"Book club?" William asked.

"Something like that."

Gabe hit the door and practically jogged toward his street, wishing he'd been smart enough to drive to work today. His phone rang when he was almost to his place. "Hi," he said as soon as he answered. "I'll be there in fifteen."

"Do you have a date, baby brother?"

He laughed in shock at the sound of his sister's voice. "Hey, Naomi. I'm heading out for a beer."

"Really? Your voice sounded *awfully* sweet," she teased.

"Shit." He shook his head. "What's up? Is everything okay?"

"Everything's fine, but I want to hear more about this date."

"It's just a date," he said, and she squealed in excitement.

"I knew it. Tell me all about her."

"I'm not telling you anything. And I'm running late. That's all you need to know."

She sighed but gave up easily. "All right. I was just calling to say I'm thinking of coming to visit sometime. Would you let me stay if I did? Pretty please?"

"I've only got one bedroom," he said.

"Pleeeeeease? Come on. You know I hate hotels."

He could perfectly picture her exaggerated pout. He shook his head. "You'd have to sleep on my couch."

"Yay! I'll probably come next week. Let all your single friends know."

He groaned as she hung up on him, but his irritation was superficial. He hadn't seen Naomi in almost nine months, and he'd be happy to have her around, though he cringed over what she'd do to his bathroom counter. This time he'd just clear his stuff out of there entirely. And she probably wouldn't stay long. She was a restless soul.

She'd had an apartment in New York for a couple of years, but she'd spent only a few nights a year there. Even when she wasn't traveling, she liked being with other people too much to live alone.

If he thought too long about it, there was no sign she'd ever be ready to settle down. His solution was not to think too long about it. Somebody had to take over the family business.

Their dad had inherited the original MacKenzie's from his father, just a little burger joint in Queens. But their dad had taken that little burger joint and all his father's secrets, and he'd turned the business into a chain of high-end retro restaurants that had gotten more popular every year since 1999. They ground their own beef, won awards for their french fries and served fifteen-dollar bourbon-spiked milkshakes to all the hipsters of Manhattan.

Gabe had worked in the restaurants from the time he could walk. He knew everything about the business. But his heart wasn't in it. Every single year, he'd put each dollar he earned at MacKenzie's in the bank to save up for summer wilderness camps. He liked the restaurants and he loved the people, but running MacKenzie's wasn't his passion.

It would just be his job.

Dad wasn't going to retire until one of his kids took over, and Gabe was very afraid his dad would work himself into an early grave. After his father had had two minor health scares in the past year, Gabe had known what he needed to do.

His dad would turn sixty in one year, and Gabe had talked him into retiring then. He'd talked him into it by agreeing to take over. He'd talked himself into it by pretending that five years from now Naomi might be willing to take the reins for a while. Hell, ten years from now even vegan Claire might get on board.

Until then...well, you did what you needed to do for your family, and Gabe's dad deserved to step down and relax for a while. He'd worked hard to pass Mac-

Kenzie's on to his kids, and Gabe would make sure that happened.

But not right now. He didn't have to think about any of that right now, because he was on his way to see Veronica.

He stepped into his apartment and shed his tension along with his work clothes. Veronica hadn't been specific, but a charity event at a gallery sounded more formal than other Jackson events, so no jeans tonight. He showered as quickly as he could, then pulled on black slacks and a blue dress shirt. He was out the door at eight fifteen and hoped the walk over would finish drying his hair.

He'd been looking forward to seeing her all day. Hell, he'd been looking forward to seeing her since the moment he'd left her place on Sunday night. He was glad she'd gotten in touch. He'd wanted to text her this morning, but he hadn't trusted his impulse. Maybe he'd wanted to speak to her, or maybe he'd just wanted to make sure she thought of him as amazing. The perfect lover. The guy who'd made her come and then texted her in the morning to say hi.

He'd never really thought of himself as...*manipulating* situations. Not until a bad breakup two years before. They'd been seeing each other for six months, and Gabe had been ready to end it, but he'd wanted to let her down gently. Eloise had been talking about love and the future, and Gabe had felt himself cringing away, but still... He hadn't wanted to be an asshole about it.

That had seemed like a kind thing until Eloise had confronted him and accused him of always wanting to be the good guy and stringing her along in the process.

If he'd just been honest, she could have moved on, and instead he'd kept her thinking there might be a chance.

"You think you're doing the right thing," she'd yelled, "but all you do is try to manipulate how I see you! Stop fucking around with my emotions and tell me the *truth*."

He'd told her the truth then, because he'd been angry enough to do it. It was only later that he'd really thought about what she'd said. It took almost a year to realize she'd been right. He liked to control what people thought of him, be their ideal. He didn't want to do that with Veronica.

Especially because he knew he was misleading her in other ways. With another woman, Gabe could keep quiet about his plans and see where the relationship led. Enjoy the ride.

But Veronica threw a huge wrench into the works. It didn't feel casual. It wasn't serious yet, but it could be. Not a problem in and of itself, but Veronica hated New York, and he was heading back there. There was no way around that. If things did get serious with her, there was no future.

Even if he set next year's plans aside and focused only on the present, he was misleading her. He hadn't lied exactly. Yes, he'd grown up in New York City, but he hadn't lived there full-time since he'd left for college at eighteen. It no longer felt like his home, but his family was still there. He still went back for holidays. Now that she was comfortable with him, he could tell her that. Let her know that not all guys from Manhattan were assholes.

Reassuring himself that she'd understand or at the very least that he couldn't control how she'd feel about it, he spotted the gallery ahead and picked up his pace.

He'd been in a couple of the Jackson galleries, but he could tell this one was way too rich for his blood as he approached. There was a huge abstract bronze statue in the window that he'd guess cost something close to six figures. This was no local artists' shop.

It was a large space and crowded with people. Gabe had assumed he'd spot Veronica as soon as he walked in, but she didn't seem to be in the front room. He passed through to a back room that was even bigger. A bar was set up in the middle of the room and dozens of people milled around. They weren't his normal Jackson crowd. In fact, he felt as if he'd been transported back to Manhattan. The women wore spike heels and lots of jewelry. Most of the men were twice Gabe's age. He had no idea how Veronica had ended up here. Maybe it was part of her gig with the paper.

He scanned the crowd as he walked slowly around the bar, watching for the bright, vibrant Veronica who made public appearances. But he didn't find her. He found a shier version.

She stood in a corner, in the shadows between two brightly lit paintings. Her teeth worried her bottom lip, and her eyes were cast down, staring at the champagne in her hand. She wore a little black dress that skimmed her body and showed off her legs. Gabe's heart skipped at the sight of her.

It did more than skip when she looked up and spotted him. The uncertainty on her face disappeared in an instant, replaced by a smile that crinkled her eyes and twisted his heart.

"Gabe!" he heard her say from twenty feet away. She strode toward him, her legs muscles tightening with the movement. He let himself watch the show.

She reached toward him as if she meant to hug him but then seemed to catch herself and stuttered to a stop a foot away. "Hi," she said.

He leaned closer, keeping his hands to himself as his mouth neared her cheek. "You look beautiful," he murmured, and watched her skin turn pink.

She touched her hair and ducked her head. "Thank you. And thank you for coming."

He meant to say something charming then, but the sight of her so close started a series of memories in his head. Quick little movies of Veronica perched topless on his lap, of her naked on the couch, of her licking him, teasing him, sucking him. "Damn," he breathed. "It's good to see you."

She glanced up, and her happy eyes held his. Her shy smile turned wicked.

Gabe cleared his throat and rocked back a little, aware that he was already on the verge of getting embarrassingly aroused. "So what are we doing here?" he asked.

"My dad's really into being a big shot in Jackson. Sometimes he wants me to come to these charity events with him. It makes him seem like a community family man or something."

Gabe was suddenly very glad he'd moved back. "Your father is here?"

"He's in front being— Oh, shit. This is weird, isn't it? I didn't mean to make this into a meet-the-family thing! Oh, God. I won't even introduce you, okay? This is…" She grimaced and shook her head. "I'm sorry."

"It's no big deal," he said, hoping he was right.

"I wasn't thinking of that. I just wanted someone to keep me company. It's always so boring. There aren't a lot of young single people at charity auctions, and there's never anyone I know, and I wanted to see you."

"Hey." He rubbed her arm. "It's fine. If you introduce me to your dad, I'll pretend we just met and I'm barely tolerating your presence. It'll be fine."

She nodded and crossed her arms tightly. "You're kidding, right?"

"Yes, I'm kidding. I'll introduce myself and then ask his permission to take your virginity. How's that?"

Her laughter started out as a shocked squeal, but it soon descended into hilarity, complete with tears leaking from her eyes. "You," she gasped, "really are the worst."

"I know. Sorry." He had a strong urge to pull her into his arms and press a kiss to the top of her head, but he didn't have that right. Not in public. Certainly not with her dad here.

A waiter approached and Gabe snagged two glasses of champagne, exchanging Veronica's nearly empty glass for a fresh one.

"Should we mingle?" he asked.

"Absolutely not," she said. "Let's look at the art instead." She moved toward a wall of photographs. "This is a local photographer. She has her own place around the corner."

He thought the photo was black-and-white, but as he studied it, he realized it was only a late fall scene of bare aspen against a hill of rock and snow. There was a hint of gold in the crushed aspen leaves that littered the ground. "It feels a little sad," he said.

"It is. But I love it. She doesn't take the most obvious photos. There are so many beautiful places here. I like that she finds the secrets, too."

He glanced at her, thinking that she was like that. Beautiful, with cool hidden secrets that others didn't notice. "Are you going to bid on it?"

"Ha! I'll leave that to the billionaires. I have been eyeing one of the small prints in her shop, though. I might be able to afford one of those someday. Are you into art at all?"

"I admire it, but I don't know much."

"Me, too. I'm in awe of artists. I always wanted to be able to draw when I was young. I used to sketch all the time, but I never got any better. It's funny that you can see something perfectly in your head, but somehow your hands can't make it."

"Right, it's like—"

"Veronica," a man boomed from behind them.

Gabe swung around to see a distinguished-looking man in his sixties. He wore an expensive suit cut to make his paunch look a little less noticeable. The man took off his glasses to give them a quick polish, then looked everywhere except at Veronica and Gabe. "I'm leaving. I put in a bid on that mixed-media piece by the door. Text me if I'm outbid. I'll have to make a donation if I don't get it."

"Sure," she said. "Dad, this is Gabe MacKenzie. Gabe, this is my father, Judge Anthony Chandler."

"Sir," Gabe said, trying hard not to think about the virginity joke he'd made as he shook the man's hand. "It's a pleasure to meet you."

"Nice to meet you," her father said gruffly, barely glancing at Gabe. He left without another word to Veronica. Gabe watched him stop on his way toward the door to clap hands with another man with great enthusiasm before hugging the man's wife. He wasn't gruff with everyone, it seemed.

"I hope that was painless," she said.

"Is he pissed at you?" Gabe asked.

"Dad? No. Just eternally unimpressed."

"Oh. I'm sorry."

She shrugged. "He's a political animal and I don't have any power, and he must have decided you were too young and harmless to merit his charm. You're not one of the silverbacks."

"Wow."

She winced. "Sorry. That was kind of a mood killer. I'm used to him, but I'm sorry if you felt snubbed. Let's get back to the art."

He followed her back to the wall of photos. "And your mom? Are they divorced?"

"My mom died when I was little."

"I'm sorry," Gabe said, feeling as though he finally got her shyness. With a dad like that and no mom around...?

"It was a long time ago," Veronica said. "She had cancer most of my life, but I still remember all the time I spent with her. We used to watch movies in her bed. She was sick, but she never let me see her down. She used to bake cookies every Friday, and they'd still be warm when I got home from school."

"She sounds amazing."

"She was. That's where New York started for me. With her. She'd been once with my father and she'd been enchanted. The skyscrapers, the taxis, the street performers, Times Square and Broadway. She wanted to take me to see *Cats* when I was old enough. But she got sick again. And that was that."

"Shit, Veronica."

"It's okay. I got my fill of New York later. It all worked out."

He didn't know what to say to that. It had clearly not worked out.

She smiled. "Do you feel sorry for me now? I hope so, because I'm going to try to talk you into coming over later and I'll use every advantage I have."

He nudged her with his elbow. "And you say I'm the worst?"

"I know, right? What are your parents like?"

Compared to her dad, they were saints. "My dad runs his own business. He's always busy, always going, big personality. My mom is kick-ass. She mostly stayed home with us, but she ran our household like the commander of an army. She doesn't take crap from anyone, including my dad."

"They sound awesome. How many brothers and sisters do you have?"

They strolled around the corner, heading toward the front room of the gallery. "Two sisters. They're both older."

"Ha! I should have known you were the baby. You're so charming and cute."

"Cute, huh? I think I've been downgraded."

"Unfortunately, you're all those things. Gorgeous, cute, sweet, sexy. Leave something for the other guys, Gabe."

He shook his head. "Is this another tactic to get into my pants? Blatant flattery?"

"It is if it's working," she said with a grin. The grin snapped to a flat line and her eyes narrowed suddenly. Gabe followed her gaze to a man who was approaching them through the wide corridor that connected the two rooms.

"Roni!" the guy called. "It's been a long time."

"Hi, Dillon," she said. "It's Veronica now." Gabe was shocked at how low her voice had gone. Not shy, really, but...cool.

"Right. Veronica. I can't believe I haven't seen you since you got back to town. You look great. Really different."

Gabe watched as her cheeks went red. She looked away, her fingers tightening around the stem of the glass. "Thanks," she muttered.

"I read your column. Amazing stuff. New York was really good for you."

"Yeah," she said. "It was a blast."

The guy cleared his throat and then turned to Gabe to introduce himself. Gabe shook his hand but kept his introduction brief. Veronica clearly didn't like this guy.

Dillon nodded as if someone had said something. "Anyway, how's Jason? I haven't seen him since he came to town on a ski trip a few years ago. I hear he's in San Francisco now."

"I wouldn't know," Veronica said. She stared down at her glass again. Bit her lip. She shifted a little closer to Gabe, and he put his arm around her instinctively.

"You don't keep in touch?" Dillon asked, sounding surprised.

"Why would I?" She looked up and stared the man straight in the face, her shoulder stiffening under Gabe's hand. "He really wasn't very nice to me, was he?"

The guy frowned and lowered his voice. "Hey, that was just kid stuff," he said. "High school. You know?"

She nodded and seemed to lose whatever emotion

had straightened her spine. She shifted toward Gabe again. He pulled her to his side and squeezed her shoulder. He wanted to ask what was wrong, but not here. Not in front of this guy. Dillon seemed harmless enough, but Gabe had to fight the sudden urge to punch him in the face for no reason.

"Yeah," she finally agreed. "It was a long time ago. Have a good night, Dillon."

"You, too. Nice to see you again. You look great."

Dillon nodded a goodbye to Gabe and moved back to the group he'd been standing with before. He said something to his date and the woman glanced over at Veronica in surprise.

"Are you okay?" Gabe murmured.

"I'm fine," she said, but she didn't shift away from him and he could feel the tightness of her body.

"Let's go this way," he said, turning her around to head back the way they'd come. He guided them toward a far corner of the temporary bar. When they got there, he took her hand.

"Hey, what's going on? Who was that guy?"

"No one," she said. "Someone I went to school with."

"Who's Jason? An ex-boyfriend?"

She shook her head, then drained her champagne glass. Gabe took the empty glass from her and set it on the bar, but he kept her hand in his.

"He was my stepbrother," she finally said.

"I didn't realize you had siblings."

"I don't. My dad remarried when I was fifteen. Only for a few years, though. It didn't work out. Jackson wasn't good enough for them. She left my dad three years later and moved back to LA."

"Ah. So I take it you didn't get along with your step-brother?"

"No. He was a spoiled, entitled asshole. And Dillon was his best friend, so…not someone I want to hang out with." She shook her head and smiled. "Do you want to go? Let's just get out of here."

"I thought your dad wanted you to watch the bids."

She waved her hand. "He doesn't give a shit about art. He just likes showing off. Let's go."

"Where to?"

She wrapped her fingers more securely in his and pulled him toward the front with a smile. "You could walk me home, or I could walk you home. I'm not drunk tonight, Gabe."

He followed her outside and they turned toward their neighborhood.

God, he wanted it. Wanted to touch her again, taste her again, make her come. And this time he wanted deep inside her. He knew he could make it good for her. But maybe… "We should wait. Just a little longer. I want—"

"Gabe." She tugged him to a stop. "I'm not a teenager. I know what I want. Do you want it, too?"

She'd been nervous at the party. Uncomfortable. But she wasn't nervous now. She looked up at him with challenge in her eyes. He backed her up until they were shadowed from the street lamps under a store awning. He pressed her back to the brick wall, but her expression didn't change. She wanted him. She was daring him.

He dipped his head to kiss her neck, and just that touch made her moan. "You never told me everything, Veronica."

"I did," she whispered.

"No—" he pressed another kiss to her throat, then brushed his lips over her ear "—you didn't. I don't want to hurt you. I don't want to be that guy who just fumbles around and hopes I've got it right."

She chuckled and wrapped her arms around his neck. "As if you'd ever be that guy."

He smiled at the compliment. "Tell me," he urged. He wanted to know, but he also liked her secrets. He liked the honesty of them and the glimpses of her that no one else saw.

She finally nodded. "You won't hurt me, Gabe. I... I've done things to myself. With my vibrator." Her gaze dropped for a moment, and his heart dropped right along with it. God, he could picture her doing that. Doing to herself what no one else had done for her.

"You won't hurt me," she repeated, her gaze slowly rising to meet his eyes again. "You don't have to be careful. I just really, really want to be fucked, Gabe. I want you to do that for me."

Her words pushed inside him and squeezed out any reason. "Okay," he whispered.

"My place?" she asked, tugging him back out to the street to make clear that she wasn't really asking.

"Hey, what's the rush?" he teased. "We could hang out at the party a little longer. Catch up with Dillon."

"You're very funny. Shouldn't you be too turned on to joke?"

"I'm trying to take the edge off. It's not easy to walk like this."

Her laughter rang out in the night, a delighted sound that made him laugh, too, despite the ache in his cock.

"Good," she said. "I'm glad I've made it difficult. But we'd better not go back to the party. It could be awkward. I made out with Dillon once, after all. Does that make you jealous?"

He followed her across the next intersection. "Do you want it to?"

"Yes! No one's ever been jealous over me."

"Then I can't stand the thought of that guy's hands on you. I want to knock him out. Then I want to touch you until you forget all about him."

She grinned. "All right, but it might take a lot of touching. He's a big real-estate guy now. Really rich. A great catch."

He caught her at the corner and leaned down to growl into her ear. "I'll fuck you until you can't remember that guy's name."

"Oh, God," she whispered. "I forgot it already."

"Good. Let's get you fucked, Dear Veronica."

"Yes," she whispered. "Let's."

CHAPTER THIRTEEN

IT DIDN'T GO SMOOTHLY, of course. It wasn't as if Veronica's terrible streak of bad sexual luck could be broken by one glorious man. Before she'd taken two steps toward her official deflowering, her phone buzzed. She winced, offered a quick apology to Gabe and read the text from her father.

Got a text from Dillon Tettering. Says he just spoke to you. Butter him up, will you? I'm playing hardball on a new investment.

Typical. I barely know him, she sent back.

So get to know him. And tell me if he says anything about Blue Sky.

Sure, she answered, then tucked her phone away without even a twinge of guilt. She cared as little about her dad's investments as he did about her life.

"Sorry," she said to Gabe. "My dad."

"Better now than later," he said, and delight bubbled up inside her again.

They had to stop at the next intersection for a fire truck. It rumbled past in a cloud of exhaust on its way back to the station. One of the men waved to Gabe, and Veronica felt immediately guilty for the hand she'd wrapped around his arm. This was a small town, after all.

But Gabe didn't flinch away. He just raised a hand and they walked on as if nothing had happened. Her phone buzzed again, but she ignored it. She couldn't handle her dad in her head when she was trying her best to get laid.

"Do you want to go climbing this weekend?" Gabe asked once they'd reached a quieter street.

"What? No!"

He looked down at her and ignored the way she shook her head. "I saw the note on your fridge. 'Try new things.'"

She felt a brief pang of mortification that he'd seen her stupid notes, but she shoved it aside. "I'm trying a lot of new things, in case you haven't noticed. I'll climb you. Isn't that enough bravery for now?"

"Aw, come on. That'll be easy."

"Not that easy. I've seen your cock." Her face flamed at her own words, but she loved saying them, and she loved his pleased grin.

"More flattery, Veronica?"

"I'm just trying to close this deal," she said.

"All right. Then say you'll come climbing with me. Nothing too hard. You can trust me. I'll keep you safe."

The strange thing was that she did trust him. She had from nearly the first moment she'd met him. He'd been talking only about climbing, but there was something honest about Gabe. Something safe.

She liked to think that her ability to be herself with him was because she was getting older and stronger, but she couldn't imagine being this honest with another man. She knew Gabe would take care of her in bed. She knew he wouldn't tell anyone her secrets. She knew she was seeing the real him when they were together.

She felt like herself with him, the person she'd always hoped was somewhere inside her.

"Why do you want me to climb with you?" she asked, genuinely curious, even if she wasn't tempted.

"I think you'll like it. It's quiet. Peaceful."

"Peaceful," she muttered. Maybe they had different meanings for the word.

"And to be honest—" he sneaked a look at her and she nudged his side to get him to continue "—I like teaching you things."

Now she was the one sneaking a look at him. She watched him, but he kept his face straight ahead, revealing nothing. "Are you talking about sex?"

He coughed a little as if he was clearing his throat. "Only if that's not weird."

She didn't know if it was weird or not, but she felt a hard shock of arousal at the thought. He'd whispered such wicked things to her. He'd guided her so carefully. Oh, God, just the thought turned her on so much.

"I liked that," she admitted, trying to get her voice above a whisper and failing.

"Jesus, you turn me on," he said quietly.

It all felt impossible to her. Wonderful and impossible. He didn't care if she was awkward. He laughed when she was weird. And his body made her mouth water. It was too good to be true and she didn't give a damn.

She slid her hand down his muscled forearm and wrapped her fingers into his. "Maybe," she said as they walked down her quiet street.

"Maybe what?" he asked.

"Maybe I'll let you teach me how to climb."

They didn't speak after that. The walk to her apartment was quiet. She rubbed her thumb over the edge of his finger, feeling the way his skin was rougher than hers, toughened by climbing.

It felt strange to know that they were going to have sex. All her previous dates had been countdowns that had hurtled faster and faster toward doubt and anxiety. But this time she calmly unlocked her apartment door and let him in. She didn't wonder. She knew. And while she couldn't help the nervousness that sizzled through her, she didn't have any doubt.

She took off her heels and suddenly he was so much bigger than her. When he bent his head to meet her eyes, his face was shadowed. His hair fell forward. She felt as if she were the only person in his whole world as she rose up to kiss him.

She'd wanted to touch him all night and now she could. She stroked her fingers down his beard, down his throat, around to the back of his neck, into his hair. She dragged her mouth from his and followed the path of her hand, rubbing her lips along his soft beard and then breathing deeply as she kissed the crook of his neck.

"You smell so good, Gabe. Your skin smells like sex to me now." Her fingers caught the top button of his shirt. "I want all of it."

His head fell back when she licked his neck. She bit him, scraping her teeth over his skin, then laughed in triumph at the groan that vibrated against her mouth.

She went willingly when he backed her toward her bedroom, but she didn't give up her quest for more of his skin. She plucked each button free, then sighed in relief when she could slide both her hands into his open shirt. Her nerves flamed with the warmth of him under her palms, the soft feel of his chest hair, the hard pebbles of his nipples.

He pulled his shirt free of his pants once they were next to the bed, but she stopped him. "I want to undress you."

Nodding, he let his hands drop and watched as she freed the last button. His crisp shirt fell open and she slid her hands around his bare waist, marveling at how lean he was, how perfect. "You really are beautiful," she breathed against his collarbone just before she licked it. She felt the texture roughen beneath her tongue as goose bumps chased over his skin. She pulled back to watch his nipples pebble with the sensation.

She circled one with her thumb, surprised when he shivered. "Does that feel good to you, too?"

"Yes."

"Really?" She ducked her head and traced it with her tongue. That didn't get the response she wanted, so she gently bit it. Gabe grunted.

"This is fun," she breathed.

"You're torturing me," he rasped. When she laughed, he took her wrist in a hard grip and moved it down to the front of his pants. They both groaned when she curved her hand over the hard bulge of his cock.

"I love that I can do this to you, Gabe."

"Just thinking about you gets me hard as a rock," he said, the words so rough it felt as though she could feel them against her. "I jerked off to you this morning."

"Did you?" she asked in shock, stroking up and down the fabric that covered him. "Really?"

"Yes. In the shower. I thought of you coming against my mouth again. And then I imagined coming in yours."

She was breathing hard now, remembering his hand on his cock, remembering his belly covered in come. "Do you want to do that?"

"Yes. But not tonight. Tonight I want to fuck you."

God, she felt dizzy with lust, as if all her blood had sunk deep inside her where her pulse beat hard between her legs. She pushed his shirt off his shoulders and tossed it on the floor, then set to work on his belt. As soon as she'd unzipped him, she wanted to tug his boxer briefs down and watch his cock rise free, but she made her greedy hands wait. She slid her hands around him and eased his pants down his hips. Then she slipped her fingers beneath his briefs and spread her fingers over the hard muscles of his ass.

"Please," he rasped. "Touch me."

"I am touching you," she teased.

In response, he pulled her tight against his hips and pushed against her with a groan. "Touch my cock. I want to feel your hand around it."

She dug her nails into his ass as he rocked against her. "Okay," she panted. "Yes."

Pushing her hands farther down, she dragged his underwear off and his cock was free. He felt hard as steel in her hand, and so hot and silky and *good*. She squeezed him as he groaned in relief.

"God, yes," he sighed as he ducked his head and kissed her. She moaned into his mouth as their tongues rubbed together. His fingers closed over hers and he stroked himself with her hand, his cock pushing against her, fucking her fist. She took his tongue deeper, pressing up to his mouth, wanting everything.

She felt wild. Desperate. Dirty. Everything she'd always wanted to feel. She tipped her head back to draw a breath, but she couldn't get enough air into her lungs. "Fuck me," she gasped.

"Yes." He stripped the rest of the way down and then turned her around to face the bed.

Now, she thought at the sound of her zipper. His knuckles brushed her spine until they stopped at the top of her ass. *Now.*

Her dress fell and pooled around her feet. Then her bra. His hands framed her ribs; his mouth brushed her shoulder. He pulled her against him and his cock was a hot brand against her back.

Veronica closed her eyes and sighed at the pleasure. The heat of him. The rough drag of his calloused hands against her bare skin.

He sucked at the curve of her neck and his hands were suddenly at her breasts, his fingers plucking at her nipples, twisting pleasure into her that somehow wound around her pussy and squeezed it tight.

She breathed his name, so new to her but so comforting. As if she knew him. As if her body knew him.

The calloused tips of his fingers drifted down her belly and sneaked beneath her panties. She'd worn black lace for him tonight, dressing just for this moment, and she watched his hand slide beneath the wisp of fabric.

Her clit felt tight and tense before he even touched it. When his fingers found her, her whole body jerked in shock.

"Shh," he whispered in her ear. "Let me touch you."

"Yes," she said eagerly, loving the way his fingers slipped into her wetness. His mouth sucked at her neck, and his hands worked her, one at her breast, the other stroking along her pussy. He teased her for a long while, brushing her clit only occasionally as he stroked, but then he finally centered there, drawing small circles of pleasure into her.

Even above all that, she could still feel his cock. It pressed rhythmically against the small of her back, his own wetness letting him slide against her skin. God, she wanted to taste that again, wanted the salty slippery feel of his precome on her tongue. His cock wanted inside her. It wanted to slide into her. Fill her up. She pictured that and the pleasure pressed harder against her clit, pushing toward his fingers.

"Yes," she murmured. She dug her nails into his wrist, trying to press his hand harder to her.

"Does that feel good, Veronica?" he whispered.

"Yessss."

"Mmm." He slid his hand deeper into her panties, and suddenly his finger was inside her, stretching her open.

"Oh, God," she sobbed.

"Are you ready to fuck?" he asked. "Are you squirming for it?"

"Yes."

His finger slid out and he was teasing her clit again, and now she really was squirming, pushing back into his cock, trying her best to torture him the way he was torturing her.

"Or do you want to come first?" he asked, rubbing more firmly into the terrible, wonderful tightness of her clit.

"Yes," she answered immediately. "Yes, I want that. Please. I want to come." She was so close. So close. If she could just stop thinking. If she could just relax. It was right there.

His fingers left her, sliding free of her panties. She felt the cool wetness of her own arousal on her stomach. "Wait," she begged.

"Shh," he said again. He slid her panties down, then cupped one of her ass cheeks in his hand. "God, you've got a gorgeous ass," he said.

If she hadn't been so frustrated, she would have been thrilled with his words, but they seemed trivial at the moment. Who cared what he thought of her ass? She wanted him focused on her clit.

"Gabe," she growled.

He laughed a little, and she was shocked by how angry it made her.

"Frustrated?" he asked as he turned her to face him.

She wiped the arrogance off his face by wrapping her hand around his cock. "Make me come," she said, feeling greedy for it now that she knew he could.

"I will. When you're ready." His narrowed eyes looked dangerous now, glinting with lust and power as he looked at her hand around his cock.

"Make me come," she ordered again.

"Not until I'm deep inside you," he growled, backing her up to the mattress.

Shocked, she felt the world tip as she fell back onto the bed. When he stepped between her knees, her legs spread for him, and she felt vulnerable, decadent, her thighs open and her panties still hanging from one ankle.

He put one knee on the bed, forcing her to move back. Then he opened a condom and knelt above her.

It hit her then, that he was big and hard and so much

stronger than she was, and he was about to be inside her. Her mouth went suddenly dry. Her heart sped. She backed up a little farther as he rolled the condom down over his thick erection. All her bravado and frustration was gone.

"Just…" she started, then had to swallow to wet her tongue. "Just go slow, okay?"

"Slow," he agreed, fisting his cock.

He was about to do it. He was about to guide himself into her and fuck her. Oh, God.

But then her world fell into pleasure again. Gabe's thumb feathered over her clit. She gasped.

"Better?" he asked. She nodded, clenching her teeth against a groan. He rubbed her clit and she arched up, eyes closed as she pressed her head into the mattress. "I like watching you, Veronica. I like the way your neck gets tight, the way you bite your lip."

She gasped as he circled her clit faster.

"Stop me anytime," he murmured. "I don't want to hurt you."

The blunt head of his cock rubbed between her lips. She felt it press against her, and then it was pushing her open, sliding inside her, stretching her. Just when the tightness became too much, he eased out again, then slid a little deeper, just a little. And the whole time his thumb rubbed her clit, making her squirm against him.

"How does that feel?" he asked, the words a little breathless.

She nodded, keeping her eyes shut tight. It felt…full.

"Raise your knees, sweetheart."

Her thighs opened wider like that and some of the pressure eased.

"Yeah," he rasped, moving slowly inside her. In and

out, just an inch at a time. She could feel it get easier, feel herself get wetter. "You feel so good, Veronica. You feel so fucking hot and tight."

"Yes," she groaned.

"Here. Feel it."

He took her hand and eased it between them. He was still kneeling, his knees spread under her thighs, raising her hips a little. Her fingers touched her clit first, and then they brushed his hard, thick shaft.

"Do you feel that?" he murmured. "How good that is?"

Yes. His cock was wet and so hot from her pussy. And she could feel how tight her own flesh was, stretched around him as he slowly pulled out and then pushed back in.

She opened her eyes. There was no mistaking any of this. Gabe hovered above her, his chest widening up to his gorgeous shoulders, his arms flexing as his hands curved around her knees and his eyes locked on her pussy as he carefully sank himself into her again. And not only could she feel him inside her, she could feel the slide of him through her fingers right where her body took him in.

She was really fucking. She smiled just as his gaze rose to her face.

His laugh sounded pained as he leaned closer, bracing himself above her. Her eyes widened at this shift of his body inside her. "You look so sweet," he murmured, bending closer to press a slow kiss to her mouth. "Now...touch yourself."

"Oh," she breathed against his lips. "Okay."

She shifted her fingers up and pressed them tight

to her clit. He withdrew and then sank himself deep. Deeper than he'd been before. Her eyes fluttered closed.

The logical part of her brain was confused. She didn't know why it should feel so good, so *needed*, but each slow, steady thrust seemed to fill up a part of her that had never felt empty until now. She knew, logically, that her sexual pleasure was centered on the stroking of her clit, but somehow his cock added to that, increasing the weight building inside her and pulling her down, down, down.

He kissed her then, kissed her deep and slow, just like his thrusts. This was *sex*. Real sex. This was the thing that made people foolish and stupid and willing to give up everything. Just for this feeling of fitting together over and over and over. This was what people risked their souls for.

She turned her head, needing to draw a deep breath. "Don't stop," she begged. "Please don't stop." She moved her fingers faster.

"I won't stop," he growled. "I'd fuck you forever if I could."

"Please," she gasped again. It was so close. Right there. But despite the way his shaft dragged over every nerve, she couldn't get there. She was outside herself, *thinking* about it. "I'm sorry," she sobbed.

"Stop." He paused, his cock pushed deep inside her. "Stop. It doesn't matter. Doesn't this feel good?"

"Yes," she sobbed.

"Look at me." He smoothed her hair back from her forehead and waited for her to open her eyes and look at him. She didn't want to, but she did. "This feels so fucking good to me," he said. "Do you like it?"

"Yes," she choked out past her frustration.

"You'd tell me if you didn't?"

"No!" she admitted. "But I do. I love it, I swear. I just can't…"

"Shh…" He kissed her forehead again, then her nose, her mouth, before he pushed up to balance on his hands. "Look at that," he whispered, gazing down her body. "Isn't that beautiful?"

He'd raised himself above her and she could see straight down to her fingers disappearing into the hair between her legs, and then she could see his cock sliding slowly out as his hips rose.

"Yes," she hissed.

"Watch that," he ordered.

She watched as he disappeared in slow inches into her body.

"Rub your clit."

She did. She rubbed her clit and watched as he moved his hips in a slow, steady rhythm.

"Does that feel good?"

"Yeah," she sighed.

"Tell me."

"It feels good," she repeated. "You feel good. You feel so big."

He growled out, "Yes."

"You fill me up."

He sighed and she felt him shake his head against hers. "Look at you," he said, his voice going dark and rough. "Look at you, Veronica."

He lifted her hips, sliding his knees beneath her thighs again, raising her up so he could crouch over her and fuck her more deeply. He curled around her, ducking his head, and he sucked her nipple into his mouth.

She cried out in shock at the new pleasure. His teeth

against her nipple, pulling too hard at her, as he fucked her faster, harder.

"Oh, fuck," she whispered, circling her clit, pressing desperately at that pleasure. "Please," she gasped, begging her own body, begging him. She just wanted this once. Okay, she wanted it a thousand times, but just one time to start. One time with Gabe, coming with him deep inside her, coming while he fucked her, while the muscles of his neck and shoulders and arms strained.

She slid an arm around his back, trying to clutch him, but he was slick with sweat and her fingernails slipped along his spine, making him grunt against her breast.

It was that one little thing that pushed her to the edge. The feel of his sweat under her hand as he fucked her, the rawness of that, the knowledge that he was fucking her so hard, that it was real for him, too.

"Gabe," she ground out, her teeth clenched against the pressure building suddenly inside her. "Oh, God... *Gabe.*" She tried to hold back a scream, but she couldn't. The cry escaped her in a ragged animal sound, and then another one as her orgasm rolled through her in waves. He kept fucking her, moving faster as she rubbed her clit until it all became too much and she had to stop. She sobbed as the orgasm began to fade.

He held himself still then, his cock tight inside her as his chest heaved. He waited until her gasps quieted to sighs. Then he raised his head from her breast and watched again. She watched, too, marveling at the sight of his body disappearing over and over into hers.

"Fuck," he finally whispered, his thrusts growing a little rougher. "Ah, fuck, Veronica." She watched his face as he came and felt so thankful she hadn't missed it. His teeth were bared in a grimace, his eyes shut tight as he pumped into her. She scratched her nails up his shoulder, then tangled her fingers in his hair. His cock jerked inside her.

He finally relaxed with a drawn-out sigh as his eyes opened. He stared at her for a long moment. She stared back.

"Please," he finally said, "tell me that qualified as really fucking."

She laughed, wincing at the strange feeling of his penis still inside her. "That definitely qualified."

"Thank God. I was going to have to write in for advice if it didn't."

She squeezed her eyes closed as he slid free of her and rolled to the side.

"Dear Veronica," he said, "I gave it everything I had, and still…"

Her laughter dissolved into giggles, and tears wet her eyes. She pressed a hand over her mouth to try to stifle her hilarity, but it took a few moments.

Gabe kissed her shoulder and got out of bed. Right. They were done now. She wiped the tears from her eyes and looked around, regretting that they hadn't gotten under the covers before they did it. Now she was just sprawled naked and wet on the bed with no defenses, and that was not the position she wanted to be in when he left.

When she heard the water in the bathroom come on, Veronica scrambled up to climb to the head of the bed and pull the covers back. Unfortunately, the bedding was caught under her knees. She shifted several times from one knee to the other, trying to tug the blanket down, and she'd just barely gotten it free when Gabe walked back in, looking lean and hot and very, very naked.

She froze, kneeling and half-bent on the bed and feeling very, very naked herself.

"Good idea," he said. "I'm freezing."

He took the blanket from her hand and held it a little higher so she could scoot in. She did, if only to get her naked body underneath *something*. Gabe followed her and even though she scooted over as far as she could, he was still pressed against her side when she stopped. She clutched the blanket tight under her chin and stared at the dark space of the ceiling.

"Are you okay?" he asked.

She could feel him watching her and she felt acutely embarrassed about the whole thing. He knew too much about her, and right now she just wanted to play it off as nothing. Just sex. Just an orgasm. Because now she felt convinced he was treating her as if she were fragile. If she hadn't revealed her secrets, would he still be here? Would he be cuddled so close? Would he be reaching up to gently tip her face toward his?

"Veronica?" he whispered.

She hoped that her expression was as hard to read as his was, but she was facing the light leaking in from the other room. He could probably see every anxious thought written on her skin.

"I'm sorry," she whispered. "This is weird."

He frowned. "What's weird?"

"Pillow talk?" she guessed.

His frown vanished and he kissed her. She could feel his chuckle against her mouth. "I guess it is weird. Do you want me to go?"

"No! I mean, only if you want to. It's just such a

weird shift. To be so utterly intimate, to be at your most…animalistic…"

"Grr," he growled.

"And then it's over and you have to be…just… normal again."

"You don't have to be normal," he said. "You know I like it when you're weird."

She laughed and smacked him on the arm. "Did you just call me weird?"

"Yes. But you called me weird first. You're supposed to tell me I'm amazing and I did a good job."

"You need reassurance? I'm the beginner here!"

"You're right." He propped himself up on his elbow and watched her, his hair flopping forward in a way that was already precious. "I don't need reassurance, but I'm just a man, and we like to be told what good boys we are."

She shook her head in exasperation, then reached up to stroke his beard. "You were a very, very, *very* good boy tonight."

He grinned, looking like a kid swelling up with praise. "Thank you."

"And me?"

"You," he murmured, the grin falling away as he leaned down to press another soft kiss to her mouth. "You were exquisite. And I lied a little. When I said I wouldn't stop, I was so close to coming that it hurt. You felt so good, Veronica. And you looked like sin."

This time her laughter wasn't amusement. It was shock. The loveliest slap of shock she'd ever felt. *Exquisite sin.* She'd never been either of those things, and tonight she was both. The idea settled in to her skin and felt surprisingly comfortable. She didn't even blush.

She didn't deny it. Maybe she should let her boss know that she was a sexual savant, after all. Maybe the world needed to know.

She was just reaching up to pull him in for a longer kiss when her phone rang. She raised her head and looked around, spotting her purse on the floor near the doorway. Exquisite or not, she wasn't climbing naked over Gabe to stroll over and retrieve it.

She waved a dismissive hand and relaxed back into Gabe's body. A few seconds later, the message chime dinged and she winced.

"Here," Gabe said, sliding out of bed to get her purse. He seemed entirely un-self-conscious, and frankly, she was happy for it. His body was a work of art. Strong thighs and a tight ass, and that lean stomach leading up to strong shoulders. She wanted to lick him everywhere. She wanted to *bite* him, which seemed like an odd impulse, but her jaw tensed with the desire.

She was so distracted by the idea that she forgot to pretend she wasn't staring at him as he delivered her purse. "Thank you," she said, eyeing his naked hip as she pulled her phone out. She felt a little sad when he was beneath the covers. Then again, she could touch him now. She could even bite him if she wanted to.

She probably wouldn't, though. Probably. She was so distracted by the thought that she barely registered that the call had come from an unknown number. The voice on the message was unfamiliar for a moment, and then her eyes widened.

"Oh, my God," she breathed as she listened.

"What's wrong?" Gabe asked.

She shook her head and listened to the rest of the message, then sighed in shock. "My dad gave Dillon my phone number," she groaned as she shoved her phone back into her purse.

"Why?"

"Something about a development deal, I'm sure. Dillon wants to get together for a drink sometime. Jesus."

"Are you going to go?" he asked. "Just to make me jealous?" He kissed her shoulder and trailed his fingertips along the skin of her chest. The blanket had been tugged down by her movements and his fingers helped it along until one of her nipples was exposed.

"No," she breathed, fighting the stupid urge to tug the blanket up again. Instead of grabbing it and hiding herself, she watched as he circled her nipple and it tightened at his touch. "No," she tried again, "I'm not having a drink with him."

"Not even for old times' sake?"

She smiled at his teasing tone. "Definitely not. We made out at a party once, and once was enough."

"Uh-oh. Not a good kisser?"

She shrugged as his fingers continued to tease her. "No, he was fine. I thought he liked me because he'd been a little nicer to me than Jason's other friends. But Jason teased Dillon after he made out with me, so Dillon played it off. He said he'd never do it again, because my flat chest made it feel like he was making out with a boy. Jason started calling me Ronald or Ron instead of Roni after that. And then a lot of people started calling me Ronald."

Gabe shook his head. "Jesus, Veronica. I'm sorry. What a fucking asshole."

"Exactly."

"And an idiot," Gabe added. "Look at you. You're perfect."

She wasn't anything close to perfect. If she could have magically wished her breasts bigger, she would have. But Gabe made her feel beautiful. He leaned in to kiss the nipple he'd teased to a tight point. "Boys are dumb," he murmured.

"They are."

"And cruel." He kissed her again, his eyes closing as he feathered his mouth over her. His beard looked so stark against her pale breast. "And you're beautiful."

Tears burned suddenly in her eyes, but she blinked them away and slipped her fingers into the soft waves of his hair. He was so sweet. She felt like a new person with him. The person she'd always hoped she might be.

"If you take me climbing," she said slowly, "I'll trust you." But that wasn't really what she was saying. Those weren't the heights that suddenly scared her. The heights that loomed before her were far more dangerous than any cliff, and she was pretty sure she was already falling hard.

CHAPTER FOURTEEN

GABE HAD NO right to feel so energetic after only six hours of sleep, but his eyes had popped open at 7:00 a.m. and there'd been no closing them again. Even the briefest memory of the night before made him smile, and some of the memories went on and on.

He knew it was partly ridiculous male ego puffing him up. After all, he hadn't just made Veronica come, he'd felt her orgasm gripping him as she'd gasped his name.

Goddamn, that had been...heartwarming.

He grinned again as he headed out an hour early for work in the hopes of getting in on a pickup game at the fire station. He needed to work off some of this energy.

The surfeit of energy wasn't ego, at least. It was something dumber than that. He was crushing. Hard. Veronica was cute and sweet and smart. And the sex was fucking fantastic.

Something about her made his mouth water and his cock throb. He wasn't sure what it was, but he knew one thing: this relationship couldn't work. Hell, maybe that was part of the attraction, that she was permanently out of his reach. He could touch her as much as she'd allow right now, but there was an end date to that. They could never belong to each other. He couldn't risk falling in love with her.

So maybe that was part of the urgency to see her again as soon as possible. All he knew for sure was that he couldn't wait for work to be over so he could meet her for dinner. More than that, he couldn't wait for it to be an hour after that, walking her home or maybe watching her sip a martini and waiting to touch her. Waiting to make her come again. Waiting to watch her face melt as he eased into her body.

Damn. He couldn't think about that as he was walking up to the municipal building. He shook off his thoughts of her and headed toward the back door of the fire station instead of the library. If William was around, Gabe would love a game. If not, he'd go for a quick run. A couple of the guys had already let Gabe know he was free to shower up at the station before work.

The door opened into a hallway and the first room he encountered was the locker area. The second was a large exercise room. One guy was lifting free weights, but it wasn't William. Gabe followed the sound of voices down the hallway and ended up in what looked to be a huge living area. He spotted William right away, planted in front of a big-screen TV that was bright with the vivid green of a soccer field.

"William," he called. "You like to play sports or just watch them?"

"Hey, Gabe!" the firefighter shouted. His eyes flicked down to Gabe's shorts and the gym bag slung against his hip. "Did you come to get your ass kicked?"

"Something like that," Gabe responded, "but not quite."

William jumped up from his chair and headed to-ward Gabe when another firefighter called out from the couch. "Hey, Librarian, who was the hot blonde we saw you with last night?"

Gabe laughed and shook his head. "Just a date."

"Nah," William said, "she looked familiar. One of Lauren's friends."

"Maybe," Gabe said, then cleared his throat, torn between protecting her privacy and not trying to sweep her under the rug. "Veronica," he finally offered.

"Yeah?" William pressed. "I'd ask for an introduction, but you two looked pretty damn friendly."

He shrugged, but his stupid face gave him away. The cavernous room was suddenly filled with echoing hoots. He waved them off and turned to head back toward the court but found his way blocked by an imposing man with a very stern look on his face. Gabe backed up a step, then recognized the man as the fire captain, Jake Davis.

"Morning, Jake," he offered. Lauren had already introduced Jake as her boyfriend, and the guy had seemed polite and friendly then. He didn't look polite and friendly now.

"Veronica?" Jake asked. "Veronica Chandler?"

"Yes?" Gabe started uncertainly.

"You're dating?"

"We've gone out a couple of times."

"So it's…*casual*?"

Gabe wasn't quite sure how to respond to that. First, Veronica might be willing to be seen in public with Gabe, but that didn't mean she wanted him discussing their relationship with other people. Second, the captain hadn't exactly asked it in a friendly way.

Gabe glanced toward the roomful of men for help,

but all their eyes were now locked studiously on the television, even William's.

"It's...um..." He wasn't sure why he was nervous, but it seemed as if he was about to answer a very important question. He finally settled on a nonanswer. "I've only been in town a couple of weeks. Lauren introduced us."

Jake Davis grunted and narrowed his eyes at Gabe, seeming unimpressed with the explanation. Gabe felt like squirming, though he didn't know why. Probably something to do with the fact that Jake was old enough to be Veronica's father and Gabe had done filthy, filthy things to her only hours before.

He felt heat creep up the back of his neck, but he held the captain's gaze.

"She's very young," Jake finally said. "I'd better not hear that you've pulled any crap with her."

"Of course not," Gabe answered.

"She's a nice girl."

Gabe offered a crisp nod. "Yes, sir."

Jake stared at him for a moment longer, then grunted again and disappeared into an office. The door slammed behind him.

Gabe felt William's hand land hard on his back. "Close one, my man."

"What the hell was that? Is he a relative?"

"To the blonde? I don't think so, but the captain is old-fashioned. No shit-talking about women around here. I mentioned *once* what I wanted to do to a certain little librarian, and he put me on toilet duty for a month."

"He caught you talking about Lauren?" Gabe asked in horror.

"No, not Lauren! I'm not an idiot. It was her friend.

The one you replaced. I asked that girl out a dozen times. Anyway, just try to avoid him for a few days. He'll cool down."

"But I didn't say anything!"

William shrugged and tipped his chin toward the door. "Come on. A little one-on-one."

Gabe shook off the encounter and followed William outside to the court. It was only 9:00 a.m., but the sun had already started to warm up the day and it melted the new tension from his muscles.

Forty-five intense minutes later, Gabe had forgotten all about the interaction with Jake, and he was ready to get to work. Hair still damp from the shower, he slung his bag over his shoulder and crossed the ten feet between the fire station door and the library.

He was supposed to get the last of the bid numbers on the digital lending system today, and once that was resolved with Jean-Marie, he could start getting down to the nitty-gritty of it. They could strike an agreement with a lending company, get the software loaded onto a test server and then start integrating it into the existing library system. Once the bare bones were in place, Gabe would work on the collection with the other librarians.

Granted, actual lending was probably months away, but engineering it all would be fun as hell.

A half hour later, he was deep into a comparison spreadsheet he planned to present to Jean-Marie at the end of the day when Lauren burst into the tiny office that was tucked behind the circulation desk.

"Oh, my God, you sneaky little bastard."

"What?" he snapped, whipping around.

"You totally pretended not to like Veronica when I introduced you!"

Gabe winced. Damn. Of course Jake had passed that information on to Lauren. Or maybe Veronica had told her? "Ah. Veronica."

For a moment, he couldn't read her narrowed eyes, but then she smiled and kept smiling until he cleared his throat.

"How many times have you gone out?" she asked.

"A couple. But you'll have to ask her anything else."

"Oh, you don't kiss and tell?" she crowed.

"No, I do not."

She shoved his shoulder, sending the chair spinning back toward the computer. "I can't believe she didn't say anything to me! You were the one texting on her birthday! Why didn't she tell me?"

He shook his head. "Maybe because you and I work together?"

She nodded. Then her face fell. "Wait a minute. Does that mean I don't get details? That's not fair."

Gabe hoped it was true. Lauren already felt like yet another big sister, as if Gabe didn't have enough of those.

"So...you like her, Gabe?" Lauren pressed.

"Yes," he answered, starting work on his spreadsheet again in an effort to stave off more questions.

"She's great, isn't she?"

Shit. A smile tugged at his mouth and Lauren was standing right next to him. No question she could see it. He tried to cover himself by changing the subject. "Jake didn't seem happy to find out."

"Oh, please," she scoffed. "He's so overprotective. His daughter is about that age, so he likes to imagine that Veronica couldn't possibly be doing anything dirty. Even though his own daughter is married now! So…is she?"

"Married?" he asked in shock.

"No. Is Veronica doing anything dirty?"

Gabe could practically hear Veronica in his ear, begging him not to stop fucking her. Somehow, he kept his eyes on the screen and breathed slowly and his face didn't betray him with a blush. "Workplace," he muttered.

"Shit," Lauren bit out. "Don't report me."

"Only because I'm scared of your boyfriend."

She walked out but almost immediately stuck her head back into the room. "So you'll be at the show Thursday?"

"I will."

"Great! You can sit at our table and convince Jake that you're good enough for Veronica." She dropped that bombshell and disappeared.

Gabe groaned. Lauren really was like a big sister: sharp and admirable and infuriating. But he couldn't keep his irritation alive for long. In any normal situation, even if he and Veronica were only dating casually, he'd get to know her friends. They'd hang out together. And he wouldn't mind that at all. He liked Lauren, and he certainly liked Veronica enough to get to know the people in her life.

The problem was that this wasn't a normal situation. He didn't want to disrupt her world. He didn't want to find himself woven into it, knowing he was going to leave so many loose ends when he moved back to New York.

On the other hand, she'd already become a new passion, and she was the perfect addition to the perfect year in Jackson he had planned. Getting to know everything about her, teaching her everything he knew about sex, finding out what made her tick.

He rolled his shoulders and told himself it was too early to matter. They'd just started dating. They hadn't discussed how serious it was or even agreed to be exclusive. He could watch her show, hang out with her friends. It wasn't a big deal. It didn't have to be.

He checked to be sure Lauren hadn't reappeared in the doorway to drop another bomb, then set back to work on the spreadsheet. The library was fully staffed today, so unless it got busier than expected, he could devote himself to the project. Good news, because it was the only thing that could keep his mind from steadily straying back to Veronica. She'd already staked out an alarming amount of space inside his mind.

After working halfway through his lunch hour without realizing it, Gabe was just about to rush out the door to grab a sandwich when Jake Davis walked into the library, looking as if he was ready for a fight. Gabe had the completely irrational thought that Jake had somehow discovered that nice Veronica Chandler had been a virgin...until last night.

Adrenaline poured into Gabe's bloodstream and he stood straighter when Jake's eyes locked on him, but it turned out that Gabe had misidentified the threat.

"MacKenzie," Jake barked. "We've got a river guide and four rafters trapped in a narrow offshoot of the Snake River. Two injuries, as far as we can gather. Quickest way in is from the top. You want to assist?"

Gabe's thinking slid from self-defense to rescue in half a second. "I'll tell Jean-Marie."

"Meet us in the station in two minutes."

Gabe had informed his new boss that he'd be serving with the rescue squad during the summer months, though he hadn't expected to be called up during training. Still, if five people needed to be lifted out of a canyon, they'd need as many hands as they could get. Jean-Marie gave her immediate okay for him to go, and Gabe grabbed his bag and rushed to the fire station. He was tugging on his workout shirt when William walked into the locker room and tossed him a pair of canvas work pants. "See if these fit and grab a sweatshirt out of one of the lockers. We roll in one minute."

Gabe's phone rang as he buttoned the pants. He saw his sister's name and ignored it to grab a fire department hoodie and jog toward the garage bays, his heart still thumping with the rush. He couldn't talk to his sister right now, but he'd have to text Veronica and cancel their dinner plans tonight. He couldn't imagine he'd be back in town anytime soon. Even with all the excitement of the shouting firefighters and gathering volunteers, Gabe still winced in regret.

Gabe piled into a Search and Rescue SUV with three other guys, and it was just pulling out when Benton jogged up. "Hey," he huffed as he jumped in next to Gabe. "What's the word?"

The guy in the driver's seat offered what little information they had.

"You guys got extra gear?" Benton asked.

"It's all in the back," the driver answered, and Gabe breathed a sigh of relief. He was new to this and hadn't even considered he might need his own gear.

Benton slapped his thigh. "Ready for a baptism by fire?" he asked Gabe. "Or white water, I guess."

"Hell, yeah," he muttered. His heart beat hard with

anticipation. If he hadn't gotten his MLIS, he might have ended up being a firefighter. He'd had the same fireman dreams so many kids had, but they'd come too late. He'd already been head over heels in love with the New York Public Library. With its white columns and stone lions, he'd always felt as though he was Indiana Jones going in to explore a long-lost temple.

He hadn't actively dreamed about becoming a librarian, but when he'd been in his IT program at college and heard about the library science master's program, the name had triggered memories of those long days of exploring the giant library. Library science... It almost sounded like a form of archeology, and wasn't that what Indiana Jones had practiced?

He'd been intrigued enough to check it out. And he'd liked it enough to take a class. And then he'd loved it. And hell, a degree in library science might not be the perfect tool for running a chain of restaurants, but he'd already had all those skills. He'd been free to get whatever degree he wanted.

It had been a perfect fit. His first love hadn't betrayed him. He loved words and books and being around people. Hell, he even liked the organization of it all.

"That *Dog in the Night-Time* book's pretty good," Benton said. "Maybe I will come by the library sometime and try something else."

"Sure," Gabe said. "I'll do some research. See what else I can find for you."

"Thanks."

Everyone was quiet the rest of the way. It was nearly forty-five minutes to the site, and it felt so long for Gabe that he couldn't imagine what it was like for the people trapped on the rocks below.

The SUV finally pulled into a rocky clearing that sat between pine trees and a steep drop-off. As soon as the vehicle stopped, they all jumped out. Captain Davis had been in the truck in front of them, and he was ready.

"We've got two casualties. One man with an ankle that's likely broken and another with a crushed hand. The female rafter is uninjured. None of the injuries are life threatening, but the paramedics are concerned about shock, so let's not waste any time. Gabe, you head down with the four experienced rescuers." He tipped his head toward William and Benton, who were already conferring at the edge of the cliff. Gabe could hear water below.

"Follow their lead," Jake said. "The rest of us will stay up here and provide muscle and backup."

Gabe got a harness and a helmet on, then waited as one of the team strapped rescue gear to his back. Lines were being anchored and strung. Everybody was ready within ten minutes.

Gabe watched William go down first, then Benton, and then he hooked into the line and headed down toward the small group of people huddled on the boulders below.

His heart was beating almost as hard as it had for Veronica the night before. Almost, but not quite.

VERONICA HAD KNOWN that her long-awaited sexual afterglow couldn't last forever, but she hadn't expected it to end quite so abruptly. First Gabe had texted to say he wouldn't be able to see her tonight. He'd been called up to help with a white-water canyon rescue, which was really hot, but not as hot as a night with him would have been.

She'd felt guilty for her immediate flash of disappointment. After all, saving people from dying was more important than giving her another orgasm, but… water rescues weren't even his area of expertise, and her sex life had been a long-term natural disaster for so many years.

She'd nearly slapped her own hand at that. What a selfish thought. She'd decided right then and there to make an anonymous donation to the rescue squad to make up for her awfulness. She wasn't a terrible person; she was just monstrously horny all of a sudden.

Finally experiencing good sex had changed her brain-wave patterns, it seemed. Everything made her think of it. Stretching under her sheets this morning, she'd noticed how smooth and soft her body was. When she'd gone to the bathroom, she'd smiled in secret delight at being tender from sex. Making her breakfast, she'd imagined making it for Gabe and then joining him back in the bedroom. Hell, even sitting at her laptop made her want to look up dirty ideas or at least type a few more sex-positive messages to herself. And then there was the bed right behind her, practically pulsing with memories of getting well and truly fucked.

"Aw, man," she breathed, squeezing her thighs together.

It had been really hard not to drop any hints in response to Lauren's texts. You have a lot of explaining to do! Lauren had written that morning.

Lauren's second text had confirmed Veronica's suspicions on the subject. About Gabe!

Veronica had laughed in delight and sent a smiley face back to her friend. Lauren's next text had made Veronica clap a hand over her mouth to stifle her laughter.

The firefighters are gossiping. I heard about it from Jake. ARE YOU DOING GABE? You'd better call me later.

"I don't kiss and tell," Veronica had said aloud as she'd typed the same to Lauren, but God, she wanted to. She stared at the rumpled sheets of her bed and thought of all the things she wished she could tell *someone*.

Veronica paged through her emails, looking for a cheerful Dear Veronica letter to answer. She didn't want to deal with questions about body odor or infidelity today. She wanted something *happy*.

Or maybe something obnoxiously fun. Something about yet another man who hated going down. Man, she could really go to town about that now.

Two more Dear Veronica emails arrived, and she immediately rejected the first one. It was a rant about American women and how they didn't seem to appreciate "real men" anymore. Not an uncommon complaint, and one that always made her shudder.

But it was the second letter that stopped her cold. As soon as she saw it, she realized she'd been waiting. Dreading. Knowing it had to come someday. Her body hummed with a terrible prickling anxiety, a combination of alarm and self-loathing and fear. The email was titled "I Don't Know How to Keep Going" and just that made Veronica break out in a sweat that chilled her whole body.

Dear Veronica,
I feel totally alone. Nobody in my school likes me and when I try to talk to my parents about it, they tell me to try harder to fit in. But you can't TRY your way to fitting in, especially when nobody wants you around.

I don't fit in and I never have. I don't care about sports or hunting or video games, so I don't know how to talk to other guys. I get sick just thinking of going to school, and most days I don't want to live anymore. I don't think I can get through two more weeks of this, much less two more years, and I don't think anything will change after high school anyway. Do you have any advice?

—Nobody

Nobody. The screen went blurry and Veronica had to wipe her eyes several times before she could see the words again.

Nobody. She knew exactly how that felt. To be nothing. No one. It had been her life in high school, too. It had been her life in her own family.

Do you have any advice?

Oh, God. She wasn't qualified for this. She was barely qualified to give advice on wedding etiquette and blow jobs. But this? This kid needed real help from a professional.

She took a deep breath. That was exactly what she'd tell him. As a matter of fact, she could still remember the language used for these kinds of letters at her previous job.

Feeling a tiny bit calmer, she read the letter again, but this time she took note of the email address and her heart fell. It appeared to be a randomly generated series of numbers and letters, and the email provider was one of the largest online sites. A lot of people used a temporary email address to submit questions. It usually wasn't a problem, because the disclaimer on the paper's website covered permissions, so she didn't have to follow up before publishing.

But this was different. She needed to reach out to this boy.

She immediately hit Reply and crossed her mental fingers as she started typing, but she hit a snag immediately. She wasn't going to call him Nobody. She refused to. So she just started with "Hello" and went from there.

I'm hoping you're still at this email address so we can talk. Could you let me know? I'd love to get some more information about what you're going through, because I truly understand. Please get in touch.

She signed her name and hit Send. When her inbox dinged just a few seconds later, she knew what it meant. Her response had been returned as undeliverable.

Veronica wiped her face again, then blew her nose and closed her eyes to try to stop her tears. If she couldn't reach him directly, she'd have to post a response on her online column, because she couldn't wait a week to answer this boy. What if things got worse for him? What if he decided to hurt himself? She knew what the suicide statistics were for teenage boys, and this boy was clearly depressed.

She needed to reach out and she needed to do it the right way. She ticked through her mental list of contacts, but she couldn't settle on one that satisfied her. There was a psychiatrist she'd been in touch with through the paper once, but she didn't trust him. He'd seemed arrogant and had even cracked a few jokes about his patients. No, she didn't trust him at all.

Her social circle wasn't very large, and it didn't include any doctors or therapists, but she knew whose would. Ironic that she might have to get in touch with him about this. Her lip curled at the thought. But this wasn't about her, and she could swallow her pride for this child.

She dialed her father and held her breath.

"Yes?" he answered curtly. He was all business with her and anyone else beneath him. If she'd been a US senator or one of the wealthy people in town, his tone would have been decidedly warmer.

"I need to ask a favor," she said, hating the words as they left her mouth.

"I hope the favor has to do with Dillon Tettering."

"It does not."

"So it's money?" he barked.

"No, it's not money. Listen, I just need to know if you have any friends in therapy or psychiatry in town. I have a bit of an emergency regarding a letter writer, and I need a little advice."

"Isn't that what you're paid for?" he said with a cold laugh.

"Dad. Just... Do you know anyone? Surely you've dealt with a lot of psychology experts from the bench." It always helped to remind him that you were aware of his very important job.

"Most of those are brought in by the feds."

"But not all?" she pressed.

"Sure," he finally said. She could hear him shuffling papers as he spoke to her. His attention was always on something else, but maybe he was actually looking for something for her this time. "I can give you a name."

She sighed and slumped into her chair. "Thank you."

"I assume you'll return the favor by having a drink with Dillon Tettering."

Unbelievable. It wasn't enough that she was his daughter; she still had to bring something to the table. Her tension over the letter snapped to anger. "You know I don't like him. You know I didn't like any of Jason's friends. Why would you ask me to do that?"

"Jesus, Veronica, that was years ago. Grow up. It's a drink."

"Yeah? What if he wants a quick lay afterward? You want me to do that, too?"

She expected him to explode. She actually winced, waiting for it, but after a brief moment of silence, he laughed, one deep, hard bark of laughter. "Get over yourself and meet him for a drink. It's a development deal, not a sex-slave ring. And I don't know what the hell you're so uptight about, anyway. You have no trouble embarrassing me with half the columns you write." He hung up without waiting for her agreement. A few minutes later, her mail dinged again, and she opened it to find an email from her father. It was just the name of a psychologist and a phone number, nothing else.

She called the psychologist's office immediately and left a message with the receptionist, blatantly dropping her father's name in the hopes that the therapist would call back quickly.

As soon as she got off the phone, she sent an email to her editor, asking if it would be all right to update the online column early this week. Then she started on the first draft of her letter.

Her father's name, as bitter as it was on her tongue, was a magic word in this town, and her phone rang just as she finished reviewing her words. Not only was he fast, but the therapist agreed to review Veronica's letter as soon as she sent it, to make sure she was offering the correct advice.

As she waited for his response, she read the letter from Nobody again, trying to puzzle out details that weren't there. If he was writing to her, he probably went to her old high school here in town, and she could perfectly imagine him wandering those halls, hoping he didn't run into anyone who'd draw attention to him.

Veronica's stepbrother had been one year ahead of her, so the only class they'd ever shared was Spanish. But that hadn't mattered. He'd been a year older. He'd corrupted everything for her, his disdain trickling down through the lower classes.

She'd hated every single day. She'd hated waking up in the morning and knowing she'd have to see him, share a house with him and then go to a school where he'd made her into a nobody.

Even now it was strange to think that her arrogant, superior stepbrother had been willing to tear her down so completely when she was related to him. She'd have thought he wouldn't want that association. But the truth was that he couldn't bear even one atom of approval or admiration being focused on anyone else, and she'd committed the biggest sin of all: she'd lived in his house, and she'd been there before him. Destroying her had been about claiming his territory, like the male lion who killed all the cubs in a pride when he took it over.

He hadn't wanted his mom to remarry, he hadn't wanted to leave Southern California and he definitely hadn't wanted to live in Wyoming. Stepping on Veronica had been his revenge, and he'd enjoyed it.

Veronica sat back and stared at the ceiling, drawing deep breaths.

Returning to Jackson hadn't brought back as many memories of her high school years as she'd feared. Jason and his mother had hightailed it out of here years ago, her dad had a new house, and most of the people she'd gone to high school with hadn't been destined to stay in Wyoming.

But now there was this letter, bringing it all back. And then there was Dillon.

"Shit," she moaned. She might as well just get that over with now, while these kick-ass memories were raining down on her.

She hit Dillon's number and opened a text box. Her lip curled again. She couldn't believe she was doing this. But if her dad's contact could help her reach out to that teenager, it would be worth it. Probably.

Hi, Dillon, she typed, refusing to add an exclamation point to her greeting. Screw this asshole. I've got a show Thursday if you want to come by after. Or we could grab a drink sometime next week.

Hopefully, he'd be busy Thursday, and then she could put him off next week, and then nothing would ever happen.

No such luck. Thursday sounds great!

"Oh, Jesus," she said. Her phone beeped again. Three Martini Ranch, right?

"Ugh," she said, but she typed, Yes. Nine o'clock. One drink. That was all. Hopefully, she could rush the meeting, and then her father's emotional ransom would be paid.

Her eyes fell on Gabe's name as she closed her texts and she felt a twinge of guilt, but it wasn't as though she were going on a date with Dillon. Far from it. Gabe would probably be right there waiting for her.

She sneered at Dillon's last text when it popped up with a cheerful Can't wait! then clicked off her phone.

No, there was nothing to feel guilty about. This was more like meeting with an old enemy to reconfirm the peace treaty.

Dillon was a handsome guy, but she would never, ever find him attractive. How could she? He'd been a worm of a boy, so he couldn't be much better than a bug of a man. And after being with Gabe, she was starting to get a new perspective on dating.

Up until now, she'd spent every date trying to figure out how to get comfortable when it felt as if she was writhing on a pin. But the point of all of it was to find a guy who didn't make her feel that way in the first place. Sure, she'd had a few anxiety attacks with Gabe, but she'd mostly had fun.

Dillon wasn't going to be fun at all. Her gut churned at the thought of sitting down with him, of having to be polite and smile and pretend he hadn't helped ruin several years of her life.

Her email chimed and she lurched forward to open it. Dillon didn't matter. He was the nobody in her life now. Veronica held her breath as she read the email, then let it out in a rush of relief. The therapist had only a few suggestions, but otherwise, she'd written the right thing. She'd reached out; she'd sympathized; she'd offered help.

If the writer saw it online, hopefully, he'd get in touch again or at least reach out to a doctor or therapist for assistance. Maybe she could truly help him. Maybe she could make his life just a little better.

Waiting impatiently for the response from her editor, Veronica paced out to the kitchen to grab a drink, but instead of opening the fridge, she found herself staring at it. It needed an addition.

She got out the paper and marker one more time.

#4—Stop being afraid.

She wasn't a teenager anymore. She wasn't nobody. And she was finally going to stop being scared.

CHAPTER FIFTEEN

"I'M ALREADY TERRIFIED," she muttered, glaring at the top of Gabe's head as he slid the loop of the safety harness over her foot.

"You'll be great."

Despite her resentment, she couldn't resist touching him. As he pulled the loop over her other foot, she reached out to stroke his hair. It was silky and hot from the sun, but the nicest thing about it was that she could touch it just because she wanted to.

And she did want to. She'd tried to talk him into forgetting about this whole climbing thing altogether and just giving in to her sexual demands, but he'd stubbornly refused. Honestly, she felt a little miffed at that. She wouldn't have had the strength to say no to him, but he'd laughed and promised "later."

In fact, he'd promised to fuck her twice when they got home. She'd tried to be content with that, but as she stroked her hand through his warm hair, she wished he were kneeling in front of her for an entirely different reason. When her hand tightened, he looked up.

She raised her eyebrows. "How about we just skip all this and I give you a blow job? There's no one else out here."

"Stop trying to distract me," he said, laughing as he

worked the harness up over her capri leggings until the
top of it was at her waist.

Crap. He was really determined to do this. He tightened the thick band that went around her waist and told
her that the leg straps should be snug. She grumbled
under her breath, but she tightened them, anyway.

"Perfect," he said. "Now I'll show you how everything works, so you'll have a good sense of how safe
it is."

She bit her tongue to stop the sarcastic remark she
wanted to make. She'd just yesterday promised herself
she'd stop being afraid, and here she was practically
shaking. She trusted Gabe, and he was obviously a good
rock climber. He'd been doing it for years and was still
walking and talking.

And she had to admit that she was slightly intrigued
by the idea of this climb. She didn't want to try this, but
she was brave, wasn't she? This was her new life, or so
her friends had assured her.

"The helmet," he said, easing one onto her head, "is
to keep you safe from falling rock. This is especially
important as I'll be above you."

"Above me? I thought you'd be *with* me."

"No, I'll climb up first and secure the anchors. This
is an established climbing spot, so there are already permanent anchors at the top, but I'll secure a few more on
my way up. Let me show you how they work."

She watched him wedge an anchor into a crack of
rock. Then he showed her how to work it back out so
she could try it herself. She could see, objectively, how
the physics of the anchor worked, but it still didn't seem
nearly secure enough for her. It was a tiny piece of
metal attached to a wire. What if it broke? What if the

rock broke? Sure, the rock was millions of years old, but rocks cracked all the time! And what if the anchor somehow slipped up to a wider section of the crack? But Gabe insisted on relying on physics instead of fear.

"And we always use double anchors, at least," he said. "Sometimes three if it's a particularly tricky section."

"But how will *you* be anchored if you're climbing up to place them?" she pressed.

"Ah. I won't be."

She groaned and shook her head. "No."

He had the nerve to laugh. "That's how it works, Veronica."

"No, I don't like it."

He grabbed something from his pack and then stood straight in front of her to give her a quick kiss on the mouth. "Done it a hundred times, and this is the easiest climb in the area."

She looked doubtfully at the face of the rock. It seemed to go straight up to her. It wasn't as if there were steps carved into the middle of it. "Easy?" she croaked.

"You'll see." He kissed her again, lingering a little longer this time, until she finally gave up her stiff stance and kissed him back.

"You just have to trust me," he murmured, the words warm against her lips.

"I do."

"And yourself."

Okay, that was a little harder to manage, but she was working on it. She listened closely as he explained the knots and the locks and the pulley system that put traction on the rope to keep her from free-falling during a rappel.

He told her the calls and responses that every climbing team used, but her brain scrambled them all up as he spoke. "What if I can't remember them?"

"The only one you need to be clear on right now is 'falling.'"

"Wait, when do I say that?"

"When you're falling."

"Are you kidding me?" she yelped.

"It's just a heads-up that I need to brace myself for your weight."

"No," she said again, but he just kept going through the safety lecture before he checked her gear once more.

"Show me how you use the carabiner," he said for the second time. She showed him. "Okay. Ready?" he asked.

She stared at the rock, then looked at him, at his kind eyes and tanned skin and the strong muscles of his shoulders.

Stop being afraid.

"I'm ready," she said.

"Take your time," he reminded her. "Find your handholds. Make sure one foot is solid before you step again. Rely on your leg muscles, not your arms."

"Not a problem."

"I'll see you in a few minutes." He didn't even give her another kiss before he disappeared up the rock. And that was exactly what he did. One minute he was in front of her and the next he was twenty feet up. He didn't seem reckless, though. She could see the way he looked at every spot he used. She eased out the length of rope coiled at her feet, hyperaware that if he fell, the rope wouldn't do anything to help him.

"This is granite," he called over his shoulder. "It's

been here for millions of years, but there are still loose bits and pieces, so always check before putting your weight on it."

No, her mind said. "Okay!" she called up to him.

And then he was really gone. Out of sight. He'd eased up over an edge or an angle or something, and now a big jut of rock kept him from her sight.

She held her breath for a long time, watching the spot that had swallowed him up. But then the rope tugged at her hands and she concentrated on not letting it get taut. What if she messed up and pulled him right off the cliff? What if she murdered her only source of penis-based sex?

Suddenly the rope stopped sliding. Veronica kept her grip loose just in case, but it stayed still.

She desperately wanted to shout up to him and ask if he was okay, but she just as desperately didn't want to distract him. He wasn't anchored in. He wasn't safe. One wrong step and he'd die.

"This is the worst hobby *ever*," she whined, stretching her already aching neck.

The other half of the rope moved, pulling up fast until it was taut and tugging at her safety belt.

"Is that you?" he called. The words floated down to her from very far away, but she nearly wept with relief. He had the rope through the anchor. He was okay.

"Um," she said loudly, "yes! It's me!"

She thought she heard a chuckle in response. The rope tugged lightly a few more times and then she heard the magic words. "Belay on!"

It was time. And she couldn't remember what she was supposed to say, but she did remember what to do. She checked that her carabiner was locked, approached the rock face and took a few deep breaths until her mind started working again. The slack in the rope disappeared even though she'd moved forward only a few inches. Gabe had her.

"Climbing," she croaked. She cleared her throat and tried again. "Climbing!"

He responded to let her know that he was ready to support her weight, and she put her hands on the rock.

The first few feet were uncertain, but she quickly realized it wasn't much harder than climbing a ladder. The rock looked smooth from a distance, but it was actually jagged. There were no steps carved into it, but she moved up at a fair pace. Gabe kept her rope nice and tight the whole time, so she knew that if she slipped, she'd fall only a few inches. Granted, she'd also smash face-first into the rock, but that kind of thing could happen on a hiking trail, too.

She was actually feeling pretty badass and confident when she reached the spot where Gabe had disappeared from her view. As she'd suspected, the rock angled slightly in for a few feet here, and she could see him about twenty feet above her now.

"There you are," he said.

She beamed up at him. She couldn't help it. He'd been right the whole time. She could do this. She was fucking amazing.

"Okay," Gabe called down, "pause there for a second."

That wasn't a problem. Her feet were on a solid lip of rock and she could rest her arms on the face that angled away. Her thighs trembled like crazy, but she didn't feel weak yet.

"I want you to do something for me now. Let go of the rock and lean back."

"What?" The muscles that had just started to relax into the climb went tight as steel, shaking even harder now. "Why the hell would I do that?"

"So that you can feel what it's like to rely on the rope."

"No!"

"Come on. It's standard training."

Now that she'd started feeling kick-ass, she didn't want to back down. She didn't want to say that she couldn't do it, because she *knew* she could. "What if you don't catch me, though?"

He shook his head. "Do you think I'd let you up here if I couldn't catch you? I've gotten pretty attached to you."

That took her by surprise. Attached? Already? What did that mean? Maybe it had only been a safety-rope joke? Shit, she couldn't even ask, because it would be weird, and she was not going to be that weird, insecure girl while she was clinging to the side of a fucking mountain. She was better than that.

He nodded as if she'd agreed to something. "Get a stable stance, legs a few feet apart so you don't swing. Then let go of the rock and lean back."

"Okay." She watched her feet as she widened her stance, but then she made the mistake of turning her head and looking behind her. "Oh, shit," she gasped. He'd been right about it being an easy climb. She hadn't realized how far up she'd gotten. She was above the tops of the cottonwood trees, and they had to be at least thirty feet tall. "Oh, God," she whispered.

She couldn't lean back. She just couldn't. But that

was stupid, wasn't it? If she didn't trust the rope, what was she even doing up here?

"Okay," she tried again, pinning her eyes to Gabe instead of the ground. "Are you sure you're ready? I'm heavier than I look. I've got sturdy legs."

"I remember that about you. I'm ready."

She forced her hands off the rock and wrapped them around the rope. She had to override every single animal instinct she had in order to force her body to ease back, but she felt the pull on her safety belt and knew she was doing it.

"Hands off the rope," he called.

"What?" she screamed.

"If you fall, you want your arms free and ready so you can hit the wall with your hands instead of your face."

Okay, that seemed like a decent idea. She got one hand to let go and held it up next to her head. The other one refused to move no matter how hard she glared at it.

"Good enough," he said. "All your weight is on the rope now. Look at me."

She looked.

"Do I look like I'm straining?"

Amazingly, he didn't. He looked totally comfortable, as if he were leaning against a brick wall instead of clinging to the side of a mountain. He held the belaying rope in one hand and watched her with a smile.

"The belay devices add enough friction to support most of your weight. I hardly have to work at all, even if your weight falls suddenly. Ready to climb up to me?"

Oh, hell, yes, she was ready for that. She pulled herself back up to the rock face and yelled, "Climbing!"

His laughing response echoed down on her.

Ten feet farther up, she looked back and was relieved she could no longer see straight to the ground. And now she was far enough up that the trees were getting small. She could pretend they were bushes. The end was in sight. She was golden.

Gabe's grin was a distraction she didn't need, so instead of looking up at him, she carefully watched every move of her hands and feet. The stepping points seemed natural, but she tested each one before she put her weight on it.

Finally, her hands were on the three-foot-deep cliff where Gabe stood. It looked insanely safe after that climb. She pulled herself up and leaned against the rock.

"Oh, my God," she whispered. "I did it."

"I told you you could do it. Not only did you get here, but you were faster than I expected."

"Really?" Her knees and hands were shaking, but that didn't matter. She'd done it.

"Yes. And you're fucking hot in those pants, too."

She was too afraid to shift close enough to kiss him, but she enjoyed the look he swept down her body. As if he could read her face, he said, "When we get to the top, I'll kiss you, but I need all my blood in my brain right now."

She started to smile, but it got caught in a strange grimace. "What do you mean 'the top'? We're at the top."

"Nope, this is the first pitch, but the second pitch is only thirty-five feet. You've already climbed sixty feet. You can do it."

Her eyes swept over the beautiful vista of sky and mountains, then dropped down to those tiny trees. "Thanks, but I'm good with this. Amazing. Really awesome climb."

"We need to hit the top to rappel down on a different face. It's a nice straight line to the ground from there."

Oh, God. She turned in to the rough granite and clung there, letting her forehead rest on the sun-warmed rock. She saw the movement of a tiny spider out of the corner of her eye and didn't even care. This cliff was her friend. She was safe here. Maybe she could live here. Gabe could climb up every few days and bring her food and water. She could curl up in the little hollow of stone at her feet and sleep at night. It would be beautiful and she'd never have to let go of the granite.

She whispered, "Okay."

"Feel good?" he asked.

"Yes," she lied. "Let's go."

He showed her how to disengage the anchor once he'd called down, explaining that he was safely attached now and even if he fell, he'd fall only so far. She felt a tiny bit more secure as he headed up to the permanent anchor at the top.

"Thirty-five feet," she whispered to herself. "No big deal."

Famous last words. It seemed as if only seconds passed before he called down to her again. She concentrated on disengaging the anchor and checking all her lines, then called up that she was climbing.

Her little cliff was blessed gravity trying to hold her down, but she forced her shaking knee to bend and found a good foothold for her toes. She only had to climb three feet up to get a glimpse of Gabe again.

He was locked in to a short tether at the very top of the rock, feet spread wide for balance and leaning his whole body back as if he were relaxing into a recliner instead of a hundred-foot void. He had complete confidence in the equipment, and she had almost complete confidence in him. Her legs felt a little stronger as she hoisted herself up.

Then the rock turned suddenly smooth. One minute there were a dozen handholds to choose from, and the next there was nothing but a shiny expanse of gray striation climbing six feet above her.

Her gaze flew up to Gabe.

"Take your time," he said. "You'll figure it out. Just make your way toward me."

Figure it out? What was there to figure out? There was nothing for her to hold on to. No purchase at all for her feet. Her ears buzzed, adding a high note to the ragged sound of her breathing. She knew there must be a way to traverse this because Gabe was up above her.

She looked left and then right, wondering if she was supposed to edge sideways before going up, but no, the edges of rock that she held on to didn't continue much farther than five inches on either side.

She was going to be stuck here. There was no way she could feel her way back down to her safe cliff, and there was no way to move up. Her fingertips went numb and she saw that she'd pressed them so hard into the rock that they'd gone white at the tips.

Gabe waited silently above. He didn't offer instruction or reassurance and she wasn't sure if she was grateful or not.

Her heart beat too hard as her eyes swept back and forth over the smooth rock. She forced herself to draw a deep breath and heard her heartbeat slow as the seconds ticked past. Her eyes locked on an incongruous sight: a tiny white flower emerging on a grass-like stem from a crack in the rock. She watched that little round-petaled flower bob in the wind and tried to let her brain work.

Okay. Gabe had told her to move toward him and he wasn't directly above her—he was a few feet toward the right. She looked down at her feet and saw that even though there was no step-like foothold, there was a slight concavity in the rock that eased up at an angle toward Gabe.

She moved her left foot carefully up and pressed down. It wasn't flat, but the soft sole of the climbing shoe seemed to stick to the curve. Her eyes rose to the flower emerging from the tiny crack. With a silent apology to the plant, she placed her fingers on top of it and clung tight as she put her full weight on that tentative foothold.

Stop being afraid.

She lifted her other foot and slid herself along the mountain, keeping her body as close to the rock as possible.

It took an eternity to ease herself up six feet of rock. She had to smother every instinct her body had in order to keep going. She wanted to stop and weep and beg for help, but she didn't. And finally, the smooth expanse of rock ended in one last sweep of amber granite and the jagged handholds were back. She put her knee against a solid lip of rock and surged up.

Twenty feet later and she was even with Gabe. He grinned at her. "You did it," he said, waving his hand toward an edge of rock a foot above her head.

Veronica couldn't speak, and she couldn't return his smile, but she nodded and climbed past him to the most beautiful sight she'd ever laid eyes on: a wide expanse of flat rock that seemed to go on for a hundred feet. She hoisted herself up and collapsed onto the ground, eyes closed against the bright sun that beat down on her face.

When she heard the clink of Gabe's gear, she opened her eyes to see him kneeling next to her.

"Okay?" he asked.

She nodded.

"You did it. On your own."

Tears welled in her eyes as she nodded again.

He lay down next to her and reached for her hand. She was embarrassed at the way her whole arm trembled but thankful for the way his fingers wrapped around hers. They stared up at the clouds together for a while. The sun soaked into her.

"It's quiet, isn't it?" he murmured.

It was, just as he'd promised, the quietest place she'd ever been. The only sound up here was the occasional whisper of breeze against her ear.

She turned her head to the side and looked out over sky and mountains. "It's beautiful."

He raised her hand to his mouth and kissed it, drawing her attention back to him. He was beautiful, too, watching her as though he had all the time in the world, his chest rising and falling in a slow rhythm that settled her own pulse. His sweet eyes and cute beard and muscled shoulders were framed so perfectly by the mountain peaks behind him, as if this was his natural place in the world.

If they'd only been dating a little longer, she'd have told him that she loved him. Loved him for bringing her up here and forcing her to be brave. Loved him for looking at her as if she was as beautiful as these mountains. She did love him a little, just for this moment, but she didn't say it. She just tipped her head back toward the sky and closed her eyes.

CHAPTER SIXTEEN

EVEN FROM NINETY-FIVE feet up, Gabe could see Veronica's wide grin when she touched down on solid ground. He checked the rope one last time, started the easy rappel down and hit the ground thirty seconds later.

"Rope!" he called, tugging it free of the loop above, then stepping aside to let it fall. He turned to see her sitting on a boulder behind him, grin still in place.

"So, did you like it?" he asked.

Her laugh was soft and breathless. "It was kind of amazing."

"Only kind of?" he teased.

"Yes. And kind of awful. I need a drink, a shower and an orgasm."

"In that order?"

"Yes." She took a deep breath and rubbed her hands over her face, laughing again.

"What?" he asked.

"I really like having someone I can finally say that kind of thing to."

Jesus, he was in deep. He'd gone climbing with a couple of girls before, but watching Veronica set her jaw and conquer that last stretch had made his heart swell and ache. He wanted to tell her he was proud of her, but you couldn't say that to a woman you'd known for only a couple of weeks. He had nothing to do with how strong she was. And "You're fucking awesome" wasn't quite the sentiment he was going for.

So he bit the words back and winked. "You've been saving up a lot of filthy thoughts, have you?"

"Maybe."

"Well, funny enough, I have all those things in my apartment right now. Booze." He ticked them off on one hand. "A shower. And an orgasm. Maybe even several."

"All for me?" she squealed.

"I'm seriously hoping you'll share."

"Okay, but you'd better not be lying about the liquor. I'm not kidding. And if you have a sippy cup so I can take it in the shower with me, even better."

He grabbed her hand and tugged her up, giving in to the urge to kiss her beautiful smile. "I've got vodka," he murmured between kisses. "And orange juice. And maybe a thermos."

"I can work with that."

Her neck was slick with sweat when he trailed his hand along her skin, and Gabe's cock started to thicken. He wanted to lick her there. Lick her everywhere.

Someday, if she wanted to climb a few more times, he'd fuck her on the highest rock, under the sun and sky. He wanted that the way he wanted life. To be so utterly alone with her, inside her, the sun and breeze the only thing on their skin.

Someday. Before all the months left to him disappeared.

She got out her phone to take a few pictures of the wall they'd just rappelled down, and Gabe went to go coil ropes. He wasn't smiling anymore. He didn't know what to do. He'd meant to tell her the truth today, but it scared him. She'd probably break it off. At the very least, they'd have to have a discussion about where this was heading, and it was heading nowhere. Could he even ask her to be exclusive when it would last for only a few months?

The idea made his muscles tight. He rolled his neck, trying to ease out the knots. He didn't want to stand by while she dated other guys. Hell, he didn't even want to imagine moving back to New York and leaving her to have new experiences with other men. Sex. Sex on a hike. Sex and camping. Sex at the top of a climb.

Maybe they could date a little while longer before they had to talk about it at all. Was that manipulating her or just taking it slow? He couldn't tell anymore.

He finished gathering the rope and they headed back to the rock face where they'd started, then packed up their gear and set off down the trail. Halfway to the trailhead, they passed a rock wall that had been empty during their hike up, but it was swarming with people now. Some stood on the ground controlling ropes that led up to anchors and then down to novice climbers.

"Wait," Veronica said, "What's that?"

"Top roping," he answered.

She stopped in her tracks and stared at the scene for a moment, her eyes widening as each second passed. *"What?"* she finally gasped. "You mean we could have done *that*? It's, like, thirty feet up at the most!"

"Oh, come on. You don't want to do that. You did a full belay climb! Aren't you proud of yourself?"

She stared bug-eyed at him, then looked back to the top ropers. "But I could have done that instead!"

"We can do it now if you want."

"Fuck you!" she yelped.

Gabe tried to look contrite, but he couldn't quite pull it off when he was laughing. "I'm sorry," he gasped.

"Liar! You're not sorry at all!"

"I told you I'd take you climbing, not to what amounts to a climbing *gym*. You did a real climb and you were a natural, just like I said."

She glared at him, but all Gabe noticed was that the breeze had finally cooled her off and her nipples were hard beneath her tank top. She shook her head, drawing his gaze back up. "You're not sorry and you're ogling my breasts!"

"Okay, you're right. I'm sorry, but they're *right there*!" He gestured toward her nipples, then forced his hand down when he realized that probably wasn't her point.

She spun and started down the trail, not looking at the climbers as she passed them. Gabe grimaced and hurried to catch up. He really should have kept his eyes above her neck. Especially when she was *maybe* justifiably angry.

"I'm sorry, Veronica. Really." The trail widened and he jogged to get even with her.

She shrugged. "Yeah, well. I guess I was pretty amazing."

"Climbing? Hell, yes, you were."

"And maybe my breasts are too pretty to resist."

A heartbeat passed before he realized that the corners of her mouth were tight because she was trying to hide a smile. "Are you screwing with me?"

Her grin was wicked. "Only a little. But you really should have told me about the top roping."

"I still would've talked you into a real climb."

"Maybe. But since you didn't ask, you'll have to make it up to me."

Lust dropped into his blood with just that one flirtatious sentence. Oh, he was going to make it up to her, all right.

Thank God he'd brought her to the one climb that was close to town. He couldn't bear a long hike and an even longer drive before he got her alone. He wanted her naked and in his shower right now. She could sip from a drink while he slid soap all over her body. She could soak in the tub while he stroked her cunt. Anything she wanted, just *soon*.

She got into his truck and crossed her arms tight, smiling at the road as he pulled onto the highway toward town. Gabe's phone beeped, and he glanced down to see that his dad had sent a text. Shit. He flipped the phone over before she could see it. If she asked about his father, Gabe would have to explain a lot of things that he didn't want to talk about today. Or tomorrow.

Maybe he could make her understand. They weren't strangers anymore. They shared secrets and pleasure and trust.

He rolled his shoulders and tried to set the idea aside. He owed her something good tonight; he'd think about all this other shit some other time.

"Do you want to grab something to eat?" he asked.

"Drinks. Shower. Orgasm," she replied. "I don't have time for food."

"Maybe we could order a pizza later?" he suggested.

"That sounds perfect. You're really good at this whole seduction thing."

"Hmm." He shot her a doubtful look, trying to cover that he'd felt a shock of guilt at her words. "I'm not sure it can be called a seduction when I'm being ordered to sex you up."

"Right. Just shut up and drive."

"Yes, ma'am," he said with complete enthusiasm. "Anything new you want to learn tonight?"

He glanced over just in time to catch the blush that stole over her cheeks. She didn't look at him. Her crossed arms tightened against her chest. "I want to suck your cock again," she said.

Gabe nearly groaned. His foot pressed more firmly to the accelerator.

"Other than that," she said softly, "I'll leave it up to you."

His hands went a little numb on the steering wheel, so he forced himself to loosen his grip. He was hard as a rock already. "I want you to suck my cock," he said, lust shooting through him as he said vulgar words to this sweet girl. "And then I want you on top of me. I want to watch you ride me."

She drew a deep breath before she nodded. "Yes. I'll do that."

He rolled his shoulders again, trying to get control of his body. They'd be in town in five minutes and at his place in ten. He couldn't get out of the car this way, not at four in the afternoon.

He wasn't sure what it was about her that turned him on like crazy. It wasn't her inexperience. He didn't give a shit about that kind of thing. Maybe it was her enthusiasm. Her strange mix of self-consciousness and knowledge. It made him want to show her every wicked thing. To watch her lick her lips in anticipation even as her face turned pink.

His line of thought wasn't helping. He shifted in his

seat and cleared his throat. Veronica glanced at him, mouth curving into a naughty smile.

"Shut up," he growled. "This is your fault."

"Good."

He laughed despite the ache in his cock, but his laughter ended when her hand slid onto his thigh.

"Don't," he groaned.

"Don't what?" she asked as her fingers slipped up to stroke over the bulge in his shorts.

He didn't have the heart to tell her to stop.

"I've written plenty of times that women shouldn't feel flattered about this kind of thing, but…I love how hard you get for me. It thrills me. Don't tell anyone I said that." Her hand pressed harder against his cock, the pleasure both a relief and a torment.

"I won't," he promised.

"I love it," she whispered. He slid a little farther down in his seat and her fingers tightened around him as much as they could through the shorts.

"Me, too," he moaned.

She laughed and let him go, and he desperately wanted to pull over and make her do it some more. He wanted to tell her to take it out and stroke it, right there in the car. Wanted to watch her bright eyes spark with wickedness as she told him they shouldn't and then she did it, anyway.

But now they were at the outskirts of town, and she probably didn't want her name in the paper quite like that. *Local Advice Columnist Arrested for Public Indecency.* Though it would destroy any doubts about her sexual experience.

Gabe concentrated on navigating through town. Veronica smiled out at the streets. It was a close call, but by the time he pulled into his parking space, he was calm enough to get out of the car and unload the gear.

She stopped him with a hand on his arm. "Thank you. For today."

"You're welcome."

"I was really scared, but I wanted to do it, anyway."

He set down the bag he'd picked up and turned to give her a hug. "It's supposed to be scary," he said. "That's why climbers do harder and harder climbs. To feel that adrenaline again. To push past their fear and instincts."

"Really?" she breathed against his chest.

"Really."

She nodded and he let her go, but she still looked uncertain. "I got a letter yesterday that scared me."

Gabe's hackles rose. "Threatening?"

"No, not like that. It was from a high school kid who felt like he didn't want to live anymore."

"Jesus," Gabe breathed, alarm spiking through his body. "What did you do?"

She shrugged. "The only thing I could do. He'd used a temporary email address, so I consulted with a therapist and then posted an answer on my site. I hope he sees it."

"He'll see it. He wrote to you because he wanted help."

"Do you think so?" she whispered.

He touched her face, but she didn't look up at him. "I told you about yesterday. My first rescue situation."

"Yeah."

"I was fine until I got down there and saw how scared those people were. In pain and freezing and terrified. That was when it hit me that I could really help them, and that if I screwed up, I'd make everything so much worse."

She shook her head. "I don't know how you do that."

He shrugged. "It was scary, but it was what I was there for. It's what you're there for, too. And I think what you deal with is a hell of a lot more frightening than a broken ankle. You're scared because you're taking it seriously and you care."

She laughed. "Is that why I'm scared? I thought it was because I was scared of everything."

"You do a good job of hiding it."

"Yeah," she breathed. "I'm good at that."

"You're good at a lot of things," he said, not meaning it as a flirtation, but she looked up at him with a wicked smile and his mind immediately turned toward the shower that was only a few dozen feet away.

"I'm a quick learner," she promised.

"Then let's get your ass inside."

She grabbed one of the bags and held out a hand. "Lead the way." He did.

Some part of his brain was aware that the knob turned too easily under his key, but he was too distracted by Veronica's naughty smile to be alarmed. The shower was only a dozen feet away now, and—

The door swung open. Someone rushed at him. And suddenly the wrong woman was in his arms.

"Gabe!" she shrieked, jumping up and hitting him with her full weight as she wrapped her arms and legs around him. He stumbled back under the assault, twisting to avoid bodychecking Veronica. His assailant's bright red hair swung into his eyes.

"Naomi?" he gasped.

"Surprise!" she yelled as another woman stepped out of his apartment and waved.

His sister was here. And she'd brought a friend.

Oh, shit. His gaze slid to Veronica's round eyes and slack jaw.

He shook his head, but there was no stopping this now. His family had dropped straight into Veronica's lap. And the truth couldn't be far behind.

THE MOST GORGEOUS WOMAN in the entire world was wrapped around Gabe's body and clinging like a vine. Or maybe the second woman standing in his doorway was the most gorgeous woman in the world. Definitely one of them was and both were focused on Gabe.

The woman draped around Gabe tossed her head and laughed, her long red hair swinging back as if she was in a shampoo commercial. "Are you surprised?" she shrieked.

Yes. Veronica was surprised. And starting to feel a little sick.

Gabe wasn't her boyfriend. She knew that. But she'd kind of been pretending that he would be.

Still, he was free to date other women at this point. Just…just not someone so utterly stunning.

The laughing redhead was disentangling herself from Gabe now as he gasped out, "Naomi?" one more time.

God, she even had a beautiful name. And as she put her feet down and stood straight, the beauty just kept going. In her heels, she was as tall as Gabe, maybe even taller. She wore red pumps and the tightest jeans Veronica had ever seen, which only made her impossibly long legs longer.

"What are you doing here?" Gabe asked, his eyes darting from Veronica to Naomi and back again. "You said maybe next week."

"I missed you and I wanted to surprise you. Surprise!"

Yes, Veronica was definitely feeling sick now. This girl had missed Gabe. He'd just moved here. She was his ex from Cincinnati. Or *not* his ex. Veronica backed up a step. She was his girlfriend from Cincinnati.

"Oh, my God," Naomi groaned, "You're not even happy to see me. It's been nine months!"

His girlfriend from somewhere else.

"I am happy to see you—I just…" His gaze focused on Veronica again, and Naomi's eyes followed the path.

"Well, hello," she said, looping her arm through Gabe's and swinging him around to face Veronica. They looked like a team. A couple. "Who's this?" she asked with a smile.

Veronica took another step back.

Gabe shook his head. "This is Veronica," he answered. "Veronica, this is my sister Naomi. Apparently, she came to surprise me."

Veronica had already taken another step back before she registered his words. "Your what?" she murmured, but her confusion was interrupted by the giant beautiful creature rushing forward to wrap Veronica in a hug. "Are you Gabe's girlfriend?" she cooed.

"No! I mean…no, I…"

"Naomi, leave her alone," Gabe said. "And tell me what the hell you're doing here."

"You said I could come." She let Veronica go and shrugged at her brother, though she kept one slender arm slung around Veronica's shoulder.

Gabe ran a hand through his wind-mussed hair, making it stick up in even stranger directions. "I assumed you would let me know in advance. You know, in case I had *plans*."

Naomi stuck out her bottom lip. "Well, jeez. We can go stay at a hotel if you want."

At the word *we*, Gabe looked toward the doorway. "Hello, Monique."

Monique waved her fingers and smiled as if she showed up on people's doorsteps every day and it had never been a problem before. It probably hadn't. Who would turn her away? She was just as tall as Gabe's sister and just as stunning. Her brown skin glowed with perfect health. Her black hair stood out in wild twists, and while a style like that would've made Veronica look like a madwoman, it somehow lent Monique's face a delicate perfection.

And Gabe knew her name.

Veronica stopped herself from backing all the way to the sidewalk so she could bolt toward home, but it was a close call. She was dressed in sweaty hiking clothes, and her face felt greasy with sunscreen. She couldn't imagine what her hair looked like, since she'd had to clip it back with three barrettes to keep it out of her face for the climb. She felt ugly, dirty and about four feet tall next to these elegant women. The perfect height to look up Monique's very short white dress.

"Maybe we should—" Gabe started, but he stopped speaking when Naomi swept Veronica closer and directed her into Gabe's apartment.

"How did you get into my place?" he sputtered, as if he'd just recognized that there'd been a little breaking and entering.

"Oh, please." Naomi waved a hand. "You always keep a spare key nearby. I found it above the patio door frame. Not very smart, little brother."

"Believe me," he muttered, "it won't happen again."

Naomi finally let Veronica go, and Veronica found herself rocking a little unsteadily without the support.

"Would you like a beer?" Gabe's sister asked, already breezing toward the kitchen, her heels clicking against the wood floors of his apartment.

Veronica nodded, then looked questioningly at Gabe. He looked a little horrified, but not nearly as shocked as Veronica was. *I'm sorry*, he mouthed as Veronica felt a cold bottle pressed into her hand. She murmured a thank-you and then sucked down half of the ice-cold beer.

"How long are you staying?" he asked.

"Just a few days. I've got a shoot uptown next week. I'm sorry, Gabe, but I couldn't handle Dad anymore. I had to get out of there. He brought home burgers every night and then acted hurt when I wouldn't eat. I told him I'm showing fall collections all month and I can't afford not to fit into the damn clothes. All he wanted to do was talk about the next MacKenzie's location. It was like he was trying to lure me to the dark side with grease. Mom sent cookies, by the way." She waved toward the kitchen, and the motion of her hand sent Veronica's head spinning.

Uptown. Fall collection. Showings.

No.

She looked at Naomi again, then Monique, who'd plopped down onto the couch to scroll through her phone.

They were tall and perfect and thin. They couldn't eat burgers. They had to fit into clothes.

Oh, my God.

"Can you excuse us for a moment?" she heard Gabe say. He took her elbow and led her toward the open door of his bedroom.

"Sure," Naomi called. "You two have fun."

Veronica heard him close the door behind her. She shook her head, trying to clear the cobwebs that had draped over her brain. "They're models," she murmured.

"I'm so, so sorry, Veronica. You have to believe me." He pulled her into his arms and tucked her head under his chin.

"Your sister is a fashion model."

"Yes," he said.

"In New York."

"Sometimes."

Veronica's mind was working again and it kept turning things over and finding new details that she did not want to see. "MacKenzie's," she whispered.

Gabe didn't have a response for that. She felt his chest rise beneath her as he inhaled.

She put her hand up and pushed him back until he let her go. "MacKenzie's," she repeated. "As in the famous New York burger place?"

He winced and let out a long breath before he answered. "Yeah."

"You said you lived in New York when you were a kid."

His head dipped in a careful nod. "I did. I left when I was eighteen. My family is still there, but I haven't lived there in thirteen years."

"Oh." The cold creeping up her fingers reminded her she was still holding the beer and she downed the rest of it. She wasn't quite sure why she felt so hurt. She couldn't get mad at him for where he was from, could she? But she was mad. She'd trusted him. Trusted that she could be awkward and honest and uncertain with him, because his world hadn't been filled with girls like the ones who were lounging on his couch right now. Girls who were everything Veronica had never been. "I didn't know," she finally managed to say.

"That's not my life," he said, and she could hear the pleading in those words.

"But…" She frowned. "Did you keep that from me on purpose? When I talked about the city, you never said anything about your parents living there. You didn't say anything about MacKenzie's. I mean, that's kind of big. Everybody goes there. *I've* been there!"

He paced over to the window of his bedroom and then back. She was in his bedroom for the first time and she wasn't even sure she should bother looking around. She might never be here again.

"Okay," he started. "When we met, I played it down on purpose, because Lauren introduced us like we had Manhattan in common. I didn't want to encourage it. I didn't want to date a girl from Manhattan."

She nodded. He'd already told her most of that.

"And then… I don't know. We haven't talked much about our families yet."

"We talked about the city," she cut in.

He tipped his head in acknowledgment. "I'm sorry. It was wrong not to be more up-front about it. It seemed like you'd think of me as one of those guys you dated in New York. And you didn't *like* any of those guys."

She hugged her arms tight together and tried to figure out what she felt. It wasn't his fault that she'd revealed so much of herself right from the start. It wasn't as if he'd demanded to know everything about her and then he'd refused to say anything about himself. "Why did you leave?" she asked. The question so many people had asked her. The thing she'd lied about a hundred times.

"Because it wasn't the right place for me. I don't hate it. I could imagine living there. It's where I grew up and almost everyone I love is there. But if I had a choice, I'd choose this."

That was what really mattered, wasn't it? He couldn't help where he was from. Hell, there wasn't even anything wrong with New York; it just intimidated her, and she didn't want to be intimidated by Gabe.

"Your sister is a New York model," she said flatly.

"She's really nice, though."

Yes, Veronica could see that. "Tell me that you never dated Monique."

"Never," he said, then added, "ever," with a hopeful smile.

"Did you date any of her other model friends?" Veronica hated the sullenness in her voice, but that was how she felt. Sullen. It was childish, but true.

He cleared his throat. "I dated one of her friends when I was eighteen. For maybe two weeks."

If Gabe hadn't been watching, she would have lifted her fists to the sky and shaken them, cursing God or the moon or the Fates.

"Other than that," he continued, "I've never shared the same interests with Naomi's friends. Or Naomi. But I love her to death."

Right. That beautiful, intimidating creature was his sister.

Veronica felt suddenly guilty. She was sure that Naomi and her friends were perfectly lovely. Veronica just…kind of didn't want them to be lovely. She wanted them to be awful. Which made her feel even worse.

"I'm sorry," he said. "This isn't the way I would've explained, obviously. I was thinking today that I needed to tell you about my family. I wasn't going to keep it from you forever. I just told myself that we'd barely started dating, so it was okay."

She nodded. "It is okay. I understand. We hardly know each other."

"I wouldn't say that."

She smiled despite her tension. "I should go."

"No, don't go. Hang out with us."

"Gabe, I'm sweaty and dirty and bruised and I'm wearing this." She swept a hand up and down her body. "I'm leaving."

"Fuck, this is not how I wanted this day to end. Not even close."

"Me, neither." She looked at his bed and wanted to kick it. She should have been naked and in his shower by now. This wasn't fair at all. Her muscles were already starting to stiffen from the climb.

"I'm going to go take a bath," she said.

"I could come over and help?" he suggested.

"No, have fun with your sister." *And Monique*, her shitty, insecure brain added. She reached behind her for the knob and pulled the door open. "I'll talk to you later."

She turned before he could talk her into staying and called out, "Nice meeting you!" as she hurried through the living room. She started jogging as soon as she hit the sidewalk, and she was home in two minutes and shutting the door hard behind her. Her apartment felt dark and safe and lonely. It was free of Gabe and beautiful women and what he might be thinking about them.

But when she rushed to the fridge to grab a bottle of wine, she saw her notes and felt immediately ashamed.

#4—Stop being afraid.

She'd actually run home as if she'd been terrorized by those perfectly lovely women. All because she was afraid that Gabe would like them more. That wasn't normal, was it? What the hell was wrong with her?

When thirty seconds of hard thought didn't solve the riddle for her, she decided wine and a hot bath couldn't hurt anything. An unquestionably less satisfying plan than the one she'd hatched at the bottom of that climb, but it would have to do.

She deeply regretted the loss of the orgasms Gabe had promised her, but as she eased her sore body into the hot bathwater, she wondered if this was just as good. She moaned so loudly she was afraid her neighbors might hear, then decided she didn't care. It felt too damn perfect.

The wine and water soaked warmth into her muscles and she slid deeper into the tub, letting go of her tension.

She didn't want Gabe to be a man who was used to hanging out with models. She didn't want him to be someone who loved the city that had scared her so much. But he probably didn't want her to be the type of girl who felt jealous and insecure, so maybe neither of them was perfect.

"No, wait," she murmured. "That's all me." She laughed and sipped her wine, stretching her tired feet under the water. He'd been pretty damn perfect from the start. Or maybe not.

Her insecurities were all her fault, but Gabe was at fault, too. He'd withheld information that he'd known was important. A mistake, but not an unforgivable one, not this early in their relationship. Assuming she wanted it to continue.

She rolled her eyes at her own thought. There was no doubt she wanted it to continue. If she'd written in to her own column, she knew the advice she'd give. *Have you told him all of your secrets? Did you sweep all the skeletons out of your closet on the first date and let him examine each one? Just because he gave you your first good lay doesn't mean you're married. Lighten up.*

Lighten up. And stop being scared. There was good news to be had here. Gabe had spent time around the sophisticated women of Manhattan. He'd hung out with models. Hell, maybe he'd even had sex with them. And he liked Veronica.

"Don't be flattered that a man wants to have sex with you," she said aloud.

She sunk her head under the water to wet her hair. "Yeah, right," she sputtered when she came up. She was so flattered she was squirming.

When the water grew cold, she forced herself out of the tub. It was still early. She could get some work done.

"Sure," she muttered, "I'll work instead of getting fucked a few times. That'll be great." Yeah, the bath definitely hadn't washed away that bitterness.

She put on her feeling-sorry-for-herself clothes: yoga pants and a big sweatshirt. Then she found her phone. Her heart skipped at the sight of two missed texts from

Gabe, but it fell to the pit of her stomach when she read the first.

We're going out tonight with some of my friends. Come with? The second one had arrived a few minutes later. Please?

She didn't want to go. She could be weird and awkward around Gabe, but she didn't want to be herself in front of his friends, and she didn't have the energy to be edgy Dear Veronica tonight. But the idea of sitting around her lonely apartment without Gabe was too much to bear.

She wrote back before she could overthink it. You promised me drinks and orgasms. I doubt I'll get the latter at a bar.

His reply buzzed within seconds. Drinks first, then orgasms, I promise.

You already promised that, and look where I am right now. She pouted at the phone.

Where are you right now? he asked.

She looked down at her fleece and the pink fuzzy socks she wore. I just got out of the bath.

Oh, God. You didn't come yet, did you?

She laughed, imagining husky desperation in his words. Not YET, no...

Please, he wrote. Tonight.

With your sister in the next room?

The phone stayed silent for a long moment, and then his reply appeared. I'll give Naomi and Monique my bed for tonight if you're willing to share yours?

"God," she sighed. She wanted that so much. Wanted Gabe in her bed, making love to her until she fell asleep and then waking her with more later.

My bed's kind of small for a big man like you.

We'll cuddle, he answered.

Laughing, she collapsed onto her bed and wished he were there already. All right. I'll see you tonight.

As soon as he sent the details about the plans, her anxiety returned, but this time instead of indulging it, Veronica jumped to her feet and stormed into the kitchen. She jerked open the drawer, got out her marker and paper, and wrote a new note.

"Perfect," she growled as she slapped it onto the fridge and used her last magnet to hold it in place.

#5—Have a little fucking confidence and enjoy yourself for once.

She was not going to be defeated by New York City. Not this time.

CHAPTER SEVENTEEN

"SHE SEEMS PERFECT for you," Naomi said. "Very sporty."

Gabe shot her a glare. He wasn't sure sporty was supposed to be a compliment in this case. "I taught her how to climb today."

"Ooh! How come you've never taught me to climb?"

"Because you said if you broke a nail, you'd make my life a living hell."

"Ah, that sounds right. So." She looked him up and down as he rolled up the sleeves of his green plaid shirt. "You're a little dressed up for a night at the bar. Are you in love with this girl or what?"

"I'm wearing jeans!" he protested.

"You're wearing *real shoes*. I've never seen you out in anything nicer than a T-shirt and sneakers." She slipped on heels and grabbed a jacket that looked as if it was short enough for a toddler.

"That's an exaggeration," he said. "And if you want to keep warm, you might want to bring a jacket that goes down farther than your...rib cage."

"You mean my boobs?"

Gabe shook his head. "No, I did not mean that."

"Stop changing the subject. Are you in love with this girl or what?"

"I've been dating her for just over a week."

"So?"

Gabe picked up the clothes his sister had tossed on his bed and moved them back to her suitcase. "How's Dad?"

"The same. He can't stop talking about you coming home, even though he pretends he hates the idea of retiring."

He sat down on the bed. "He does hate the idea of retiring. He only agreed to it because I agreed to take over. For now."

Naomi sat next to him, dropping hard enough to make him bounce twice before she settled an arm around his waist. "I'm sorry, Gabe. I've only got about five more good years left in modeling, if that."

"Yeah. I know." They'd had this talk a thousand times. "I don't blame you, Naomi. I'm the one who pushed for him to retire at sixty instead of sixty-five. He's slowing way down. His doctor keeps telling him to lose some weight, change his diet, and Dad's never going to do that when he's in the restaurants every day."

"Do you really think he's going to stay out of the shop just because you've taken over?"

Gabe groaned and fell back on the bed, dragging Naomi with him. "I don't know. But I can always threaten to leave again if he doesn't behave."

"You won't do that," she sighed.

"I know." He wouldn't. He and his sisters were their Dad's whole world. He'd started training them in the restaurant business from age three up, finding jobs that even toddlers could help with. His dream had been for the whole family to work together, but then his kids had scattered like leaves on the wind, and his wishes had disappeared along with them.

"I just want him to be happy," Gabe said. "And healthy."

"I'll help in a few years," Naomi promised. Gabe didn't voice his doubts. She'd promised that before. And whether she was modeling or not, his sister wasn't the type to put both feet firmly on the ground. But maybe she'd pull through. She had to settle down sometime.

"Why did Claire have to become a vegetarian?" he groaned.

"Vegan," Naomi corrected.

It didn't matter to Gabe. He didn't care what she ate or didn't eat; he only cared that she'd walked away from MacKenzie's. "Yeah. By the way, Mom's cookies are great. Cherry thumbprint. Your favorite."

"Shut up!" She slugged his arm. "You're just as bad as they are."

"I'm just giving you the option."

They lay silently together for a few heartbeats, reminding Gabe of the many summers they'd spent on beaches as kids. There'd been so many evenings of trying to eke out the last few minutes as their mom called from the porch of the rented house. Their dad had sometimes come for a few days, too, but he'd always needed to get back to work. Gabe was just starting to relax into the mattress when Naomi bounded up. "All right. Just one cookie."

She disappeared, and Gabe hauled himself up to follow her into the living room. Monique appeared from the bathroom, wearing sparkling purple eye makeup now with little bits of glitter that danced over her cheekbones. She'd clearly never been to a bar in Jackson, but Gabe was sure she'd be popular, regardless of the sparkles. She slipped on silver heels that set off the skin of her legs and then held her arms up to the sky. "Ready?" she asked.

He was ready to see Veronica, so he nodded and grabbed his keys. Naomi hurried out and handed him a half-eaten cookie. "Finish this," she ordered.

"Come on, Naomi, you can have one cookie."

"It's my second one!" she screeched. Monique just followed silently as usual. He'd rarely heard her speak. Some guys seemed to be enchanted by that, but Gabe couldn't figure it out. How were you supposed to be interested in a woman who didn't even talk, much less one who didn't babble funny, awkward things whenever she got nervous?

Veronica had insisted on meeting them at the bar, but Gabe still had to fight the urge to swing by her place and see if she wanted to walk with them. A glance at his watch told him she'd probably left ten minutes before, so he led the two women straight toward a place two blocks off the main square. Not quite a dive, but definitely a locals' place.

He spotted Veronica at a table with a few of his friends as soon as he walked in. They must have called her over to join them. She was deep in conversation with Benton, and even when Gabe sat down next to her, she only offered a wave before carrying on. She looked as pretty as ever, but tonight she was wearing a black tank top and tight jeans. Gabe introduced Naomi and Monique to the others and then leaned a little closer to Veronica.

"I'm not an expert in education or autism," she said, "but I have an idea. If you can't afford to go back and visit very often, maybe you could send a recording. I know you said he doesn't want to talk on the phone, so maybe something playable would be better. A video of you reading a story or singing a song or just talking about something you like. That might help him hear you without having to engage on the spot."

"That's a great suggestion!" Benton said, slapping his hand on the table. "I know repetition can be important to him. And I play a little guitar. I think he likes the Beatles."

"That's perfect," Veronica said.

"I just don't want him to forget me, you know? I'm the only uncle he has, but I can't get back to visit more than once a year." Benton nodded to himself before his gaze shifted to Gabe. "Man, I can't believe you're dating Dear Veronica! She's a genius. How did you pull that off?"

"Just lucky, I guess."

She turned to him with a smile, and Gabe was struck anew by how sexy she was. Her big eyes were painted dark and smoky again, and her earrings were long strands of silver that moved with every breath she took. "Hey, beautiful," he said as his gaze fell to her rosy pink mouth. "Thanks for giving me another chance."

"Stop being charming," she said, but her gaze was on his mouth, too, as if she wanted to taste him just as much as he wanted to taste her.

He tipped his head toward her ear. "Give me thirty minutes. I just need to be sure Naomi is comfortable, and then she won't care if I'm here anymore. We can go."

Veronica shook her head. "No, I want to stay and have fun. It's been a long week already."

"Did some jackass make you try rock climbing or something?"

She laughed, throwing her head back the way she did when she relaxed, and Gabe watched the curve of her neck and remembered that he'd planned to lick her there this afternoon. That had been hours ago. He might start to twitch if he didn't touch her soon.

"Yes," she laughed, "some jackass made me try rock climbing. But after that stress with the column, I'm down for a little fun."

He brushed his thumb against hers. "You haven't heard back?"

"No, and I'd like to forget it for a little while."

"I'll do anything I can," he said.

While she was laughing, Benton caught Gabe's eye. "Hey, you didn't tell me Naomi was here," he said, his best charming-bartender smile in place.

Gabe groaned, but there was no keeping those two apart. "She wanted to surprise you." Within minutes Benton had gotten up and planted himself in between Naomi and Monique.

"Gabe!" Naomi called as the crowd got louder. "Why does Benton keep referring to your girlfriend as Dear Veronica?"

"She's the local advice columnist," he said with a proud grin.

Naomi's mouth made a perfect O of surprise, as if she were posing for the camera, but her shriek wasn't quite as elegant. "Are you kidding me? Like Dear Abby?"

"Well," Veronica answered, "a little younger, I hope."

"That's so cool!" Naomi leaned past Gabe, forcing him to edge back in his seat. He tried not to resent it. "I need some advice! Can you help me?"

"It depends on your problem," Veronica answered. "But I'll try my best."

Naomi glanced at Gabe, then looked over her shoulder at Monique before leaning in closer. "I have a friend who's getting married in a month. Great guy, big wedding, expensive honeymoon, all that. But here's the thing... Three months ago, she accidentally texted me when she obviously meant to text someone else, because, you know...she mentioned his dick."

Gabe groaned and leaned farther back as Naomi shot him an irritated look. "I know what a dick is, Gabe."

"Shut up."

"Anyway," she huffed, "she immediately texted again and said, 'Sorry, that was for Oliver, LOL!' Except I know it wasn't for Oliver. We were all at the same party together, and she was texting and I could see Oliver across the room and he was talking to someone else the whole time! His phone wasn't even in his hand!"

Veronica winced. "Yikes."

"Exactly!" Naomi said, then glanced back at Monique again to be sure she wasn't listening. "Monique knows her, too," she whispered. " I don't know what to do. On one hand, it's not my business. On the other, she clearly shouldn't be getting married when she's fucking someone else! Should I say something?"

Veronica frowned, her head cocking to the side as she seemed to puzzle it over. "Are you absolutely sure they don't have an open relationship?"

"Believe me, I'd know if they did."

"Okay, then I'd say that you should talk to her. Not to try to force her hand about calling off the wedding or coming clean, but just to say, 'Listen, I know that text wasn't to Oliver and I wondered if you wanted to talk.' Sometimes people get really caught up in the idea of the wedding and they don't know how to get out of it."

"Yes!" Naomi said. "She talks about the wedding all the time, and she's almost manic about it."

"If she's someone who's aware of status and appearance—"

Naomi nodded frantically at that.

"—then she might feel like she's not allowed to back out of the wedding. So you could start that conversation. Ask if she's freaked out. Ask if she's really ready to get married, considering the text you saw. Tell her that Oliver is going to be a lot more hurt by an ugly divorce than he will be by a broken engagement. That may be the prompt she needs to reevaluate what she's doing."

Naomi grabbed Veronica's hands. "Thank you! That's such a good idea. It's been driving me crazy. I haven't told anyone, because it would ruin her life, but I can't just let her go on like everything is fine!"

"She might be relieved. And maybe she'll make the right choice."

"God." Naomi sighed, "she's amazing, Gabe. Maybe she could solve all *your* issues." She squeezed Veronica's hands. "You look amazing tonight, by the way."

"Thank you," Veronica said. "You look great, too." Then her gaze slid to Gabe. "What issues are those?"

He kicked his sister under the table. He knew she was talking about their dad and Gabe's insistence that he could fix everything by coming home. But he wasn't going to have that conversation here. "Oh, you know," he said. "She worries about me rock climbing."

"She should worry. It's insane!"

Gabe's tension melted away as Veronica began describing their day to Naomi. She was still calling it insane, but her eyes sparkled with excitement as she described the climb. Her hands flew as she gestured, shaping the details with her hands. "It was the most terrifying thing I've ever done. By far!"

"You're proud of yourself, though," Gabe said softly.

"Are you kidding? I'm so proud of myself! I totally kicked ass!"

Naomi gave her a high five. "Sing it, sister! Let's get another round of drinks!"

Gabe didn't talk much after that. He mostly just watched Veronica shine the way she did in front of that microphone during the live performances. But this was a little different. It didn't seem like a show. She laughed and told stories and she teased Benton about flirting with Naomi, and…she looked relaxed.

Gabe wanted to watch her like this for hours, and he wanted to take her home right now and make her come. Mostly he just wanted *her*.

And he wasn't the only one, apparently. Someone stepped up behind him and Gabe turned to see Dillon Tettering standing there, hands in his pockets and charming smile in place.

All of Gabe's muscles went tight. He wanted to punch that fucking smile off the guy's face. Sure, he'd been just an idiot teenager when he'd betrayed Veronica's trust, but as far as Gabe was concerned, little assholes just grew up to be big assholes. Granted, there were exceptions. People changed. But it was telling that this bastard still thought Veronica might be interested in him. What an arrogant dick.

"Hi, Roni," he said. "I didn't expect to see you here."

She stiffened before she turned slowly around. "It's Veronica," she reminded him.

"Right, sorry." He rocked back on his heels at her clear reluctance to talk. His eyes swept over the table and lingered for a moment on Naomi and Monique. What a dick.

"Well, I can see you're busy," he said. "I'll see you tomorrow. Can't wait." He walked away after dropping that bomb. Naomi caught Gabe's gaze and raised her eyebrows, but then she turned back to the others to join in the conversation.

Veronica sank a little in her seat. "I needed a favor from my dad."

Gabe wasn't sure he had a right to feel pissed, but he did. Dillon made his skin crawl. "What does that mean?"

"I asked my dad for the name of a therapist for help with that letter I told you about. And my dad asked me to see Dillon in exchange."

"I see. So you're going on a date?"

"No!" Her eyes jumped to the other people at the table and she lowered her voice. "It's not a date. I said he could come by the bar after my show for a drink. That's it."

"You said you didn't want to have a drink with him," Gabe pressed.

"I don't!"

"Then why don't you just tell your dad no?"

"It's complicated, okay? Nobody tells my dad no."

"Veronica, come on. You're not just anyone—you're his daughter."

She barked out a humorless laugh. "Like that makes it easier. It's just a drink. It's not worth fighting my dad over this."

"It's not just a drink," Gabe snapped.

She pulled back and stared at him for a moment. "You're asking me not to go have one harmless drink?"

"No, I just can't stand the thought of you with that asshole!"

Veronica rolled her eyes. "Are you kidding me? Monique is *living* in your apartment and she's the most beautiful woman I've ever seen!"

"That's not what I meant." He tipped his head back and took a deep breath. "He was an asshole to you, Veronica. He hurt your feelings. I don't want you forced to spend time with a guy who hurt you."

"Oh," she said.

"And if your dad knew, he wouldn't want you to see that guy, either. So just tell him."

"Gabe…" She shook her head and crossed her arms tight over her chest. "That's what you don't understand. My dad does know, and if I complain, he'll tell me to grow up and stop worrying about high school bullshit. To be fair, that's also what he told me when I was in high school, so at least I can count on his consistency."

Gabe couldn't wrap his head around what she was saying. "Your dad knows that Dillon made out with you and then made fun of you?"

She let go of the death clasp on her own arms to reach for her martini glass. She didn't gulp it down, though; she took a very careful sip. "I asked him to get my stepbrother to stop calling me Ronald. I mean, he said it constantly. At school, in the house, around the dinner table. It wasn't something my father could have missed. So yeah, I explained what had happened."

"What did he do?" Gabe asked, though he now felt sure he didn't want to know the answer.

"I already told you. He said I should grow up and stop letting people use my weakness against me."

"What weakness?" Gabe asked.

She shrugged and took another sip. "Who knows. Sensitivity, shyness, small breasts? Any weakness. All of them. My dad is not a big fan of weakness. Or me."

"Veronica," Gabe breathed. "That's ridiculous."

"Yeah. It is ridiculous. So it's just not worth saying no over something so small. I save up my resistance for more important things."

"Maybe that's a mistake. Maybe that's why he pushes you around."

"Do you think I haven't considered that? I just... I can't ask for his help and then tell him to leave me alone! What don't you get about that?"

He put his hand over hers. He wanted to tell her that it wasn't like asking for help with an apartment or money, but she was already upset, and this wasn't the place. "Okay," he said, "I'm sorry."

She shook her head.

"I get why you said yes. I just hate it."

She didn't look up when she spoke. "I live in his building. I don't pay rent. I put my foot down and refused to move back home with him, but I still live off his generosity. So I can complain about him all I want, but look where I am. It's like I never left home at all."

"Bullshit. You took a risk and went after something you wanted. Not many people actually do that, you know. It didn't work out, but at least you *tried*."

"Yeah," she breathed. He watched her paste on a smile before she met his eyes. "That's what I've been trying to tell myself. I just have to figure out what to do now."

"What do you want to do?"

Her fake smile softened into something more genuine. "Long term? I'm not sure. But I have definite goals for tonight. Want to get out of here?"

"Oh, hell, yes," he said. He threw some cash on the table and leaned close to Naomi. "You good here? I'm thinking of taking off with Veronica."

"Oh, yeah? Hang a tie on the door until you're done."

"I'm staying at her place. You can have the bed. You and Monique, I mean, not one of these horny bastards."

"Party pooper."

He stood and said his goodbyes as he took Veronica's hand.

"Have fun, you two!" Naomi called.

Veronica's face blazed, but she waved good-naturedly as they left. Once they were out the door, Gabe stopped her for a quick kiss. "You look pretty," he said, sweeping his eyes down her skinny jeans to her heels, "but I miss your legs."

"I was not wearing a short skirt around women with four-foot-long legs, thank you."

"Fine. Save your shameless nudity for me."

She tossed him a coy smile and began walking away. "Deal."

He let her stay a few steps ahead of him for a minute, admiring the sight of her ass in those jeans. Sure, he missed her bare thighs, but this was a nice treat, too. She glanced back at him with another coy smile.

"I've been thinking," he said, "that you rescue a lot more people than I do even though I'm on a search-and-rescue team."

"I don't rescue people. Not most of them, anyway."

"Sure you do," he insisted. "It's not just the life-changing stuff. It's smaller things, too. Just helping Benton out with his nephew. That's important."

She ducked her head. "I don't know. I was thinking of going back for a master's in psychology. I think maybe I could be a therapist, but I'm not sure I've been successful enough to guide other people."

"I don't believe that's a requirement."

She laughed. "I guess it's not."

"You're good at listening. Good at seeing what people are saying."

"I guess." She shrugged off the compliment. "I had fun tonight," she said. "And today was pretty nice, too. You're very sexy climbing up those rocks, you know."

"Am I?"

"Yes." She sneaked her hand around his arm and squeezed his biceps. "You're very strong. I like your arms. And your hands." Her fingers slid down the inside of his arm and over his palm, leaving his skin tingling with pleasure. "I like seeing what makes your fingers so rough. It makes me think of how your fingertips feel against my nipples."

"Jesus," he breathed.

"What? I had my bath and I finally got my drinks."

"I wanted to give you a bath," he growled.

"Then I guess you shouldn't have ditched me for a couple of hot girls."

"You're cruel. You know I had no choice."

"You still have to make it up to me," she sang, dancing across the street toward her apartment. "Drinks, a bath, you know what's next on the list."

Yes. An orgasm. And he couldn't wait to make her come again.

VERONICA FELT AS if she were floating as she breezed into her apartment. Strange that this already felt normal, bringing Gabe home to have sex with him. She hardly felt shy at all. In fact, she felt almost confident.

She'd started the evening off with fear, but she'd gotten through it. She'd gone out instead of staying in. She'd gotten along with his friends. She'd even had *fun*.

And the best part of all was that it was going to be okay. It really was. He was from New York. He was sexy and smart and accomplished. His friends were beautiful and charismatic and confident. And Veronica had fit right in. She'd never had that in the past.

It felt like a miracle. And now she wanted another one.

She locked her door and walked toward her bedroom, smiling over her shoulder to be sure Gabe was following. "Tonight I want to touch you," she said.

His gaze had focused on her ass, but he looked up at that. "Yes," he said, the slight darkness in his voice making it sound more like an order than permission.

God, she liked that. She liked his confidence. She liked him teaching her, because she knew if she wasn't doing something right, he'd tell her. And if he didn't tell her, then she knew everything was just the way he liked it.

Veronica shucked her jeans before she even reached the bed. She hoped he liked the black panties she wore. They were boy shorts, not that revealing, but she liked the way they rode up to expose the bottom of her ass.

Gabe did, too, if the heat in his eyes was any indication when she turned around and caught him looking.

She stroked her hands up his chest. "Have I ever mentioned how hot you are?"

"Yes, but you should probably mention it again."

"Mmm." She let her hands follow the contours of his

muscles, up and over his pecs, and then curving over his strong shoulders. "You're so sexy," she whispered. She slid her hands back down, over his chest and belly. She began unbuttoning his shirt. "I want to touch you everywhere."

He sucked in a breath and she wondered if her knuckles had tickled his stomach. She'd find out later. Right now he was shrugging his shirt off and he was entirely exposed to her from the waist up.

"God," she murmured, brushing her mouth over his chest as she breathed in the scent of him. He tugged up on her tank top then, and she barely paid attention as she raised her arms. She just took the opportunity to nudge him toward the bed.

He backed up until his legs hit the mattress and when she nudged him again, he fell to his back. The sight of him bare chested and prone on her bed made her laugh with delight. "I love this," she said, then felt a brief explosion of panic in her veins. "I love having you here," she clarified so that he wouldn't get the wrong idea. "I love fucking."

He grinned as she straddled his thighs, but his grin snapped to a hiss when she traced her fingernails down his belly. "Are you ticklish?" she asked.

"A little." He sucked in his stomach when she did it again.

"I like that, too," she responded, but she showed him mercy and pressed her palms against his warm stomach. He was so flat compared to her body, so different. Tightly muscled and lean and dusted with dark hair. She leaned down to lick the thin line of hair that ran from his waistband to his navel. He hissed again and the power of it swept over her as she pushed her hands up over his ribs and then the hard muscles of his chest.

"Come 'ere," he murmured, his hands rising to cup her face and bring her toward his mouth. She braced her hands on his chest and leaned down to kiss him, only because she liked his hands guiding her. She gave him one long kiss, sweeping her tongue slowly over his before she pulled away. She wanted to taste him everywhere.

She let her cheek drag down his furry jaw, then sucked at the delicate skin just past his Adam's apple. His hands framed her waist and he sighed as if he'd found a comfortable spot.

Veronica was so turned on she felt almost lightheaded. She wasn't sure why. He'd barely even touched her. But something about the smell of his skin and the feel of his body had everything inside her pulled so tight that it almost hurt. Her heart drummed hard and fast, adding to the dizziness. She loved it.

She tasted her way down his neck to his chest, swirling her tongue around one of his nipples just to watch it tighten for her. She grazed her nose over his chest hair and kissed her way along his ribs.

When she sat up and grinned down at him, he wasn't smiling anymore. He looked slightly pained.

She looked down to the very significant rise in his jeans. "What's the matter? Are you uncomfortable?"

"Yes." When he reached out, she assumed he meant to unbutton his jeans, but instead his hands rose and he very slowly unfastened the front clasp of her bra and spread the straps down her arms. Goose bumps chased over her skin where he touched her, and then his calloused fingertips traced gently around her areolas. She shivered.

"Are you done touching me?" he asked, the words a low rasp.

"No," she whispered.

"Then touch me."

She shivered again. She couldn't help it. His words were as rough as the edges of his fingers where they teased her nipples.

Her hands felt clumsy now, but she did as he'd ordered. She spread her fingers along his ribs, then slid them down to his hips. She'd meant to tease him a little longer, but now she was the one who wanted his jeans off. They were in the way. She wanted all of him.

She unbuttoned his jeans and slid the zipper carefully down. Her mouth went dry at the sight of the erection outlined so clearly against his gray boxer briefs. It was difficult to believe that she had access to a cock like that after so many years of celibacy. Maybe it was her reward for waiting.

She wanted to touch him then, but she didn't. Instead she shifted aside and tugged his jeans down.

"Wait," he said, startling her, but he only dug into his pocket for a condom. Then he helped push the jeans off and raised his hips so she could slide his underwear off, too.

She couldn't help the breathy *Oh* that escaped her mouth once he was fully naked. His cock looked so thick framed by his narrow hips. Her fingers curled, but she still didn't touch him.

She straddled his thighs again, loving how hot his naked skin was against hers. "Look at you," she breathed, taking in the sight of him beneath her.

"Look at you," he countered.

She smiled because she didn't have the slightest desire to cover herself. He could look all he wanted.

Leaning forward, she kissed his ribs again, loving the way his cock pressed to her breasts. Apparently, he loved it, too, because he gasped in shock. She slid a little lower on his legs, pressing her body along his erection, and he cursed under his breath.

God, sex was so much *fun*.

When she kissed his belly, she teased him by dragging her open mouth along his skin only inches from the head of his cock. A glance up told her that he was watching intently. Waiting. Smiling, she ducked her head and kissed a path to his side. There was one last thing she wanted to do before things got serious.

His hips were tight with muscle just like the rest of him. She licked the V-shaped line that crossed down his hip. Then she did what she'd been wanting to do for days. She bit him.

He jerked in shock beneath her mouth. "Mmm, sorry," she murmured. Then she pressed her teeth to him again, more slowly this time, feeling the give of him under her teeth. She left the faintest of imprints there, but she licked him in apology. "I've been wanting to bite you," she said.

When he pushed her hair off her face, she bit the ball of his thumb, too.

Gabe gasped out a shocked laugh. "Fine, but just watch where you're biting."

"Oh, you mean when I'm sucking your cock?" she asked.

"Yes," he said, and now the hand in her hair was guiding her toward him.

"You want to feel my mouth?" she whispered.

"Yes."

Her heart fluttered, her nervousness trying to make a comeback. She tried to hide her uncertainty with boldness. "Tell me you like it."

"I love it," he said. She pressed a kiss to the crown, then circled it with her tongue. "I love your mouth," he groaned.

That was all she needed to hear. She didn't start out slow the way she had the first time. Instead she took him deep into her mouth, her heart speeding at his grunt of surprise.

"Oh, fuck, I love your mouth," he groaned as she sucked at him. He seemed inclined to skip the preliminaries tonight, too. He framed her head with both hands and eased her down until he hit the back of her throat. Veronica was relieved to find that she didn't gag. She liked him that deep. It made her feel…triumphant. Maybe she'd unpack that ridiculous thought later, or maybe she'd just enjoy it, because she loved his breathless words right now, whispering, "Just like that. God, just like that. It feels so good."

She slid up and down, not needing the guidance of his hands anymore. She could tell he liked it by the way his thighs tightened with every draw of her mouth, the way he pushed up to meet her, the way he groaned with pleasure. She slipped her hands down his hips and dug her nails into his ass.

He cursed, but before she could take him deeper again, his hands lifted her head. "I'm sorry. It feels too good. And I really want to fuck you."

She laughed at that, because there were a couple of options here and both of them were good. She could refuse to comply and keep doing this until he came, or she could climb a little higher on his body and fuck him.

The second thought made everything inside her tighten. Yes. She wanted that. She'd had it only once, after all, and she had so much catching up to do.

She rose up and slid her panties down. Gabe's eyes were focused between her legs, but his hand swept the bed beside him for the condom. He put the condom on as she crawled higher on the bed. Then he fisted the base of his cock as she straddled him again.

He stroked a hand between her legs, making her gasp. "That got you wet," he murmured. "Doing that."

She nodded, but she just stayed poised above him. She wasn't sure what to do, or maybe she was only too intimidated to try. It was hardly a puzzle, after all. The penis went into the vagina. Basic biology.

Gabe's free hand settled on her hip and he eased her down as if he knew she needed help. His cock only brushed against her pussy at first. Then it pressed against her. She held her breath, and her body began to take him in, stretching tight around him. Just as the pressure began to overwhelm her, he guided her up again, then back down. This time it was easier. She closed her eyes and sighed as though his cock were taking all the space for breath inside her.

This was basic biology, yes, but it somehow still felt miraculous. That another person was in her body. That it felt *right* instead of strange.

Finally, she was settled tight against his hips, her body filled with him.

His hands swept up her sides. "I love this, too," he said. She opened her eyes, startled by the mix of shock and dark pleasure that flashed through her at his words.

It was so close to "I love you." And so close to what she was feeling as she looked at him beneath her. His thumbs brushed over her nipples and she sighed.

"You're so beautiful, Veronica."

Was she? She didn't know, but he made her feel needy and wild and sexy.

"Just ride me," he said. "Whatever you do will feel good for me."

She nodded and pressed her knees hard to the mattress, sliding up only an inch, her eyelids fluttering at the strange feeling. This was different from being on her back. This was *her* doing the fucking. She moved very slowly, trying it out. It felt...nice.

Gabe's eyes focused first on her face, but as she moved on him, his gaze fell to her breasts. His thumbs brushed her nipples again, and then he squeezed them.

"Oh," she sighed, her eyes fluttering closed. The feeling shot straight to the nerves stretched tight around him. "That feels good," she whispered.

She kept riding him slowly, her thighs already shaking from the effort. Her legs were weak and tired after today's climb, but she wouldn't let that stop her. She wanted it just like this, filling herself over and over again with his cock.

But eventually, her shaking legs refused to hold her. She braced her hands on either side of his head and opened her eyes. "I'm tired," she said with a frustrated laugh.

"It's okay. You were busy being kick-ass all day."

He held her face between gentle hands and pulled her down for a kiss, his warm mouth like a gift for hers. His beard tickled her chin. Then he moved beneath her, and even though she was on top, he was the one doing the fucking now, tipping his hips up to slide deeper. She sighed in pleasure, but the sigh turned to a moan a moment later. His hands slid down her body and gripped her hips as he fucked her faster.

"Gabe," she gasped. His cock felt huge now as he held her open above him. His hips slapped into her. "Oh, God," she groaned. "Oh, God."

"Fuck. Veronica. I can't..."

His muscles went tight; his thrusts grew rougher. When his fingers dug hard into her flesh, she realized he was coming and raised her head a little to watch his face as the pleasure seemed to contort into pain. Breath hissed through his teeth until his hips finally slowed.

"I'm sorry," he gasped.

"It's okay," she said, only now realizing that it wasn't okay. She wanted to come. Hadn't that been the deal after that climb?

He opened his eyes and smiled. "You just looked so fucking hot above me. I couldn't help it."

Well, she couldn't resent that. And he had let her do whatever she'd wanted to him. She'd get off next time. The sex had still been fantastic.

She gave him a quick kiss and slid off him to give her still-shaking legs a rest.

Despite the near-liquid state of her thigh muscles, she felt tense as she collapsed into her blankets. Restless. Still, she smiled at the sight of Gabe's ass when he got up to go to the bathroom. She'd have to bite that one day, too. It looked made for biting.

She stretched hard and tried not to feel disappointed. He'd fucked her well and thoroughly with that beautiful body. And it had felt wonderful.

The day finally caught up to her. Despite the slight

vibration of tension in her muscles, she closed her eyes and sank into the pillows. She felt as though she could sleep for twelve hours. Even that might not be a relief, because she knew her arms and legs would be sore from the—

"Ah!" she shrieked when a hand grabbed her ankle and tugged it wide. Her eyes flew open to find Gabe dropping to his knees between her spread legs.

"Now let's get you that orgasm," he said with a grin.

"What?"

One of his eyebrows rose. "Don't tell me you're too tired. All you have to do is lie there."

"I—" she started, but he'd already ducked down and dragged his tongue over her clit. "Oh!" she gasped at the hard shock of pleasure. For some reason, she hadn't imagined he'd want to do that after he'd fucked her. She already felt wet and warm and slightly used, but he put his whole mouth over her and sucked at her clit.

"Oh, God," she groaned, raising her knees and spreading them wider. "You're like my own personal fantasy, Gabe MacKenzie."

His mouth left her for the barest moment. She glanced down to see him watching her, the naughty smile gone from his face. But he didn't say anything, and then his tongue was on her clit again, and Veronica let her head fall back and her eyes close as she tangled her fingers in his hair.

He was her fantasy, and even better than that, this was all going to be okay. She could feel it. And then all she could feel was his mouth.

CHAPTER EIGHTEEN

VERONICA WOKE TO a sensation of being bound by something hot and heavy and comforting. When she stretched, Gabe's hand spread over her naked waist and pulled her more snug against him.

"Mmm," she sighed as she turned her head into his shoulder and inhaled the scent of his sleep-warmed skin. He smelled like spice and sex. Despite that she'd come right before falling asleep, lust still settled into her belly as she breathed him in.

"I'm sure it's just my sister," he murmured into her hair, and she realized what had woken her as his phone gave another brief buzz. His hand stroked her hip, then stilled again.

Veronica entertained the idea of rousing herself enough to initiate sex, but she must have fallen back asleep before she could act on it, because the next thing she knew, she was jerked awake again.

Gabe's phone was buzzing again.

"I swear to God," he rasped, "if she's calling because she can't find the bottle opener…"

Cold seared her back when he left the bed, and she quickly rolled over into his spot. He cursed and she heard something on the dresser fall over, but then he must have found his phone, because the glow of the screen lit his naked chest.

"It's my mom," he said, all the sleepiness leaving his voice.

Veronica sat up and turned on the lamp next to her bed, sheet clutched to her chest in deference to his far-away mother.

"Mom?" he said. "What's wrong?"

When Veronica saw the way fear fell over him, taking all the color in his face with it, she almost wished she'd left the room dark.

"You're at the hospital?" he asked. "What are they saying?" He paced toward the dark doorway that led to her living room, then back, scrubbing his free hand over his hair.

"I…I don't get it. Didn't he just go to the doctor last month? I know, but— Okay. Okay."

Veronica watched his eyes search the room until they found the clock.

"I'll get a flight out for me and Naomi, but it won't be for at least six hours, and we'll have to connect. I'll call as soon as I have something. Leave your phone on, Mom, okay? Let me know if anything changes."

Veronica was already out of bed and pulling on clothes when he hung up. "What's wrong?"

"My dad. He had a heart attack."

"Oh, Gabe." He looked so lost, just staring at her, the hand holding the phone still raised halfway to his ear. She crossed the room and wrapped her arms around his waist. "I'm so sorry. Is he going to be okay?"

"I don't know. They said he's critical but stable. Stable is good, right?"

"Yes," she agreed, "stable is really good."

"His doctor has been warning him to get healthier, but he was just there a month ago and he was fine."

She squeezed him harder. "Does your sister know?"

"I'm not sure. I'd better go." Still, he didn't move; he just held tight to her, heart thundering against her ear.

"He's going to be okay," she said, wishing out loud for him.

She felt the movement of his muscles as he nodded. "You're right. He'll be okay."

She kissed his shaking heart and whispered his name before he took a deep breath and let her go. "I'll let you know when I'm leaving and when I can..." His words trailed away as he looked down at the shirt he'd picked up.

"Don't worry about that," she said.

His forehead creased and he shook his head, but he couldn't seem to speak.

"It's okay, Gabe. Just go tell your sister and get back to New York."

He nodded and finished getting dressed, then gave her a quick kiss before leaving.

It was only 3:00 a.m., but Veronica knew she'd never get back to sleep now. She pulled on warm clothes and made herself tea to try to shake off the chill that had settled beneath her skin. Poor Gabe. And his poor family. It was so awful that this had happened while Naomi was away, too.

She hoped Gabe's mother wasn't all alone. Surely they had more family there? Everyone she'd ever met from New York had had cousins stretched throughout the boroughs.

She wanted to call Gabe and see what was happening, but she was in a very strange position. She wasn't his girlfriend. They'd barely started dating. She had no right to insert herself into this tragedy or distract him while he was worried. She didn't even know his parents' names.

Feeling awful about that, she curled up in bed with her cup of tea and looked up MacKenzie's.

She immediately recognized the pictures of Gabe's dad. He looked like a bigger, bulkier version of Gabe. The man was clean shaven, but the kind brown eyes and sturdy nose were the same. He smiled in every single picture she found. A fantastic smile that said he loved the world and everyone in it.

Blinking back tears, she found a history of the business. Gabe's dad was named James, and he'd taken over the business from his father, who'd started the first MacKenzie's in 1970. The family's love for the place was evident in the stories on the website. And right there in the About Us section was a picture of Gabe's whole family. It must have been taken years ago, because Gabe was a teenager, gangly and thin faced. His two sisters framed him, both of them tall and beautiful. His dad had one big arm around Gabe's mom, a woman in her late forties who wore her hair in a ponytail and her sunglasses perched on top of her head.

They looked so happy. Veronica crossed her fingers and hoped hard that everything would be okay. It wasn't fair that a family like that could be broken up so early.

This kind of family had been Veronica's fantasy her whole life. Even when her mom had been alive, she'd watched other kids' fathers and wondered what it would be like to have a big laughing dad who was willing to take off work to come to the school musical performances.

After her mom had died, Veronica hadn't really dreamed much about family at all, until the day her

dad had announced that he was remarrying. His court-
ship had taken place entirely out of Veronica's sight, so
she'd had no picture of who this new woman would be.
But her mind had formed someone a lot like that picture of Gabe's mom. Pretty and funny and a little no-
nonsense. A woman who would come in and organize
their sterile little household into a real family.

Veronica had been utterly off base. Her stepmother
had swept into Veronica's life and reorganized the
household, all right, but her main goal had been reset-
ting the flow of the home so that it all revolved around
her and her son. If Veronica had had a stepbrother like
Gabe, everything would have been different.

Okay, maybe not like Gabe. That would have been
an awful made-for-TV movie. *My Brother, My Lover*.
So someone just as kind as Gabe but without Gabe's
lust-inducing pheromones. That would've been perfect.

She did a load of laundry and made herself breakfast, checking her phone about five times a minute to
be sure Gabe hadn't texted.

At 6:00 a.m. just as she was dozing off on her couch,
there was a quiet knock on the door. She raced over and
jerked it open.

Gabe's heavy eyes widened for a moment. "I didn't
want to wake you," he said.

"I couldn't sleep." She opened the door wide and
pulled him in out of the predawn cold. His fingers felt
chilled. "How is he?"

"The same. Still stable, though. They think it was
a pretty minor heart attack as far as damage, but he'll
still be in the hospital for a few days."

"Thank God." She put her arms around him and tried
to absorb some of the cold from his body.

He kissed the top of her head. "Veronica, I'm so sorry."

"Don't be silly. There's nothing to be sorry for. Did you get a flight?"

His chin rubbed her head when he nodded.

"What time?"

"Nine-thirty. We should get in by 5:00 p.m. Someone offered Monique a free tour of Yellowstone, so she's going to stay at my place for a couple more days. But she won't eat these, so I brought them for you."

She pulled back to see a plastic container in one of his hands.

"My mom's cookies," he explained.

"Oh, Gabe. That's so sweet." She blinked hard, but she still had to wipe a tear from her cheek as she took the cookies to the kitchen.

"She's a great baker. Not so great at cooking, but my dad took care of that. He *does* take care of that, I mean. He'd come home to make us dinner sometimes before going back to work. He's always worked way too hard."

She nodded. She knew what that was like, at least. "Do you want some tea or coffee? Do you need to go?"

"I should go," he said, but he didn't move.

"How is Naomi?" she asked.

He shook his head. "She's okay," he said, but then his words went quick and hoarse. "I need to tell you something. Can we sit down?"

Fear shot through her at the hopeless look in his eyes. She took his hand and led him to the couch. His fingers squeezed hers too hard, but then they slipped away. He spread his hands out against his own thighs and stared at them for a long moment.

"I'm really sorry," he said again.

"Why do you keep saying that? Your dad had a heart attack. Why would you apologize for something like that?"

He took a deep breath. "Because...I don't think I'm coming back."

She froze and her heart held still for a long moment before it raced to catch up with her anxiety. "What?"

"My dad... He's going to need help."

"Gabe, you don't know that yet. He could be back to normal soon. Try to be positive."

But he was shaking his head. "He won't be able to keep up this pace."

"He has managers and people to help him, doesn't he? Maybe it'll take a few weeks to get everything running smoothly, but—"

"You don't understand," he interrupted. "I was worried about something like this. He works too hard. He doesn't take care of himself, but he won't sell the company to anyone else. He's determined to keep it in the family, so I told him I'd take over when he turned sixty."

"How old is he?" she asked.

"Fifty-nine."

"Fifty-nine?" She didn't understand what he meant. "That's... You just moved to Jackson. That doesn't make any sense."

"I have a one-year contract with the library."

"What?" she breathed.

"It wasn't a permanent position. I was brought in to get digital lending up and running, because..." He glanced at her face and stopped talking. "Veronica. I was going to tell you..."

She stared into his sad brown eyes and shook her head. "Another thing you meant to tell me and didn't?"

He winced.

"It doesn't matter," she managed to say despite that her throat was closing up. "I get it."

"I came here to live the life I wanted for a year," he explained.

"Right," she said. "Of course."

"But now I don't think I can wait a year. If Dad's okay... I need to make sure he stays okay. I need to go back."

"Sure." Her whole body buzzed with the shock of it. He was leaving. He'd always been leaving. That was all right, though, wasn't it? They weren't in love.

"I'm sorry. I didn't want to tell you over the phone from New York. I just—"

"It's fine," she cut in. "You didn't promise anything. I told you this wasn't that kind of first time. It was casual."

"It wasn't," he said immediately. "It wasn't like that for me."

"Then why didn't you tell me?" she snapped. "Either it was casual and it didn't mean anything, or it meant something and you lied to me. Again."

"I..." He scrubbed his hands over his face. "I'm sorry. This whole thing got away from me. It's been intense from the start, and I didn't know when to tell you."

Intense. Right. She stood up. "We can't do this right now. You need to go make sure your dad is okay. The phone will be better, anyway."

"No, it won't. I want you to know that I wasn't lying to you. I want to stand here and tell you that if I don't come back, it's not because I don't want to."

She backed up because he was standing now, too, and she just wanted to hug him. She wanted to cry, and she didn't know why. "It doesn't matter. It was only a few dates."

"That's not true."

"Then you were *lying*!" she yelled, wishing she could take it back even before her words settled over them. He didn't need this right now. She didn't even know why she felt so angry. It pushed at her skin like panic, trying to claw deeper. "You let me feel things for you," she said, trying to keep her voice low. "Things I wouldn't have let myself feel if I knew you were *leaving*."

"I know," he groaned. "But I knew I was leaving and I still felt those things. I don't think it would've mattered, Veronica."

"You should have let me decide that!"

"I'm sorry." He pressed his hands to his forehead and cursed. "I thought we'd have time. I thought we could figure it out."

"Well, we don't have time." Pain raked at her insides. She crossed her arms hard and tried to push it down. "You didn't have to ask me to trust you, you know. You didn't have to act like you were being so honest, because I believed you, and now I feel *stupid*."

"Please don't. You're not stupid."

She laughed. "Thanks."

"I'm sorry, Veronica. I just… My family needs me." He moved toward her, his hands reaching out. "But if I can find a way—"

Veronica backed up, afraid for him to touch her. If he touched her, she'd start crying. She'd cling to him and breathe him in and she'd never want to let him go. There was no reason for that, she told herself. She barely knew him.

He dropped his hands. His face fell.

"You need to go. We don't…we don't need to talk about this again, but please let me know how your dad is, okay? And tell Naomi I'm thinking of her, too."

He watched her, his hands still open at his sides, as if he was pleading.

If he moved toward her again, she wouldn't have the will to say no. She didn't want to. This might be her very last chance to touch him, and she didn't have the strength to reject that chance.

But he didn't move closer. His hands turned slowly back in toward his body. He took a deep breath and closed his eyes as he exhaled. "I'll call you as soon as I can."

She would've told him that wasn't necessary, but maybe he needed someone to talk to. She couldn't be so harsh when he was scared for his father. "Do you need a ride to the airport?"

"No. Monique will take us in my car."

They stood in silence for a few seconds, tension drawing so tight between them she thought she might snap, but then he nodded and turned. "Goodbye," he said. "I'm sorry." And he was gone, shutting the door behind him before she could even respond.

She pressed her hand to her mouth, holding back a cry or a sob or some word she couldn't even anticipate.

She shouldn't have let him leave like that. Not with his father still in danger. "I'm sorry," she whispered against her own skin. She wanted to chase after him and hold him and tell him everything was fine, that she was fine. But she felt stupid for even considering it.

This wasn't a movie, and he wasn't her boyfriend. They'd had sex a few times and they hadn't even pretended to be in love. It had been a hookup. Now it was over, and his mind was already back in New York, where he belonged.

Gabe had been an amazing lover. More than she'd ever hoped for. But it was over now, so she let him go. For good.

CHAPTER NINETEEN

THE SHOW WENT well as far as Veronica could tell. She talked. People laughed and cheered. A martini was delivered but she just let it sit. She'd lost her taste for fun pink drinks. She had no idea what she was saying, but she wasn't the least bit scared this time.

She wrapped up the evening by offering a quick answer to one extra note, figuring she might as well take advantage of her sorrow-fueled bravery. "Yes, of course," she started, "you should write thank-you notes. Everybody should still write thank-you notes, preferably on real paper! But here's the flip side of graciousness. If you want to be a gracious person, you don't get to be shitty about other people not writing thank-you notes. Sorry, but that's the way it works."

Several people loudly disagreed, but most cheered. Veronica waved goodbye and promised to see everyone next week. Then she escaped to the office.

She didn't collapse into the chair with relief as she usually did. Instead she sank slowly down and stared at her hands, at a loss for what to do now. She'd have to see Dillon for that drink, but she still had ten minutes to waste. She could just stare at her phone.

Suddenly alarmed that she might have missed Gabe's call, she dug her phone out and checked, but no, there were no messages or texts or missed calls.

When a shadow fell over her, the stupid sudden thought that Gabe was back flashed through her mind, but she looked up to see Lauren. Of course. Lauren had said that she and Jake were coming, and Isabelle had joined them, as well.

"That was even better than the first night! Are you coming out?"

"Yeah, absolutely," Veronica answered, trying to look cheerful.

"Hey, are you all right? Is it Gabe's dad? I know he's in the hospital."

"I haven't heard anything yet. He said he'd get in touch when he could, but…" Everything else welled up, wanting to spill out of her mouth, but Veronica held it back. She couldn't hold back the tears, though.

"Oh, sweetie," Lauren cooed, crouching down to wrap her arms around Veronica. "It's going to be okay."

She nodded, because it would be okay. Gabe's dad would be fine. He had to be, because his family needed him.

And she'd be fine, too. Gabe had been her first lover, and it was over now, and she'd be fine. She should just be glad it hadn't gone on longer, because it would've hurt so much more.

But God…she'd wanted it to go on longer. It would all be okay, but it wasn't *fair*.

She nodded and moved away from Lauren. "I'll be out in a few minutes. I promised to have a drink with someone, but it should be over with quickly. Will you wait for me?"

"Absolutely." Lauren pulled some tissues from her purse and handed them to Veronica. "I'll see you in a few."

Back to feeling numb again, Veronica dabbed at her damp eyes and then got out her makeup bag.

She didn't want to see Dillon at all, but she refused to let him see her upset. She wasn't weak and scared anymore. She was brave and real and confident. There was nothing Dillon could say to make her small again. She was *above* him. Whatever she'd failed at in life, she'd never, ever been cruel.

Treating it as war paint, she darkened the liner around her eyes and glossed her lips with a shiny red that made her look as if she'd just snacked on some poor man's jugular. Fuck all of them.

She was glad she'd gotten good at wearing her clothes as a costume. Or maybe armor. Whichever it was, she felt protected from the world as she stood and opened the door. She was tall in her heels and cool as a winter wind in her midnight-blue sheath. Nothing could hurt her.

Dillon was seated in the front of the room, near the bar. She'd spotted him smiling at her during the show and then refused to look in his direction again. Now she stared dead into his eyes as she approached, letting her lip curl a little when his gaze swept down her legs. Apparently, he'd gotten over his aversion to her body.

"Veronica!" he called out, standing as she approached. He reached out as if he meant to give her a hug, but she stopped at the chair opposite his and sat down.

"Dillon. What can I do for you?"

He looked confused by the question as his hands fell back to his sides. Frowning, he took a seat. "I just wanted to see you again. Catch up a little."

"Why?"

He sat back in his seat and studied her for a moment. "What can I get you to drink?"

"Ginger martini," she said without hesitation. She suddenly knew what she wanted, and it was something with bite.

"Sounds interesting. I'll try it, too." He raised a hand, and a server immediately appeared, as if his finger were a rich person's version of the Bat-Signal. "Two ginger martinis, please."

At least he said *please*. She'd gone on a date with a guy in Manhattan who'd called every server *chief* and never once said *thank you* or *please*. Veronica had wondered if she could ever be attracted to a man in a suit after that, but she'd worked through it.

Dillon wasn't wearing a suit, but he was wearing jeans that looked very expensive and polished loafers with no socks. She missed Gabe and his beat-up trail shoes.

No, you don't, her brain scolded.

"That was an amazing show," Dillon said. "Even better than your columns, which are hard to beat."

"Thank you."

The server returned in record time with the drinks, and Veronica noticed that the woman didn't mention anything about the drinks being on the house. Veronica winked at her. Hopefully, Dillon was a big tipper.

When she took a sip of her drink, Dillon mirrored her. "Good," he said. "Not too sweet."

She nodded, enjoying the way the spice of it burned her throat. And ginger was good for the stomach, so maybe she could drink ten of them and suffer no ill consequences.

Dillon leaned back in his chair again, looking more

relaxed now, as if buying the drinks had returned control back to him. "I wanted to catch up because I liked you in high school and I like you now."

Well, that was to the point. He watched her as if he expected her to be aroused by his confidence, but she still felt icy cool. He was an investor. He was into the game. He wanted something and he'd go after it. Simple and efficient. An admirable business strategy, really, but she wasn't any of his business.

"You're interesting," he said when she didn't respond.

"Dillon…" She twirled the stem of her glass in her fingers, watching the candied ginger at the bottom bounce off the glass. "Do you know why I liked you back then?"

He shook his head, his face a blur past the rim of her drink.

"Because you were the only one of Jason's friends who was ever nice to me."

"Like I said, I liked you."

"Right," she murmured. "I thought you were sweet. That's why I let you kiss me. Touch my breasts. Put your hand down my pants."

She finally looked up and saw that he'd lost a little of his confidence. He was frowning again.

"But you weren't sweet, were you?" Veronica asked.

The perfectly smooth skin of his cheeks turned a little pink. "Roni, I'm sorry about that. Jason was… I don't know. I guess I told myself it was just normal sibling-rivalry stuff."

"He wasn't my sibling."

"Right. Well, stepsibling, then. I don't know. He was my friend, and you were his little sister. I was embarrassed that he called me out on messing around with you. I didn't know what to say."

"So you made fun of me," she said.

"It wasn't like that. I was just making excuses. Trying to get him off my back."

"Right. Off your back and right onto mine. He made my life a living hell for three years, Dillon. And instead of making things better, you made them worse. So I don't understand why you think I'd be interested in dating you now."

"Because I've grown up," he answered without hesitation. "We both have."

She laughed. "The first thing you asked me about was Jason! Like he's still your hero. Like you still think it was excusable high school stuff. I was nobody before he moved to town, but he made me into *nothing*. Do you get the difference? He mocked me and bullied me and encouraged everyone else to do the same. Because if a girl is so low that even her own brother treats her like shit, she must be worthless, right?"

His cheeks weren't pink anymore. They'd gone pale. "Roni, I'm sorry. I honestly didn't know it was that bad for you. I was young and clueless."

She nodded. He was right. She knew that. He was probably a lot nicer now, but he could never be her hero. She couldn't trust him with her body or her heart. She didn't even know why he'd ask such a thing. Boys were stupid, just as Gabe had said.

"Thank you for the apology. And the drink." She'd barely touched it and she felt satisfied with that. "I know this wasn't what you were expecting tonight. My dad really wanted me to meet with you because of that development deal. You and he are in agreement that this isn't high school anymore, so in that spirit, I hope you won't let my bad memories ruin any deal with my father."

"No, of course not, but—"

"Thanks, Dillon. I appreciate the effort, but I just can't let those memories go. But it was good to catch up."

Even in the midst of walking away, she wanted to go back and apologize. Maybe he hadn't deserved that. He wasn't Jason. He hadn't meant to be cruel. And she really didn't want to make him feel bad. But she straightened her spine and kept walking toward her friends' table.

"Have a little fucking confidence," she whispered to herself.

Ask your friends for help, her brain fired back, but she ignored it and smiled at Lauren and Isabelle. Gabe was gone. There was no help for that.

"If that was a date," Lauren said, "it doesn't look like it went well."

"It definitely wasn't a date," Veronica said, taking the empty chair that Lauren patted.

Jake glared at the table Veronica had come from. "I thought you were dating Gabe."

"I thought you didn't like that," Veronica countered. Lauren had filled her in on Jake's reaction.

"I like Gabe a lot more than I like the looks of that guy."

"It wasn't a date," Veronica repeated.

"Good," he muttered.

"Shut up, Jake," Lauren said, though she kissed his cheek when she said it. "Whoever Veronica says is good enough for her is good enough for her."

He didn't look the least bit convinced by that, but he shrugged. "Gabe is okay."

She didn't want to talk about Gabe. She couldn't. To her horror, she felt tears welling in her eyes again. Lauren snapped into action. "Jake, could you go somewhere else for a minute? I think we need some girl talk."

He jumped up as if he was relieved. "I've got to be at the station in thirty. I'll just head over early."

"Thanks, sweetie," Lauren said. She let him give her a kiss on the cheek then turned his head for a kiss on the mouth, as well. "Be safe. I'll see you in the morning."

Veronica wiped her tears away and glanced around to see if anyone was watching.

"What's really going on?" Lauren pressed.

Veronica shrugged. Everything inside her was telling her to keep quiet, but she was tired of keeping quiet. Tired of handling all her stresses and sorrows alone. Gabe was gone, and now her friends were all she had. She didn't want to be alone anymore.

Veronica swallowed back the urge to cry. "Did you know he only had a one-year contract?"

"Gabe?" Lauren asked. "No, I didn't hear anything about that. It's unusual, but maybe Jean-Marie wasn't sure he'd work out. Why?"

"He has a one-year contract because he's moving to New York in a year."

"Oh," Lauren said.

"And he didn't tell me."

Isabelle cleared her throat. "Maybe he was going to."

"He says he was, but he didn't and it looks like he's not coming back."

"Shit," Lauren said. "I'm sorry."

"Don't pass that on to Jean-Marie," Veronica added

quickly. "It was a personal conversation. But…I just feel so stupid. Like he was playing me this whole time."

"But was he?" Isabelle asked. "You just started dating. Were you guys serious yet?"

That was the question, wasn't it? She'd felt serious things for him, but they'd never once talked about it. She'd never even asked if he was seeing other people. Maybe she wasn't being rational, but feelings weren't supposed to be rational, were they? And maybe it had meant too much to her, after all.

But she couldn't explain that to Lauren and Isabelle. She'd confessed that she was a failure in New York, but she couldn't confess *this*.

"Did he lie to you?" Lauren asked, putting her hand over Veronica's. "Because that's really shitty if he did."

Not quite. Not really. "I can't say he lied to me. It's just that he only told me the easy things and not the difficult ones."

Lauren nodded. "But didn't you do the same? Isn't that what people do when they're first dating? Put on their best face?"

"Maybe that's my problem. I told him things I'd never told anyone. But that was my fault, right?"

Isabelle shook her head. "You were open. There's nothing wrong with that. You trusted him."

"That's the thing!" she said. "He *asked* me to trust him, and I did. I honestly did. I trusted him to be honest and I even trusted him with—" She snapped her mouth shut, hoping she'd caught it in time, but both women were eyeing her intently now. Waiting.

"Is there something you're not saying?" Lauren asked quietly.

Veronica glanced around again. No one was paying attention besides these two women. Her friends. People who hadn't batted an eye at her last confession. She squeezed her eyes closed. "He was my first," she whispered.

"What?" Isabelle asked. Veronica felt her lean closer. "Your first what?"

Determined not to be a complete coward, Veronica opened her eyes. "My first time."

Lauren frowned. "Back in New York, you mean? You knew him before?"

"No. I mean here. A week ago."

It finally hit Lauren. Her eyes went wide. She sat back. Isabelle was still frowning, but a few seconds later she slapped a hand over her mouth. "You're kidding," she said past her fingers.

Veronica shook her head.

Lauren looked around as if she was confused. "But you're…you're an expert."

"Yeah. I read a lot."

"He was really your first?" she asked, looking as if the shock was still sinking in.

"Yes."

"Did he know?" Lauren asked.

"Yes. And he made it perfect. So completely perfect. Maybe that's why this is so hard to take, because it's not perfect anymore. He's *gone*."

Lauren's mouth went tight. "I'm going to kill him."

"No! It's not his fault. I didn't want it to be something weird and meaningful. I just wanted to do it. God, this is so fucking embarrassing. I can't believe I'm telling you."

"Shut your mouth," Isabelle snapped. "Didn't we already have this conversation? You don't have to keep your weird crap from us."

"Ha!" She managed that one laugh, but then tears welled in her eyes and spilled over her cheeks as if someone had switched on a fountain. "I don't want him to be gone," she admitted, which didn't help slow her tears at all. "Shit, is everyone looking at me?"

"No one is looking at you," Isabelle said, but Veronica felt a cocktail napkin thrust into her hand. She dabbed at her cheeks.

Lauren patted her arm. "Did he break it off? Because maybe you could still see each other if you like him that much."

"I can't. I can't go back there."

"To New York? Come on. It's not that bad. You're just being a wuss."

She laughed again, though the sound was a little clogged with tears. "I hate that place."

"You lived there for years. You're telling me there's nothing you like about it?"

Veronica shrugged. "The food is good. And I like Central Park."

"Well, there you go. Dinner and brunch and walks in the park and sex. Come on. That's a long weekend right there."

Isabelle nodded. "If the sex was worth it, anyway."

"Oh, it was worth it," Veronica said. Then she growled in frustration. "God, it was so worth it and I hate him for that, too. He was…" She waved a hand, trying and failing to find the words, but her friends nodded as if they understood.

"Maybe I won't kill him, after all," Lauren said.

"So you both think I shouldn't be mad at him?"

Lauren scoffed. "I think you should be as mad as you want. He asked you to trust him and he knew he wasn't telling the whole truth. Fuck that shit. We'll all hate him with you if you want."

That sounded good. Helpful. But…no. She didn't want that. She didn't really hate him at all, so she couldn't stand the thought of her friends hating him. "No. But thanks for listening."

Isabelle poked her arm. "We expect more details later, you know. But for now, would another drink help?"

Veronica took stock of her insides and shook her head. She wasn't in the mood. Just saying it all out loud seemed to have helped. She was starting to let go of a little of her shock, and she found herself laughing with Lauren about the letters they'd heard during the performance. A few minutes later, Lauren was trying to bribe Veronica into letting her see the night's letters that she hadn't used, but before Veronica could finish saying no, her phone buzzed.

"Hold on," she said, pulling it out of her purse.

"Is it Gabe?"

It wasn't Gabe. It was only her email alert, but Veronica still held up a hand and read the email. "Oh, no," she breathed.

Lauren grabbed her hand. "What is it?"

"It's not Gabe," she said immediately.

Lauren slumped with relief.

Veronica read to the end of the message. It wasn't Gabe, but it was bad news. The teenager had finally written back, and even though he thanked her for the advice, he didn't think it would help him. You don't understand, he said. Nothing good will ever happen for me.

Veronica pushed back from the table. "I'm sorry. It's something to do with my column. I need to take care of it."

"Do you want us to walk you home?" Isabelle asked, but Veronica was already moving toward the door.

"No, thanks!" she called. "Lauren, I'll let you know when I hear about Gabe's dad!"

As soon as she was outside, Veronica toed off the heels she'd been so happy with earlier and jogged toward her place in her bare feet.

Nothing good will ever happen for me. I don't want to talk to anyone about it. It'll be better for everyone if I'm gone.

She paused halfway to her apartment and wrote a quick reply.

Are you there? Can I write back to you at this address? I really want to talk to you.

Hitting Send, she took off for her place again. Her phone buzzed just as she reached her front door. "Please, please, please," she whispered, but she didn't get her wish. Her email had been returned as undeliverable just like last time. "Shit!" she cursed as she struggled with her keys and finally got the door open.

Her next email was to her editor. She forwarded the message she'd received from the boy calling himself Nobody and added only Calling you now! to the subject.

The call went to voice mail. "I know we've already discussed the protocol for receiving Dear Veronica letters about suicide, but I wanted to give you a heads-up. I just got a letter from the teenager who wrote last week, the one who says he's being bullied. He wrote from another random address. I can't get in touch. He didn't give any specific plans, but it's clear that he's considering hurting himself. I'm going to call the police and see if there's a way they can track him down. Please let me know if there's anything else we should do."

She dropped her purse and shoes and raced to her laptop to find the phone number for the Teton County Sheriff's Office. It took only a few minutes to get through to a deputy.

"Oh, hey!" he said. "Dear Veronica! I read your stuff."

"That's good, because I need a favor. I received a letter indicating that a teenage boy is having suicidal thoughts, but it came from a fake email address and he didn't give a name or number. I have no idea how to get in touch, and I'm really worried. I think he needs help. If I forward you the email and file a report, can the sheriff's office do something?"

"Absolutely. We can try to track down the IP address, see if we can get in touch with the kid that way."

"Thank you," she sighed. "All I know is that he's in school. I suspect he's a sophomore here, but that probably only narrows it down to a couple of hundred kids, and I have no idea what to do."

"We'll be happy to help," he said, giving her his email address so she could forward everything she had. He asked her to come in to the station and fill out a report also, though he said it could wait until morning. There was no way she was waiting until morning.

She hung up, sent the emails to the deputy, then wrote to the therapist, forwarding the letter and letting him know the steps she'd taken. Her heart beat so hard it hurt, her body telling her to take action, to make this better. But how could she make it better when she couldn't even find him?

She read through the letter one more time, hoping she'd gotten it all wrong, but it was only worse on the second read.

Dear Veronica,
Thank you so much for writing back to me. I'm sorry I used a fake email address. I don't want my parents to find out and freak.

I know you think things can get better, but they can't. You don't know what it's like. Everyone hates me. Someone spit on me in the hall last week. They call me gay, but I don't even think I am. Not that it matters, cuz no one will go out with me.

I'm not going to college. My grades suck cuz I'm so screwed up. It feels like I'm never getting out of this place, but I can't stand it here any longer.

You say everything can change for me but you don't understand. Nothing good will ever happen for me. I don't wanna talk to anyone about it. I don't want therapy. I just want everything to stop.

I'm sorry I dragged you into this. You seem like a really nice person.

He hadn't signed it this time, maybe because she'd told him not to call himself Nobody. The only positive thing she could see was that he'd reached out again. But everything else about it scared her. She knew the statistics for teen boys and suicide were high. Higher than other demographics. They couldn't see that life might get better. They didn't have the ability to think ahead.

The therapist wrote back quickly to tell her she'd done the right thing.

If the police track him down, I'd be happy to help. Please give his parents my number, or the hospital can get in touch with me if he's checked in.

Veronica changed into jeans and a sweater and pulled on her running shoes to head to the sheriff's office. It was only a short walk. She was filling out her report within fifteen minutes. Unfortunately, there wasn't anything to do after that. She had to wait to hear from the deputy. All she could do now was repost the suicide hotline information to the website.

She started to head home, then found herself stupidly turning corners and walking down random streets, hoping that…what? She'd see a distraught teenage boy and ask if he was the one who'd written to her?

She'd never felt so helpless in her life.

When her phone beeped, she pulled it out with a sudden rush of relief, but it wasn't the police. It was Gabe.

Spent the evening with my dad. He's in good spirits and his condition has been upgraded to serious. I never thought I'd see that as great news.

She smiled as another text popped up.

I'm going to try to get some sleep. Hopefully, we'll know more in the morning. He looks good, though.

Before she could respond, a final text popped up.

I'm sorry, was all it said.

She broke down in tears. Uncontrollable tears. She was so mad at him, but she wanted to call him. She wanted to hear his tired voice and tell him it would all be fine. She wanted to tell him about the letter she'd gotten and how worried she was. But he didn't need her problems tonight, and he didn't need to listen to her cry. He needed sleep and time with his family.

And Veronica didn't need him. How could she? She barely knew him.

She cried for a few more minutes, thankful that it was pitch-dark on this street. When she finally managed to wipe away enough of her tears that she could see, she wrote back. Such good news! she typed with damp fingers. I'm so, so happy that he's improving. I'm keeping all of you in my thoughts. Get some sleep and things will look even better in the morning. Good night.

Then she went home, ate five of Gabe's mom's cookies and waited by her phone all night.

CHAPTER TWENTY

"DAD, COME ON," Gabe groaned. "I don't want to talk about the restaurants right now. Every time you start getting into it, your blood pressure goes up. I can see it right there!" Gabe pointed at the machine that tracked his dad's life in impersonal lines and numbers.

Could die any moment, it all seemed to say, no matter what the numbers read. *Could die, could die, could die*, over and over. Gabe had thought it would be less scary in the morning, but it wasn't.

"But you haven't even seen the new location in Brooklyn! It's two stories! Amazing place. If your mom would bring my iPad like I asked her to—"

"Mom doesn't want you talking about the business any more than I do. You're retiring now, anyway."

"I never agreed to that!"

Gabe watched the numbers rise. "Fine. We'll talk about it later. But I'm moving back regardless. The details can wait."

His dad grinned. "Good. I like seeing that face every day. Especially now that I can see it." He smacked Gabe's naked cheek, then pulled him in for a brutal hug, not paying any attention to the wires and lines that tangled every time he made a sudden movement.

Gabe just shook his head at how *normal* his dad seemed. As if nothing had ever happened. Until he had to get up to use the bathroom. Then he looked like a man who'd aged twenty years overnight.

His dad patted his cheek again. "You look good, son. I'm glad your mom got you to shave the beard."

Gabe rolled his eyes. "She guilted me into it this morning. Told me it would make you happy."

"Did you buy that?"

"No, but I wanted to make her happy, too." He rubbed a hand over his bare jaw. After three years, it felt like someone else's face. It was for the best, though. He damn sure wasn't going to wear one of those beard nets in the kitchens.

He winced at the thought of spending his days—and nights—in MacKenzie's, but he didn't let his mind shy away from it now. If he returned to Jackson at all, it would be only to pack up his stuff. Maybe it was easier this way. If he'd settled into his life there, if he'd settled into his feelings for Veronica...

Shit. Too late for that.

"Naomi says you have a girl out there in Wyoming," his dad said as if he'd read Gabe's mind. His elbow hit Gabe's ribs. "Says she's famous."

He laughed, thinking he'd tell Veronica that the next time he talked to her. If she was willing to talk. "She's kind of famous. Writes an advice column for the local paper."

"You serious about this girl?"

"Dad, I just met her."

His father shrugged. "I knew as soon as I met your mom. Asked her to marry me a month later."

"Sure, but she was smart enough to say no."

"Only the first time! So is it serious?"

Gabe forced a smile. Fuck yes, it was serious. "No,"

he said, rubbing at the strange ache that had popped up in his chest. "We were dating. No big deal."

His mom came in just in time to save Gabe from what felt like his own heart attack starting. He'd already fucked with Veronica's emotions, and now he felt as if he was betraying her in different ways.

"Did you bring my iPad?" his dad yelled.

"Oh, my God, calm down, James. I've got your stupid iPad right here. Why don't you get right back to working on your next heart attack? What could possibly go wrong?"

"She's never going to let this go," his dad muttered.

"No, I'm not," Mom answered as Gabe stood to give her a kiss.

"Gabe's moving home," his dad said. "You should thank me."

"Do you want to start another argument?" she snapped. "Gabe should do what Gabe wants to do."

His dad just grinned again. "He wants to be here, helping me run MacKenzie's."

Gabe stayed silent while his mom sighed. "I made chicken salad," she said. "It's in the fridge. Go home and make yourself lunch. Take a nap. I'll be here all day with this stubborn bastard."

"I need to show him the new Brooklyn location!" his dad yelled, but his mom shooed Gabe toward the door.

"Go on before he gets all riled up," she whispered. "And make sure your sister eats, too."

Gabe waved past his mom's shoulder. "I'll see you in a few hours, Dad. Show me the pictures then." Hopefully, he'd get some rest in the meantime. Gabe had thought it was still morning, but it was already noon. Even with the windows, he had no sense of time in here.

The day was gray and dreary. Drizzle dampened his head as he stepped onto the street. His cheeks felt cold.

His clean-shaven face was the most foreign thing about being home, though. The screeching, roaring, rumbling sound of the streets was already background noise. Unnoticeable. In a few months, he wouldn't even remember what silence sounded like.

His mind flashed on that moment with Veronica at the top of the climb. Of lying there, his hand wrapped around hers, the sun seeping through his muscles and straight into his bones.

Maybe he could get back there for vacations. Maybe she'd see him again. If he could just talk her into coming out to New York sometime, if he could go out and see her a few times a year... Now that he was back in the city, he could think of so many things to show her. So many things that she would love if she just gave it a chance. New York had been her dream for so long. There was no way she'd purged it from her heart so completely.

He grabbed a cab home, thinking of Veronica the whole way. He'd been too wrapped up in worrying about his father yesterday. He hadn't thought much about what he'd said to Veronica, how she'd felt, the look in her eyes.

He'd assumed that when he told her the truth, he'd have time to lay it out as gently as he could and time afterward to try to make it up to her. But he felt as if he'd slapped her. As if he'd hurt her and then walked away without a backward glance.

He stared out the window at the buildings he recognized from his teenage years. He had a lot of planning to do. He had to find a place. Had to resign from the library. Had to sink himself back into MacKenzie's and hope he didn't drown. But all he wanted to think about was the top of that climb and watching Veronica smile up at the sky.

He skipped the sandwich and didn't bother harassing his sister about eating, either. He just went to his room and fell onto his bed. He felt as if he'd missed a week of sleep instead of just a few hours. The thought of eating made his stomach turn.

A dark veil of sleep was just slipping over him when his phone rang. He raised it to his ear without opening his eyes. "Hello?"

"Gabe?"

His eyes popped open at the sound of her voice.

"I'm sorry," Veronica said, whispering as if she were invading his dad's hospital room. "Are you busy?"

"No. I'm alone."

"I didn't want to bother you, but..."

"No, it's fine. It's good to hear your voice." The twist in his stomach seemed to unravel itself. "Really good."

"How's your dad?" she asked.

"Already trying to get back to work. This morning the doctors said he could go home in two days if he continues to improve. But it's going to be a long road to recovery. He'll probably need stents. Maybe a bypass if he doesn't clean up his act."

"I'm sorry."

He sighed. "At this point, I'm thankful that it's all 'maybes.' He looks good, and I think my mom is already planning a party for him when he gets home. My older sister should be here from India tomorrow."

"Good. That's great."

He waited for her to say more, but all he got was silence. "Veronica—"

"I didn't want to bother you," she jumped in. "You have so much going on, but you're the only person I know who works with computer systems and stuff, and I just…"

Gabe frowned at the rough edge to her voice and sat up on the side of his bed. "What's wrong?"

"You know that email I got from the teenager? The one who was being bullied at school?"

"I remember."

"He wrote back and he's talking about ending it and I don't know what to do," she said, her words running together on a long breath. "I went to the police and they tracked down his IP, but it didn't tell them anything. There's only one major internet provider here, so they can't even narrow that down, and I don't know what to do! They told me they could try to get a search warrant from the internet provider, but that will take days. Do you have any ideas? I can't just hope he doesn't kill himself, Gabe. He wrote to me for *help*."

"Shh. It's okay." He hated hearing the pain in her voice. "Listen, maybe there are a few ways we can work on this. Do you have the IP?"

"No! Should I call the deputy? Maybe he can—"

"Hey," Gabe interrupted. "It's not hard. I'll walk you through it."

"You don't have time for this," she insisted, her voice cracking a little and breaking his heart. He should be there with her.

"I have plenty of time. I was just lying down in my old bedroom staring at my ceiling. No big deal. Now, is your email program open? What's the email address?"

Luckily, the address was from one of the big providers that embedded IPs in the header. He walked her through how to grab the hidden information. "Okay, now it gets trickier," he said. "You don't even know a first name?"

"No!" she cried. "Nothing! The deputy said if I could just get a little more out of him, maybe they could help, but I already tried to get him to contact me. He hasn't."

"Are you a monitor on the Dear Veronica blog?"

"Yes."

"Okay, listen," he said. "I was stalking you a little last week, reading through your old columns, trying to figure out the best way to seduce you."

Her laugh sounded like a little hiccup of relief.

"It seems like there are a *lot* of comments for every post."

"There are. Yes. I delete the ones that are abusive."

He smiled, thinking of how hard she must frown going through comments like that. "And you have to register to comment, right?"

"Yes, but people use fake names all the time. Almost everyone does."

"But they have to use a real, verifiable email address," he said. "So if you can find a user with the same IP address as your teenager—"

"Then I might find a real email address!" she gasped.

"Exactly. There are some pretty simple search functions you can use." He promised to send her a link that would tell her exactly how to search the blog for that IP address.

"Gabe. Thank you. I just...I was afraid to call and bother you, and—"

"You don't ever have to be afraid to call me. I'm just happy you're still willing to talk to me."

He'd been vaguely hoping that she'd reassure him. That she'd laugh and say, "Of course I still want to talk to you!" But she didn't say anything.

"Let me know what happens with the IP search," he said.

"Sure. Yes. If I can get a real email address, my friend Isabelle has a boyfriend who's a US marshal. Maybe he can push the sheriff's department a little harder."

"That sounds like a good plan," Gabe said.

"I'll let you know. Thank you, Gabe."

He hated the way she said it so formally, as if he wasn't expected to help her. He collapsed back onto his bed, but this time he didn't close his eyes. The knot retied itself tightly in his stomach.

He could have his family or he could have Veronica. It was as simple as that, and he couldn't walk away from his family. Not even for her.

CHAPTER TWENTY-ONE

HE WAS A SOPHOMORE at her old high school just as she'd suspected. When the police had arrived, his parents found three half-empty bottles of his mom's old Valium prescription in his bedside table. He hadn't taken any yet, but he'd been saving up. They'd also found the *Dear Veronica* blog open on his computer.

The police told Veronica that the boy had denied everything at first, but then he'd broken down in tears and cried in his mom's arms. He'd said that he was miserable and wanted to be dead, but he didn't want to make his parents worry. He'd said he was sorry he'd caused all this trouble.

That had made Veronica break down and sob. That he'd thought killing himself would have been less trouble for his parents and the community than just asking for help. That he hadn't wanted to bother his family with his pain. That he thought he wasn't worth it.

She'd cried because if she hadn't had an escape plan already in place, maybe she would have thought about hurting herself, too. After all, she'd had nowhere else to turn. She had asked for help, and her father had ignored her.

A week later, Veronica was only more angry. Angry for that boy and herself and everyone else like them. But she didn't know what to do with that. She wrote to the school to ask how she could help. There were already bullying programs in place at the school. They taught suicide awareness and prevention. But the principal admitted that with budget cuts, the school counselors focused mostly on getting kids ready for college and addressing problem children.

"They simply don't have time to meet with kids unless those kids are acting out. We've only got two counselors for the whole school."

But one of those counselors wrote back with an idea that got stuck in Veronica's mind like a bur.

There's a program designed to reach out to kids who are going through depression or anxiety, but it costs a lot to fully fund. We've only been able to scrape up the money for brochures and a few lesson plans. If we could do the whole month-long program every year, I bet the kids would take it from there. There are clubs they can organize themselves, to get together and feel like they belong to something.

Money. The one thing Veronica didn't have. But she knew who had plenty of money and nothing worthwhile to spend it on. And she was feeling way too angry to be afraid of him anymore.

She knew her dad was home tonight. He'd asked if she was coming for dinner. Funny that he asked her about dinner at least twice a week. Maybe there was something inside him that loved her. Maybe he got lonely. Maybe late at night he wondered if he'd focused on the wrong things in his life and felt regret. She'd never know, because he'd never admit it.

She couldn't remember her dad being any softer, but

her mom had loved him and her mom had been a gentle soul. She must have seen something tender in the man she'd married. Perhaps her struggle with cancer had changed him. Veronica didn't remember what he'd been like before those years of illness.

She tried to keep that in mind through dinner, waiting until they were halfway through their silent meal to bring up her request. "Dad, I have a proposal for you."

He grunted as he scrolled through something on his phone.

"There's a program I'd like to get started at the high school. It helps kids with mental health problems recognize what's going on and teaches them to reach out for help. Kids really struggle with things like anxiety and depression."

"Another thing you won't get paid for?"

"I get paid for my job, Dad. And no, I wouldn't get paid for this. In fact, the program would need money. Lots of money. Eight thousand dollars a year for the full program."

"Eight grand a year to make posters for crazy kids? Good luck with that."

She stared at him until he looked up from his phone. "Eight grand a year," she said, "to help kids who are suffering the way you let me suffer all through high school."

"Now you're telling me you were depressed?"

"I don't know if I was depressed, but I know I was scared and anxious, and I could have used someone to talk to. God knows you didn't want to hear it."

"Jesus, Veronica. Do you know what my teen years were like? Growing up on a farm in Nebraska? You want to know how many times my dad asked about my *feelings*?"

She could practically feel the sneer slide over her skin and she was transported back to her childhood, to her dad dismissing everything. Her grief, her loneliness and then her despair over the new family he'd delivered to her. Her emotions had always been an inconvenience, a nuisance, a weakness.

"He tortured me, you know," she said calmly.

"Who? Jason? Now you're saying he abused you?"

"No, he never *touched* me. He just ruined my life. He didn't want to live here, he didn't want to be here, so he took it out on me, and you never did a damn thing about it."

He waved his fork. "I told you not to let him see you sweat. You let him get to you."

She laughed. The smell of the lasagna her father's housekeeper had cooked was making her nauseous, so she pushed her plate away and scooted her chair back. "This wasn't some asshole in my algebra class, Dad. He lived with me. He was around twenty-four hours a day. He called me ugly. He called me stupid. He told everyone at school that I was creepy and disgusting and that he moved to a room on the other side of the house so he wouldn't have to be near me!"

"So?" her dad muttered. "None of that was true."

"So?" she cried. "I was fifteen! Do you think my classmates cared if it was *true*?" She slammed her hands on the table. "This was in my home! I didn't have a safe place anywhere. He never touched me, Dad, but he violated me over and over. He took pictures of my ugly cotton underwear and posted them online. He made fun of my flat chest. He made sure other people made

fun of my flat chest. It wasn't enough to make sure I wasn't popular—he wanted to *hurt* me, and you just sat there and let him."

Her dad didn't look so arrogant now. He hunched over his plate, pushing bits of tomatoes around. "You never told me about the pictures."

"He called me an ugly cunt right in front of you, and you did nothing! *Nothing!*" This time when she hit the table, he looked up and seemed to snap out of his brief remorse.

He glared at her. "Stop being hysterical."

Her palms stung, tingling with bright pain. "Three years," she said softly. "They were only here for three years, Jason and his icy bitch of a mother, but he's been in my head since then, reminding me that I'm not like anyone else, that I'll never fit in, that I'll never say or do or be the right thing. And you were right there with him, letting me know that I'm not quite good enough to be your daughter."

"That's not true," he grouched, reaching for his wine-glass. "I've never said that."

"You never had to. But you know what? None of it matters anymore. I am good enough. I'm good at my job. I'm funny. I'm smart. And I fucking *care* about people."

He stared at her for a long time, still looking perturbed, but really looking at her. Maybe he'd truly get it this time. Maybe he'd finally acknowledge just how thoroughly he'd failed to protect her.

"Fine," he finally said. "You want me to contribute to this fund for troubled youth? Is that what all this is about?"

Her shaking heart fell as if she'd just dropped down

the hill of a roller coaster. She was falling and her dad refused to catch her. She took a deep breath, stretching her fingers out on the dark wood of this huge dining room table that no loving family was ever going to gather around.

But she wasn't falling, was she? She was flying, and no one needed to catch her. "Yes, Dad, that's what this is about. But you're not going to contribute. You're going to fund the entire program. Every year."

He scoffed. "I'm not paying tens of thousands of dollars just so you can—"

"Yes, you are," she snapped. "You can make a big deal out of it. Look how much Judge Chandler cares about our children! Look what a wonderful member of the community he is! You can have a glamorous party. Raise money for the school. And in return, I won't write a column about what a crappy father you were."

His jaw dropped. "You little shit. You're *threatening* me?"

"No. I'm telling you how you can start making this right. Because if you won't do this, then it's clear that there's no hope for us. That you'll never understand. That you don't regret anything about how I was treated and won't ever admit that you failed me. And if all that is true, Dad...then you don't deserve me in your life."

He shook his head, still outraged, still in disbelief.

"Helping these kids is important to me," she said. "I'm asking you to do this for me. If you do, then we can start working on having a different relationship, one where you show me respect and I behave like an adult instead of a scared little girl. If you won't do this, then we're done. Maybe not forever, but for a while."

"An ultimatum isn't a negotiation," he snapped.

"This isn't a negotiation." She put on her sweater and gathered up her purse and phone. "It's an offer. Take it or leave it. I'll either be writing a column about the wonderful new school program or I'll be writing about exactly why I needed something like that when I was a kid." She stood. "You decide what you want people talking about, Dad."

Her knees were shaking when she walked out, but her steps were steady. Technically, she supposed she was blackmailing her own father, but surely there was another term when you wanted the money to go to a good cause? More important, she suspected her dad would actually respect a demand more than a request. He'd always admired ballsiness. It was so much less messy than dealing with ovaries.

Her threat was an empty one, though. She was going to write the same column regardless. As a matter of fact, she'd already written it. Whether her father funded it or not, she was going to bring this program to the school. The therapist had already agreed to be the local contact for the group. If she had to raise money for it herself, she would. She had a platform, and the newspaper would consider it good publicity.

Her dad texted her before she even made it back to town. She couldn't resist peeking at her phone.

Well? Am I supposed to put a goddamn blank check in the mail or do you have more details?

She laughed. She laughed so hard she had to pull over. It was probably not the sane response to your father giving in to your blackmail demands, but normal people didn't blackmail their relatives, did they? So she let herself laugh, and then she turned up the crappy stereo in the same crappy old car she'd had in high school and sang triumphantly along to Beyoncé.

As soon as she got home, she forwarded all the information she'd gathered about the program to her dad, along with a specific amount. Then she opened her column and read through it one more time to be sure it was perfect.

…And that's why I believe so strongly in this program. Because I was one of those kids. I felt alone and scared all through high school. In fact, I still feel like that a lot today. But the truth is I'm not alone, and I never was; I just didn't know who to reach out to.

The reason I've become a decent advice columnist is that I've lived through so many of the things the rest of you have. Low self-esteem, loneliness, body-image issues, bullying, communication problems, family tensions. I've spent too many years thinking I'm not good enough for love or my job or success, and my only defense was to pretend I was fine so that no one else would see the truth: that I wasn't enough.

But the real truth is that I am enough, and when I read your letters I see myself in them, in your problems with anxiety and self-doubt and depression and love, and these kids deserve a chance to see themselves in others, too.

The column went live on the website the next day and was printed in the paper the day after that. Her stomach never stopped aching. She felt naked and exposed and dangerously vulnerable. As if she'd stripped off all the protection she'd so carefully layered over herself. After all, the key to faking your way through life was that you didn't admit you were faking it.

But it was a relief, too. She didn't have to pretend anymore. The next column she worked on was her easiest yet, because she wasn't worried that she might reveal too much. She could be herself. Her *real* self. The woman she was finally getting to know after twenty-seven years.

The response was overwhelming. The online comment section exploded with people telling their own stories. Stories that made Veronica break down and cry, and stories that made her cheer. She'd always felt that she didn't fit in anywhere, that she was different, but she was starting to realize that *everyone* felt different.

Her next Dear Veronica Live was overflowing with people, and even though she had stage fright, it wasn't nearly as crippling as it had been. After all, she didn't have to fear that they'd see through her facade; she'd already let them in.

She wrapped it up a little more slowly than normal, pausing just as she set the microphone down to pick it up again. "I already thanked you guys for coming out tonight, but I also wanted to thank you for the responses to my last column. It meant a lot to get that kind of support for the new program at the high school. And if there's anyone here who was brave enough to share their story in the comments, thank you so much for that, too. I'm honored."

The applause was overwhelming, and before she could retreat to the office, several women approached to give her hugs. She wasn't sure how to handle that, so she just hugged them back. All these years of hiding, and she could have just been herself the whole time. The knowledge was bittersweet.

Still, she wasn't going to beat up on herself. Her method of coping had gotten her this job and her new friends, and it had even gotten her Gabe.

Though that was bittersweet, as well.

She finally made her escape and closed the office door firmly behind her before collapsing into a chair. She dug through her purse for her phone, though she wasn't sure why. Gabe had left a beautiful message about her new column, but she hadn't called him back, and that felt almost like a betrayal. After all, he'd played a part in bringing out the real Veronica. She should thank him for that, or at least let him know how much he'd helped.

But she couldn't call him. Some of her anger had faded in the past week, but she still felt betrayed. And what did any of that even matter? The relationship wasn't going anywhere. It couldn't.

But her doubts disappeared when she saw she had a message. Excitement shot through her veins, but it dried to ash when she realized the message was from an unfamiliar number. It wasn't Gabe.

Expecting a random marketing call, she barely listened at first, but as the woman on the line kept talking, Veronica sat up straighter. Then straighter still.

"Holy shit," she whispered, blinking hard. Things had been changing quickly in her life in the past few weeks, but this was a seismic shift she could never have anticipated. She just wasn't sure if it was good or...too terrifying to contemplate.

CHAPTER TWENTY-TWO

"HAVE I MENTIONED how much I loved the column?" Gabe asked.

Veronica smiled up at him as they strolled along one of the quieter paths through Central Park, and his pulse sped. She looked so beautiful. And a little different, despite that they'd only been apart for two weeks. She wore just mascara and lip gloss as far as he could tell, instead of the smoky shadow and dark liner she often wore. Her short black skirt was topped by a casual T-shirt. "You've only told me about ten times. Thank you."

"When we talked on the phone... I'm sorry you went through that. When you said your stepbrother was an asshole, I didn't realize you meant that it went on for years."

She nodded. "It's okay. I'm finally learning to let it go."

"You seem different," he said.

"Do I?"

"Yes." He watched her until she crinkled her nose at him. "You seem more like you were with me in private. Like your guard is down, even here in your least favorite place."

"Maybe. And speaking of...how's life in the city?"

He looked around them at the huge ancient trees and

the walls of gray rock. "Noisy," he said. Even here he could hear the sound of distant construction and impatient taxi drivers.

"Yeah. I assume this is still your favorite part of New York?" she asked.

"Of course. Well, this and the library. I haven't been there since I've been back. I'd love to go with you. But here...these were the first rocks I ever climbed." He gestured at the rocky hill ahead of them. "Seriously. I would spend hours here as a kid, pretending I was in a deep, dark jungle. Pretending I was an explorer."

"It's beautiful here," she said, sighing, even as someone jogged between them, forcing them to step quickly apart. Veronica tilted her head. "Was that guy using an actual Walkman?"

Gabe squinted and shook his head. "If nothing else, this town is truly interesting."

"It is," she said, her voice carefully neutral.

He wanted her to give the city a second chance. More important, he wanted her to give him a second chance. "So..." he ventured, "I wasn't expecting to see you so soon. Are you ever going to tell me why you came?"

She shrugged, her lips pressing together in a secret smile. "Maybe I just missed you."

The words stabbed him in the heart, because the teasing in them was so at odds with his own ridiculous hope. "I was actually kind of hoping that was it, you know. It feels like a lot longer than two weeks since I left."

She laughed as if he were joking. "No, I came because I figured you must be lonely without my expert sexual skills. How would you ever find another girl that has to be taught how to have sex?"

"Now you're just fishing for compliments, Ms. Chandler. Not very subtle."

She blushed, and Gabe felt as if he were having yet another dream about her. Veronica, here in the city, blushing and laughing as though they were back to normal. But they weren't. She hadn't touched him once.

"You look so strange," she said, her brow creasing. "Like you're a different person now. You look like you belong here."

That hurt almost as much as her joke that she'd missed him. He ran a hand over his jaw. "My mom made me do it."

She laughed so loudly that a pigeon flapped up into the air and moved its plump body five feet farther up the path. "That's what happens when you move back home at thirty-one."

"Shut up. I'm looking for my own place right now." The words eradicated the laughter between them.

"Right." She nodded. "So you're really staying."

The traffic noise grew louder as they moved toward the edge of the park. Veronica crossed her arms and squeezed them tight to her chest as if she was cold. He recognized the gesture now. She felt insecure or uncertain. She was unhappy. He wanted to put his arms around her, kiss her, tell her how sorry he was. But all he could do was talk.

"I haven't given my notice at the library yet, but… My dad won't stop working unless I take the reins. He'll kill himself. I can't let him do that."

"I know," she whispered.

"I was hoping maybe you'd come over and meet him."

"Gabe—"

"He's up and around now. He'd love for you to come by. It's almost like nothing happened. And my mom is kind of counting on seeing you."

She groaned. "They know I'm here?"

"Of course."

"Why would you tell them that? I'm just a girl you dated for a couple of weeks!"

"That's not all you are."

"Yes, it is!"

"Then why are you here?" he challenged.

They stopped at a curve in the path. The trees were still thick here, but you could see the silver-and-white faces of the buildings beyond them. There was no illusion left here. No pretending that they could be anywhere.

"I got an offer for syndication," she said. "A couple of days ago."

"What?"

"My column. It's going to be syndicated."

"Here?"

"Not here," she said, laughing. "There are enough advice columns in New York. But it will go into a few smaller newspapers in the West and Midwest, and it'll be featured on a big online news source. I'm meeting with an agent tomorrow. That's why I'm here."

"Holy shit, Veronica," he breathed. Then he said it louder. "Holy shit!"

He finally hugged her and she hugged him back, laughing when he picked her up and spun her around. "You're amazing," he said.

"I'm terrified," she admitted, but she didn't look terrified. Her eyes glowed as he set her down. Her wide smile softened. And when he ducked his head, she watched his mouth come closer instead of saying no.

He kissed her lightly, just a brush of his lips, but when he felt her sigh against him, he tried again.

"Oh, God," she whispered against the kiss. His heart felt thin, fragile. As if the ache inside it might tear open at any moment.

"You smell so good," she murmured. Her hands rose to press against his cheeks. "That's weird to say, isn't it? But I missed your smell."

Gabe made himself laugh instead of groaning in pain. "It's not weird. I missed everything about you. Your taste, your scent, your touch. The sound of you sighing."

She shook her head. "Don't say that."

"It's true."

"I barely know you," she countered.

"This is real."

"You live in New York," she said, and he couldn't think of anything to say to that. He lived in New York, and she despised the city. Then again, she was here.

"Just come home with me," he said. "My dad just got out of the hospital, you know. He needs cheering up."

"God, are you guilt-tripping me?"

"Yes. Plus, you never thanked my mom for those cookies."

She shoved him. "You're awful!"

"Come on. It's only a few blocks up."

He wasn't sure what he was doing, luring her home. He'd spent the past couple of weeks blowing off any mention of her, but his parents had kept needling him, egged on by Naomi. When he'd mentioned Veronica was coming to town, they'd practically swooned. Gabe was already in too deep, halfway in love with this girl he might never see again, and now he was introducing her to his parents.

Idiotic, like every other step he'd taken with Veronica. Idiotic, but somehow inevitable. *Come home with me and break my heart. I'll do my best to break yours, too.*

For some reason, she came with him.

They waded through the busy streets that bordered the park, but a few blocks in, the streets grew narrower and almost quiet. "Upper East Side," she said. "Very nice."

"Not *upper* upper," he said. "Come on."

"Where are we heading? Seventy-second?"

"Sixty-eighth," he said. "Barely respectable."

Laughing, she touched his arm and then left her hand there. Gabe felt like a teenager cataloguing every inch of progress with the girl he liked. *She let me kiss her. She put her hand on my arm.* He felt dizzy with it.

"Hello, Gabe!"

"Mrs. Tran," he called out to the woman sweeping the steps of a little shop. "Good afternoon."

"Pretty girl," she said with a grin.

"I'm a lucky guy." Veronica elbowed him, but her hand wrapped more securely around his arm.

They passed a tiny park wedged between two tall buildings. The screams of the kids crawled up the bricks and echoed above the trees. "This is a nice street," Veronica said.

"You know, New York isn't so bad. It can be just as nice as any other place if you find the right people."

"I know that," she said quietly. "I know that it was me and not the city."

"I didn't mean it like that."

"Maybe not, but it's true. I came here running from my life, but my life came right along with me."

"So you don't hate the city?"

She shot him a careful look. "It's not the right place for me. It's not the right place for you, either."

"I can make it the right place. For a little while."

"Here?" she pressed, looking pointedly up the fifteen-story building they were passing.

He didn't look with her. He'd passed it a thousand times in his life. Instead of answering, he pointed to the next building. "This is it."

She smiled at the elaborate five-story brick facade. "This is where you grew up?"

"Yep. We moved here when I was nine."

"Which floor?" she asked, craning her neck as they climbed up the stairs to the entry.

"Fourth," he said, then added, "And fifth."

"Oh, my God!" she gasped. "You're filthy rich!"

"We had a big family. And my dad was expanding the business."

"I guess so!"

He unlocked the door and waved her in. "Ready?" he asked as they stepped onto the elevator.

"This is a terrible idea," she said, then set her jaw as if she were heading into battle.

She was probably right, and he couldn't care less.

VERONICA'S FACE FLAMED with embarrassment as she was enveloped in yet another hug. "She's the cutest thing I've ever seen!" Gabe's mom said.

"Mom," Veronica heard Gabe groan, though the

word was muffled since his mom's arms were wrapped around Veronica's head.

"Well, it's true. Look at her!"

"Thank you, Mrs. MacKenzie," Veronica said as she was set free.

"Oh, my word, call me Mary."

"Mom, please stop embarrassing Veronica. And me."
I'm sorry, he mouthed when Veronica caught his eye.

"Don't sass your mom," his dad said. "That girl is clearly the cutest thing we've ever seen."

Gabe shook his head. "Unbelievable. Really."

"Are you hungry?" Mary asked.

Veronica had been trying to edge closer to Gabe, but his mom put an arm around Veronica's shoulders and guided her deeper into the apartment. "You must be exhausted, flying all the way from Wyoming."

"I'm fine. Honestly."

"A cappuccino, then. I just bought one of those new cup brewers with the steamed-milk attachment. You won't believe how good it is, and a fraction of the price of Starbucks."

Veronica looked back until she spotted Gabe and his father following.

"Veronica!" a familiar voice cried as they walked into the huge kitchen.

Naomi bounded across the tile and swept Veronica into yet another hug. "It's so good to see you again!"

"Nice to see you, Naomi. You look great."

"Oh, my God, my roots are a mess. Don't even look. Claire is meditating but she should be down soon. It's only her fourth meditation of the day," she added with a roll of her eyes.

"Leave her alone," Mary said. "It helps her chakras or something."

"Sure, Mom."

Gabe drew near and Veronica reached desperately out to clasp his hand before she got swept into a river of his relatives.

"Mary," his dad said, "make her one of those cappuccinos."

"I'm doing it right now." Mary rushed over to the machine and started opening little latches and inserting tiny plastic cups of coffee grounds.

"You know," his dad said, "Gabe's never brought a girl home until now."

Veronica shook her head frantically. "I'm just in town for a business trip."

"Dad," Gabe said hoarsely. "Please. Don't."

"It's true!" Naomi cooed. "Look at his face. He's blushing!"

He rubbed his face with both hands. "This is literally the worst idea I've ever had."

His dad slapped him on the back. "Or the best, eh?"

"Mom…" Gabe took a deep breath. "Maybe hold off on the coffee for a bit. I'm going to show Veronica around."

"Oh, take her up to the garden!" his mom suggested. "She'll love it. It's just like being in the country."

"It's not like being in the country," Gabe muttered as he tugged Veronica toward a staircase. She happily followed. "My family doesn't understand wide-open spaces," he explained as they hit the stairs. "They find the idea of Wyoming vaguely sinister."

"Oh, wait a few minutes!" Mary yelled. "Your sister is meditating!"

Gabe pulled Veronica faster up the stairs. "That was the stairway," he said as they reached the top floor. "Hall bathroom," he said, gesturing toward the first door before pulling her down the dark wood of the hallway. "My bedroom." He tugged her inside. "With a door that locks."

The door closed solidly behind her.

"Oh, my God," she whispered.

"I know."

"Your family is a TV family."

He cringed. "Which TV family?"

"I don't know. All of them at once?" She started laughing, then laughed so hard that she snorted. "I'm sorry," she sobbed, covering her mouth to quiet the noise. "Your sister is meditating."

Gabe fell back onto his bed and stared at the ceiling. "You were right about this being a terrible idea. They're a bit much. Maybe."

"Maybe," she gasped, giving in to one last bout of hysteria before she got her laughter under control. "But, Gabe, honestly…they're wonderful."

He raised one eyebrow and glared at her.

"I'm serious. They're everything I always imagined about other people's families. When I was, like, eight years old and watched too much television."

"Shut up."

"Don't sass me, Gabe."

He groaned and made a lunge for her, pulling her down on the bed beside him. "I've never made out with a girl in this bed," he said, rising up on his elbow above her.

She wanted to tell him no. She meant to. But he looked so sweet above her, his hair flopping down to shade his eyes. Eyes that were looking at her mouth as she licked her lips.

This was a terrible idea. Even now she had no idea what she'd come here to say to him. That it was over forever. Or that maybe—just *maybe*—they could see what happened long-distance.

Whatever her decision, it wouldn't be made clearer by making out. But...

"You have dimples," she whispered, reaching up to touch his cheek. Of course he did. She should have known. It would've been strange if Gabe MacKenzie *didn't* have adorable dimples. They flashed when he smiled, but then he kissed her and she closed her eyes.

Oh, God, he tasted so good. So right. She tangled her hands in his hair and pulled him tighter to her. She was instantly aroused, despite their weeks apart, despite her anger and hurt. She wanted nothing more than to pull up her skirt and tell him, *Hurry, shh, hurry. Just be quick before somebody knocks.*

She'd never sneaked up to a boy's bedroom before, never let him run his hand over her breasts with his family only one floor away. She'd never groaned into his mouth and hoped that the sound was soft enough that his parents wouldn't hear.

"God, I want to fuck you," he murmured against her lips. "I don't know if I should say that or not, but I do."

She didn't answer, because she was thinking the exact same thing, but her lack of objection seemed to encourage him. His eyes darkened and he kissed her again.

"We shouldn't have come here," he growled. "We should have gone to your hotel. Will you take me there later? Will you let me touch you again, Veronica?"

His fingers sneaked down her leg and under her skirt and he pressed his hand to her panties.

She gasped and pushed up toward him.

"I know you're mad," he whispered. "I know you're pissed, but you feel so good." He stroked her through the material until her hips rocked in time with his touch. His fingertips dragged over her clit.

"Will you take me back to your room, Veronica? Let me fuck you? Make you come?" He slipped beneath the fabric and she groaned at the new brightness of the pleasure.

"Yes," she said. "Yes." And then she was saying the things she'd imagined. Things she'd never say to someone else. "Here. Do it now. Just hurry. Before someone comes up."

"Now?" he rasped as his fingers pressed inside her and she arched up to meet him.

"Yes. Please. I missed you."

"Yes," he agreed. He rose up and frantically unfastened his belt and pants, but before he could do more than tug his underwear down, a knock thumped at the door.

They both froze. She was sure her eyes were as wide as his.

"Gabe?" his mom said through the door. "Come on down—the coffee is ready!"

"Okay," he said, the word unnaturally bright.

"We're going to walk to the restaurant afterward, show Veronica around."

"Uh," he croaked. "Sure."

Her quiet footsteps moved away.

Veronica and Gabe stared at each other until she

looked down to see half of his cock exposed. She couldn't help it. She started laughing again.

"Oh, Jesus," he groaned.

"I'm sorry!"

"Now you know why I've never made out with a girl in this bed. Please tell me you'll invite me to your hotel."

He started to tug up his pants, but Veronica stopped him. "Just let me..." she murmured, then leaned forward to press one very chaste kiss to the warm skin of his cock.

"Fuck. Veronica."

"You taste so good," she whispered.

"Stop," he begged.

"Okay. Don't tell your mom I did that."

He collapsed onto the bed with a desperate moan and tugged up his pants. "I distinctly remember telling her to wait on the coffee."

She felt a sadness that wasn't only about her unrequited lust. "They're so sweet, Gabe." She slipped her fingers into his hair just to remind herself how soft it was. "I can see where you got it."

He turned his head to watch her, his big brown eyes melting everything inside her into something dangerously soft. She sat up quickly before she could throw herself into his arms and confess her terrible, stupid love for him. "Let's go. What if your parents think you were fingering me in here?"

"They know the cutest girl they've ever met would never let me do something like that."

Oh, God, she loved him so much. Him and his beautiful eyes and his stupid dimples and his ridiculously perfect family. She shouldn't have come here. She had to let him go.

Gabe checked his clothing and disappeared into his bathroom to wash his hands and then they tiptoed down the hallway as if his mom didn't already know they'd been locked in his room.

The party started again as soon as they stepped into the kitchen. There were stories and pictures and cups of coffee and an introduction to Claire, who was as beautiful as Naomi but calm and quiet. Gabe's dad showed her pictures of the new location he had planned. It wasn't that far from where Veronica had lived in Brooklyn, though in a much nicer neighborhood.

She noticed that Gabe said nothing about the restaurant, though. His dad did all the talking. Gabe changed the subject as quickly as he could. When everyone began getting ready to walk her over for a tour of MacKenzie's, Gabe whispered, "Sorry about this."

Not exactly the response she'd expect from a man about to take over the business.

Still, he seemed cheerful as they stepped into the warm, sunny evening. Veronica felt cheerful, too, which was strange. She was in the city she hated, after all, with a man she'd been fighting with, and all while taking a slow stroll with his big family.

But it felt…cozy. Even the city felt cozy, as if she were cocooned in a warm family bubble that colored everything around her. Still, this wasn't the New York she was used to. There was no garbage piled on the curb. No men calling come-ons from across the street. This was a privileged part of New York she'd never been part of.

Granted, she knew there were nice working-class neighborhoods in the outer boroughs, but she hadn't even had the money to upgrade to working class. Hell, if she moved here today, she wouldn't be able to afford her old neighborhood.

But this part of the city...it was awfully nice if you could afford it, and she could imagine visiting. Spending time here. Walking to dinner with Gabe.

"Here it is!" his dad called out from ten feet ahead of her and Gabe. He swung an arm toward the glass-doored entrance of MacKenzie's. "Our third location. Unfortunately for them, it's my home base now."

But the employees didn't seem to feel put-upon. The hostess gave both James and Mary big hugs when they came in, and several others gathered around to pat James's back and tell him he looked great.

It was only five-thirty, but the long bar was starting to fill with people ordering drinks or sipping spiked milkshakes. The hostess led the way to a big round table. "Who wants a drink?" James boomed.

"Not you," said Mary. "And no sneaking a burger in the kitchen."

"Why don't I just lie down and die right here, then?" he grumbled.

"That is not funny!" she snapped.

"Aw, I'm sorry, babe." He kissed her cheek and all seemed forgiven. "No burgers today, all right?"

Naomi and Claire both ordered vodka sodas, but Veronica wasn't missing out on a spiked milkshake. She shoved down her self-consciousness and ordered a vanilla bourbon milkshake, happy when Gabe did the same. Before the drinks even arrived, though, she was scooted from the table by Gabe's dad.

"Take her on a tour!" he said to Gabe. "Show her around. This was the first location we designed from scratch. It used to be a shoe factory, if you can believe that. We gutted the whole thing, what…twenty-eight years ago now? Gabe was just a baby. We still had that place over on the West Side."

Gabe took her hand, sending sparks up her arm as he led her through the dining room toward the swinging kitchen doors.

"Well," he said as they walked into the white-tiled kitchen space, "this is it."

The area was smaller than she'd expected. Space was at a premium in the city, of course, but the design of the big dining room made the public area feel expansive. As small and crowded with kitchen staff as it was, the area looked spotless. A couple of the guys on the line waved spatulas toward Gabe. He waved back. Two of the dishwashers burst out laughing at something. Gabe didn't seem interested. He guided her toward a big glass door at the back.

"My dad's office," he said. "He likes to see what's going on."

Small as it was, the office was comfortable. There was a desk and a couple of chairs and even a love seat pushed up against a wall. A big bouquet of fresh flowers sat in the middle of the desk with a note perched in the middle. The door closed behind them, shutting out the noise of the kitchen.

She looked around, trying to picture Gabe here at this desk. "Is this where you'll work?"

"I suppose," he said. "I'm hoping I can have an office in my apartment, though. Get some quiet. I should probably rent out an official office, though. My dad liked being in the thick of things and he was always moving from location to location. But we need something more central."

His voice was flat. Tired.

"The employees seem pretty happy," she tried.

"Yeah, Dad likes to hire the best, so he doesn't pay minimum wage, even to the dishwashers. He has high expectations. He gets people who care. I think it's a great business strategy, but it's really just who he is."

Gabe glanced up and Veronica realized someone had signaled him from the other side of the door. "Hold on," Gabe said. "The manager needs something."

She looked around the office for a moment, wondering what James would've pointed out if he were giving the tour. The original blueprints were framed and hung behind the desk. She studied those for a moment but then she caught sight of Gabe again and watched him instead.

He was flat mouthed. Tense. With his beard gone and that resigned expression on his face, he looked like a stranger. Something twisted deep in her chest, something close to fear. This wasn't right. He didn't belong here, but there was nothing she could say to change that. She couldn't come between him and his family. Gabe would die for them. She knew that. And this wasn't dying. Not quite.

He opened the door and flashed that familiar carefree smile she remembered. "Come on. Our milkshakes are melting."

Yeah, so was her heart. Because she realized now that this was her last night with Gabe MacKenzie.

CHAPTER TWENTY-THREE

GABE'S HEART STARTED beating faster. Then it gained strength, the quick beats now thick with blood. And he and Veronica had only stepped onto the elevator.

They stood an inch apart, both facing the door, neither speaking as they rose toward the twelfth floor of her hotel. It was early yet. Still bright outside. After the milkshakes, he'd suggested they grab dinner later. Much later. She'd agreed.

Gabe was half-hard already, his body already imagining the moment when her hotel room door locked behind them. But it wasn't just that. She'd had fun tonight. She'd enjoyed his family and his neighborhood. She'd held his hand on the walk to her hotel.

She'd forgiven him.

The elevator doors slid open, and Veronica stepped out to lead the way. He followed, his hands tightening with the urge to touch her.

As she stopped in front of a door and got out her key card, Gabe told himself to go slow, be careful, but then he remembered her desperation back in his bedroom. Her dirty words urging him on. The way she'd pressed a sweet, small kiss to his cock and sent him to a new level of painful arousal.

Veronica being shy had turned him on. This new needy Veronica made him crazy. So as soon as he'd followed her through the door, he backed her against the wall and kissed her.

She didn't hesitate. She kissed him right back, moaning into his mouth as she twisted her fingers into his hair to pull him closer. He was rock hard in two seconds flat and tugging Veronica's shirt up with his next breath.

Do it now. He heard her breathless words again. *Just hurry.*

Yes. He needed to fuck her, taste her, remind her how good things were between them.

When he swung her toward the bed, she helpfully fell right into it, already kicking off her shoes. "I want you naked," she said.

He stripped out of his shirt and pants, feeling a violent jolt of lust at the way her eyes glittered with hunger when they locked on to his cock. She slipped off her bra and reached to unbutton her skirt, but Gabe couldn't wait. He hooked his fingers beneath the fabric and peeled her underwear down her legs and when the skirt slid off, she was naked.

He moved between her thighs, his shoulders pushing them open. She gasped his name, a protest or a plea, he wasn't sure, but when he put his mouth to her, she was already wet, already flooding his tongue with that taste he'd been wanting.

She cried out sharply, her back arching as he found her clit with his tongue.

"Oh, fuck," she groaned. "Oh, God, I missed that so much."

So had he.

She planted her feet to the mattress and tipped her hips up to his mouth. He felt the sting of her hand gripping his hair and smiled against her. It hadn't taken her

long to get over any shyness about this. She wasn't quiet
anymore. She moaned and sighed as he licked her. Her
thighs shook. "Yes," she urged. "Yes."

Gabe's cock throbbed at the way she began to work
herself against his mouth, as if she couldn't wait to get
fucked. And despite that she'd warned him just a few
weeks before that she had trouble climaxing, she was
coming now. Even she seemed surprised by how quick
it was, her cry of release more a shocked gasp. Thighs
still shaking, she muttered, "Oh, my God," over and
over, even as her orgasm subsided.

Gabe found the condoms he'd stashed in his pocket,
rolled one on and slid back between her legs. Her eyes
opened when his cock notched against her. They widened as he pushed in. Her tight heat squeezed him. He
sighed with relief.

"I spent the past two weeks fantasizing about this,"
he rasped as he pushed deeper. "How fucking wet you
get for me. How hot your pussy is. How much I love
filling you up."

She moaned and wrapped her legs around his hips.

"You're perfect, Veronica." He was finally pressed as
deep as he could get. He closed his eyes and held himself still for a moment, feeling her body ease around
him.

"I'm not," she whispered.

"Yes, you are. So fucking perfect."

"No," she insisted, but when he moved within her,
she stopped denying it. She only moaned and wrapped
her legs tighter.

"Don't you feel perfect?" he growled. "Don't you
feel like everything I want?"

She shook her head, but he kept fucking her until

she said yes. *Yes*, she was perfect. *Yes*, she was everything he wanted. *Yes*, he loved filling her up more than he loved anything in the world.

He loved her pussy and her breasts and the way her sweet face melted into carnality as he sank his cock into her over and over. The way she dug her nails into his back. The way she began to meet his thrusts. The way she got wetter and wetter the longer he fucked her, her body wanting more, more, more.

Yes.

The pleasure descended over him, pushing against the pressure building inside until he couldn't bear it anymore. His orgasm seized him tight. With a gasp, he sank himself deeper, faster, coming so hard that he felt dizzy with it. Everything went dark except that painful pleasure. It felt like a full minute before it faded.

He opened his eyes to find Veronica watching with a strange, tender look on her face. She stroked a hand over his cheek, and he turned to press a kiss to her palm. "I love you, Veronica," he said against her skin.

She let her hand fall away. "Don't say that."

"I know it's too soon. But it's true." When he leaned down to kiss her, she kissed him back. He didn't need her to say it. He didn't even need her to feel the same right now. But he wanted her to know how he felt.

He slid free of her body and went to the bathroom to clean up. When he got back, he slipped under the covers with her and pulled her into his arms.

"It's strange," she whispered, "how quickly someone else's presence becomes comfortable."

"It doesn't always happen," he said, and felt her nod against him. "Sometimes you just want to get away from the other person as soon as you can."

"Yeah, I remember that even from my few false starts. But it never felt strange with you. I always wanted to get closer."

"I'm so happy to hear that," he said with a chuckle. "How long are you staying?"

"Here? I leave tomorrow."

The shock of that was almost a physical pain. "What?"

"I have two meetings in the morning, and I fly out around three. I didn't want to stay long. You know how I feel about the city."

He scooted higher on the bed, sitting up so he could look at her. "But you had a good time today. Everything seemed…good."

She looked up at him for a moment, but then she sat up, too, dragging the sheets high to cover herself. "It was good. Obviously. This was *really* good. But, Gabe… I'm going home."

"Okay, fine," he said, the warmth in his body starting to replace itself with something hotter. Anger or panic. "This was a preliminary trip. But I don't want this to be over. I meant it when I said I missed you. Being with you here feels right. Like I never left."

She shook her head, still not looking at him. "I can't do this."

Yes, the heat was definitely panic. "I know you're angry. You have a right to be."

"That's not it," she started, but he cut her off.

"You're in Jackson, yes, but I'll come out as often as I can."

"What, twice a year?"

He took her hand. "We could do that for a little while. It could work. You like my family. You had a nice time today. I have friends here, and you could fit right in. You can't tell me there isn't still something you love about this city."

"Gabe." She shook her head.

"It'll be a few years. That's all. We can try it this way for a while, and you never know—maybe you'll come back to the city for a little while. With a syndicated column, you could work anywhere. A few years, Veronica. Then one of my sisters will step up."

"Do you honestly believe that will happen, Gabe?"

"It has to," he answered.

"No," she said, pulling her hand away. She climbed from the bed and pulled her shirt on, then her skirt. He just sat there, dumb with shock. One minute everything had been perfect, and now...

"I'm not doing this," she said. "I can't. And it's not because I'm afraid to live in New York again or because you lied to me or because it will be long-distance."

"Then why?" he pressed. "And don't tell me it's because you don't feel it, too. There's something special between us. In bed, yes, but out of it, too."

"There is," she agreed. "It's special and good and it *hurts*, Gabe." She swiped at a tear that escaped her eye. "Because I want it so much and I can't have it."

"You can." He stood up and pulled on his pants, then reached toward her, trying to offer comfort, but she shook her head.

"No. I've spent my entire life pretending. Pretending I wasn't shy and scared and lonely. I faked my way through high school and college. I faked my way through New York City. I've faked my way through Dear Veronica, too, and I'm not doing it anymore. Not ever again."

He shook his head. "I'd never ask you to be someone you're not."

"No. Not *me*, Gabe. *You.* You want me to come here and live your fake life with *you*."

His head drew back as if he were trying to escape a blow. "What?" A huff of breath escaped him on a laugh. "Me?"

"You're always telling me to be myself," she said, "but how can you say that? You're planning a whole fake life for yourself, doing something you hate in a place you don't want to be."

"I don't have a choice!"

"Fine, but I'm not going back, and I'm not going to watch you do that to yourself."

"I'll still be me, Veronica."

"No, you won't. Everything about you was different at the restaurant today, and that will hurt you the same way it hurt me. I won't encourage it. I won't be a part of it. Claire isn't going to walk away from her life and run a burger place. She's a vegan, Gabe! And Naomi? You think she's going to run MacKenzie's? She just told me tonight that she wants to buy a place in Paris!"

She wiped another tear from her cheek, but this time Gabe was too shocked to try to comfort her. His limbs felt numb. "What the hell am I supposed to do?" he asked. "Just watch my dad work until he dies?"

"I don't know!" she cried. Then she took a deep breath and seemed to calm. "I have no idea, but I don't think the answer is to give up everything you are because he's stubborn. I've tried that kind of thing. It doesn't work."

He snatched up his shirt, the panic finally flowing into fury. "I don't have any choice. Don't you get that?"

"Okay," she whispered. "But I do."

Wow. She was really walking away from him. How could she not understand? "You don't even like your dad and you can't stand up to him. I'm doing this out of love, at least." As soon as the words left his mouth, he hated himself for them, but she nodded.

"That's changing," she said. "I'm learning. But for you… It's like you only want people to know the good things, Gabe. You did that with me. You're doing that with your dad. It's protective, I think. You want to take care of the bad stuff yourself. You want to shield them. But you're shielding yourself, too. Nobody has to be disappointed with you, because you'll make it all okay."

"I'm not one of your columns," he snapped.

"Right. I'm sorry. That was…" She shrugged. "I'm sorry."

Gabe fastened his belt and shoved his feet into his shoes. "Call me if you change your mind," he said.

Lips pressed tight together, she nodded.

"Good luck tomorrow."

"Thank you."

He left before he said something else that was hurtful. Something he wouldn't be able to take back.

She couldn't understand family, because her dad had never done the things he should have. But Gabe's dad was different. He'd always taken care of them. Always watched out. Always made sure they had the best. He'd *protected* all of them, and now it was Gabe's turn to do the same.

He couldn't walk away from that, not even for Veronica. So he rode down the elevator and felt another thing he wanted dropping away, and he knew there was nothing he could do about it.

HE DIDN'T SLEEP a wink. He dragged himself from bed at 5:00 a.m. to go for a run and try to get Veronica out of his head, but all he thought about while running through the dawn streets was how much she'd like it this time of morning. How clean it all was. How the birds were singing and the pink sun glinted off the river and how much he wished she were with him.

He was cleaned up and on the subway by seven, heading to Brooklyn to check in on the new location. His dad had been begging him to, and frankly, Gabe needed off the island. Veronica was only a few dozen blocks away. If he stayed that close, he'd go see her. So he went to Brooklyn and watched the contractors work for a while, pretending he gave a damn about it all.

But her words stung him as if they were new wounds on his skin. Maybe it was pretending. He'd told himself sacrifice was just part of growing up, but now he didn't know if he was sacrificing his happiness for something good or if he was just giving in.

He wasn't bad at this job. He could do it. He was organized and sharp and dedicated to keeping his father's vision going. It was a lot of work, but he was young and healthy—he could push himself just as hard as his dad had.

And then what? Do the same thing year after year until he had a heart attack, too?

Shit.

At 10:00 a.m. Gabe shook the general contractor's hand and made a quick escape from the newly gutted space. He felt as if he'd been working for ten hours instead of two and a half. The cacophony of the subway station seemed to bore through his skull. When the train pulled up, Gabe caught sight of himself in the reflection of the window, neck bent, shoulders hunched up. He looked miserable.

Veronica was right. He wasn't himself here. He couldn't be. But he didn't have any fucking choice.

The fury was there again as he boarded the train. It built as the car picked up speed, the roar of noise like fuel on a fire. Gabe closed his eyes and imagined feeling like this again tomorrow, and the day after that, and the *year* after that.

He opened his eyes and glanced at the people surrounding him. They looked as exhausted and miserable as Gabe felt. His dad was different. If James MacKenzie had been here, he'd have struck up three different conversations and had the whole damn train car laughing. That was his happiness in life. Being around people, cheering them up, whether that was with a good burger or a bad joke. He loved what he did, and even with that, the business had worn him down with stress. How would Gabe survive it?

Because Veronica was definitely right about one thing. Claire wasn't going to step up in a few years and neither was Naomi. If Gabe took this on, he'd be taking it on forever.

If. That word meant he had a choice. Did he?

When he got back to his family's place, he wasn't surprised to walk in on an argument. His mom and dad were both stubborn and strong, and they'd never spent this many hours of the week together.

"You've been putting me off for decades," his mom snapped, "telling me we'd travel next year or the year after that. I want to go to the Bahamas. I want to go to Europe. I want to go on a cruise. And you *have* to take time off. The doctor said so."

"I'm taking time off. Don't you see me sitting here being useless? I'll travel with you, Mary, I swear to God, but right now I need to be here to help Gabe. You think he's just going to step right in and things will go smoothly? I may not be able to work sixty hours a week, but I can damn sure be here to offer guidance."

Gabe waved as he walked into the kitchen. "Hi, Mom. Dad."

"Gabe," his mom said, "tell your father you don't need him here."

"Of course he needs me here," his dad snapped.

"Watch your blood pressure!" she yelled back.

"Guys," Gabe said, holding up his hands in a plea.

His dad scoffed. "There will be plenty of time to travel later. I can't just leave Gabe with a mess. What's the point of leaving my kids the business if it's in chaos?"

What was the point exactly? Gabe took a deep breath. "Dad, did you ever consider that maybe the legacy your kids would rather have is you?"

His dad's face creased with bafflement. "What are you talking about? You've got me. I'm right here."

"None of us are married yet," Gabe said. "None of us have kids. If we could trade the restaurants for another twenty years with you, all three of us would make that choice in a heartbeat. Sometimes it seems like you care more about MacKenzie's than you do about time with any grandkids you might have."

"Gabe," his Dad growled. "That's ridiculous."

"I want you around to see my kids, Dad. I can't imagine a better grandfather than you."

"What's all this about? Is Veronica pregnant?"

His mom stepped forward. "Gabe? Is that true?"

He laughed. "No, she's not pregnant. She'll be back in Wyoming tonight and I'll probably never see her again."

His mom tsked, but his dad shook his head. "That's nonsense. She'll be back. I could see in a second how good you were together. I haven't seen you that relaxed and happy since you got home. You were like the old Gabe again."

"Ha. Right." He looked at his mom, the lines around her eyes tight with worry and resignation. She'd been waiting her whole life for the man she loved to stop working so hard and give her some real time together. And she'd keep waiting.

And his dad, so determined to make everything perfect and so sure of what was right for everyone that he couldn't see how wrong he was. Even a brush with death hadn't changed that. He was as stubborn as ever and Gabe was going to allow that to continue.

He looked at both his parents and stood up a little straighter. "We need to talk," he said. He was going to have to tell the whole truth. The kind of truth that no one wanted to hear. And for once, he couldn't try to cushion the blow.

CHAPTER TWENTY-FOUR

SHE WAS PROUD of herself. Truly, unequivocally proud. She'd met with her brand-new agent, recommended by a contact at her old paper, and they'd gone into that syndicate office with a strategy. Veronica hadn't accepted a deal yet—waiting a week was part of the strategy— but she had an offer for fourteen newspapers, and she was going to take it. One more day and her agent would make the call.

Veronica could move out of her dad's apartment. She might even take a few classes toward that degree in psychology she'd been considering.

And if she'd left a part of herself back in New York, well…there was nothing to be done about that.

Losing Gabe made her happiness bittersweet, but she felt thankful, too. Thankful she hadn't had him longer. Just a few weeks of Gabe and she was already marked, as if her body were covered in memories. She wondered if she'd still be able to feel him on her skin a year from now. Ten years from now. She wondered if she'd want to.

She tugged on jeans and pulled on a tank top, hoping tonight's crowd would accept a more casual Dear Veronica. Only slightly more casual, though. Her tank top sparkled with tiny black crystals and she added her blue half boots to dress the whole thing up.

If Gabe were going to be there, maybe she'd have worn a dress, but the thought of showing off her thighs to a room without Gabe made her sad.

Just as she was grabbing her purse to walk to the bar, her phone rang. When she saw it was her father, she almost didn't pick up.

She finally answered after the fourth ring. "Hello?"

"I suppose you want me to come to the show," her father said gruffly.

Veronica frowned at her door. "What?"

"Your show. I guess I should come and support you or you'll accuse me of not caring."

"Dad…" She shook her head in utter confusion. "I don't think that would be a good idea. My show can get a little inappropriate."

"Yes, I've noticed that from your columns," he snapped.

She took a deep breath and braced herself for the lecture. But it didn't come.

"I guess you know what you're doing," he grumbled. "Give the audience what they want. That's why you got that offer."

"Um…yes?" she agreed, hating the doubt in her voice but too confused to leave it behind. She tried to think of something else to say into the silence, but he finally filled it.

"All right. Just remember that I offered. Are we still on for dinner tomorrow?"

"Of course."

"See you then," he said, and hung up. She pulled the phone from her ear and frowned at it.

"Okay," she whispered. That had been really weird. Her dad was actually *trying*. Maybe she should have stood up to him a long time ago. Maybe he really hadn't known how terrible he'd been to her.

Veronica set off for the Three Martini Ranch with a quick prayer of thanks that her dad hadn't simply shown up to hear her opinions on open relationships or safe sex. But she was glad he'd called. It was a nice confidence boost even if she didn't need one. He was her only family and he was *trying*.

The bar was as crowded as she'd ever seen it, but for the first time, Veronica didn't rush to the office to hide. She walked around and said hi to a few people, then found herself at a table of Gabe's friends, talking to Benton about his nephew.

She felt normal. Not terrified. Not even nervous really, though she was a little afraid that Benton might ask about Gabe. She couldn't talk about Gabe.

Compared to that prospect, getting up to give live advice to an audience was easy.

Half an hour later, she was at the microphone talking about the complicated mechanics of negotiating holidays when both partners had step-children and in-laws and former in-laws. She wished she'd brought a chalkboard so she could diagram it. Modern holidays could be a minefield.

The next question was from a bride who was trying to plan a wedding while feuding with her sisters, and Veronica was beginning to feel as though she'd gotten a good deal by not having a big, raucous family like Gabe's. If she ever got married, it would likely be a quiet ceremony in her dad's courtroom. Unless, of course, her future husband came from a New York family and had older sisters and— She shoved that thought away and moved on to a query about female orgasms.

That question took a while to answer thanks to a few shouted follow-ups from the crowd, and by the time it was done, Veronica realized that she was already forty-five minutes into the show. She'd normally start wrapping it up now, winding down with one last question or maybe two if she had to. But tonight she spread another five questions out on the table. Tonight she wasn't just getting this over with. She wasn't eyeing the hallway and planning her escape. She was *loving* it.

Laughing, she read a question about safe sex aloud and said another silent thank-you to her dad for not just showing up.

"Here's the thing. If your partner is that adamant about not using condoms, then he's the guy who talks every single partner into not bothering with a condom. He's also the guy who's happy when his random hookup doesn't ask for a condom. That's who your man is. That's what you're putting your mouth on. Would you put your mouth on a bathroom doorknob? Would you put your vagina on that doorknob? Well then, don't put it on his penis."

She cringed a little when she saw the reaction of a couple at a front table. The man's arms were crossed tight and he was glaring at the floor. The woman with him wasn't smiling, either. Her mouth was twisted in disgust, and her eyes slid to the side to watch his reaction. Veronica had never so clearly identified one of the writers before. She cleared her throat and reached for the next letter.

She paused when she saw Benton approaching. "Oh, hi," she said in surprise when he stepped up to her.

"I have an emergency Dear Veronica letter. Would you read it? As a favor?" He made a begging motion with his hands and gave her a puppy-eyed look that she suspected had charmed many a woman.

It totally worked. The man was damn near irresistible. "Okay," she said, taking the letter carefully from his fingers.

"Well, this is a surprise," she said into the microphone. "But you have to take a few chances in life." She unfolded the paper and smiled.

"'Dear Veronica, I've completely screwed up with a woman I really like. We've only known each other a few weeks, but I think we've got something truly amazing.'"

The crowd reacted with an "Aww" that she joined in on.

"That's sweet," she said, "But I have a feeling there's a plot twist coming. 'She's perfect. Beautiful and smart and a little dorky.'" Veronica laughed. "Oh, my God, she is perfect!" She looked quickly over the room, trying to pick out Benton and see the girl he was with, but she couldn't find him.

"'But...'" she started again, then shook her head. "See, there is always a 'but'! 'But I wasn't completely truthful when we started dating, and worse than that, I was a coward. I walked away from her when I shouldn't have. I gave up on myself and on her. So here's my question, Veronica...'"

The nape of her neck started tingling. She swallowed hard and swept the room again, not even sure what she was looking for.

"'If I...'" The words were hoarse. She cleared her throat. "'If I left New York and moved back to Jackson, would she give me another chance? Just a small one?'"

Her heart felt as if it weighed a hundred pounds as she looked up. As if it was falling and pulling her stomach and her breath and her thoughts down with it. This time she didn't have to look around the room. Gabe was standing right there in the middle of the tables. She stared at him. She couldn't move. Her heart was too heavy to lift.

The crowd began to murmur. All eyes turned to Gabe as he stepped forward.

"Would she give him another chance?" Gabe asked just loudly enough for her to hear.

Veronica shook her head.

"No?" he asked softly.

She felt the eyes of the crowd focus on her now. She set down the letter. "I suppose they... I suppose they'd need to talk."

"But she'd be willing to listen?"

Her mind spun. She pulled her gaze off his pleading brown eyes and looked around. Several of the women in the audience nodded at her. She thought she might faint. She thought she should be mortified. But all she felt was a terrible, rushing hope. Her head spun with it. "All right," she finally answered. "She'd be willing to listen."

Applause broke out and then spread to cheers of encouragement. She shook her head. "But not until after the show. Go sit down."

Gabe grinned and waved good-naturedly at the howls of laughter. Several people patted him on the back as he made his way toward Benton's table. Naomi was there, too. Had Gabe picked up his whole family and brought them here?

Head buzzing with fear and joy and that stupid hope, Veronica quieted the crowd and forced herself to read two more letters before she admitted defeat and gave up. "Okay, readers, thanks for another great night. Now if you'll excuse me, I need to follow up on one of tonight's questions."

"You make him pay, girl!" a woman called as Veronica passed her table. Veronica gave her a thumbs-up.

"He's too cute to give up on!" someone else added. Veronica grinned and shook her head and wondered if she should kill Gabe. Not until after she hugged him, though. And then shook him. And then kissed him and asked what the hell he was up to.

She escaped to the office, and suddenly he was there in the doorway. Right there.

His hands were in the pockets of his jeans, his neck slightly bent, but he watched her, his eyebrows rising in question.

"Hi," he said.

"Hi." She didn't know what to say. She'd meant never to see him again, but he looked so sweet and sad, and he was *here*, and she desperately wanted to throw herself into his arms. But she didn't move. She couldn't. "What are you doing here?"

She'd been strong when she'd said goodbye in New York. She couldn't do that again. His face had been so stiff with hurt and anger, and she'd hated it. She liked him too much. And he was *here*.

God. He was here.

His wide shoulders rose as he took a deep breath. "I took your advice."

"What advice?"

"I told my dad he was being a stubborn ass."

"What?" she gasped.

"Okay, I didn't say it like that. Well, maybe I did

at one point when it got a little heated. The important thing is I told him the truth."

"What truth?" she breathed, as the hope rushed faster through her veins.

"The truth that I was giving up my life for his. The truth that his kids would rather have him than a hundred restaurants. And the truth that he needed to step up and sell the business like a responsible adult."

Her heart pounded hard. She pressed a hand to it. "He… You *said* that?"

"That and more. You were right. About everything. The thing is, it was my fault. I told him that, too. Naomi and Claire were smart enough—and *honest* enough—to say no. But I wanted to take care of it for him. The same way he'd always taken care of stuff for me. I wanted to give him his dream so I never even told him the truth about mine."

"But…" She felt dizzy and surprisingly angry. Why was he doing this to her when she'd done her best to give him up? She'd been strong. Done the right thing. She shook her head. "What did he say?"

Gabe smiled. "I won't repeat most of it. He was shocked and fighting for the future he'd always planned. I let him yell. I deserved it. But the truth is…he's like me. He wants me to be happy, and he saw how happy I was when I wasn't thinking about MacKenzie's. He saw how happy I was with you. He saw that, and he wants that for me."

Veronica sat down hard on the desk. "I don't understand. What does this mean?"

"It means I've moved back to Jackson. You were right. I can't live in New York. I'm not myself there. I'm lucky I put off resigning at the library. I took it as

family leave. Hopefully, Jean-Marie will have me back."
He paused. "And I'm hoping you will, too."

She shook her head and watched him frown.

"Just a small chance?" he pressed. "A couple of
dates?"

She looked away.

"Do you want me to beg? I will."

"No."

Gabe ducked down to catch her eye. "You could add
me to your list. Make me a project. Number six—give
a stupid boy one more shot?"

"No, Gabe!" she snapped. "This isn't funny. I can't…
I can't be the girl who made your dad go back to a
stressful job! I'm not coming between you and your
family. I would never ever do that!"

The worry fell from his face. "That's not who you'll
be. You'll be the girl who challenged me to be myself.
My honest self. And my dad… I can't make his decisions for him. I have to accept that."

"So you're just going to let him take over again?
Work himself to death? I don't believe you. You'll never
be okay with that."

"No. That's not how it's going to be. We all sat down
together. All five of us. My sisters felt the same way I
did. And my mom cried. She wants to travel. She wants
a living, healthy husband. This time, Dad didn't blow
her off. Maybe the heart attack scared him or maybe
he just needed to hear the truth from all of us at once.
I don't know why, but in the end, he agreed to bring
on a partner."

"Really?"

"Yes. He doesn't want to give up control. I get that.
It's our family name. But he agreed to look for some-

one to take over a minority stake. He'll have veto power over decisions, but he won't have to be there day to day."

"Really?" she repeated.

"Really. He still thinks one of us will want the business one day, and that's fine. You never know. And if that makes it easier for him to give up some control, then it's a good thing."

"But…"

He grinned at her, his eyebrows raised in question, and that sweet smile melted her heart.

"No!" she said. "No, I already gave you up. I already did that and I was strong and it hurt so much and I can't do this again!"

"But you don't have to give me up again. I'm here."

"That's not what I meant." She held strong in the face of his hopeful brown eyes. She could do it. He was practically a stranger without his beard. Those dimples meant nothing to her.

"Okay," he finally said. "I understand. But if you change your mind, if you get lonely, I'll just be a block away," he teased, trying a different tack. "Day or night. Text or call and I'll be at your door in—"

"Shut up," she said. She crossed her arms tightly and his gaze dropped to her breasts.

He stopped talking and waited.

She glared. "We both know I won't be able to resist."

His eyes rose to meet hers. He smiled. "Yeah?"

"You know how beautiful you are, you bastard."

His smile spread to a grin. "Is that all you care about? My good looks?"

She raised one shoulder. "That and your cunnilingus skills. I guess I'll give you another shot."

He stepped closer. His hands settled on her arms.

When he pulled her toward him, she let him. Then his hand was cradling her cheek as he kissed her.

"Jesus, Veronica," he breathed. "You had me scared there for a minute."

She wrapped her arms around him and pulled him down for a longer kiss. When he finally lifted his head, she stared up at him. "Are you really here?" she asked, and tears were suddenly falling down her cheeks.

"I'm sorry," he said. He kicked the door shut behind him and then they didn't say anything for a long while. She kissed him, tasted him, touched the hard, wide muscles of his shoulders. She'd missed him so much. It felt as though it had been weeks instead of days. How had she gotten so accustomed to him so quickly?

When they emerged from the office five minutes later, Veronica was sure she'd feel embarrassed. She didn't like to be the center of attention, after all, and she wasn't exactly used to people knowing about her personal life, if only because she'd rarely had one.

But the brief round of applause that greeted them felt friendly. She blushed, but she held tight to Gabe's hand as they worked their way over to Benton's table so Veronica could give Naomi a hug.

"Thank you for giving him another chance," Naomi said as she squeezed Veronica tight. "Men are idiots sometimes. *Most* of the time."

"I know," Veronica said. She noticed that when Gabe's sister sat back down, her thigh was pressed tightly to Benton's leg, and his hand settled over her knee.

Interesting, but Veronica was too wired to think about catching up right now. That could happen later. Right now all she cared about was being alone with Gabe.

Gabe slapped Benton's back. "Thanks for delivering my note. We're heading over to Veronica's place to talk."

Naomi arched an eyebrow. "I won't wait up."

"I didn't think you would," he said, his gaze going pointedly toward Benton's hand. Naomi put her hand over Benton's and laced their fingers together.

Gabe nodded and turned Veronica toward the door.

"Are they an item?" Veronica whispered as they walked away.

"Maybe. They've been talking a lot over the past few weeks. They had a thing a few years ago, and I guess the spark hasn't died."

"That's nice."

He shrugged. "I suppose. Benton's a bit of a player, but when I pointed that out to Naomi she reminded me that she hasn't exactly been a wallflower. She'll give him a run for his money."

"They're cute together."

He shot her a smile. "True. And it won't be hard for me to keep an eye on my best friend."

"But who's going to watch your sister?"

"Good question. Maybe it's Benton's heart I should be worried about."

The night was quiet and warm, but thunder rumbled beyond the mountains. As they walked, Gabe looked over the town square, which was still bustling with people. "It's starting to get busy around here. Feels like I've been gone a long time."

She nodded. It had felt like months.

He breathed in deeply as they drew closer to her apartment. "God, it smells good. I can't believe I was going to give this up."

Now that she wasn't kissing him, it was a little easier to think, to consider what he'd said and what he'd done. She turned it over in her head, trying to figure out if she was making a mistake. He'd betrayed her, yes, but his heart had been in the right place. He'd wanted to do the right thing for his family, even though it was wrong to keep the truth from her. Still, she hesitated at her door.

"Gabe, this is only a chance. I'm not promising anything. It'll take me a while to trust you again."

"I know," he said.

"How will I know when you're telling me something I want to hear and when you're being truthful?"

"I'll be honest to a fault."

She eyed him doubtfully.

"I'm serious. Like, I'll tell you right now that I'll deny being your boyfriend if it will save me getting beat up by Jake Davis."

She laughed and let him bend down to kiss her before she shoved him away and unlocked the door.

"And," he continued as he followed her inside, "I'm really not a fan of your dad. Sorry. That's just the truth."

"Oh, that's a shock."

"Lastly—and this is tough to say…"

"Yes?" she pressed, though the word was a little breathless because she'd just realized they were now alone in her apartment. And they hadn't really come here to talk.

"The truth is," he said, his breath warm against her neck as he slipped up behind her, "I think your bedroom skills need a little work."

"What?" she cried.

"I know. It's really one of the main reasons I came back to Jackson." His fingertips whispered down her bare arms and Veronica shivered. "It wasn't fair to abandon you in the middle of our lessons. I was thinking I could give you a few more pointers. Try it out again. See how it goes."

She laughed in scandalized delight. "You really are the worst, Gabe MacKenzie."

"Really? Then maybe I'm the one who needs a few pointers. In fact, we could start right now. If you're willing to give me another shot." Yes, she was willing to give him another shot. She'd risk her heart for this man.

Standing behind her, he slid his arms around her waist and unbuttoned her jeans. Veronica choked on her own laugh. "I guess we could…try it again."

A few minutes later, she was deadly serious and gasping out instructions. Gabe was an incredibly quick learner. And she was the happiest teacher in the world. The truth was she trusted him with everything. Her body, her heart, her happiness. She didn't need time.

She decided right then and there to add a new note to the collection on her fridge.

#6—Take a chance on loving Gabe MacKenzie with all your heart.

Maybe her best advice yet.

* * * * *

*If you enjoyed Veronica and Gabe's story, you'll love
the complete GIRLS' NIGHT OUT series:*

*"FANNING THE FLAMES" eNovella
LOOKING FOR TROUBLE
FLIRTING WITH DISASTER
TAKING THE HEAT*

*Available now from Victoria Dahl
and HQN Books.*

*Keep reading for an excerpt of
FLIRTING WITH DISASTER!*

ISABELLE WEST EDGED her SUV up the steep driveway and winced as she heard a grocery bag tip over. She tried to identify the dull rolling sound that followed. Probably the cantaloupe. But maybe just a can of soup. It'd be a little surprise for her when she opened the hatch and saw what sprang out and tumbled through the snow toward the trees.

She was getting tired of that particular surprise and promised herself she'd order the cargo net as soon as she got inside. She'd been meaning to do it for…maybe two years now. But today she'd remember. She was trying to teach herself to be proactive. Or at least to manage the small things that every other adult seemed to have no problem with.

As she rounded the last curve of the drive and spied her little cabin, she wrinkled her nose. Not because of the cabin. She loved that. It was perfect for her in every way with its dark log walls and big windows and front porch. What made her wince was the sight of the manual garage door past the haze of snow sifting from the sky, a reminder that she'd also been meaning to call about getting a garage-door opener installed. That one had been on her mental to-do list for at least four years. Definitely not five.

"I'll do that, too," she said to herself as she pulled

close to the garage door and tugged up the hood of her coat. "As a matter of fact…" She dug her phone from her pocket and held down the button. "Phone, remind me to order a cargo net and call a garage guy."

The phone beeped and said, "I'm sorry, I didn't catch that."

Gritting her teeth, Isabelle hit the button again. "Remind me to buy a cargo net and call the garage guy."

"I'm sorry, did you need me to find a mechanic?"

"Fuck you," Isabelle growled. She ducked out of her car, thankful that the giant, wet flakes of this morning had given way to the dry Wyoming snow she was more used to. The snow sounded like sand as it bounced off her jacket and slid to the ground.

She wrenched up the garage door and got back to her car without getting wet at all. But she couldn't say the same about her cantaloupe. As soon as she opened the gate of her SUV, it rolled past her outstretched hand and straight into a snowbank.

"Fuck you, too," she said to the cantaloupe, then felt immediately guilty. It only took her a minute to rescue the melon and dust off as much snow as she could. It hadn't really caused that much trouble. It took a lot more time to repack the bag that had tipped over and haul it inside.

Next time, she'd remember to put the boxes of art supplies she'd picked up from the post office into the back; then she'd have room to store the groceries on the floor of her backseat, where they'd be less likely to—

"Art supplies!" she gasped, and rushed back out to the truck to haul in the boxes of goodies.

She grinned as she set the first box on the kitchen table and slit the tape to reveal the treasures inside.

She'd been out of yellow ochre for three days now, and even though she hadn't needed it, the lack had hovered at the back of her mind like a foreshadowing of tragedy to come. She snatched up the tube and breathed a sigh of relief. Disaster averted. She was whole again.

After unpacking the box and carefully laying out each precious item on the kitchen table, she retrieved the other two boxes from the backseat and went through the same routine. She beamed at the sight of the bounty spread over the table. Seven more tubes of color, a new studio light to get her through the winter, a dozen pre-stretched canvases and her favorite brush conditioner that smelled like something close to sandalwood. It made the task of looking after her brushes almost soothing. Discovering it last year had been a treat.

Satisfied with her unveiling of the goods, she made five trips to the room she used as her studio, shelving the paints she didn't need yet and getting the new lamp set up at her current workstation. She played with the LED settings for a while, still dubious about the idea that she could get good color temperatures, but the settings seemed sufficient. Nice, even.

"Hmm." Isabelle crossed her arms and stared at the unfinished painting, trying to decide if the daylight setting was pure enough. There weren't new technological advancements in the world of oil painting very often, so she'd be happy if she could get excited about this one. Still, she'd have to work under the light for a couple of hours and see how it felt.

During the summer, she wouldn't need it much at all. This room was meant to be the great room of the cabin, and windows climbed up the two-story wall to the peak of the roof. The windows faced south, and during the summer, she had good light here for nearly twelve hours of every day. But during the winter, there were only a few decent hours of sunlight, and that was assuming the sky was clear.

As a matter of fact… She glanced out, hoping to spot an approaching break in the clouds, but it was solid white out there. A good time to try the lamp, then. It was almost two, so she should force herself to grab lunch first, but then she'd have hours to work.

Her thoughts were interrupted by the heavy slide of fur against her ankle. "Hey, Bear," she said to the cat, surprised by his affection. He was an ornery twenty-pound stray who'd wandered into her cabin three years before, and he didn't cuddle often.

He meowed loudly for attention, but when she leaned down to scratch his chin, he sidestepped and eyed her scornfully. "I suppose you just want food?" she asked. She'd run out of wet food yesterday, which was why—

"The groceries!" she gasped, but her heart barely managed a quick leap before she calmed it down. The bags in the SUV were fine. It was cold enough that she could leave them overnight and not lose anything. Except bananas, maybe. Those weren't as hardy as people thought, not in the cold. If it were summer, though… Yeah. She'd lost hundreds of dollars of food that way over the years. But this time the only bag in danger was the one on her kitchen counter.

She rushed to the kitchen and unpacked that bag, happy to find that, aside from that damp cantaloupe, everything else was perfect. She shoved a frozen meal into the microwave, opened a can of food for Bear and went to haul in the rest of the bags. Half an hour later, she was organized, full of chicken piccata and happily

planted in front of her canvas, adding a glistening high-
light to a long stretch of a man's triceps.

Glancing from the canvas to a spread of photos hung
on a board next to it, she nodded. "Perfect." Her eyes
swept down the triceps muscle to the hard knot of elbow
beneath it. What a beautiful line.

Her attention twitched for a moment, and Isabelle
glared at the gleam of the light on wet paint, but then she
shook off the random irritation and dipped her brush in
white again. Just the tiniest drag of paint, just—

Her hand jerked, nearly touching the canvas before
she pulled back. "What the hell?" she snapped as she
finally registered that a sound had interrupted her. A
loud sound. The staccato knock of some stranger come
to screw up her workday.

She wanted to ignore it. It definitely wasn't Jill, her
neighbor and the only person who dropped by unan-
nounced. Jill didn't knock like that. She rarely knocked
at all, because she knew Isabelle wouldn't hear it. But
it could be one of Isabelle's other friends. Lauren. Or
maybe even Sophie, who was supposed to be back in
town soon.

Had Isabelle forgotten another meetup? It was possible. She vaguely remembered Lauren mentioning something about a new girl they might be able to bring in to
their little group of friends since Sophie was usually
on the road these days.

Isabelle set down the brush, wiped her hands on a rag
and decided she'd have to answer the door, just in case.

Whoever it was knocked one more time, just as Isabelle reached for the door. She yanked it open, ready to
apologize to Lauren, but it wasn't Lauren. Or Sophie.
Or any other girlfriend. It was a man, taller than she

was, snow dusting his short, dark hair and drifting in on the breeze as she frowned.

"Sorry to disturb you, Ms...?"

Really? He was going to start this off by asking for *her* name? "Yes?" she responded, tempted to close the door on his face and march right back to her studio. Whatever he was selling, she didn't want it.

His gaze sharpened a bit, but his chin dipped in acknowledgment, and he reached into the pocket of the nondescript navy blue parka he wore. "I'm Deputy US Marshal Tom Duncan."

Her hand tightened on the doorknob, and something went wrong with her ears. His lips kept moving, but she couldn't hear the words. Then he paused, watching her as if waiting for a response.

Isabelle cleared her throat, hoping the noise would force her ears back into working condition. "I'm sorry," she said with more calm than she could believe. "I wasn't paying attention. Who are you?"

His brow tightened with irritation. "I'm Deputy Marshal Tom Duncan."

"I got that part," she bit out, her veins too flooded with fight-or-flight to keep her voice even now.

"I'm in the neighborhood as part of a protection detail, and—"

"This isn't a neighborhood," she interrupted, angry that he couldn't come up with a better excuse. Did he think she was an idiot?

"All right," he said carefully, his jaw clenching around the words. She'd made him mad. Good. She hoped he was cold, too. Because he was ruining more than her day. He was ruining something much larger than that.

He tried again. "I'm in the immediate area with a protection team, and I wanted to make contact with each of the residents. First—"

"What immediate area?" She glanced pointedly toward the one other house on her road, knowing damn well that Jill didn't need the sort of protection a US marshal provided. This was ridiculous. Why was he even pretending?

"Ma'am," he snapped, the word crisp with impatience. "We're on Judge Anthony Chandler's property. I understand that he may not live on your road, but his residence is only a half mile through those trees. I'm informing you and all of your neighbors in case you see anyone from the marshal service near your property or on the road. If you see anyone you don't recognize, please give me a call."

He held out a card, and Isabelle glanced at it. She didn't take it. "You want me to call you."

"Yes. If it's one of my people, I'll confirm that. However, if it's not one of my people, then it could be the fugitive who's threatened Judge Chandler's life." He held up a creased photo of an unremarkable-looking white man in his forties.

Isabelle finally took the card and examined it as she spoke. "Someone threatened Judge Chandler, so I should expect a team of marshals hanging around my property. That's what you're telling me?"

"Yes." His gaze drifted past her shoulder, looking into her house. "Are you the only one living here at this time?"

"That's not your concern."

His eyes snapped back to her. "It's very important for your safety and for ours that we be aware of any unusual activity. Trespassers, items missing from your home or property, even trash you might find on a trail. Have you seen anything unusual?"

Isabelle gave him a flat look. "Just you."

His jaw tightened again. It was a nice jaw. A nice face altogether, lean and angled and just starting to show his age around his eyes. Too bad he was a liar.

"The man who threatened the judge is a survivalist, the brother of Ephraim Stevenson, whose trial begins on Monday. I'm advising you to be aware. And please notify any other residents of your home to do the same."

She held his gaze for a long moment, trying to give nothing away while still conveying that she knew this story was bullshit. That he wasn't fooling her. That she wasn't scared.

But she was.

"Sure, Marshal," she finally said, forcing a patently pleasant smile. "I'm happy to cooperate with any reasonable law enforcement requests. But I'd appreciate it if you stayed off my property. If I need your help, I'll let you know."

She stepped back and closed the door. Hard. The defiance dropped from her shoulders. She covered her eyes with one shaking hand. For a moment, there was silence outside, then she heard the crunch of his boots on her snowy porch steps. Isabelle leaned her back against the door and slowly slid down until she hit the floor.

They'd found her.

The ax had always been hanging over her, waiting to drop. In this day and age, you could never truly disappear. Not for good. But she'd tried.

For a girl like her, it hadn't been easy. She'd been

sheltered. Twenty-two years old, but still a child in important ways. Always taken care of, always protected.

Still, she'd managed to hide for fourteen years. She'd moved several times, assumed a new identity, built a successful career. But they'd found her.

So why hadn't Deputy Marshal Tom Duncan arrested her immediately?

Surprised to find her eyes were blurry with tears, Isabelle wiped the wetness from her face and pushed up to her feet. She slipped over to the front window and carefully peeked outside.

The only sign of him was the set of footprints that led up to her porch and the set leading back down to her drive. There wasn't quite enough fresh snow that she could track his prints down her driveway, but he hadn't sneaked off into the deep snow at the side of her house. He was gone. Which didn't make sense.

She wasn't a dangerous criminal. She hadn't even been a criminal at all until she'd purchased fake IDs and changed her identity. If he'd come here to arrest her for that, he would've just arrested her. He didn't need to retreat to assemble a backup team or call SWAT. A set of handcuffs would've done the trick. Even one of those plastic zip ties would've incapacitated her.

So they weren't here to make a simple arrest. There was only one explanation. Her father must be back in the country, and they assumed he'd be in contact with Isabelle. They were going to watch and wait.

"Asshole," she muttered as she closed the curtains and locked her door. She hadn't bothered with that kind of thing in years. She'd finally felt safe from the world up here in the mountains outside Jackson, Wyoming. What the hell was she going to do now?

She stood in her entry for a moment with no clue what her next move was. She couldn't run again. She didn't want to. This was her life. Her *real* life. The world she'd chosen for herself.

She wouldn't run.

Fuzzy with shock, she headed back to her studio, feeling like a toy that was slowly winding down.

Did that guy really think she'd fall for such a flimsy story? She'd been around cops all her life. A protection detail was a protection detail; they didn't canvass neighborhoods asking who you were hiding in your house.

Her head buzzed with the noise of a thousand memories as she stopped before her easel and took up the brush. She held it poised above the line she'd painted earlier, but the color wasn't alive anymore. It wasn't good. She looked at the photos again, trying to absorb the life captured there, but when she looked back to the canvas, her mind gave her nothing. Nothing except Chicago and her parents and her old home and friends and *Patrick*.

She set the brush down and switched off the lamp. She wouldn't be able to work this evening. And she wouldn't be able to relax. That was the reason she'd started this new life in the first place. For peace and quiet and *forgetting*. And now he'd blown it up with a casually dropped bomb. Deputy Marshal Tom Duncan, asshole extraordinaire.

Heading toward her tiny living room and the ancient laptop she kept there, Isabelle pulled his card from the pocket of her jeans and shot it a nasty look. She'd find out exactly who he was and what he wanted, and she'd figure out if there was any way to make it better. And then she'd get back to painting.